**"Do you want to learn how to protect yourself?"
Stephen asked.**

Green eyes sparking with fire, Isobel raised her sword and said, "Teach me."

"You should carry a short blade as well," he instructed as he fended off her attack.

"Why? You think you can knock my sword from my hand?"

"I can. But I will not have to. You will drop it."

He forced her to step back, and back, and back again. She threw her hands up, sending the sword clattering against the wall as she tumbled backward.

"I'm afraid you have the advantage of me," she said, reaching her hand up for him. He took it and sank to his knees beside her.

"Not true, Isobel," he said in a harsh whisper. "'Tis I who am at your mercy."

His eyes fixed on her lips, full and parted. The moment their lips touched, fire seared through him. She was kissing him back, mouth open. Slowly, he lowered his body...

He froze the instant he felt the prick of cold steel against his neck.

"You are right," Isobel said so close to Stephen's ear that he could feel her breath, "'tis wise to carry a short blade."

*Please turn this page for praise
for Margaret Mallory...*

ALSO BY MARGARET MALLORY

Knight of Desire

Knight of Pleasure

MARGARET MALLORY

FOREVER

NEW YORK   BOSTON

Copyright © 2009 by Peggy L. Brown
Excerpt from *Knight of Passion* copyright © 2009 by Peggy L. Brown
All rights reserved. Except as permitted under the U.S. Copyright Act of 1976, no part of this publication may be reproduced, distributed, or transmitted in any form or by any means, or stored in a database or retrieval system, without the prior written permission of the publisher.

Book design by L & G McRee
Cover illustration by Alan Ayers

Forever
Hachette Book Group
237 Park Avenue
New York, NY 10017
Visit our Web site at www.HachetteBookGroup.com.

Forever is an imprint of Grand Central Publishing. The Forever name and logo are trademarks of Hachette Book Group, Inc.

Printed in the United States of America

First Printing: December 2009

10 9 8 7 6 5 4 3 2 1

For my parents, Norman and Audrey Brown,
who gave me my love of history, books,
and foreign places.

Acknowledgments

I will be forever grateful to Alex Logan at Grand Central Publishing for plucking *Knight of Pleasure* from the vast sea of manuscripts before her and saying, "Yes, I want this one." A special thank-you also goes to my agent and friend, Kevan Lyon, for her faith in me.

When I started my first novel, my favorite librarian (my sister) told me to join Romance Writers of America (RWA). Thanks to her sage advice, I am part of the generous community of romance writers. I am grateful to the members of my local RWA chapters, who cheer me on every step of the way; to my critique buddies, who always tell me what they really think; and to the published authors who were exceedingly kind in their support of my first book, *Knight of Desire*.

I beg forgiveness of my friends and family for neglecting them while I wrote this book. (We all know I will do it again.) My love and thanks go to all of them, especially my husband.

Knight of Pleasure

Prologue

Which of you brave Knights of the Round Table will fight me?" Isobel called out.

"Me! Choose me! Isobel, choose me!"

Isobel ignored the shouts of the boys jumping up and down around her and rose up on her toes, searching for her brother. Where was Geoffrey? When she spotted him in the tall grass, she dropped to her heels and sighed. Her brother was gazing at the sky, a smile on his face, happily talking to himself.

She pointed instead to a frail-looking boy at the back of the circle. "You shall be Gawain."

The other boys groaned as Gawain stepped forward, dragging his wooden sword behind him.

"Sir Gawain," Isobel said, giving him a low bow. "I am the evil Black Knight who has captured Queen Guinevere."

The little boy scrunched up his face. "Why do you not play Queen Gui-, Gui-, Gui-"

"Because I am the Black Knight." At thirteen, she was the eldest here and got to set the rules.

She glared up at the gray stone walls of Hume Castle. The boys her age were inside, practicing with real swords in the castle's bailey yard. 'Twas so unfair! For no cause at all, her father forbade her to go off with the boys—or touch a sword—while they were at this gathering. She was to sit quietly and keep her gown clean.

She turned back to Gawain and raised her sword. "Will you not fight to save your queen?"

Gawain stood frozen, his eyes round with panic.

Quickly, she leaned down and cupped her hand to the boy's ear. "The Knight of the Round Table *always* prevails, I promise."

She did her best to make his clumsy swings look skilled. When that proved hopeless, she jumped about, making faces and acting the fool. Soon, even Gawain was laughing. She finished with a most worthy death, moaning and clutching her chest before sprawling full length on the ground.

She lay, sweaty and breathless, listening to the boys' cheers. The rare sunshine felt good on her face. When a shadow passed over her, she opened her eyes. She squinted at the tall figure looming over her and groaned. Would Bartholomew Graham not leave her alone? He plagued her!

"Go away, calf brain," she said and stuck her tongue out.

She pushed herself up onto her elbows. More ill luck. All the older boys had come out to watch.

"You've changed since last summer," Bartholomew Graham said. He moved his eyes deliberately to her chest.

" 'Tis a shame you have not." She batted away the hand he offered and scrambled to her feet. "Or have you ceased to cheat at games and bully the younger boys?"

"I have a real sword, pretty Isobel," he said with a wink. "If you'll go into the wood with me, I'll let you play with it."

The older boys guffawed at this witless remark. Praise God, she would marry none of them! Her father would find a young man as noble and worthy as Galahad for her.

"Isobel!"

The boys' laughter died as her father's voice boomed out across the field. Isobel was the apple of her father's eye, and woe to any boy caught offending her. Boys, big and small, began slipping away through the field. All save one. Her brother looked about him as though awakened from a dream.

"Geoffrey, go!" she hissed at him. "It will not help to have you in trouble, as well."

Isobel waved to her father. Ah, she was in luck. The man lumbering beside him with a gait like a pregnant cow was their host, Lord Hume. Her father would keep his temper around the old man. All the same, she opened her other hand and let the wooden sword slip to the ground beside her.

When the men finally reached her, she gave Lord Hume her best curtsy. She wanted to make a good impression, since her father said Lord Hume could help them regain their lands.

"I am most sorry for your loss," she said, pleased with herself for remembering the recent death of his wife.

What an old man he was! 'Twas hard to look at him with all that loose skin hanging from his neck and those puffy bags under his eyes drooping halfway down his cheeks. But he must be wealthy. As wealthy as her father said, to own a jeweled belt that could reach around that immense belly of his.

"Your daughter is the image of your lovely wife," Hume said. "And she has spirit enough to keep a man young."

How often did her father say she would make him old before his time? A smile tugged at the corners of her mouth as she slid a look at him, hoping to catch his eye.

"Aye, she is a lively girl," her father said.

The cheerfulness of his reply gave Isobel hope she might escape a scolding for her swordplay with the boys. While the men talked on and on about some event that would take place in the autumn, she grew bored and tried not to fidget.

"'Tis settled then," Lord Hume said, taking his leave at last. "You will want to speak to your daughter now."

Lord Hume took hold of her hand before she could hide it behind her back. She tried not to make a face as he slavered on it. As soon as his back was turned, though, she wiped it on her gown.

She stood beside her father, waiting to be chastised about swords and dirty gowns. When Hume finally hobbled through the castle gate, she turned to face her father.

To her amazement, he was hopping from foot to foot, doing a little dance!

"Father, what has happened?"

He picked her up and swung her in a circle. Then he did his little dance again. Seeing him so gloriously happy made her heart swell with pleasure.

"Tell me, tell me!" she said, laughing.

He raised his hands toward the heavens and shouted, "God forgive me for ever wishing you were a boy!"

Her father grinned down at her, eyes shining, as if she had just handed him the moon and stars.

"Isobel, my girl, I have such good news!"

Chapter One

Northumberland, England
September 1417

The cold from the chapel's stone floor seeped through Isobel's knees. Her every bone and muscle ached with it. 'Twas not the cold, however, that caused her to pause in her prayers. Once again, she ran her eyes over the shrouded corpse surrounded by tall, flickering candles.

When her gaze reached the corpse's belly, high and wide beneath the cloth, a small sigh escaped her. The body was, indeed, Lord Hume's.

This need for reassurance was childish. Chastising herself for her lapse, Isobel returned to her prayers. She would fulfill this last duty to her husband.

And then she would be free of him.

When next she opened her eyes, it was to find the pinched face of the castle chaplain leaning over her.

"I must speak with you," he said without apology.

She nodded and held her breath until he straightened. Did the man never bathe? He smelled almost as bad as Hume.

Whatever the priest had to tell her must be important. As her husband's confessor, he had reason to know Hume's soul was in need of every prayer. Still, she was reluctant to leave the servants to keep vigil without her. Despite the extra coin she gave them, they would cease their prayers the moment the door closed behind her.

Hume had not been a well-loved lord.

When she attempted to rise, her legs failed her, and the priest had to grasp her arm to keep her from falling. She let him lead her out of the tower that housed the castle's small chapel. As she stepped out into the bailey yard, a gush of wind cut through her cloak and gown. She waited, shivering, while Father Dunne fought the wind to close the heavy wooden door.

As soon as he joined her in the yard, she asked, "What is it, Father Dunne?"

Father Dunne pulled his hood low over his face, took her arm, and started walking her toward the keep. "Please, let us wait to speak until we are inside."

"Of course."

The frozen ground crunched beneath their feet. Thinking of the blazing hearth in the hall, Isobel quickened her steps. Food would do her good, as well. She'd missed the midday meal.

As they went up the steps of the keep, she noticed two of them were cracked. She added the repair to the list in her head. The castle was hers now. No more begging Hume's permission to take care of what needed to be done.

As she entered the hall, she saw their nearest neighbor warming his hands at the hearth. She gave Father Dunne a sharp look. The priest was sorely mistaken if he thought the arrival of Bartholomew Graham was good cause to draw her from her vigil.

"Isobel!"

It set her teeth on edge to hear Graham address her by her Christian name, despite her repeated requests that he not.

"My most sincere regrets at Lord Hume's passing," Graham said as he rushed toward her, arms extended.

She offered her hand to prevent his coming closer. Fixing fine gray eyes on her, he pressed his lips to it. He lingered unnecessarily. As he always did.

She should not have been shocked when Graham pursued her during her marriage. After all, he'd been a liar and a cheat as a boy. But how he could still not know his good looks and easy charm were lost on her—that was a mystery.

"Thank you for your concern, but I must speak with Father Dunne now," she said, tugging her hand from Graham's grip.

She clenched her jaw to keep from snapping at him. Usually, she handled Graham's attentions with more grace, but she was tired and her patience short. The last days of Hume's illness had not been easy.

"If you wish to wait," she made herself say, "I will have some refreshment brought."

Father Dunne cleared his throat. "Forgive me, Lady Hume, but I must ask that he join us." Her face must have shown her irritation, for Father Dunne hastened to add, "I have good cause, as you shall see."

She could not very well argue with the castle chaplain in front of the servants in the hall. Biting back her temper, she turned and led the two men up the circular stairs to the family's private rooms on the floor above.

She added replacing the castle chaplain to her list.

Once they were in the privacy of the family solar, she did not bother to keep the sharpness from her tone. "Now, Father Dunne, what is so important that you have seen fit to call me away from my prayers for my husband's soul?"

The chaplain bristled. "I felt it my duty to inform you of a document your husband entrusted into my care."

"A document?" She felt a pang of anxiety in the pit of her stomach. "What sort of document?"

"'Tis a conveyance of certain properties."

Just how large a sum had Hume given to the Cistercian monks at Melrose Abbey to say Masses for him? She did not begrudge the monks, but she hoped there would be sufficient funds left to make the long-neglected repairs to the castle.

"You speak of his will?" she asked.

"A will could not serve this purpose," Father Dunne said in his ponderous voice. "A man may give his gold, his horse, and his armor to whomever he chooses in his will—but not his lands. Upon his death, his lands pass to his heirs."

Father Dunne coughed, looking uneasy for the first time. "To give his lands to anyone else," he said, drawing a rolled parchment from inside his robe, "a man must do it *before* his death."

Isobel had tried for months to convince her husband to let Jamieson buy the small plot he worked so he could marry the miller's daughter. With death knocking at his door, Hume must have finally done it. Good deeds, like prayers, could reduce his time in purgatory.

This must be what the priest was fussing about. She smiled and reached her hand out. "Let me see it, then."

Father Dunne stepped back, clutching the document to his chest. "I suggest you sit first, Lady Hume."

Isobel folded her arms and tapped her foot. "I prefer to stand." Truly, the man did bring out the worst in her.

The priest tightened his mouth and began unrolling the parchment. "'Tis a simple document," he said, still not giving it to her. "In essence, it grants all of Lord Hume's lands, including this castle, to Bartholomew Graham."

The priest had to be mistaken. Or lying. Still, the smug look on his face sent a wave of fear through her.

She ripped the parchment from his hands and scanned the words. She read them a second time, more slowly. And then again, a third time. She looked up, unseeing, and tried to take in the enormity of what her husband had done to her. Surely he would not do this. Could not do it. Not after all she had given up, all she had done for him.

For eight long years she was at the beck and call of a peckish old man who wore her down with his whining and constant demands. Day after day after day. Listening to his tedious conversation. Trying not to watch as food and drink dribbled down his chins and onto his fine clothes.

And then there were the nights.

She put her hand to her chest, fighting the feeling of suffocation. Once again, she saw him huffing and puffing over her, red-faced and sweating. God's mercy! How she feared he would fall dead on top of her and trap her beneath his enormous weight. After years without conceiving, she finally convinced him the risk to his health was too great.

She resented every day, every hour, of her marriage. Still, she had done her duty by her husband.

"It must be a forgery," she murmured, looking down

at the parchment again. She recognized the script as the priest's, but that meant nothing. With shaking hands, she uncurled the final roll of the document.

She ran numb fingertips over the familiar seal.

She watched as the parchment slipped from her hand and fluttered to the floor. The ground shifted beneath her feet. As she reached out to catch herself, the room went black.

Isobel awoke to the nightmarish sight of Graham and that weasel of a priest hovering over her. Before she could gather her wits, Graham lifted her to the bench, his hands touching her in more places than necessary for the task.

As she looked down, a deep red drop hit the bodice of her gown. Bewildered, she touched her finger to it.

"You struck your head on the bench when you fell," Father Dunne said, handing her a cloth. "I did warn you to sit."

"Leave us, Father Dunne," Graham said, as if he were already lord of the castle.

The priest's eyes darted back and forth between them as he backed out of the room. Isobel suspected he went no farther than the other side of the door.

She glared up at Graham as she dabbed at the cut on her forehead. "How did you get Hume to do it?"

Graham dropped next to her on the bench, sitting so close that his thigh touched hers. Too light-headed to stand, she slid to the edge of the bench.

"Hume came to believe I was his son," Graham said, smiling at her. "You know how much he wanted one."

"So you lied to him!"

"Well, it certainly *could* be true," he said with a shrug. "Fortunately, the conveyance is not dependent upon it."

Graham's mother had been a wealthy widow, notorious in this part of the Borders. When she became pregnant, more than one man stepped forward, claiming to be the father and offering to marry her. She disappointed them all by keeping her property—and the secret of her son's parentage—to herself.

"I gave my husband no cause to punish me," Isobel murmured to herself. She could not believe Hume would leave her destitute.

"In sooth, the old man was most concerned for your welfare." Graham stretched his legs out and crossed his arms behind his head. "It gave him great comfort to know I would wed you after his death."

"You would do what?" She must have misheard him.

"Finally, you shall have a man who can please you." His hot breath was in her ear, but she was too stunned to move. "I've wanted you since you were a girl, still playing at sword fighting with the boys."

Coming back to her senses, she slapped at the hand creeping up her thigh. "What would make you believe I would agree to marry you?"

"You would prefer," he said in an amused tone, "to return to your father's house?"

The blood drained from her head. 'Twas true. If she could not remain at Hume Castle, she had no place else to go. She sank against the stone wall behind her and closed her eyes.

"Do not fret—your father would not keep you long," Graham said, patting her knee. "Though you are no longer an untouched girl, he'll have no trouble finding another old man to pay to have such a beauty in his bed."

She swung her arm to slap him, but he caught her wrist.

"'Tis always exciting to be with you, Isobel." With his eyes hot on hers, he pried her fist open and ran his tongue over her palm, sending a quiver of revulsion through her.

All these years, she had sorely misjudged him. She had considered him a mere annoyance, fool that she was. Only now did she see he was not merely shallow and selfish, but ruthless and cunning. The handsome face and easy manner hid a man without honor.

A man who would take what he wanted.

"I shall return in a few days to take my place here," he said.

Isobel's limbs went weak with relief as he rose to go.

At the door, he turned. "Send a message," he said, giving her a wink, "if you cannot wait so long."

Chapter Two

$\mathcal{A}$s soon as Graham was out the door, she raced to it and slid the bar across. Rage pulsed through her now, blurring her vision. She paced the room, clenching her fists until her nails cut into her palms. What could she do? Surely there must be some way to challenge the theft of her property. But how would she go about it? Who could help her?

The only person she trusted was her brother. But Geoffrey was in Normandy with the king's army. She covered her face in her hands, not wanting to think now how worried she was about him. Her sweet, dreamy brother was no soldier. Sending him off to fight was one more thing she would not forgive her father.

Her father. In this alone he would be her ally. He would care if she lost her property.

In the end, she sent for him, for she had no one else to ask.

An hour later, her maid poked her head through the solar door. "M'lady, Sir Edward awaits you in the hall."

Her father must have set out as soon as he received her message.

Isobel hurried down the stairs to the hall. At the entrance she halted, caught off guard by the wave of loss that hit her at the sight of the familiar bullish frame. Her father stood half turned from her, surveying the imposing hall with a smile of satisfaction on his face. After all these years, it should not hurt this much to see him.

With a growing tightness in her chest, she remembered how she used to think he caused the sun to shine. She was the favored child, the adored daughter he took with him everywhere. If it had been otherwise, she would not have felt so betrayed.

What a foolish girl she was. She had believed her father delayed betrothing her because he could not find a man he deemed worthy. Galahads are hard to come by.

Then he sold her like cattle. To a man like Hume.

She recalled how her legs shook and her breath came in gasping hiccups as she climbed down from Hume's high bed to wash that first night. Behind the screen, she lit a candle and poured water into the basin. As she wiped the blood smeared along the inside of her thigh, it struck her: her father knew what Hume would do to her. He knew, and yet he gave her to the man anyway.

"Isobel, 'tis good to see you!" Her father's booming voice jarred her back to the present.

When he came toward her as though he would embrace her, she stopped him with a lift of her hand.

"'Tis a shame," he said, "it took your husband's death for you to receive me in your home."

Isobel resented both the criticism and the hurt in his voice. "Come, we must speak in private."

With no further greeting, she turned and led him up the stairs to the solar. Here, too, he looked about with a proprietary air, admiring the rich tapestries and costly glass window.

"Who would have thought the old man would live so long?" he said, his good cheer restored. "But now this fine castle and all the Hume lands are yours! I told you marriage was a woman's path to power."

Before Isobel could step back, he took hold of her arms. "With what Hume has left you," he said, his eyes alight, "who knows how high you may reach next time?"

Isobel could only stare at him in horror. Could her father truly believe she would let him plan a second marriage for her?

"I know 'twas not easy," he said, his voice softer. "But now you shall reap the reward for your sacrifice."

"My 'sacrifice,' as you call it, has been for naught—at least, naught for me!" Isobel was so choked with emotion, she could barely get the words out. "Hume gave you what you wanted the day the marriage was consummated, but he's left me with nothing."

"He what?"

As she looked into her father's face, her rage returned full force. "My lord husband gave away all the lands I was to inherit." She wanted to pound her fists against her father's chest like the willful child she once was. "You promised I would have my independence once he died. You promised me!"

His fingers dug painfully into her arms. "You are mistaken. Hume had no children; his lands must come to you."

"He has given it all to Bartholomew Graham!" she shouted at him. "My home. My lands. Every last parcel."

"The devil take him!" her father exploded. "What reason could Hume have?"

Isobel covered her face with her hands. "Graham tricked the old fool into believing he was his son."

"This will not stand!" Her father stormed up and down the room, eyes bulging and hands flying in the air. "We will take this up with Bishop Beaufort. Then we shall see! Surely the king's uncle can cure this fraud. I swear, Isobel, we shall see young Graham imprisoned for this."

Before the last shovel of dirt covered Hume's body, Isobel and her father set out for Alnwick Castle. Bishop Beaufort was at the castle on business for the king.

Isobel pulled her horse up at the bridge and eyed the sprawling stone fortress above her. As a child, she had come here often. But that was in the days when Alnwick was home to the Earl of Northumberland—before Northumberland attempted to wrest the crown from Henry Lancaster.

Northumberland escaped to Scotland. The more important of his co-conspirators were beheaded, the lesser dispossessed. Foolish men, every one of them, to take on the Lancasters.

Her father, heedless as ever, spurred his horse over the river that served as Alnwick Castle's first line of defense. Isobel followed more slowly. Bishop Beaufort was the wiliest of all the Lancasters.

"I hear Beaufort is the richest man in all of England," her father said as they neared the gatehouse. "God's beard, he's loaned the crown vast sums for the king's expedition to Normandy."

"Hush!" she whispered. "Do not forgot he was half

brother to our last king." *The king you committed treason against.*

"I have my pardon from young King Henry," he said, but he was not as confident as he pretended. Beads of sweat stood out on his forehead as they rode through the barbican, the narrow passage designed to trap an enemy inside the main gate.

They were escorted into the keep and shut in a small anteroom to await the bishop's pleasure. Almost at once, an immaculately dressed servant came to usher her father into the great hall for an audience. Isobel was left to stew while two men discussed her fate.

She was surprised when the servant returned a short time later without her father.

"His Grace the Bishop wishes to see you now, m'lady." She must have been too slow to rise to her feet, for he arched an eyebrow and said, "His Grace is a busy man."

She walked through the massive wooden door he held open for her and entered an enormous hall with high ceilings that drew the eye ever upward like a church.

There was no mistaking the man behind the heavy wooden table near the hearth. She would have known Bishop Beaufort by the power he exuded, even if he had not worn the vestments of his office—a gold silk chasuble over a snowy white linen alb with apparels worked in silk and gold at the wrists.

The bishop did not look up from his papers as she crossed the room. When she took her place before the table beside her father, she saw that the parchment in the bishop's hands was her copy of Hume's property conveyance.

Her father poked his elbow in her side and winked. His

conversation with the bishop must have gone well, praise God!

"I do not believe," the bishop said, his eyes still on the document, "the transfer of Hume's property can be challenged."

Stunned by the bishop's swift dismissal of her cause, she shot a look at her father. His nod did not reassure her.

"Your father suggests a reasonable solution," the bishop said, snapping her attention back to him. "Under the circumstances, the only honorable course open to Graham is to wed you. I shall see that he makes the offer."

The bishop picked up a new sheaf of papers, dismissing both her and her problem.

"But I have already refused him." Her voice seemed to echo in the cavernous hall. "I do not mean to be ungrateful for your kind assistance, Your Grace," she added hastily. "But I could not marry the man who stole my property. He is wholly without honor."

The bishop set his papers aside and truly looked at her for the first time. Powerful as he was, he could not move her; she met his eyes so he would know it. Instead of irritation, she saw keen interest in the sharp gaze he leveled at her.

"Let me speak alone with your daughter," he said without taking his eyes from hers. Though spoken politely enough, it was not a request.

When the door closed behind her father, the bishop motioned for her to sit. She sat, hands clasped in her lap, and willed herself to stay calm as the bishop inspected her.

"Let us review your choices, Lady Hume," he said, touching his steepled fingers to his chin. "First, you can accept Graham. With him, you keep your home, maintain your position."

She opened her mouth to object and snapped it closed again.

"Second, you can return to your father's care. With the generous dowry your father will provide"—the pointed look he gave her made it clear he knew the humiliating terms of her first marriage—"I am confident the next husband he finds for you will be as suitable as the last."

He paused, as though to give her time to consider. Time, however, could improve neither choice.

Please God, is there no escape for me? None at all?

"I can offer you a third choice," the bishop said in a slow, deliberate voice. He reached out and rested his long, tapered fingers on a rolled parchment at the side of his table. "I just received a letter from my nephew. He has taken Caen."

"God preserve him," she murmured. Desperately, she tried to think of what reason he could have for telling her of King Henry's progress in reclaiming English lands in Normandy. The bishop did not seem like a man to speak without purpose.

"The king is anxious to strengthen the ties between England and Normandy. Come spring, Parliament will offer incentives to English merchants to settle there."

Merchants? What could this have to do with her?

"Alliances among the nobility are even more important." He tapped the rolled parchment with his forefinger. "The king asks for my assistance in making such... arrangements."

Her thoughts seemed thick and slow as she struggled to understand the import of his words.

"I offer you the opportunity to enter into a marriage advantageous to you," he said. "And to England."

Her breath caught. "In Normandy?"

"You must marry someone," the bishop said, turning his palm up on the table. He leaned forward a fraction and narrowed his eyes. "I think perhaps you are a woman who would prefer the devil you do not know over the devil you do."

Knowing she was being played by a master did not help her one whit.

The bishop drummed his fingers lightly on the table.

She tried to think it through. A stranger could hardly be worse than Graham. And if she were in Normandy, she could watch over her brother. But how could she agree to wed a man she knew nothing about?

The bishop drummed his fingers again.

"Would I be permitted to meet the French 'devil' first, before committing to marry him?"

An appreciative smile briefly touched the bishop's lips, but he shook his head. "Even if you leave before a betrothal can be arranged, you will be bound by your pledge to the king." He arched one thin eyebrow. "Do you have some ... *requirement* ... you wish me to pass on to the king?"

A knight, brave and true, good and kind. The description of a Camelot knight came to her, quite inexplicably. Flushing, she shook her head.

"After your father's ... misjudgments ... of the past," the bishop said, his nostrils flaring ever so slightly, "such a marriage would do much to restore your family to the king's good graces."

"May I have time to consider, Your Grace?"

"Of course." With a glimmer in his eye he said, "Soon the crossing will be impossible until spring, but I am sure you wish to spend the long winter months here, with your father."

Oh, he was a clever man.

The bishop rose to his feet. "I leave for Westminster in three days. Until then, you may send a message to me here."

With no further word, he swept out of the room.

Chapter Three

Duchy of Normandy
October 1417

Sir Stephen Carleton awoke to a blinding headache. He lay still, listening to the distant sound of wind and rain, and tried to recall where he was. Aye, he was with King Henry's army in Normandy. In the town of Caen, in fact.

But where, precisely, in Caen?

Giving up, he slit one eye open and winced at the dim light. It came through an arrow slit, so he was somewhere in the castle. But this was not his bedchamber. And what was he doing in bed when it was yet daylight—

He groaned. Gingerly, he turned his head for confirmation. Upon seeing the bare shoulder and tousled blond hair, he squeezed his eyes shut again. Marie de Lisieux. God help him, she was a lot of woman to forget.

He edged his arm out from under her, taking great care not to disturb her. Pleased at his success, he sat up and swung his legs over the side of the bed—much, much too quickly.

Resting his head in his hands to recover, he looked

down at his limp member and wondered if it would ever rise again. The woman was insatiable. No wonder her husband turned a blind eye to her infidelities; the man was grateful for the respite.

How had he ended up in bed with her again? A wave of self-loathing washed over him, making him desperate for a drink. Ironic, since drink was what had gotten him here. But drink kept at bay the visions that plagued him.

Aye, drink helped. And women, of course.

There were plenty of men to drink with in a town overrun with soldiers. And, for him, there were always willing women. Which one hardly mattered. He had even less expectation of finding a woman who could make him happy than he did of achieving knightly glory in this wretched war.

He wondered what it would be like to be with a woman who was strong and brave and clever. A woman who would not settle for him being less than the man he could be.

Could she save him? Was he worth saving?

He knew only one woman like that, and he did not expect to meet another. Still, he enjoyed women. Talking with them. Flirting with them. Bedding them. He did not have to be fully sober, however, to know the one asleep beside him was a mistake.

Keeping a watchful eye on Marie's still form, he eased himself down from the bed. She slept like the dead, the saints be praised. When he leaned over to gather his clothes, his head throbbed so violently he feared he would be sick. He waited for his stomach to settle before pulling the shirt and tunic over his head. Teetering on one foot, he nearly fell as he struggled into his leggings.

He grabbed his boots in one hand, his belt and sword in the other, and made his escape.

God's beard, the corridor was freezing!

He could see now he was in the castle's keep. But whose bedchamber was that? It would be just like Marie to take him to another lover's bed. The woman thrived on trouble.

Caen Castle was huge, with numerous buildings scattered across acres of bailey yard. The walk to the main gate was almost long enough to clear his head. When he finally crossed the bridge into the Old Town, he entered the first public house he found.

He was still there hours later, drinking with a boisterous group of soldiers, when he felt eyes upon him. The familiar form of his half brother, Lord William FitzAlan, filled the doorway. When the other men noticed the great commander, they fumbled to their feet and offered to make room. William kept his gaze on Stephen.

Stephen poured more wine into his cup and ignored his brother. When one of his companions called out, "May God bring us more victories," he did not raise his cup with the others. But he drank it down all the same.

He poured another and decided to make his own toast.

"God grant us victory," he said, clutching the edge of the table, "even if we must starve women and children to achieve it."

Before he saw William move, his brother had an iron grip on his arm and was leading him out the door. Outside, William slammed him up against the wall.

William cupped Stephen's chin and jaw in his hand. With his face so close their noses nearly touched, he said, "God in heaven, Stephen, what am I to do with you?"

Drunk or sober, Stephen would not let any other man lay hands on him. But this was William. "'Tis a long time since I've been your responsibility, big brother."

"I have served as both father and brother to you for far too many years to stand by and let you do this to yourself!"

William released his hold and leaned heavily against the wall beside Stephen. In a quiet voice he said, "We did what we could. You must try to put it behind you."

Stephen did not want to talk about what happened the day the siege of Caen broke and the English army swarmed through the town. By the time he and William reached the market square, English soldiers were massacring the crowd of women, children, and old men gathered there. He and William rode through the melee, swinging their swords in the air, shouting and pushing, until at last the order to halt was heard and obeyed.

The images of that day would not leave him.

When it was over, Stephen walked through the carnage in the square. The wails of women filled his ears, and the smell of blood choked him as he stepped over broken bodies of children and old men. When he looked down, a child's severed arm lay before his bloody boot. He leaned against a wall and vomited until his knees were weak.

"This is not the path to glory I expected when we came to fight the French," he said.

"King Henry's army slaughtering old men, women, and children!" William said, his voice hard with anger. "I never thought to see it."

"You must have known. Why else did you order Jamie to remain outside the city walls that day?" Despite the accusation in his voice, Stephen was immensely grateful his nephew did not witness the slaughter in the square.

"The lad is only fifteen," William objected. "'Tis true I suspected trouble, though not as foul as that. The men were full of bloodlust after our knight was burned to death."

The city defenders had thrown bales of burning straw onto the knight, who lay injured in the ditch at the base of the wall. Unable to reach their man, listening to his screams, the English sat by their campfires in frustrated rage.

"And the king?" Stephen asked, though he knew the answer.

"He believes the people brought the wrath of God upon themselves," William said in a grim voice. "They had only to submit to him as their rightful sovereign to escape their fate."

"The women and children had no part in the city's decision to hold out against us."

"The killing was against the king's orders, and he'll not allow it to happen again." William took in a deep breath and let it out. "The other towns will fall quickly now."

"So the slaughter served a purpose," Stephen said, his voice tight. "Our king is nothing if not strategic."

"You are incautious with your opinions," William said, though without much force. "If the people here had the sense God gave them, they would welcome us. The French nobility are a blight upon the land. Both Burgundy and Armagnac factions pillage the countryside for their own enrichment."

"'Tis a shame the French armies will not fight us. I hoped to win great battles for England." Embarrassed, Stephen elbowed William and tried for a lighter tone. "Like my famous brother."

"By God, I never thought I would miss fighting the Scots," William said as he heaved himself away from the wall. "Come, I'll walk with you to the castle. You need to get your sleep—you have an appointment with the king early on the morrow."

Stephen felt the remaining effects of the drink drain out of him. "Called in a favor for your feckless little brother, have you?"

"Feckless perhaps, but hardly little." William clouted him on the back. "And I called in no favors. God knows why, but the king has seen something special in you since you were a lad. He says he has an assignment for you."

"What is it?"

William shrugged. "He did not say."

They walked in companionable silence through the castle gate and into the castle grounds. During the day the bailey yard was busy with soldiers, but it was peaceful this time of night. They were nearly to the Old Palace, where Stephen shared a chamber with his nephew, before William spoke again.

"You should ask the king's permission to return to Northumberland. 'Tis time you claimed the Carleton lands."

"I am not so foolish as that! Mother and Catherine will be relentless, once I have the property, to make a good match." Why was his unmarried state such a thorn in their sides?

"They want to see you settled before you fall into serious trouble over some woman." William shook his head. "And they are right. 'Tis bound to happen."

Stephen ignored the remark; he'd heard it before.

After a time, William said, "There is much to be said

for a life with wife and children, on lands of one's own. God knows, Catherine is the source of all my happiness."

"As I've always told you," Stephen said, forcing a laugh, "if you find me a woman like her, I'll be wed as soon as the banns can be posted."

Catherine was beautiful, courageous, full of opinions and laughter. He'd adored her from the age of twelve, when his mother sent him to live with William and his new wife.

"I wish to God Catherine were here now," William said, his tone sour. "You would not behave like this if she were here to see it."

Stephen shrugged, acknowledging the truth of it. In his youth, it had always been easier to face William's anger than Catherine's disappointment. Even now, he would do anything to please her.

Well, almost anything. At least here in Normandy, he was free of her attempts to get him betrothed to some pliant and exceedingly dull young lady of good family and fortune.

Aye, he knew he must marry. But he was only five and twenty! With luck, he could put that duty off for many years.

Stephen sat in the Great Hall of the Exchequer, drumming his fingers. Damn. He should have risen early enough to join the king for Mass in the chapel.

At the sound of boots, he jumped to his feet. King Henry swept into the hall, trailed by several soldiers who served as his personal guard. With a curt nod, the king released Stephen from his bow.

Stephen sighed inwardly as the king scrutinized him in the long silence that followed. Though he had taken care in dressing for this ungodly early appointment, there was naught he could do about his bloodshot eyes. King Henry indulged in neither women nor drink; he had little tolerance for those who did.

"How can I be of service to you, sire?" Stephen smiled and gave a deferential nod to temper his boldness in speaking first.

"Perhaps you could explain to me," the king said, clasping his hands behind his back, "why a man who is so easily amused must devote so much time to seeking amusement."

Stephen dropped the smile. Had he been so indiscreet that word of his behavior had reached even the king's ears?

"I have better use for your talents, Stephen Carleton."

Stephen detected no trace of sarcasm in the king's tone. A good sign, perhaps. "I am, as always, at your disposal, sire."

He wondered again what assignment the king had for him. He desperately wanted a military command, but he would be satisfied with rounding up renegades. Anything, so long as it was dangerous and diverting.

"My subjects here must see that I come not to conquer, but to rule as their rightful sovereign. 'Tis time to establish order and good governance in the lands we have thus far reclaimed. To that end, I have appointed Sir John Popham as bailli of Caen. I want you to assist him."

Stephen could not believe what he was hearing. "You want me to be...to be..." He had to grope for the word, and it felt distasteful in his mouth when he found it. "An *administrator?* But I am a skilled knight, sire."

"You would make a fine commander, as well," the king said in a flat voice. "But until a French army is willing to face us in battle, I have more commanders than I need."

Two years before, the English army decimated the cream of French chivalry at the Battle of Agincourt in a defeat so resounding it would be remembered through the ages. The French commanders had studiously avoided fighting the young English king head-to-head ever since.

"What I need is a man of wit and charm who can earn the people's trust," the king said. "Your charge is to hear their complaints, resolve their disputes fairly, and convince them they are better off under English rule."

Sweet Lamb of God. "I am glad to be of service, sire."

"Leave us," the king called out. When the heavy doors closed behind the soldiers keeping guard at the entrance, the king said, "I knew I chose the right man. No one would guess from your countenance you are seething."

The smile on the king's face brought to mind a cat with an injured bird under his paw.

"That deceptive charm," the king continued, "and your much-lauded talent for learning secrets, will prove valuable in your second assignment, as well."

It was a family joke that no secret was safe from him. Stephen tried to guess which of his loved ones saw fit to share this with the king. His musings were stopped dead as a panel in the wall behind the king swung open. When a tall, elegantly dressed man with distinctive white-blond hair stepped through the opening, Stephen re-sheathed his sword.

"Robert!" Stephen shouted. "What are you doing in Normandy? Does William know?"

He and Robert thumped each other on the back, then

stepped back to look more closely at each other. Though Robert's face showed a few more laugh lines, Stephen didn't doubt women fell at his feet—and into his bed— with the same regularity.

"*Sir* Robert now," the king said. "After twenty years, our friend has given up the guise of traveling musician. He has returned to claim his rightful place as a nobleman of Normandy."

"You are full of surprises," Stephen said, laughing.

Robert grinned back. "How it would grieve my uncle to know I've inherited his estates! I went into hiding because he was determined to have me murdered." Robert leaned close to Stephen and whispered, "His second wife favored me a bit too much."

"Despite his change in circumstances," the king said, "Robert has agreed to continue his service to me."

Steven knew what that "service" was. As a troubadour, Robert traveled widely and was welcomed everywhere. That had made him a useful spy in the years when England was roiled in rebellion and King Henry was yet Prince Harry.

"I cannot tell you how many evenings the family spent speculating about who you truly were," Stephen said.

Robert's eyes crinkled with good humor. "We can speak more of that another time. Now we must discuss the king's plans for you. We shall be working together, my friend."

———

When the king dismissed Stephen and signaled for him to remain, Robert felt no sense of alarm, no foreboding.

Though they were very different men, their relationship was one of long-standing and mutual respect.

"Order and good government will not be enough to bind Normandy to England," Harry began. "We must have marriage alliances among the nobility, as well."

Apprehension crept up Robert's spine. Marriage alliances? Could the king mean—good God, the saints protect him!

"I received a letter today from my uncle, Bishop Beaufort, regarding one such young lady. If the weather holds, she could arrive any day."

A drop of sweat trickled down Robert's back. "A young lady, sire? How young?" Please God, not some young innocent. He was years and years too old for that.

"She is a widow of two and twenty."

Better than fifteen or sixteen. But only slightly. He must think of an excuse, but what? Blast it, if he were yet just a troubadour, the king would never ask this of him.

"I want your advice," Harry said, touching the points of his steepled fingers to his chin. "Which of the French noblemen who have pledged loyalty to me should I bind more closely through a marriage alliance?"

Praise God! Relief coursed through Robert's body. He hoped it did not show in his face.

"The only city that lies between my army and Paris is Rouen," the king said. "I want a man with influence in that city. A man who might convince them it is in their interest to surrender quickly."

Robert sucked in a breath to steady himself and set his mind to the king's question.

"Philippe de Roche," he said, glad the answer was so easy. "He is a powerful man in Rouen. And, as a member of the Burgundy faction, he is allied with us for the time being. From what I hear, his only true loyalty is to himself."

"Then he is no different from most of these French nobles," the king said, disapproval heavy in his voice.

"De Roche will not wish to bind himself to an English lady," Robert said, "until he is certain which way the wind blows."

"Since most of his lands are under our control, he will agree to the marriage," the king said with a smile. "But will it keep him loyal?"

Robert shrugged. "It will, at least, preclude him from making a marriage alliance unfavorable to us."

"I have reason to hope for more," the king said. "My uncle reports that this particular lady is blessed with both a strong will and great beauty."

Robert had no interest in the young widow's attributes.

"Perhaps you met her in your travels?" the king said. "Her name is Lady Isobel Hume—her father is Sir Edward Dobson."

The blood drained from Robert's head so rapidly he swayed on his feet. Margaret's daughter. The king was speaking of Margaret's daughter. Coming here. To Caen.

" 'Tis many years since I traveled to the north," Robert said, struggling to keep his features smooth. "But I believe my troupe did perform for her father's household once or twice."

Pretty little Isobel, so like her mother. She sat at his feet for hours listening to him sing ballads and recite tales. Her favorites were those of King Arthur.

"She was a lovely child," he said and regretted the wistful tone that crept into his voice.

"Well, she is no child now," the king snapped. "I do not know what I shall do with her until the marriage can be arranged. There are no English noblewomen here into whose care I may put her. She has a brother with Gloucester's army, but it will take time to bring him to Caen."

"Put her into my care until the brother comes." The words were out of Robert's mouth before he thought them.

"A young lady? In your care? Do you take me for a fool!"

"Believe me, I do not want this burden," Robert said, putting his hands up. "If you had anyone else, I would not own up to my obligation."

"Obligation?" the king demanded. "What obligation?"

Obligations. Consequences. What lad of sixteen considers these when he believes himself in love? That summer in Flanders, he and Margaret sneaked off every chance they got.

"We are distant relation, through our families in Flanders," Robert said, knowing bits of truth always improve a falsehood. "If you doubt it, ask Lady Hume if she has a Flemish grandmother."

The king narrowed his eyes at Robert, considering.

"She is a widow, not a young girl," Robert reminded him. "She does not need a guardian."

"Still, I must do something with her," the king grumbled.

"I give you my pledge, the lady will be safe with me."

The king nodded; Harry always did like a pledge.

"But you shall watch over her," the king said, shaking his finger in Robert's face, "as a father watches over a daughter."

Robert's throat tightened. God knew, he was late to the task. And wholly unsuited.

But he would do his best.

Chapter Four

November 1417

Stephen strode through the bailey yard, his thoughts sour after spending an entire morning resolving a dispute between two whining merchants. Praise God, he had the afternoon free to train with William and Jamie. He needed to wield a sword until his muscles ached and the sweat poured from his skin.

This evening, like all his evenings now, belonged to Robert. God help him, his king valued him for the secrets he could wheedle out of people. What honor was there in that?

The king should be pleased to learn Stephen was employing his "special talents." So far, there was no shortage of local men who wished to drink with him or women who wished to bed him.

"Stephen!"

He did not see Marie de Lisieux until he had to grab her to keep from knocking her to the ground. God in heaven, the woman was always underfoot. She pursued him with a persistence that had long since ceased to be flattering.

Marie pressed her hand to her ample bosom. "You must come sit with me while I recover."

The spark in her eyes told him sitting was not what the lady had in mind. Keeping her marriage vows was just the beginning of the scruples the voluptuous Marie de Lisieux did not have. The woman was trouble. But who was he to deny the king's command to "insinuate" himself with the local nobility?

"I cannot now." Over her shoulder, he saw William and Jamie coming across the bailey yard. Robert was with them.

Marie tugged on his arm. "Then when?"

"Saturday," he said and waved to the others.

"But that is days away!"

Her perfume was so strong it made his eyes water. Odd he never noticed before.

"Tonight," she insisted. "You must come to me tonight."

"Late," he said, prying her fingers from his tunic. He gave her a wink and ran off to join the others.

His mood lifted as the four of them walked in the direction of the Old Palace. Between it and the Exchequer was an open space where they usually practiced.

"I am pleased you are joining us," he said, clamping his hand on Robert's shoulder. "After all you've done for me, I shall make it my personal duty to keep you in fighting shape."

Robert laughed. "I should enjoy the challenge, but I cannot today. I've come to ask a favor."

Stephen threw him a black look. "What is it?"

"A noblewoman from Northumberland arrived by ship this morning," Robert said, turning to address William

and Jamie, as well. "The king has put her in my care.
Since she is here without friend or family, it would be a
kindness if you would talk with her."

The back of Stephen's neck prickled. He could think of
only one explanation for the arrival of a lone English lady
in Caen.

"If this is some foolish girl my mother and Catherine
have sent, I will send her back. No matter the consequences." His suspicion shifted quickly to outrage. "Robert, how could you be party to this scheme of theirs?"

"Afore God, I am innocent!" Robert said, putting his
hand over his heart and laughing. "This lady is here to
make a political marriage. Believe me, I shall have to
answer to the king if anything more than friendly talk
occurs between you."

Stephen's good humor returned at once. "What was the
king thinking, putting her into your care?"

"As it happens, her mother is a distant cousin of
mine."

"The king believed that?" Stephen said, grinning.
"What of her betrothed? Surely the man does not know
you, to allow it."

"The lady is safe in my hands," Robert said. "As for the
man, he is in Rouen—and has yet to learn of his impend-
ing betrothal."

———

Isobel tried to ignore her maid's fidgeting as she watched
for Sir Robert. From their bench in front of the Old Palace, she could see most of the buildings enclosed within
the castle's outer walls. The Exchequer Hall, where Sir

Robert said King Henry held court, was to her right. If she leaned forward and looked the other way, she could see past the curtain wall of the keep all the way to the eastern gate, Porte des Champs.

Soldiers were everywhere she looked.

"There are so many men here," her maid said. "Are we safe, m'lady?" The woman's eyes flitted from side to side, as though she expected to be attacked at any moment.

"Hush!" Isobel was exasperated with the woman's endless questions. Since she had no servants of her own now, she was forced to bring this silly woman from her father's household. "The men guarding us wear the king's livery. We could not be safer."

The unease that gnawed at her stomach had nothing to do with finding herself in the midst of hundreds of armed men. All her anxiety centered on one man.

"But where is your intended?" the maid asked. "When will he come for you?"

"You know very well Sir Robert has gone to ask for news of him." So long as her Frenchman was not here, she did not care where he was. *Please, God, let him never come.*

"Have you ever seen a man so handsome?"

Isobel knew the maid was no longer speaking of her intended, but of Sir Robert. The woman was so agog when he met them at the ship that Isobel had to give her a firm shove to get her down the ship's ramp.

"He is more beautiful than handsome," Isobel said, more to herself than the maid. "Like the angel Gabriel."

"Just so, m'lady!"

He'd been kind as an angel, too. After making sure she was comfortably settled into a chamber in the keep, he devoted the rest of his morning to walking her about the castle grounds.

'Twas odd, though. Bits of song kept coming into her head when he spoke. As she puzzled over it, she gazed at the lovely chapel dedicated to Saint George that stood midway between her bench and the main gate, Porte Saint-Pierre.

Her jaw dropped when she saw Robert striding toward her with three other men. Like the waters of the Red Sea, the crowds of soldiers parted before them, leaving her with a clear view. The four tall, formidable, well-built men looked as if they stepped out of the magical tales of her childhood.

One of them was of an age with Sir Robert and looked precisely as she always imagined King Arthur: dark golden, commanding, grave. Next to him was a dark-haired youth of perhaps sixteen.

She shifted her gaze to the last man, who was talking with great animation. Judging from how the others turned their heads to listen, it was a good story he was telling. All four men were handsome, but there was something about this one that held her attention.

That rich auburn hair, which he wore to his shoulders, must be the envy of every woman who saw it. She liked his long, lithe frame and the way he walked with an easy, catlike grace despite the wild gestures he was making.

"M'lady, could one of these fine men be your intended?"

Isobel turned to stare at her maid. Could it be true? Could he have arrived already? Alarm coursed through her limbs and settled in a knot in her belly.

"One of them is the right age, aye?" the maid persisted.

Sir Robert said her Frenchman was but a few years older than she.

When she turned back to look at the men again, her throat closed in panic. They were nearly upon her!

"See, m'lady, the one on the end with the lovely hair—"

Out of the corner of her eye, she saw the maid's arm rising and grabbed it before the woman could point.

She was not ready to meet him, she was not, she was not. She busied herself brushing her gown, trying desperately to calm herself.

With a burst of male laughter, the men surrounded her.

Robert greeted her with a warm smile and helped her to her feet. Tilting his head toward the man who looked like King Arthur, he said, "Lady Hume, let me present Lord William FitzAlan."

FitzAlan looked as though he slayed dragons for breakfast. But when he greeted her, she saw kindness in his eyes.

"And this is FitzAlan's son, Jamie Rayburn," Robert said, turning to the dark-haired youth.

Young Jamie Rayburn seemed unable to keep his eyes from running over her, head to foot, despite the fact that it caused him to blush furiously.

She had no time to wonder how it might be that father and son had different family names before the third man eased the youth aside. All else faded away as she looked into the face of the man she was to marry.

Could it be true? Could this man with the laughing eyes be her new husband?

She'd prayed for a man who did not disgust her. Never did she dare hope for this. The man was so handsome he took her breath away. Every feature was pleasing: the black slash eyebrows; the hard planes of cheek and jaw; the strong, straight nose; the wide, mobile mouth.

But his eyes would always be her favorite part. Amazing how the color almost matched his hair—just a few shades darker and more deep brown than chestnut.

And his voice. So melodic.

As she listened to it, she imagined a row of pretty children with the warm brown eyes of puppies.

And almost failed to catch his words.

"...a delight to meet you. I am Sir Stephen Carleton."

She blinked at him. "But that is an English name."

"Aye, 'tis," he said with a grin that drew her gaze to his even white teeth. "I am from Northumberland, just as you are."

Northumberland? But...good heavens! She felt herself blush to her roots, mortified by her mistake. What must the man think?

"I've spent little time in Northumberland since I was twelve," Carleton continued, smooth as silk. "Still, I expect we have some acquaintances in common."

She caught the devilish twinkle in his eyes, and her humiliation was complete. Did he guess she mistook him for her Frenchman? Or was he merely amused by her wide-open stare?

What had come over her? She thought she gave up those childish dreams of Knights of the Round Table a long, long time ago.

In sooth, this Stephen Carleton was as handsome as any of the knights of legend. She was quite sure, however, none of the Camelot knights had the mischief she saw in the eyes of the man grinning down at her.

Unbidden, the image of Bartholomew Graham flitted across her mind. A reminder that good looks and easy charm could hide a very black heart.

———

Stephen watched, amused, as Jamie gawked helplessly at the dark-haired beauty. His nephew appeared incapable of speech. Before the poor boy could embarrass himself further, Stephen stepped forward to introduce himself.

He did not anticipate the effect those green eyes would have on him when the lady shifted her gaze to him. God in heaven, she was looking at him as though he were the answer to her prayers. It made him almost wish he were.

The undisguised longing in her eyes sent a bolt of desire scorching through him. The look was gone so quickly he might have imagined it.

Except he knew he had not.

Hoping to strike the spark again, he gave her the smile that usually got him what he wanted. Cool as ice, she turned and took up conversation with Robert.

He found himself behaving as badly as Jamie, taking her in from head to toe. The braids wound in gold mesh attached to her headdress were dark. She had pale skin and lovely delicate features that made her appear fragile. But there was something about the way she held herself that told him she did not consider herself weak or in need of protection.

He followed the elegant line of her neck. Breathing hard, he worked his way down her slender, shapely form. He was grateful for the unseasonably warm weather that had led her to remove her cloak. Grateful, indeed.

His slow, thorough perusal was interrupted by a hard jab to the ribs. When he sent a questioning sideways glance at the offender, William gave his head an almost imperceptible shake and mouthed, "Nay."

Stephen almost laughed aloud. Aye, there were many reasons he should not look at Lady Hume like that. That she was to make a political marriage for the king was reason enough for a wise man to keep his distance.

He bit back a smile, considering the dangers. Catherine always said he was drawn to trouble like a bear to honey. She was right, of course.

Chapter Five

"Try to remember," Robert said as they walked down a dark street to yet another gathering, "you want to get the men drunk enough so they speak freely, while only *pretending* to be drunk yourself."

Stephen had sipped watered wine like a grandmother all night, but he did not bother to defend himself. He felt restless, despite the late hour.

"Tell me about this Lady Isobel Hume." He kept his voice casual, although he'd been thinking about her all day.

"She is virtuous and unmarried," Robert said. "Not your sort at all."

Stephen laughed. "Come, Robert, a man can be curious, can he not?"

"So long as you do not attempt to satisfy your 'curiosity' with this particular lady."

Some undeserving Frenchman would have that pleasure. For some reason, that galled Stephen to no end.

"Speaking of women," Robert said. "By the saints, Stephen, can you not show some discretion in the women you bed?"

This, just after he'd fended off their last host's buxom and oh-so-willing daughter. "How can you, of all men, lecture me about women?"

"Who better?" Robert said. "I do not suggest you be celibate, God forbid. Only do try to exercise better judgment."

"Did William ask you to speak with me about this?"

Robert's laugh rang out through the empty street. "William would sooner put you in chains as a remedy than have me advise you about women!"

Stephen sighed. "Not that it is your concern, but I am finished with Marie." Of course, Marie did not know that yet.

Marie. Good God, he'd forgotten their liaison tonight. Marie was not a woman easily deterred. When he failed to come to their meeting place, she would seek him out. Even go to his bedchamber—

"St. Wilgefort's beard!" He abandoned Robert in the middle of the dark street and took off running.

Luckily, the men on duty at the gate were drinking companions of his. With a few ribald shouts, they waved him through. He raced across the endless expanse of bailey yard to the Old Palace. Breathing hard, he took the steps to the second floor two at a time and sprinted down the dimly lit corridor to the chamber he shared with Jamie.

If he was too late, William would have his head, for sure.

When he burst into the chamber, two heads popped up from the bed. Marie lay sprawled over Jamie, her gown pushed down below her breasts. But God was with him; the bedclothes were still between Marie and his nephew.

Jamie bolted upright, sending Marie rolling sideways.

With a dramatic sigh, Marie raised herself up on one arm and looked at Stephen. She did not cover herself.

"He is a bit young for you, Marie," Stephen said, keeping his tone light. "You must be twice his age."

A smile twitched at her lips. "I swear, Stephen," she said, widening her eyes, "he gave every sign he was old enough."

He closed his eyes briefly. Would this night ever end? "Time to go, Marie."

She took her time squeezing her breasts back into her tight bodice—a process Jamie followed closely. When she slid down from the high bed, she made sure her gown rode up high on her thighs.

Stephen picked up her cloak from the floor, draped it around her shoulders, and led her to the door.

"The three of us?" she whispered close to his ear.

He gave his head a firm shake. "How does your husband handle you?"

"Not nearly as well as you do," she said as he eased her out the door.

He bolted it behind her, then turned to face his nephew, who sat on the bed looking shamefaced and disheveled. "Stay away from that woman."

"I was asleep—she was on me before I knew it," Jamie fumbled. "She thought I was you, at first. I did not mean to...I...I know she is yours..."

"She is not mine, praise God. Marie has a husband." He sank onto a nearby stool. Wearily, he pulled his boots off and tried to think of the right words. "You are but fifteen—"

"Nearly sixteen," Jamie interrupted. "Surely you'll not tell me I am too young. She would not be my first."

Stephen lifted his eyes heavenward for help that did not come. "Believe me, you are too young to bed this particular woman," he said. "And much too good a man."

He looked at his nephew, trying to see him as the young man he was now, without also seeing the boy who used to toddle after him. Deep blue eyes, dark hair. Too handsome for his own good.

"Many women will want you," he said at last. "That does not mean you must bed them all."

"You do."

Stephen rubbed his temples. "Nay, not all of them."

God in heaven, he was a fool to think Jamie had been unaware. Forget William's wrath, Catherine would skin him alive. How many times had she admonished him that Jamie looked up to him? Lately, he had not believed it possible his nephew still did.

"Aye, there have been a lot of women lately," he admitted, exhaling a long breath. "And I can tell you, there is no lasting satisfaction in meaningless affairs with frivolous women. 'Tis much better to look for what your parents have."

"Then why do you not seek it for yourself?"

Jamie's face was so serious Stephen had to fight not to smile. God, he loved this boy.

"For the right woman," he said, meeting his nephew's eyes, "I would give up all the others without regret." He thought it might even be true.

"So, while a man waits for the perfect woman, he is free to waste time on frivolous ones," Jamie said with a grin. "Then I say, do not hurry, Perfect Woman. Take your time!"

Jamie ducked as Stephen's boot sailed over his head.

"Move over, you lout!" Stephen said, crawling into the bed.

Long after Jamie's breathing grew steady, Stephen lay awake, thinking. When Catherine came into his mind, he smiled. The one perfect woman. He missed her.

With an enormous sense of relief, he realized he'd not imagined taking his sister-in-law to bed in years. Not since he was Jamie's age—and everyone knew what youth of that age were like!

Perhaps he was not as bad as he thought.

His mind drifted to the lady from Northumberland... and to that look she gave him in the first moment they met.

A man might do a lot to see that look again.

Chapter Six

Stephen cursed Sir John Popham as he followed the path along the castle wall to the bailli's residence. With mist hovering over the ground, the bailey yard was eerie at this hour. Did Popham set their appointments earlier each day just to spite him?

He tried to turn his thoughts to the business of the day, but they kept returning to the more interesting subject of Lady Isobel Hume. The more he saw of her, the more intrigued he became. And he saw her often; he made sure of that.

Flirtation seemed not a part of her social repertoire. Unusual, especially for such a pretty woman.

Her smiles rarely reached her eyes. He'd yet to hear her laugh. As with flirting, his efforts there came to naught. He tried to imagine what her laugh would sound like. A tinkling? A light trill?

Aye, he was intrigued. Almost as much as he was attracted. It was not just that she was beautiful, though she was that. He wanted to know her. And her secrets.

Curiosity had always been his weakness.

A peculiar sound interrupted his musings. Peculiar,

at least, to be coming from one of the storerooms built against the wall. He went to the low wooden door and put his ear to it.

Whish! Whish! Whish! The sound was unmistakable. Drawing his sword, he eased the door open to take a look.

"Lady Hume!"

She looked as surprised as he was to catch her alone in a storeroom attacking a sack of grain with a sword.

"The poor thing is defenseless," he said, cocking his head toward the sack. Grain was seeping onto the dirt floor from several small tears.

"Close the door!" she hissed. "I cannot be seen here."

And what a sight she was, with her cheeks flushed and strands of dark hair sticking to her face and neck. *God preserve me*. He stepped inside and firmly closed the door behind him.

"I meant for you to remain outside when you closed it."

Though she took a step back as she spoke, she kept a firm hand on her sword. As she should.

With her glossy dark hair in a loose braid over her shoulder, she looked even more beautiful than he imagined. And he'd spent hours imagining it. No man saw a grown woman with her hair uncovered unless he was a close family member. Or a lover. The intimacy of it sent his pulse racing.

Aye, the lady had every reason to feel nervous at finding herself alone with a man in this secluded place.

"That sack cannot provide much of a challenge," he said, trying to put her at ease.

"You make fun of me." There was resentment in her tone, but he was pleased to see her shoulders relax.

"I believe I would serve as a better partner, though I must warn you"—he paused to glance meaningfully at the sack of grain—"I will not hold still while you poke at me."

Her sudden smile spilled over him like a burst of sunshine.

"But I wonder," she said, raising her sword in his direction, "will you squeal like a pig when I do stick you?"

He laughed out loud. "I am shamed to admit this is my first time matching swords with a woman, so please be kind."

She barely gave him time to take up position before she attacked.

"You have natural skill," he allowed after a few parries and thrusts. "All you need is more practice."

"But you, sir, are astonishing," she said, a little breathless. "Quite the best I've seen."

His chest swelled as if he were a youth of twelve.

"And I thought you excelled only at drinking games."

Ouch. "So you've been watching me. I am flattered."

The deep flush of her cheeks pleased him to no end. He deflected a determined jab to his heart.

He played with her as he did with the younger squires—hard enough to challenge, but not so hard as to discourage. When she pulled her skirt out of the way with her free hand, though, he missed his footing and very nearly dropped his sword.

She stepped back, her brows furrowed.

"Showing your ankles was a clever move," he said, giving her a low bow. "A trick I've not seen before."

"It was not my intention to rely on anything other than my skill." Her tone was as stiff as her spine. "I would not be so dishonorable as to stoop to tricks."

Good Lord. "If your opponent is both stronger and more skilled than you are," he said, keeping his voice even, "then you must use what advantages you do have."

Sword arm extended, he motioned with his other hand for her to come forward. He suppressed a smile when she took up her sword again and came toward him.

"Then, once you have an opening, you must use it," he said. "Never give up your moment, as you just did. Do not hesitate. Your opponent may not give you a second chance."

"You do not care how you win, sir, so long as you do?" Her tone was scathing.

He sighed inwardly. How naive could she be?

"Use whatever rules you like when you are playing, Isobel. But if a man less honorable should find you alone as I did today, you will wish you knew how to fight without the rules."

She narrowed her eyes at him but did not speak.

"It would be preferable, of course, if you did not wander about alone. You forget you are in dangerous country here."

"'Tis not your place to lecture me."

Someone should. "Now, do you want to continue playing at sword fighting?" he asked, deliberately baiting her. "Or do you want to learn how to protect yourself from someone who intends you harm?"

Green eyes sparking with fire, she raised her sword and said, "Teach me."

Oh, what he would love to teach her! God help him, she was breathtaking like this.

"You should carry a short blade, as well," he instructed as he fended off her attack.

"Why? You think you can knock my sword from my hand?"

"I can." He saw a half-empty sack on the floor behind her. "But I will not have to. You will drop it."

She fought better angry, a good quality in a fighter.

Still, he was better. Much better. He forced her to step back, and back, and back again. Once more, and her heel caught on the sack. She threw her hands up, sending the sword clattering against the wall as she tumbled backward.

The next moment, she was lying back on her elbows, her hair loose about her shoulders, skirts askew, chest heaving.

He could not move, could not even breathe.

She looked like a goddess. A wanton Venus, sprawled on the dirt floor at his feet. Then she threw her head back and laughed. Not a light trill, but a full-throated, joyful laugh that made his heart soar.

What he would not do to hear her laugh again!

"I'm afraid you have the advantage of me," she said, her eyes dancing. She reached her hand up for him to help her to her feet.

He took it and sank to his knees beside her. "Not true, Isobel," he said in a harsh whisper. "'Tis I who am at your mercy."

His eyes fixed on her lips, full and parted. Well beyond thought now, he gave in to the inexorable pull toward them. The moment their lips touched, fire seared through him.

He tried to hang on to the thin thread of caution tugging at his conscience. But she was kissing him back, mouth open, her tongue seeking his. His ears roared as she put her arms around his neck and pulled him down.

He cushioned the back of her head with his hand before it touched the dirt floor. Leaning over her, he gave himself wholly to kissing her. He splayed his hands into her hair and rained kisses along her jaw and down her throat, then returned to her mouth again.

The sweet taste of her, the smell of her, filled his senses. He was mindless of anything except her mouth, her face, her hair, his burning need to touch her.

He ran his hand down her side to the swell of her hip. When she moaned, he knew he had to feel her beneath him. Beneath him, pressed against him. Skin to skin.

Slowly, he lowered his body until he felt the soft full-ness of her breasts against his chest. Sweet heaven! Oh, God, the little sounds she was making. He let himself sink down farther and groaned aloud as his swollen shaft pressed against her hip.

There was a reason he must not do what he wanted to do, but he could not recall it. And did not want to try.

He buried his face in hair that smelled of summer flow-ers and honey. "Isobel, I want you so much."

The breath went out of him in a whoosh as he cupped the rounded softness of her breast in his hand. It fit per-fectly. And felt so wondrously good he had to squeeze his eyes shut.

He froze the instant he felt the prick of cold steel against his neck. All the reasons they should not be roll-ing around the floor of an empty storeroom came flooding back to him.

"You are right," she said so close to his ear that he could feel her breath, " 'tis wise to carry a short blade."

"Forgive me." He breathed in the smell of her skin one more time. Then he made himself get up.

As soon as he set her on her feet, she began to vigorously brush off her clothes. She was quite obviously embarrassed, but did she regret the kisses? He wished she would speak.

"Isobel?" He stepped close and touched her arm, but she would not look at him. "I cannot say I am sorry for kissing you"—*kissing* seemed hardly to cover it, but he thought it best to leave it at that—"but I do apologize if I have upset you."

"The blame is not all yours," she said, face flushed and eyes cast down, "though I might like to pretend otherwise."

Ah, an honest woman. And a fair one, too.

"You know I am soon to become betrothed."

"I did forget it for a time," he said, hoping in vain to draw a smile from her.

"It was very wrong of me," she said, lifting her chin. "It shall not happen again."

"If it will never happen again," he said, "then let me have a last kiss before we part."

He thought his outrageous request would cause her to either laugh or shout at him. When she did neither, he put his hand against her soft cheek. He leaned down until his lips touched hers. This time, he kept the kiss soft and chaste. He would not upset her again.

But when she leaned into him, he was lost again in deep, mindless kisses. When they finally broke apart, they stared at each other, breathless.

"I must leave now!" she said, backing away.

He caught her arm. "These things happen between men and women," he told her—though it had never happened quite like this to him before. "Please, Isobel, you must not feel badly or blame yourself."

The huge eyes she turned on him told him his words had done nothing to reassure her.

"Come, you will want to put this on," he said, picking up the simple headdress he saw lying on the ground.

She snatched it from his hands, slammed it on her head, and began shoving hair into it.

"'Tis a shame to cover such lovely hair." Unable to keep his hands from her, he helped push loose strands under the headdress. He let his fingers graze her skin as he worked. And tried not to sigh aloud.

"Let me go first to be sure no one is near," he told her. "Watch for my signal."

He felt her close behind him as he eased the door open. "I am happy to practice with you whenever you like," he said as he looked out into the yard. "Sword fighting or kissing."

He spun around and gave her a quick, hard kiss, looking straight into her open eyes.

———

Isobel touched her fingers to her lips as she watched him go. Her breasts ached, and her whole body still thrummed with sensation.

What happened to her? She was stunned by her body's response to his touch and by how it addled her mind. Judgment—indeed, all thought—left her the moment his lips touched hers.

Thank God, the shock of his hand on her breast finally brought her to her senses. She could not fool herself—she knew what path they'd been racing down. And, God help her, she'd been right beside him, matching him step for step.

Out in the yard, Stephen waved for her to follow. As if this were a game! She slipped out the door with her head down and walked as fast as she could in the opposite direction.

So, this must be what it is like to have an affair. Sneaking about, taking pains to be sure no one sees you coming from a place you should not be with someone you should not be with. She swallowed hard. Stephen was so practical about it all. Retrieving her headdress, tucking her hair in, keeping watch for her. So practical. And practiced.

She picked up her pace. 'Twas no comfort to know she was one of many women foolish enough to fall for Stephen Carleton's charms. No comfort at all to know others had fallen further. Fallen? Nay, jumped.

She put her hand to her chest. At least he had listened when she told him to stop. Aye, she asked him with the point of her blade on his neck. But they both knew he could have taken it from her easily enough.

Another man might have felt justified in taking her. For she was brazen, opening her mouth to him, pulling him down on top of her. Good heavens, she was a woman possessed! Even when he covered her with his body—good as that felt—she pressed into him, unable to get as close as she wanted.

Her breath quickened as she recalled the feel of his hands moving over her.

Without a speck of doubt, coupling with Stephen Carleton would be an altogether different experience from having Hume sweating and grunting over her. Just his kisses told her that. His kisses! Remembering how their tongues moved against each other, she could almost imagine—

"Isobel."

She jumped at the sound of Carleton's voice beside her. "What are you doing here?" Good God, she'd just imagined the man naked and—oh, she would not think of it more!

"You can slow down. No one saw us leave the storeroom," he said. "Let me escort you back to the keep."

"Leave me. I can find my way alone."

"Isobel, you are going the wrong way."

She looked around and found she was nearing the Porte Saint-Pierre, the main gate into the town. "Thank you," she said in a tight voice and turned on her heel.

"Truly, it is not safe for you to go about without an escort," he said, keeping pace with her. "Promise me you'll not do it again."

Promise? He had the gall to think he could exact promises from her? She kept her eyes fixed on the keep across the bailey yard and marched ahead.

She knew just what sort of man Stephen Carleton was. Did he think she did not notice how women fawned over him? She was not blind. Even when he was so drunk she was sure he could not tell one woman from another, they looked at him as if he were a gift sent by the angels.

These things happen between men and women. It was as good as saying it was nothing at all. Perhaps "these things" happened to Sir Stephen Carleton all the time, but nothing like it had ever happened to her before.

God's mercy, the man must think she was one of those widows who will allow a man liberties simply because he is pleasing to the eye. She would never stoop to being one of his many women. Someone he forgot as soon as he dressed and left the room.

Never. Never. Never.

Carleton attempted to engage her in conversation, but she ignored him. Idle chatter was well beyond her now.

They were passing the Exchequer, nearly to the keep. Escape was within her reach.

"Good morning, Robert," Carleton called out beside her.

She turned to see Robert bounding down the steps. Damnation! Robert's eyebrow went up a bare fraction as he looked from her to Carleton and back again. It took an act of will not to check her clothes again for bits of dirt and straw.

"I was just coming for you, Isobel," he said. "The king wishes you to serve attendance upon him."

The king? Although she saw King Henry every day in the hall, she'd yet to have a private audience with him.

"When shall I come?" *Please, please, not today.*

"He awaits you now."

"Now?" This time, she did look down at herself. Her cloak was clean, but God knew what her gown looked like underneath.

"You haven't time to change," Robert said, interrupting her harried thoughts, "and you look lovely as you are."

She colored, almost certain Robert guessed the cause of her dishevelment. Yet his eyes showed nothing but kind concern as he reached up and gave her headdress a firm tug to the left.

"There, now you are perfect."

Robert, of course, was as practiced as Carleton at helping a lady with her headdress.

"I very much enjoyed our walk," Carleton said and turned so Robert would not see his wink. "I look forward to the next time."

If Robert were not there, she would have kicked him.

"The king wishes to see you alone," Robert said.

"Alone? But I thought you would—"

"Believe me, this will be no more difficult than your meeting with Bishop Beaufort." Robert took her arm and turned her toward the steps. "You do know Beaufort was his tutor?"

No comfort there! She wanted to protest, but she could hardly tell Robert she was not yet recovered from an early-morning fit of madness.

"Best not keep the king waiting," Robert said, his hand at her back.

Above her, a guard held the door open. She took a deep breath and went up the steps to face the lion. Before going through the door, she glanced back just as Carleton turned to leave. She gaped in astonishment as Robert grabbed Carleton's arm and spun him back around. With no trace of his usual bonhomie, Robert poked a finger into Carleton's chest.

"Lady Hume?"

She dragged her gaze from the scene below and nodded to the guard. God help her, but she hoped Stephen Carleton was a good liar. Very likely, he was exceptional.

She had no time to dwell on it. After passing through a second set of doors, she was in the hall where King Henry held court in Normandy. A man in a simple brown cloak stood looking out one of the tall windows that faced the Old Palace. A monk?

She expected to find the hall full of people, with the

king on the dais, dressed in his bright gold, red, and blue tunic emblazoned with row upon row of lions and fleurs-de-lis. She glanced up and down the enormous room. Not a soul was here, save for her and this monk.

Her breath caught. This was no monk, but the king himself.

Her hands shook as she sank into her curtsy. Only thirty years old, and he was legend. At thirteen he led men into battle. At sixteen he commanded entire armies. After being crowned at twenty-six, he unified the nobles and brought an end to the years of chaos and rebellion.

He created a common link among the classes by making English the language of his court in England. For the first time since before the Conqueror, royal edicts were in the language of the common people.

All of England lauded Henry for his skill at governing and admired him for his piety. But what they loved him for were his victories. He was their young warrior king. England was strong again and ready to face her enemies.

"You may rise," the king said.

His cheerful countenance reassured her.

"Caen Castle was the favorite residence of my ancestor, William the Conqueror," he said, letting his eyes travel along the beams overhead. "He built it more than three and a half centuries ago, not long before he crossed the channel to conquer England."

"Then I can see why you made the castle your headquarters, sire," she ventured.

He rewarded her with a smile. "Richard the Lionhearted met here with his barons before going on crusade."

Isobel turned with him to gaze down the length of the hall. She imagined the room crowded with knights preparing to leave for the Holy Land. Men with serious faces and crimson crosses on their chests. The rumble of deep voices, the clang of metal.

"The man I have chosen for you is Philippe de Roche."

The king's words brought her back with a start. Of course, the king had not called her to discuss history. How foolish of her to forget.

"I summoned de Roche here from Rouen," the king said, all trace of his former cheerfulness gone.

She fought the urge to run from the room. How much time did she have? It could never be enough.

"De Roche replies that he will come as soon as the roads are safe to travel," the king said, biting out each word. "And he doubts they will be safe for some weeks."

Whether the king faulted de Roche's excuse as insincere or cowardly she could not tell. Liar or coward, the king was angry. Heaven help her.

"This from a man who rides with a guard of twenty!" The king took a deep breath, then spoke more calmly. "I hope the wait will not be a trial for you."

"Not at all, sire." *Let him stay in Rouen forever.*

"What has Sir Robert told you about Philippe de Roche?"

"Only that he is an important man in Rouen." She willed the king to tell her more. Something to reassure her.

"Tell me, Lady Hume," the king said, "do you know the reason your father turned traitor?"

The king's words hit her like a blow. Her palms went damp with sweat. "I was only a child at the time..."

But the king was giving no reprieve today. He leaned forward, waiting for her answer.

"I believe he sided with the rebels because...
because..." She licked her lips. Did he expect her to
defend or blame her father?

"Because?" the king prodded.

What should she say? Was any answer safe? She could
not think with her head pounding and the king staring
at her.

"He did it because he thought the rebels would prevail,"
she said, giving him the truth, "not because he thought
they should."

The king nodded his head vigorously. The right answer,
thank God! She swallowed and wiped her palms on her
cloak.

"It was a practical decision he made," she said, then
hastily added, "though grossly misguided, of course."

"Then you will understand Philippe de Roche, for he is
just such a man." The king's voice held such enthusiastic
approval Isobel nearly staggered with relief.

"I have cause to suspect that his loyalty, like your
father's," he said, cocking his head, "is based upon self-
interest alone, rather than honor and duty."

Isobel was reeling from the unexpected turns of the
king's conversation. Why speak to her of the reason for
men's loyalty?

"If the people of Rouen accept me as their sovereign
lord, I shall welcome them to my bosom," he said, crossing his hands over his heart. "But it is my duty to rule
Normandy. If they do not open their gates to me, I shall
starve them into submission."

Anyone who saw the fire in King Henry's eyes would
be foolish not to believe he would do it.

"Philippe de Roche will save the people of Rouen

much suffering if he can persuade them to avoid a siege," he said. "But for de Roche to play his part, he must be kept loyal."

She agreed to this marriage as a lesser of evils. Only now did she understand the responsibility that came with her choice.

"Your charge is to bind him to us," the king said, pointing his forefinger at her. "Do not allow de Roche to misjudge where his interest lies."

"I will do my best, sire," she said, though she despaired of knowing how she would accomplish it.

"Still, he may work against us," the king said. "If you discover he does, I must learn of it at once."

Just what did he expect of her? Isobel ran her tongue over her dry lips again. "Do you mean, sire, I should attempt to learn his true loyalty before the wedding?"

"If de Roche changes his allegiance, you shall send word to me," the king said, his eyes boring into her. "Whether it is before or after your marriage."

Chapter Seven

From the corner of her eye, Isobel watched Stephen Carleton laugh and talk with English knights, common soldiers, and local nobles as he wove his way through the crowded hall. People turned to him like iron filings to a lodestone as he passed.

He sidestepped the voluptuous Madame de Lisieux; the woman tracked him like a hound. In another moment, he was tête-à-tête in a corner with another fair-haired woman. From their frequent bursts of laughter, it was plain the two enjoyed each other's company and knew each other well. Very well, indeed.

"Who is that?" she whispered to Robert.

Robert turned to follow her line of vision. "Who? The woman next to Stephen Carleton?"

"That is the one." Isobel took a drink of her wine. "She is quite beautiful." In sooth, the woman was exquisite.

Robert took a handful of sugared nuts from the bowl on the table. "Aye, Claudette is as lovely as her famous cousin."

"She has a famous cousin?"

"Odette de Champdivers, mistress of the king of France."

Isobel shook her head. "I have not heard of her."

"You know King Charles is mad?" he said, eyes twinkling. "Well, Odette has been his mistress for twenty years without his knowing it."

She laughed; she could listen to Robert spin tales all night.

"Odette was first the mistress of the king's brother, Louis d'Orléans. When the queen took the dashing Orléans as her lover, the two of them sent Odette to the king's bed in her stead—dressed in the queen's clothes."

"The king was deceived?"

"Every night for twenty years!" Robert shook his head. "They say he's never been the wiser, and no one will risk the queen's wrath by telling him."

"And Claudette?" Isobel asked, bringing the conversation back to the woman whose hand rested on Carleton's arm.

"Claudette is more clever than her cousin. She's saved her money and kept her independence." Robert gave Isobel a rueful smile. "But I forget myself, speaking so freely with you."

"I am glad you feel you can," she said. "I do not like being treated as a child."

"Then I will tell you," Robert said, turning his gaze to Carleton, "a man may enjoy a courtesan's company in public without also employing her services in private."

How did Robert always guess what she was thinking?

"Still," he said, a smile lifting the corners of his mouth, "Stephen is not a man afraid to play with fire."

Playing with fire. Heaven help her. Each time she saw him, the episode in the storeroom came back to her. She could almost feel his mouth on hers again, his body pressed against her, his hands...

God help her, she could think of little else. Was it possible her new husband could make her feel like that? Was it a sin to hope so fervently it might be so?

She reached for her cup and tilted her head back to take a large gulp.

"Stephen's family is anxious to get him settled," Robert said, "before some husband kills him."

She choked, almost spitting wine across the table. Between coughs she asked, "He has affairs with married women?"

"I shock you again," Robert said, patting her back. "A fine chaperone I am proving to be."

It came as no surprise Carleton had affairs. What made her inhale her wine was the sudden image of him actually kissing another woman the way he'd kissed her.

"For a man who wishes to avoid a wedding at all costs," Robert explained, "married women are the safest choice."

"He could abstain."

Robert's burst of laughter caused heads to turn in their direction, including Carleton's. "That would not have occurred to me, but of course you are right." He took her hand and kissed it as he met Carleton's eyes across the room. "I do hope I am there when you suggest it to him."

As if in answer to the challenge, Stephen Carleton left the exquisite Claudette and strode across the room to them. His words of greeting were polite, but the devilish smile he gave her made it impossible for Isobel to utter a single word.

He sat on the other side of Robert and fell into easy conversation with him. "By summer we will control most of Normandy, including your ancestral home."

"It will be strange to return after so many years,"

Robert said. "And what of you, Stephen? When will you go to Northumberland to reclaim your family lands?"

Isobel could not help herself. She leaned forward and asked, "Your family lost their lands?"

Carleton's eyebrows shot up. "You did not know? My father joined the northern rebels, same as yours."

So he knew about her father. "But your brother is close to the king, is he not?"

"Lucky for me, William fought for the Lancasters," Stephen said, grinning at her. "William is my half brother. Since he was the only relative not tainted, our mother sent me to live with him when I was twelve."

"But your father's lands were confiscated?"

"Of course." He shrugged as if it were no concern to him.

"You've only to ask," Robert said, "and the king will grant them back to you."

King Henry was allowing most of the former rebels, or their families, to buy back their lands. She had paid the price for the return of her family's lands. What price did Stephen pay? What would cause the king to forgive such a debt?

"We have more in common than you knew," Stephen said, raising his cup to her. "We were both born of foolish, traitorous fathers."

Was his father's treachery not a burden to him? What of his mother? Isobel longed to ask...

The person sitting on her other side tugged at her elbow. She turned to find the pleasant, round face of Sir John Popham, a boring man if there ever was one.

"Have you a guess as to how many English merchants will come to Caen to set up shop in the spring?"

When she shook her head, the man began to talk at length about trade. Since all Popham required of her was an occasional nod, she could give most of her attention to the conversation between Robert and Stephen.

"William says he intends to return to England in the spring," she heard Robert say.

"Aye," Stephen said, "he'll not be away from Catherine any longer than he must."

"And who can blame him? Your brother is a lucky man."

Robert was saying this?

"That he is," Stephen agreed, "that he is."

Who was this woman that she had these two philanderers sighing and envying her husband?

Isobel remembered to give Popham another nod and leaned closer to Robert.

"William says you delay because you fear Catherine."

Stephen's laugh rang out. "I do not fear Catherine, I adore her! But she is intent on seeing me married—and you know how she is."

"That woman has an iron will," Robert said, "and she will bend you to it."

The two men laughed again! Despite the disparaging words, there was nothing but affection and admiration in their voices.

"My only hope is that William will get her with child again." Isobel heard the smile in Stephen's voice. "A new baby might divert her."

"Pray for twins," Robert said. "Pray for twins."

The next thing Isobel knew, Carleton was standing behind her. Her breath caught as she tilted her head to look up at him. Why must he be so handsome?

"Popham, you are boring this lady to death," Carleton said. "If you truly must talk all evening of barrels of wine and bales of wool, let us go off to a corner and spare the others."

Isobel was shocked by Carleton's directness, but Popham laughed.

"You are right, of course." Popham stood and said to Isobel, "I don't know what I would do without him."

She had no notion what Popham was talking about.

Without warning, Stephen leaned down to her. His hair brushed her cheek, making her heart race.

She felt his breath in her ear as he whispered, "You owe me for this."

Before she could recover, he took her hand. She looked at the long, strong fingers and remembered them in her hair. On her breast. She swallowed and looked up into Carleton's face. His eyes went dark; he was not even trying to mask that he was thinking the same thoughts as she.

Heat seared through her body as he pressed his lips to her fingers. He held her hand a trifle too long for courtesy, but she did not pull away.

———

Robert sat back and watched the pair. Stephen, who was usually so good at maintaining a facade, was no better than Isobel. He had never seen Stephen like this over a woman before.

The two of them were playing with fire, all right. No matter the king's affection, he would not take it lightly if Stephen jeopardized his plans. Stephen would find a cuckolded husband was nothing compared to an angry king.

Robert suspected things had not gone too far—yet. Still, the two were courting disaster. The fools may as well have been shouting it from the rooftops.

Claudette saw it, of course. There was not much that remarkable woman missed. And Marie de Lisieux, who had none of Claudette's subtlety or discretion, was watching the pair like a hawk.

Not for the first time, he wondered which faction Marie was spying for. Tonight, however, a baser motive even than politics drove Marie. 'Twas a wonder Isobel did not feel the scorch of Marie's eyes on her skin.

Praise God, William was no more perceptive than the king in such matters. The situation was far too delicate to bring William into it. A subtle hand was needed, not a storming of the gates.

He might need William's help. But not yet.

Chapter Eight

*I*sobel dropped her embroidery in her lap, annoyed her thoughts had drifted again to that damn Stephen Carleton. Small wonder, really. She had little else to occupy herself.

Where was de Roche? She stared out her narrow window, trying to imagine him riding through the keep's gate with twenty men behind him. Each day he did not come, she was torn between injury and relief.

She'd been a traitor's daughter; she did not want to be a traitor's wife. What would she do if de Roche changed allegiances after they wed? Caught between duty to husband and king, which would she choose? Either choice would be dangerous for her.

Her attention was caught by a lone rider trotting into the inner bailey yard below. There was something familiar about the way he sat his horse...

"Geoffrey!" She let her needlework fall to the floor in a tangle and flew to her door. In her hurry, she nearly tumbled down the stairs, which were built at uneven heights to trip attackers. A moment later, she was out of the keep and running across the yard to her brother.

"I am filthy," Geoffrey warned as she leapt into his arms. He held her close and said against her hair, "I came as quickly as I could."

"Thank God you are safe," she said, her eyes stinging. "I have been so worried."

"You should not fret so over me, Issie, I am a grown man now." He set her on her feet and took her hands. "Is it possible my sister has grown still more beautiful?"

"Would you scold me if I said my husband's death was good for my health?"

"I would," he said, "though I know you suffered with him."

As a man, Geoffrey could never understand how much she suffered. She did not want him to.

"Come," she said, taking his arm, "I will show you the way to the stables. Then I want you to meet Sir Robert, the kind man who has been looking after me."

She paused to lean her head against his shoulder and smile up at him. "I am so very glad you are here."

"He certainly took his time in coming."

The unexpected voice came from behind them. Isobel whirled around to find Stephen Carleton standing a few feet away, hands on hips, looking anything but his usual good-humored self.

"What kept you?" Carleton demanded, his eyes hard on Geoffrey. "Your delay has been a grave insult to this lady."

She'd never seen Carleton angry before. With temper sparking in his eyes, he looked different. Dangerous.

He turned his searing gaze on her. "I did not take you to be such a forgiving woman."

"I am sorry if I have offended you in some way," Geoffrey said, drawing Carleton's attention back to him. "I came as soon as I received the news my sister was here."

"Your sister?" The expression on Carleton's face showed first surprise, then delight.

"I thought you were that unworthy Frenchman of hers," he said, coming over and clapping Geoffrey on the back. "Welcome to Caen! I am Stephen Carleton, a friend of your sister's."

"You thought he was—" She choked on her words as anger, hot and dark, rose in her chest. "You thought I would embrace a man I did not know in the middle of the courtyard!"

"Better in a busy courtyard than a quiet place," Carleton said with a wink. "Luckily, I did not see you embrace him, or your brother would be dusting off his backside—if he could get up at all."

She wanted to slap him. "What concern is it of yours?"

Geoffrey, ever the peacemaker, said in a soothing voice, "He was only being chivalrous, trying to protect you." He took hold of her arm and began pulling her away. "Come, Issie, it was a hard ride, and I've not eaten in hours."

When she glared at Carleton over her shoulder, he blew her a kiss. The man was maddening.

———

What madness, Stephen asked himself, had taken hold of him? When he walked through the keep's gate and saw her clinging to a stranger's arm, her face lit by a rare, radiant smile, he stormed across the yard intent on beating the man to a bloody pulp.

Good God, he could hardly credit it.

Nay. He knew damn well what made him do it. Mindless, raging jealousy. He thought the man was de Roche and that Isobel was looking at him the way she looked at Stephen the day they met.

And he simply could not bear it.

He did not want to contemplate what that meant. Regardless, he intended to get to know her brother.

———

Isobel drew her cloak close against the early morning chill. "I was afraid you would forget your promise to practice with me before breakfast," she said, squeezing Geoffrey's arm.

"And risk my big sister's wrath?"

They walked in companionable silence, their feet crunching on the frozen ground.

When Geoffrey spoke again, his tone was serious. "Have you been going out alone, Isobel?"

There was only one person who could have told him. "Did that Stephen Carleton say something to you?"

"Aye, Sir Stephen gave me quite a lecture on the risks," he said, "and on my duties as a brother."

"How dare he!"

"There was no mistaking the man's message, but he was quite cordial," Geoffrey said. "He is an engaging fellow. Both he and his nephew seem to be good men."

She snorted her disagreement. "Stephen Carleton lacks all seriousness of purpose."

"He seemed quite serious about wishing to kill me yesterday," Geoffrey said, fighting a smile.

She remembered how dangerous Stephen had looked. Dangerous, and impossibly handsome.

"A vile temper does not improve a frivolous man." She sounded insufferable, but she couldn't stop herself. "He is, by all accounts, an unrepentant adulterer and drunkard. For all your piety, I am surprised you are willing to overlook his sins."

"You should not believe all you hear," Geoffrey said. "And 'tis not your place nor mine to judge. 'Let he who is without sin cast the first stone.' "

She decided not to test her brother's grace by telling him that the man he was defending had lain on top of her and kissed her senseless. That was a secret best not shared.

"What makes you smile, Issie?"

"Nothing." God help her, but she did not regret those kisses nearly as much as she ought. "Let us speak no more of Stephen Carleton."

"But he—"

She held her hand up. "Please, Geoffrey, do not."

When they reached the storeroom, she ducked through the low entrance and removed her cloak. When she turned to find a place to lay it down, she was so startled she screamed.

Stephen Carleton sat perched atop a stack of grain sacks.

"Good day, Lady Hume," he greeted her, as if he were quite used to women shrieking at the sight of him. "You remember my nephew, Jamie Rayburn?"

Noticing the young man now, she gave him a stiff nod.

"I meant to tell you that Sir Stephen kindly offered to practice with us today." Ignoring her glare, Geoffrey added, "We are fortunate, for he is well known for his skill."

"Please just call me Stephen," Carleton said, dropping down to the ground. "Your sister does."

She was going to argue, but this little falsehood was the least of his crimes.

When her brother went to chat with Jamie, Carleton came to stand beside her. "Stop scowling," he said in a low voice. "You are safe with both Jamie and your brother here. I promise, you will enjoy yourself."

She was tense and distracted at first, but after a time she became absorbed in the play. They traded partners frequently, so she had opportunity to practice with each of them. Stephen—despite herself, she did think of him as Stephen now—was by far the best swordsman and teacher.

"I'm starving! 'Tis long past time for breakfast."

Jamie's announcement caught Isobel by surprise. The hour had passed so quickly.

Jamie sheathed his sword and picked up his cloak from the corner. "Shall we meet again tomorrow?"

Geoffrey gave her a sideways glace and waited.

She smiled and nodded. So long as Geoffrey and Jamie came, too, what could be the harm?

Chapter Nine

November 1417

As Robert helped her into her cloak, Isobel heard the bells of L'Abbaye-aux-Hommes, the great abbey William the Conqueror built west of town, calling the monks to compline. Geoffrey was there tonight, praying with the monks. He would rise with them twice in the night, for matins and for lauds, then again at dawn for prime, before returning to the castle.

"How did you persuade me to go with you to one of your social gatherings in the town tonight?" she said. "I am sure I shall hate it."

"Who knows? An evening with the rich and dissolute may hold surprises," Robert said as he opened the door for her. "What do you say to walking? The night is fine and clear."

She enjoyed the long walk through the Old Town. By the time they crossed the bridge into the New Town, however, her feet were frozen. They were nearly to the far wall of the city before Robert stopped at the gate of an enormous house.

"Did I mention," Robert asked without looking at her, "that our hosts are Lord and Lady de Lisieux?"

"Marie de Lisieux! You know very well I would not have come if you told me."

"Come, you must admit to some curiosity," Robert said, giving her a wink. "I promise it will be entertaining."

As soon as they entered the house, Isobel noted with satisfaction that it was garishly decorated, with costly but unattractive tapestries and too much furniture.

"Hideous, isn't it?" Robert said in her ear. "Wait until you meet the husband."

Isobel had to struggle not to laugh. "You are a wicked man, Robert."

The food at supper was like the furnishings: rich, but tasteless. The bread was not quite fresh, the fruit green, the meats undercooked and laden with a heavy gravy with an unusual gray cast to it. Isobel was as hungry when she got up as when she sat down.

After supper, the guests dispersed into small groups throughout the public rooms of the house. Robert settled with Isobel on a bench at the back of the largest room and proceeded to tell her unseemly tidbits about the people in the room.

"Do keep your voice down!" she admonished him.

Her laughter caught in her throat when she turned and saw a late guest entering the room.

"You did not tell me Stephen was coming."

Robert raised his eyebrows. "You need to be warned?"

"Of course not."

Still, the very last thing she wanted to do was watch Marie de Lisieux drape herself over Stephen all evening. The woman had her hands on him already.

"You seem tense, my dear," Robert said.

"You are mistaken."

Over the weeks, she'd become accustomed to Stephen's company—and to ignoring the attraction between them. Of course, she'd not been foolish enough to risk being alone with him again.

Geoffrey and Jamie met her for sword practice every morning, regular as rain. Stephen came less often—no doubt it was difficult to rise early after a late night of drinking... and God knew what else. Despite her caution, she found herself warming to him each time he joined them. He was a patient teacher and had charm and wit enough for two.

How could a man of such talent fritter his time away with the most degenerate members of the local nobility? It was such a waste! And there was always some woman at hand, tittering at his jokes and giving him meaningful glances.

Robert raised his arm and called out, "Stephen, over here!"

Stephen distracted Marie de Lisieux with a blinding smile as he removed her hand from his shoulder and squeezed past.

Isobel took a deep breath to fortify herself. Was it to annoy her or to tease Marie that he wedged himself between her and Robert on the bench rather than take the chair opposite? He would amuse himself.

"I am glad you are here," Robert told him. "I must leave for a time, and I do not like to leave Isobel alone. You know what these people can be like."

"I am surprised you brought her." Stephen's tone was sharp.

"Stop talking as if I were not here," Isobel snapped. "I am not a child to be passed from nursemaid to nursemaid."

She was so annoyed she could almost forget the heat of Stephen's thigh against hers. Almost.

"Where are you going?" she asked Robert.

He winked one sea-green eye at her. "I'd rather not say."

An assignation. Was he not getting a bit old for that? Of course, men like him—and Stephen—never stopped.

The two men stood and spoke in low voices. As they talked, Isobel noticed the lovely courtesan Claudette walk past the entrance to the room and catch Robert's eye. Robert took his leave then, and Stephen slumped into the chair opposite Isobel and folded his arms across his chest.

To make conversation she said, "Sir John Popham mentioned again how much he values your assistance with the administration of the town." She'd been surprised by Popham's effusive praise. Apparently, Stephen did more with his time than charm women and drink to excess.

Stephen shrugged and scanned the room. Obviously, his work with Popham was not something he wished to discuss with her. He did not, however, have to be rude. What was the matter with him tonight? It was not her fault he was stuck with her.

Despite herself, she felt hurt. She thought they'd become friends, of sorts, over the weeks.

A handsome older woman bedecked in jewels and crimson silk appeared at Stephen's side. When the woman leaned down and whispered in his ear, he squeezed her hand and nodded.

"Do not move," he told Isobel as he got up. "I shan't be long, but there is someone I must speak to."

Speak to? Ha! She watched Stephen saunter out of the room with the woman. Who did these men think they were, telling her to stay put while they cavorted with all manner of women?

She felt awkward sitting by herself. She had little experience with gatherings such as this. Visitors to Hume Castle were few, and her husband rarely took her anywhere else. She was immensely grateful, then, when Monsieur de Lisieux rushed over to join her.

"To abandon such a beautiful lady!" de Lisieux said, throwing his hands up. "Truly, your friends do not deserve you."

The broken veins and blotchy color of his face showed the signs of excessive drink. Who could blame the poor man, married to that wretched Marie?

"Perhaps you will let me show you the house while they are gone?" de Lisieux suggested.

"You are too kind." She took the arm de Lisieux offered and smiled at the thought of Stephen returning to find her gone.

De Lisieux stopped at a side table to pour her a large cup of wine. He filled it so full she had to drink several large gulps for fear of spilling it. As they moved through the crowded rooms, de Lisieux pointed out various features of the house. Isobel made polite noises of appreciation.

Stephen was certainly taking his time.

She had a nodding acquaintance with a number of the guests from their visits to the castle. De Lisieux, of course, knew everyone. Their progress was slow as they stopped to chat with other guests milling about. Along the way, de Lisieux picked up a flagon of wine, and she let him refill her glass from it.

When neither Stephen nor Robert had returned by the time she and de Lisieux circled back to the front of the house, she was angry enough to spit. Where were they? She was more than ready to leave. If she had to "ooh" and "ahh" at one more ugly family portrait, she might scream.

"You must see the new stained-glass window I had put in the solar," de Lisieux said as he led her toward the stairs. "The craftsmanship is exquisite."

Better a window than another portrait. De Lisieux must have refilled her cup, for she had to drink it half down again so she would not spill it on the stairs. At least her host's wine was better than his food. It took the edge off her hunger.

From the top of the stairs, she turned to look at the people milling about below. She did not see Stephen—or the woman in crimson silk.

"The solar is here," de Lisieux said, drawing her away.

Inside the solar, scarlet pillows with heavy gold tassels were strewn haphazardly across the floor. How odd, with guests coming. Was it overly warm in here? She fanned herself with her hand. The servants must have made the brazier too hot.

"Excuse my pride, but is it not lovely?" de Lisieux said, leading her around the pillows to the window.

"Nice, very nice," she murmured, though there was nothing special about the glass, save for its size.

Ha, Stephen would not think to look for her in here. *If* he was looking for her. The swine. She narrowed her eyes, thinking of what he was likely doing with the woman in the crimson silks. She gulped down the rest of her wine. Without turning, she held the cup out for more.

What was de Lisieux saying? Something about tapestries? She'd ceased listening to his drivel some time ago.

"The one in the next room is most unusual," he said, pulling her through another doorway. "You must see it."

Her head began to spin. "I would like to sit, Monsieur de Lisieux." She was embarrassed that his name came out sounding like "Mi-shoe Di-shoe," but he did not appear to notice.

Good heavens, could she be drunk? Hume's drinking so disgusted her, she never overimbibed. How—

"Of course." De Lisieux's voice was solicitous.

Of course, what? She'd forgotten what she asked him.

"But first, look at the design of this beautiful tapestry."

It was difficult to make out the pattern in the dim candlelight of the room, but Isobel dutifully put her nose close to it and moved along the wall, squinting. A grimacing face, a horse's haunch, a woman's breast... Quite suddenly, she saw it as a whole and for what it was. Too shocked to speak, she stared open-mouthed at the obscene mythological scene of satyrs having intimate relations with human women.

With a sinking feeling, she looked over her shoulder. She was, as she feared, in a bedchamber. She had not heard him close the door behind them. But closed it was. How had she gotten herself into this?

"You should not have brought me here," she said and started toward the door.

De Lisieux tightened his grip on her arm, jerking her back.

She swallowed back her rising panic. Surely he would not dare—the house was full of people. And Stephen was here. Somewhere.

"Let me go," she said as calmly as she could. "Sir Stephen is waiting for me."

"Believe me, Carleton is busy elsewhere, my dear."

Before she knew it, de Lisieux was on her. Wet lips against her neck, rough hands pulling at her gown. She screamed against the hand clamped over her mouth. As she struggled to get her hand through the fichu of her gown to reach her hidden blade, she could see it in her mind's eye lying on the chest in her room. Damnation!

She kicked and clawed as he dragged her toward the bed. At last she managed to sink her teeth into his hand. She had only a moment to savor his howl of pain. The slap was so hard her ears rang, and she saw bright pinpricks of stars.

As her knees gave way, de Lisieux released his hold, and she fell hard against the floor. She struggled to her hands and knees and scrambled across the room, frantic to get away. A rhythmic smacking sound behind her caused her to look over her shoulder.

Stephen was here! He had de Lisieux against the side of the high bed, pummeling him. De Lisieux's head flopped like a child's rag doll with each punch.

"Stephen, stop it!" she screamed. "Stop it!"

Stephen shook his head, as though coming out of a daze. He stepped away, letting de Lisieux slide to the floor.

Isobel sank back onto her heels and pressed her hands over her mouth. She was dimly aware of hearing high-pitched whimpers before she realized the sounds were coming from her.

Stephen knelt in front of her and gripped her shoulders. "Did he hurt you?"

She shook her head, unable to speak.

Stephen pulled her hard against him. "Are you sure?" he asked against her hair.

She squeezed her eyes closed and nodded.

Abruptly, Stephen pushed her back to arm's length and fixed scalding eyes on her. "Sweet Lamb of God," he said, his voice shaking, "what were you doing in here with him?"

"Why are you yelling at me?" To her dismay, she was very near to tears. "You've no need to blashpheme." Frustrated, she tried again. "Blaphsheme. Blapsheme."

"You are drunk?" he said, his eyes wide.

"You dare to criticize me"—she slapped her chest at the word "me," to emphasize her outrage—"for too much drink! And 'twas not my fault. Every time I turned my head, de Lisieux poured more wine into my cup and—"

"Come," Stephen said, pulling her to her feet. "I cannot bear to be in this vile man's bedchamber another moment."

As he half carried her out of the room, she glanced at de Lisieux's body slumped on the floor. "Is he ... ?"

"He isn't dead," Stephen said, his voice hard.

He led her to the window seat in the solar. After barring the outside door, he sat beside her and took her hand.

"I am sorry I got angry with you, but you frightened me half to death." He stared straight ahead, jaw muscles tight, clenching his teeth. Despite his obvious effort to be calm, his voice rose when he spoke again. "What were you thinking, getting drunk and coming to de Lisieux's bedchamber with him?"

"He was showing me the house."

"Good God, Isobel, you are not a girl of fifteen! How can you be so foolish?"

"That is so unfair!" She wiped her nose on her sleeve and sniffed.

His shoulders sagged. "You are right. I should never have left you. I had business to attend to, but that is no excuse."

"'Tis not your fault." Even if it had been, what woman could not forgive Stephen when he turned those liquid brown eyes on her? It would be like kicking a dog.

He gathered her in his arms and rested his chin lightly on the top of her head. Encircled in his arms, her cheek resting against his hard chest, she felt safe. Protected.

"Why were you so vexed when Robert left me with you?"

"Because you and I should not be alone." His chest rose and fell beneath her cheek as he took in a deep breath and let it out. "You see, I am not good at resisting temptation."

She leaned back to look at him. Truly, he had a beautiful face—the wide, expressive mouth, the hard planes of cheek and jaw. She put a hand to it, wanting to feel the rough stubble against her palm.

For a long moment, he looked at her, eyes troubled. Then he whispered, "Sweet, sweet temptation," as he lowered his mouth to hers. This time they kissed not with the wild passion of that other time, but with a slow melting that made her insides feel like warm honey.

When he ended it and tucked her head beneath his chin again, she heard his heart pounding in his chest.

"We should return to the castle now," he said.

"Not yet." She pressed against him to feel the heat of his body through his clothes. "Not yet."

He unwound her arms from around his waist and kissed the top of her head. "'Tis wrong to take advantage of you when you've had a shock and too much to drink..."

She let her head fall back, hoping for another kiss. "But I hardly feel the wine anymore."

"You lie, Isobel," he said with a grin. "You are drunk as a soldier after a night in town. Come, I must take you back before I forget all sense of honor."

———

Stephen hoisted Isobel up onto his horse and held her there as he swung up behind her. Good Lord, she was soused. She was going to feel wretched in the morning. When she fell back against him, she felt so soft and yielding he had to pray to Saint Peter to give him strength.

"What about Robert?" she asked without opening her eyes.

"To hell with Robert."

Stephen was going to strangle him. If Robert knew he must leave for one of his clandestine meetings with the king, why in God's name did he take Isobel with him tonight? And to de Lisieux's, of all places! The only explanation was that Robert planned to leave Isobel with Stephen all along.

Now, that was curious.

Of course, Robert did not anticipate that de Lisieux, that horse's arse, would attack Isobel under his very roof. But he did know Stephen would be forced to escort Isobel back to the castle alone and late at night.

Nothing got by Robert. The man had eyes in the back of his head. Despite Stephen's denials, Robert knew damned well something had happened between Stephen and Isobel the morning he saw them just after... well, just after they rolled around on the floor of the storeroom.

Was Robert deliberately putting temptation in his way? For the life of him, Stephen could not figure out why.

He tried to feel virtuous for withstanding the temptation. But what else could he do with Isobel three sheets to the wind? Still, it was not easy with the smell of her hair in his nose and her backside jostling against him with every step of the horse. He was hard as a rock—and desperate for some distraction.

"When I was little, I used to ride like this with my father." Isobel's voice had a plaintive, faraway quality. "He took me everywhere with him."

Stephen checked his conscience; taking advantage of her drunkenness to learn her secrets did not trouble him at all.

He took the opening she gave him. "Was it your father who disappointed you?" he asked softly. "Tell me your story, Isobel; I want to hear it."

She was silent so long he thought she had dozed off. When she finally spoke again, she seemed to have forgotten Stephen's presence altogether.

"Father told me I was to save the family..."

Isobel spoke in fits and starts, as if giving voice to only a part of her thoughts.

As she told her tale, Stephen saw her clear as day: a girl on the brink of womanhood, standing in the tall grass with a wooden sword in her hand and laughter in her eyes. A headstrong girl, used to getting her own way.

Old Hume should have had his member cut off and fed to the pigs for lusting after such a girl. He must have been older than her grandfather.

When her voice faded into silence, Stephen prompted her. "Your father must have had his reasons for agreeing to the marriage."

"Hume gave him the money to buy back our lands," she said.

So Isobel was her family's sacrifice—her virginity sold to satisfy an old man's lust, her happiness traded for land.

Isobel's head rocked softly against Stephen's chest. Since he'd get no more of her tale tonight, he turned his horse toward the castle gates. Isobel barely stirred as he carried her up the back stairs to her chamber in the keep.

Would that useless maid never open the damned door? He rapped a second time and a third. When she finally let him in, she giggled at the sight of Isobel, loose-limbed in his arms.

"Don't you breathe a word of this to anyone," he told the maid as he carried Isobel to the bed. He did not like bullying servants, but he had to ensure the woman's discretion. "If you do, I swear I will have that archer you're so fond of sent to join Gloucester's army."

He looked down at Isobel and felt a surge of tenderness for the girl she once was, the girl whose father broke her heart.

When he brushed his knuckles against her cheek, Isobel smiled in her sleep. How he longed to lie beside her! To enfold her in his arms and drift to sleep with his face in her hair. To awaken to that smile in the morning and make love to her. And then to stay in bed with her the whole day through.

The maid would leave if he told her to...

He let out a deep sigh. She was not his. And could not be.

Chapter Ten

December 1417

Geoffrey sent word he could not join them for practice, so it would be just her and Jamie. Stephen had not come once since . . . Isobel shook her head to clear it of the memory of her night of wanton drunkenness.

She sent her maid back when she reached the storeroom. Though it was not precisely proper to be alone with Jamie, he was still a boy, to her mind.

As soon as she ducked through the low doorway, she realized her mistake. Stephen stood—quite alone—in the center of the room, sword in his hand. He must have come early to practice on his own. Puffs of steam came from his mouth as his breath hit the cold air. His white shirt clung to his skin.

Isobel remained by the door, her feet rooted to the ground.

"Your brother is not coming?" Stephen asked.

She shook her head. "What—what of Jamie?"

"He could not come, either," Stephen said. "Isobel, do stop looking at me as if I were the Green Knight come to cut off your head. I did not know your brother would not be here. Surely you know by now I would not harm you."

She knew no such thing. He looked dangerous, casually twirling his sword. His gaze took in every inch of her.

"Come, let us begin," he said and went to retrieve her sword from its hiding place. When she hesitated to take it from him, he asked, "Are you afraid that without the others here, you will be unable to keep your hands off me?"

Not once had Stephen said anything to embarrass her about what happened that night at the de Lisieuxs'. Not one word, not one veiled remark. Nothing at all to remind her of her drunkenness. Or her foolishness in following de Lisieux into his bedchamber. Or how she begged Stephen to kiss her.

Truly, she was grateful he waited until now, when they were alone, to tease her. That did not mean she liked it.

"You have quite enough women throwing themselves at you, Stephen Carleton." She took her sword from his outstretched hand, whipped it through the air, and pointed it at his heart. "'Tis my sword, not my hands, that should worry you."

They practiced hard. Once again she was struck by his grace and beauty with a sword. His movements were fluid and effortless as he drew her toward him, letting her attack, but always in control.

"How many women are 'quite enough'?" he asked.

"What?"

"You said 'quite enough' threw themselves at me," he said, all feigned innocence. "I assume you were counting."

Stephen seemed not the least bit winded, which only added to her irritation with him.

"One may as well attempt to count the stars," she said, attacking once more. "I prefer to devote myself to some useful purpose. Perhaps you should try to do the same."

He stepped into her thrust to block it. For a long moment they stood inches apart, the tension of sword pressed against sword between them.

"To what use would you put me, fair Isobel?" Stephen asked, then waggled his eyebrows at her.

She laughed and stepped back. "You are impossible!"

"You should laugh more often." He wiped his brow on his sleeve. "Come, let us take a rest."

He spread his cloak on the dirt floor where they could rest their backs against sacks of grain piled high against the wall.

"Now," he said, stretching his legs out, "will you tell me the rest of your story sober, or must I ply you with strong wine to get it?"

Isobel closed her eyes. "I hoped I had not truly said all those things to you."

He picked up a loose straw from the floor and twirled it between his thumb and finger. "What of your mother? Did she argue against the marriage?"

"My mother could not be bothered to leave her prayers long enough to speak for me." Hearing the bitterness in her voice, Isobel pressed her lips together.

Stephen touched her arm. "It might help to speak of it."

Would it? She never had anyone she could tell it all to. There was so much she could not share with Geoffrey, even now that he was grown. Why did she feel she could tell Stephen now? She did not understand the reason, but she did.

"It was for her that he did it," she said in a whisper.

Isobel watched bits of dust floating in the air as she tried to recall the laughing mother of her early childhood.

"After we lost our lands, my mother wanted to escape this life. She devoted herself to prayer, morning to night...until she seemed to forget us altogether."

After a time, Stephen asked, "Your father thought regaining your lands and position would restore her?"

"I knew it would not, but he would not hear me." In her frustration, she'd screamed at him that he could increase their lands a hundredfold and still she would not change.

"Did your mother say nothing to you about the marriage?"

The memory always lay just beneath the surface, scraps of it coming to her unexpectedly and catching her unawares. For the first time, she tried to recall the whole of it.

She remembered her heart pounding in her ears as she ran across the field and through the castle gate.

"I found her on her knees in the castle chapel." Chest heaving from running so hard, she stood waiting for her mother to acknowledge her until she could stand it no longer.

"You will let him do this to me?" she asked, her voice coming out high-pitched and shaky.

When her mother's lips continued moving in silent prayer, Isobel clenched her fists to keep from taking her mother by the shoulders and shaking her.

Finally, her mother lifted her head and looked at Isobel. Except for the lack of expression, her face was as lovely as ever beneath the plain headdress.

"I asked your father," her mother said in a quiet voice, "to delay the marriage until your next birthday."

"He would do anything—*anything*—you ask of him," Isobel said, her fingernails digging into her palms, "and all you can ask for me is three months!"

"Your father says Lord Hume will leave you a wealthy widow. That is the most a woman can hope for in this world."

"You could save me from this, Mother!" Isobel's words echoed off the stone walls of the small chapel.

Her mother remained placid, hands folded in her lap.

"Can you not help me this one time?" Isobel pleaded.

Her mother turned her head and her gaze grew unfocused. "I am sorry you must pay for my sins."

What sins did her pious mother imagine she had committed?

"Isobel." Stephen's voice pierced through the veil of her memories. "Take this," he said, pressing a kerchief into her hand.

Only now did she realize tears ran unchecked down her face.

"I should not have pressed you." Stephen rubbed his hand up and down her back, soothing her as if she were a child.

But she was determined to finish it now. "Do you want to hear the last words my mother said to me in this world?"

"Only if you want to tell me."

"She said, 'We women are born to suffer.' Then she went back to her prayers."

Isobel remembered swallowing back the sobs that threatened to overtake her and turning her back on her mother. Her breath came in hiccups as she marched, stiff-legged, across the bailey yard. With each step, she willed herself to harden her heart.

"I did not have a choice, of course," Isobel said to Stephen. "But I told myself I would do it for my brother—and not for that useless, pathetic woman who was my mother."

Stephen enfolded her in his arms. After a time he asked, "The marriage was very hard?"

She nodded against his chest. He tightened his hold; his arms felt good around her.

"You did not forgive your father."

"I refused even to see him." In that, at least, her husband had indulged her. The only time she saw her father during the years of her marriage was at her mother's funeral.

She should not let Stephen comfort her like this. But after the intimate story she shared with him, it seemed ridiculous to fret over his being too familiar. Even his smell—horses and leather and just Stephen—comforted her.

"You deserve to be happy," he said.

"What if de Roche is horrid?" she blurted out. "He does not want me or this marriage, or he would have come by now."

Why, after holding self-pity at bay for so long, should she suddenly give way to it now?

"The fool does not know the prize that awaits him," Stephen said in a soft voice. "Once he meets you, he will regret every moment he wasted."

She sighed and rested her head against his chest again. "My father told me not to believe in fairy tales."

Stephen brushed a loose strand of hair from her face and kissed her forehead. "There is nothing wrong in hoping for something rare."

She felt his breath in her hair as he held her.

Unleashed emotion swirled inside her. She heard the change in his breathing and felt the tension grow between them. She waited, expectant.

She nuzzled her head against his shoulder, hoping he would kiss her hair again. When he did, she sighed and lifted her face to him. His eyes locked on hers, but he made no move to kiss her. She slid her hands up his chest and rested them on the back of his neck.

He shook his head. "This is not wise, Isobel."

Neither was it fair that she might spend the rest of her days married to a man whose kiss, whose every touch, was hateful to her. "'Tis just a kiss, Stephen."

"I do not think just a kiss is possible between us."

Since the day her childhood came to a crashing end, she'd done what she should and what she must. She was sick to death of it.

She pulled Stephen to her and pressed her mouth to his. The kiss was at once all heat and passion, tongues moving, bodies rubbing, hands searching. When his hand covered her breast, she let her head fall back and closed her eyes. She felt the softness of his lips, the heat of his breath on her skin, as he moved down her throat and back up again.

"What makes me want you so badly?" he breathed against her ear. "Is it that I know I cannot have you?"

But he could have her.

She had no will to stop him. Nay, she would not let him stop. When she ran her tongue across his bottom lip and slipped her hands under his shirt, he understood the invitation. He leaned her back onto the floor. She loved the feel of his hands in her hair, the urgency of his kisses.

She raked her fingers down his back, reveling in the feel of tight muscles beneath the cloth. When she reached his buttocks, he groaned and pressed his hips hard against her. He held her face and covered her with kisses: her mouth, her cheeks, her forehead, her eyelids, her temples.

All she wanted was for him to keep on kissing her, touching her. She deserved this. She needed this. They rolled and kissed beneath the curtain of her hair. And then rolled again. His tongue was in her ear. The unexpected sensation drove away the last bit of guilt nagging at the edge of her mind.

Her every muscle tensed as he made his way, sucking and kissing, down the side of her throat and along the edge of her gown. She arched her back, wanting without knowing what. When his mouth found her breast through the cloth, she had her answer.

She felt drunk, mindless. When he moved toward her other breast, she jerked her bodice down. A groan came from deep within him. As he caressed and kissed her bare breasts, sensations ripped through her. She entwined her fingers in his hair and wrapped her legs around his waist. She cried out as he sucked on her breast, pulling sensations all the way from her toes.

Then his mouth was on hers in deep, frantic kisses. She held on as he moved against her, her arms and legs wrapped around him like a vise.

Abruptly, he pulled away. He hovered over her on his hands and knees, looking down at her with eyes dark and wild. He was breathing as hard as she was.

"I am sorry," he said. "We cannot do this."

She clung to him even as he pulled her to her feet. Of their own accord, her arms went round his waist. She moaned at the feel of the rough cloth of his shirt against her sensitive breasts.

Dropping her hands to the tight muscles of his buttocks, she pulled his hips against her. She felt the hardness of his member. His ragged breathing told her he could not hold out against her.

Suddenly, his mouth was on hers again, hot, hungry, demanding. Her knees grew weak under the assault of sensations pounding through her. His hands were on her breasts, her hips, her thighs. Squeezing, stroking, kneading.

When her feet left the ground, she wrapped her legs around him. Without lifting his mouth from hers, he carried her backward until she felt the wall against her back. Deep, deep kisses. She was dizzy with them, drunk with them. And still she wanted more.

As he ran his hands under her skirts, along the bare skin of her thighs, an aching need grew inside her. She felt his desperation rise with hers as they moved their hands frantically over each other.

He reached between them and touched her center. The jolt of sensation made her cry out. Even through the cloth, the place he rubbed was so sensitive it was almost more than she could stand.

And yet she was pleading, "Please, please, please."

His breathing was harsh against her ear. "I must be inside you."

His raw need for her caused a responsive spasm deep inside her. He was tugging at her skirts. *Please, Stephen.*

Please. Please! She grabbed a fistful of cloth caught between them and jerked at it, trying to help him. In frustration, she bit his shoulder.

She opened her eyes as the door to the storeroom flew open and crashed against the wall. A huge man entered.

She was too startled to move. But with the lightning reflexes of a fighter, Stephen turned, retrieved his sword from the ground, and pulled the knife from his belt. All the while, he kept his body between her and the intruder.

Almost at once, Stephen relaxed his stance and let the point of his sword drop to the ground.

"Hello, William."

How Stephen managed that flat, even tone she could not imagine.

Lord FitzAlan swung the door closed and moved inside the room. Though he had not yet said a word, he fairly vibrated with anger. He seemed to fill the small space to bursting.

"Get your armor, Stephen. The army leaves within the hour. Lady Hume, I will escort you to your chamber."

Over his shoulder Stephen said in a low voice, "Are you covered?"

Belatedly, she jerked her bodice up and began straightening her gown. Never in her life had she been so embarrassed.

Stephen placed her headdress in her shaking hands, wrapped her cape about her shoulders, and pulled her hood up.

He lifted her chin with his finger, forcing her to meet his eyes. "I hate that you feel shamed," he said in a soft voice.

"Stephen, the men are gathering."

The commanding voice behind them made Isobel jump, but Stephen showed no sign he heard it.

"'Tis lucky William came when he did," he whispered, touching her cheek. He broke into a devilish smile that squeezed her heart. "But I wish to God he hadn't. How I want you, Isobel!"

Before she could catch her breath, he kissed her cheek and was gone.

FitzAlan gave her a curt nod and held out his arm. Without glancing to the left or right, he led her out into the bright sunshine, a man sure of himself and his virtue.

Humiliation, loss, and longing warred inside her as she walked beside him. The keep seemed miles away.

"Keep your head up," FitzAlan ordered.

She did as she was told. FitzAlan did not break the silence again until they passed Saint George's chapel.

"I apologize for my brother's behavior," he said, looking straight ahead. "'Tis not like him to force his attentions."

She made herself say it: "He did not force his attentions on me."

FitzAlan gave a slight nod, still not looking at her. "The king has other plans for you, Lady Hume. But if things went...too far...with my brother, Stephen will marry you."

"They did not proceed 'too far,'" she bit out, surprised at her sudden anger. It did nothing to soothe her temper to know FitzAlan's suspicions were reasonable, given what he saw. "And I would not force Sir Stephen to marry me—or have you force him—if they had."

The corner of FitzAlan's mouth lifted briefly in what looked suspiciously like a smile. It was the first she saw the slightest resemblance between the two brothers—and she did not like it.

"My brother would do as honor required, regardless of my wishes," FitzAlan said. "Or yours, Lady Hume."

It sounded like a warning.

———

"By all the saints, Stephen, are you possessed?" William thundered at him as soon as they had ridden out of the city gates.

The main force was a quarter mile ahead. William, however, rode at a pace that signaled he was in no hurry to catch up.

"Possessed or mad," Stephen replied. There was no other explanation.

"Do you not have enough women?" William shouted. "This one you cannot have without marriage. And the king has already chosen a husband for her!"

"I did nothing that might require marriage." A brief moment more, and he very likely would have. Sweet Jesus! He'd been swept in a raging lust that left no room for thought of consequences.

"She said the same," William said, his voice calmer.

"You should not have embarrassed her by asking," Stephen snapped. "I wish you would not meddle in my affairs."

"I am inadequate to the task," William said, "but Catherine and our mother would be displeased if I did not make some attempt to guide your love life in their stead."

Stephen was not amused. He kept his silence for a

good long time. But, as always, it was impossible to out-last William.

"We march to Falaise?" he asked. He'd known for some time the king would break tradition and campaign through the winter, but no one knew where Henry would attack first.

"Aye," William said. "The king decided last night."

"The people here believe the city walls of Falaise are impregnable," Stephen said. "The city will hold out."

"Aye, it will be a long siege," William agreed.

The prospect of spending weeks camped out-of-doors in midwinter, bored silly, dampened Stephen's spirits further.

"Perhaps we shall be gone long enough for you to get back what little sense you once had," William said. "But I shall put my hope in her new husband taking her away before our return."

Isobel, gone from Caen? Stephen needed to see her at least once more. Backing her against a wall and very nearly ravishing her was hardly a proper farewell. Proper farewell or no, sweat broke out on his forehead thinking about it.

When he could still smell her hair, her skin, how could he imagine her gone? Or worse, with her new hus-band. He could imagine that. His jaw began to ache from clenching it.

Yet the Frenchman seemed in no hurry to claim her. Perhaps she would still be there when he returned. Per-haps the fool would never come...

"De Roche will come," William said, interrupting his thoughts. "Henry has him by the balls."

Chapter Eleven

January 1418

Isobel controlled her thoughts during the day. But her dreams betrayed her. Some nights, she dreamed of Stephen telling her stories and woke up smiling. Other times, she awoke hot and breathless with the memory of his lips on her mouth, his hands moving over her body.

Last night she had one of those dreams that drove her from her bed. She stared out her window into the darkness and imagined herself in a river, the dark water running over her, until the desire to have him touch her lessened enough for her to sleep again. This morning, wisps of the dream still floated in her head. A vague longing and a heaviness in her heart remained.

Looking out her window in the harsh light of day, she lectured herself on how lucky she was Stephen was gone from Caen. She prayed she would recover from her madness before he returned. For it was madness. Madness to risk angering the king. Madness to risk being sent home to England in disgrace. And where would she have to go but to her father's household?

Humiliated, dependent, wholly subject to her father's will. Her father would not even permit her to escape to a nunnery. He would deem it a waste of an asset, however reduced in value. After sullying her reputation and earning the king's ill will, what sort of marriage would her father broker for her this time?

It was past bearing.

Her father's treason brought them enough dishonor; she could not add to her family's shame.

For her to risk so much—ach, and for such a man! It was beyond foolishness. Even if she were a wealthy widow who could choose a man to please herself, she would be wise to stay away from the likes of Stephen Carleton.

She did not hope for a man she could love. Indeed, love would give a man far too much power over her. All she wanted was a man she could respect. A man devoted to honor and duty. Not someone who frittered his talents away on frivolous pursuits—especially the pursuit of beautiful women.

Ha! Stephen did not pursue women—he drew them like flies to a dead fish. She blew out her breath in a huff. Aye, she was just one more fly buzzing, no better than the rest.

What if FitzAlan had come to the storeroom a short time later? She put her hand to her chest. No matter what she told FitzAlan, she and Stephen would have been forced to wed. Stephen seemed no more sensible of the consequences at the time than she. But marriage was like the plague to him. Why, he went so far as to delay claiming his family lands to avoid it. How he would resent her! He would grow to hate her.

And there would always be those other women, buzzing

about. She knew infidelity was commonplace among men of her class. Why, then, did imagining Stephen being led off discreetly by one lady or another leave her seething?

What was she doing, wasting her time thinking of Stephen and getting upset? She snapped up her sewing from the table and set to work.

She was diligently stitching when Robert knocked on her chamber door.

"Where is your maid?" he asked when she let him in.

She shrugged. "I do not know half the time."

"We shall deal with her later," he said, taking both her hands in his. "Isobel, he is here."

Stephen was back! The smile froze on her face. Robert would not seek her out to tell her Stephen Carleton had returned to Caen. Nay, Robert did not know—could not know—she waited every day, every hour, for Stephen's return. Foolish, foolish woman that she was.

If not Stephen, then who? Her spirits plummeted further as the answer came to her. "De Roche?"

Robert pressed his lips into a line and nodded. "The king has just come from Falaise to meet with him. You are to join them in the Exchequer hall."

She dropped her eyes to hide her rising panic and pretended to fuss with her gown. When Robert lifted her chin with his finger, she saw sadness in his face.

"Is—is he so terrible?" she asked.

Robert squeezed her hand and said, "'Tis only that I let myself forget you would eventually leave my care."

Tears stung at her eyes. "How I shall miss you!" she said, surprised by the strength of her feelings. "Surely it will take a good deal of time to settle the marriage contract. And then we must wait for the banns to be posted."

He touched her cheek. "If the king wishes it to be done quickly, it shall be."

"But suppose I do not like him? What if he is a hateful man?" The words tumbled out of her in a rush. "What if he is a traitor? Would the king still make me—"

"Hush, hush," Robert said, enfolding her in his arms. "Let us meet the man first."

She rested her head against his chest, crushing the velvet of his beautiful tunic, but he didn't seem to mind. Having Robert hold her like this reminded her of how her father used to comfort her when she was a little girl. Her stomach tightened with unexpected longing for the father of her childhood.

"I am glad you will be with me," she whispered.

Robert leaned back and held her at arm's length. "Your new husband cannot help but adore you," he said, his eyes crinkling at the corners. "I predict your new life will be one of love and grand adventure."

A short time later, they were ushered into the Great Hall of the Exchequer. Isobel clutched Robert's arm as he led her to the far end of the room, where King Henry sat on a raised chair. No one would mistake the king for a monk today. For this occasion, he wore an ermine-trimmed robe over a tunic emblazoned with his royal herald, the lion and fleur-de-lis, in gold, red, and blue.

They halted a few paces behind a man with whom the king was speaking. As they waited for the king to acknowledge them, Robert squeezed her fingers resting on his arm. When she raised an eyebrow at him, Robert tilted his head toward the man and nodded.

This, then, was the man who would be her husband for the rest of her days. Even from the back, she could tell he was young and strongly built. He was well dressed, from his colorful silk brocade tunic and matching leggings down to his magnificent high black boots. Beneath the elaborate liripipe hat, his hair was almost black. He wore it long, fastened with a bloodred ribbon.

She leaned to the side and craned her neck, trying to catch a glimpse of his face. Warts. Boils. Pox. Blackened teeth. She tried to prepare herself. It simply was not possible that he could be wealthy, well connected, young, *and* handsome.

The king's next words jarred her from her observations.

"We are pleased, Lord de Roche," the king said, sounding anything but pleased, "that you have seen fit to heed our summons. At last."

"I apologize for my delay, sire."

De Roche did not sound any more contrite than the king sounded pleased. This did not bode well.

"I assure you, I spent the time on your behalf," de Roche continued. "I've devoted myself to persuading the men of Rouen of the wisdom of recognizing you as our sovereign lord."

"They should not need so much persuasion." The king gave him a hard look and added, "You must tell your compatriots not to try my patience—or God's."

"Of course, sire."

De Roche's complacent reply did not sound as though he took the king's warning as seriously as Isobel thought he should.

"I assume," the king said, the sharp edge still in his tone, "you are prepared to enter into a marriage contract?"

Isobel dropped into a low curtsy as the king shifted his gaze to her.

"Lady Hume," the king said, signaling for her to rise. "May I present Lord Philippe de Roche."

When the man turned, Isobel drew in a sharp breath. God's mercy! He was a vision of masculine beauty. An Adonis—an Adonis with a mustache and trim goatee that matched his dark hair. She snapped her mouth shut and forced herself to drop her eyes.

"'Tis good to meet you at last," de Roche said in a deep, rumbling voice as he stepped closer to greet her.

Blushing fiercely, she risked another glance as she held her hand out to him. Cool gray eyes swept over her from head to toe before fixing on her face.

"An English rose," he said as he bent over her hand.

A nervous ripple ran through her as she felt the warmth of his breath and the tickle of his mustache on the back of her hand. Oh, my.

"You are more beautiful than I had hoped," he said in a low voice meant for her ears alone. "And I assure you, Lady Hume, my hopes were high."

Though it was midwinter, she suddenly felt so warm she wished she had a fan. This handsome man was looking at her with the intensity of a hungry wolf. A good sign, surely, in a future husband. Aye, she was flattered. And pleased. A little breathless, too.

She managed to murmur a greeting of some sort.

"Since Lady Hume's father cannot be here to negotiate the marriage contract..."

At the sound of the king's voice, Isobel dragged her gaze away from de Roche's face.

"...that responsibility falls to her brother. Since he is young, however, I have asked Sir Robert to assist him."

The king stood. "Now I have other matters to attend to."

Despite the king's unmistakable signal the interview was at an end, de Roche spoke again.

"My king, I am grateful for the opportunity to serve you. I do so out of deep concern for the welfare of the people of Rouen—and, indeed, all of Normandy. Neither French faction is capable of bringing us peace and prosperity. I praise God you have come to save us."

"'Tis God's will that I do," the king said.

Heads bobbed as the king swept out of the hall.

Isobel cast a nervous glance at de Roche. Neither the king's irritation nor meeting his future wife appeared to have ruffled him. A confident man, to be sure. A bit arrogant, perhaps.

His unequivocal profession of loyalty to King Henry relieved her. Though his speech lacked subtlety, he sounded sincere. She prayed he was.

Isobel took the arm de Roche held out to her. As they made their way down the length of the huge hall together, she listened to the rhythmic tapping of their feet on the stone floor. She was keenly aware that this was the first of many times she would walk at this man's side.

How many times would she do this in her lifetime? A thousand? Ten thousand? How many times would she do it before de Roche did not feel a stranger to her?

How many times before Stephen did not cross her mind as she did it?

Chapter Twelve

Stephen huddled further under his blanket and cursed himself. He had no one but himself to blame that he was here freezing his buttocks off. The midwinter siege was every bit as miserable as he had thought it would be. 'Twas the coldest winter in memory. So cold, in fact, that the king ordered huts built so his army would not freeze to death before the city succumbed.

Worse than the icy rain outside his hut was the foul smell of the men crowded within. Few washed, and most still wore the clothes they arrived in more than two months ago. If he was not sure to be a frozen corpse by morning, Stephen would sleep outside to get away from the stench.

Yet he chose to be here. In weekly missives, Sir John Popham begged the king to send Stephen back to Caen. The king, however, acceded to Stephen's request to remain until the city surrendered.

Each time Stephen thought of leaving, the slaughter at Caen came back to him: the women's screams, the old men hacked to death, the blood of innocents splattered on his boots.

Nay, he could not leave. He must stay and do what he could to prevent a recurrence of that horror when Falaise fell.

How he longed for the siege to be over! The tedium nearly drove him mad. The day-and-night bombardment against the city walls gave him a constant headache. Weeks of abstinence made him more irritable still. Under such conditions, the camp women did a lively trade. But Stephen was never one to use whores. Even if he were fool enough to risk the pox, just the sight of those sorry women depressed him.

With so much time on his hands, little wonder his thoughts were so often on Isobel. But why no other women? Even his dreams were all of her. He would lie on his cot and try to imagine other women, but their features always faded into hers. Serious green eyes were the only ones he saw.

He missed her.

What was that? He sat up on his cot and listened to the strange quiet. The bombardment had stopped. Tossing his blanket aside, he drew his cloak on and left the hut.

He found William warming his hands at one of the fires that were kept burning day and night.

"We've smashed a breach in the walls," William said by way of greeting. "The town has agreed to surrender at first light."

"Will the king speak to the men?"

William knew what he was asking. "The king will remind them he will tolerate no rape or murder," William said. "Still, there are always some who will do it."

An hour after dawn, the king led his army through the city's open gates. Stephen was relieved the soldiers appeared to take the king's warning to heart, for they remained orderly. Perhaps the men were too cheerful at the prospect of sleeping in the warm houses of the town to commit mayhem. The soldiers did comb the city for valuables, the legitimate spoils of war. Though "the lion's share" went to the crown, the finders got a percentage of the value.

As he and William continued patrolling the streets without incident, Stephen began to relax. Men were help-ing themselves to drink, waving swords, and bashing in doors, but there was no real harm in that. He and William turned their horses down a quiet street of well-kept houses and shops.

Stephen heard a muffled sound; he could not tell if the yowl was dog or human.

William pulled his horse up beside Stephen's. "What was that?" he asked, cocking his head.

When the high-pitched cry came again, they bolted from their horses. William kicked open the door to the house, and Stephen rushed in. The room was empty. Hearing the clomp of boots overhead, Stephen crept up the stairs with William hard on his heels.

As soon as his head was above the floorboards, he signaled to William that there were three men. The men had their backs to him. Their attention was on the prey they had cornered, a boy and girl of eleven or twelve who looked so remarkably alike they had to be twins. The boy stood in front of his sister, holding a sword a foot too long for him.

"Halt!" William's voice filled the room.

The men, rough-looking foot soldiers, spun around with their short blades ready in their hands.

"Did you not hear your king's command?" William shouted.

The men showed no inclination to slink away or beg forgiveness.

"Since the king's punishment for rape is death," Stephen said, "you should be grateful Lord FitzAlan and I have come in time to save your miserable lives."

He used his brother's name deliberately. Upon hearing it, the three men exchanged nervous glances.

"Still, it seems to me the mere intent to commit the offense is deserving of some punishment," Stephen said. "We should at least give them a serious beating, should we not?"

From the sidelong glance William gave him, his brother did not think the beating strictly necessary, but he said, "Let us be quick about it, then."

Stephen called out to the twins to stand back as the first man charged him. Stepping to the side, he knocked the knife from the man's hand, grabbed him by the collar, and threw him against the window. He heard the satisfying crunch of the wooden shutter breaking as the man fell through it.

He turned around in time to see William send the other two men sailing down the stairs.

"Damn, you always outdo me," he said. "Could you not have left the third one to me?"

Before the words were out of his mouth, two streaks of blond hair shot past him. He caught the two children and held them, one under each arm. As they kicked and bit at him, he shouted at them in French that he would not harm them.

He looked up to find William watching him, a glint of amusement in his eyes.

"Damn you, take one before I drop them!"

William took the boy, held him firmly by the shoulders, and leaned down until the two were eye to eye. "We do not mean you harm, son," he said. "Where are your parents?"

From what Stephen saw in the boy's eyes before he dropped his gaze, he could guess the answer.

"Is there someone else looking after you?" William asked.

"I look after my sister."

"And I look after him," the girl spoke for the first time, her voice equally defiant.

William straightened and sighed.

They had been speaking to the children in Norman French, the language the English nobility shared with Normandy, but they switched to English now so the children would not understand them.

"Have you taken a good look at this girl?" Stephen said. "She is far too pretty to be safe here with only a boy to protect her."

"The boy is almost as pretty as his sister," William said, shaking his head. "Come, Stephen, do not give me that look. Do you think those men did not intend to have him after the girl?"

His brother had lived with armies years longer than he had, so Stephen did not doubt him. Still, he was profoundly shocked.

"What do you suggest we do with them?" William asked.

"We could take the boy to a church or monastery."

"You think a boy with those delicate looks is safe with priests?"

Stephen clamped his mouth shut as he absorbed this latest remark. "I will take them with me to Caen," he said after a moment's reflection. "The boy can serve as my page."

"And the girl?" William said, raising an eyebrow. "You cannot keep her. People will think the worst."

Stephen scowled at the notion anyone could think him so depraved. The girl was, what, eleven?

"I suppose we can find someone to take her in as a kitchen maid," William said, sounding dubious.

"I know a lady who needs a new maid," Stephen said, brightening at the thought. "And she will be kind to the girl."

It was only when the girl turned her startling blue eyes up at him that Stephen realized she'd stopped squirming long ago.

"Who is this lady?" she asked in accented English.

Stephen laughed. "So you speak English, you rascal?"

"But of course." The girl did not add "you fool," but it was implied in her tone. "What is the lady's name, *s'il vous plaît?*"

"Lady Isobel Hume," he said, grinning down at her.

He heard William curse under his breath, but he ignored it.

Chapter Thirteen

February 1418

Isobel felt like Job. After her years of suffering, God was rewarding her. De Roche was young and handsome. Respectful, attentive. A man of honor, bent on doing good in the world.

He was solicitous of her, sharing a trencher with her at every meal, taking afternoon walks with her when the weather permitted. When it was too wet for strolling, as it was today, he sat with her by the keep's great hearth and talked with her while she sewed.

De Roche was a serious man, and he talked of serious matters.

She stifled a yawn as he spoke yet again of his responsibility as a man of rank and fortune to help bring peace and prosperity to Normandy. She agreed wholeheartedly. His determination was admirable. Still, she found the repetition, well, a trifle tedious.

Damn that Stephen Carleton! If not for him, she would not even notice de Roche's lack of humor.

She had every reason to be content. She would be content.

'Twas true, de Roche never made her laugh. But duty weighed heavily upon him. He had an important role to play in the service of his country; it would gratify her to support him.

"Now, King Henry—there is a man born to lead armies," de Roche was saying. "A man born to command."

De Roche sang the king's praises so often her mind began to wander.

When would he kiss her?

Would his kiss make her feel the way Stephen's did? She stared at de Roche's mouth as he talked. Wondering. Longing to find out. Perhaps, once de Roche kissed her, she could stop thinking about Stephen.

A full month since his arrival, and de Roche had not kissed her once. He often looked at her as if he wanted to. On more than one occasion, she thought he tried to separate her from her guardian. Robert, however, took his duty more seriously than before, for he was there at every turn.

The thought niggled at her that de Roche could have found a way around Robert if he wanted to badly enough.

Stephen would have.

A sudden clamor of voices from outside drew her attention toward the hall's entrance. As she watched, a man burst through the door and shouted, "The army returns! Falaise has fallen! Falaise has fallen!"

They were back. Praise God! A laugh of relief caught in her throat when she turned and saw de Roche's face. The man had gone pale as death.

"Have you taken ill?" she asked. "What is—"

"I must see what has happened," he cut her off. Without a backward glance, he left her and rushed out of the hall.

The hall was soon flooded with soldiers. After the quiet of the last weeks, it felt chaotic and much too crowded. Servants scurried about, setting up the tables and carrying great jugs of ale and wine and platters piled high with roasted meats.

Isobel stood, craning her neck. Despite herself, she searched the room for a glint of auburn hair. Hearing her name above the din, she swung around to see Geoffrey making his way toward her through the throng.

When had her little brother grown into this barrel-chested man, so like their father? He reached her in three long strides and lifted her into a bear hug.

"You look in such good health!" she said, standing back to drink him in. His skin was as tan as in high summer. Perhaps he was not ill suited to a soldier's life, after all.

"You must tell me of your adventures," she said, pulling him down to sit beside her on the bench.

"I had time to write a great many poems during the siege."

To her dismay, he pulled a roll of parchment from the pouch at his belt and began at once to recite aloud.

Geoffrey was not a bad poet. But why must he write these dreary poems of martyred saints? After two or three, she caught herself searching the room again.

"You are usually better at pretending an interest in my poetry," Geoffrey chided with his usual good nature.

"Of course I want to hear them," she lied.

"Issie, who are you looking for?"

"De Roche," she lied again. "I want to introduce you."

"He is in Caen? Why did you not tell me at once!" Geoffrey leaned forward, face earnest, and took her hands. "Is he a good man? Can you be happy with him?"

She bit her lip, trying to think what she could tell her brother that would be truthful. De Roche was so much more than she had dared hope for. But sometimes...well, it mattered naught. And after Hume, she should be happy married to a toad.

"De Roche is a fine man of serious purpose," she said at last. When the worry did not leave Geoffrey's face, she gave him a bright smile. "He is also the handsomest man I've ever seen."

De Roche was pleasing to the eye, but it was a third lie, nonetheless.

"Now go and eat," she said, giving Geoffrey a gentle shove. "You must be as hungry as the rest."

She let her shoulders slump as she watched Geoffrey's broad back disappear through the crowd. For the sin of lying to her brother, she could at least claim good intent. For her sinful thoughts of Stephen, she had no excuse.

She could not even claim repentance.

————

Stephen kept the reins to the twins' horse wrapped around his fist as they rode through the streets of Caen. With their striking fair hair and near identical faces, the two children would draw glances anywhere. The sight of them astride a single horse in the midst of a line of armored knights caused the townspeople to stop and gape open-mouthed.

Stephen was taking no chances with this wily pair. After an all-too-brief pretense at docility, they tried to escape. Repeatedly. He would gladly let them go if he thought they would be safe. But no family member came looking for them before he left Falaise. If there was anyone in the whole of Normandy willing to take responsibility for them, the twins were not telling. They refused even to give him their names.

Once inside the castle gates, Stephen parted from the other men and rode straight for the keep, twins in tow. He needed to get this girl off his hands. He smiled to himself, pleased to have a good excuse to seek out Isobel at once.

Now he just had to figure out how to look for Isobel without losing one of these troublemakers. He swung off his horse and grabbed the girl as her feet touched the ground. Once he had her, the boy came easily.

"You're hurting me!" the girl whined as he dragged the pair up the steps of the keep.

"If you would quit pulling, it would not hurt," he said evenly. "Now, I want you to pretend that you are a very good girl so Lady Hume will agree to take you. Believe me, she is much nicer than I am."

The girl gave a loud snort to let him know what she thought of his request. A little wistfully, he thought of his gaggle of nieces and nephews. They could be a handful, but he never had this much trouble with them.

He paused inside the entrance of the busy hall, a twin on either side, and searched the crowd for Isobel. He found her almost at once, across the room near the hearth. When she looked up and met his eyes, his throat went dry.

Her face glowed, as though she were truly pleased to see him. Suddenly, he had a vision of her as she was the last time he saw her. Hair loose and tangled, lips swollen from his kisses. He strode across the room, seeing nothing and no one but her.

A sharp tug on his hand saved him from sweeping Isobel into his arms in full view of everyone in the hall.

He looked down, surprised to see he still held the twins. Recalled to his purpose, he turned his attention back to Isobel.

And at once forgot what he meant to say. How could she have grown still lovelier? The green velvet gown made her eyes a deep forest green.

"I am glad for your safe return, Sir Stephen."

His stomach tightened at Isobel's formal greeting. *Sir* Stephen. So that was how it was.

"And who is this lovely girl?" Isobel asked, touching the child's arm.

To his astonishment, the devil girl gave a graceful curtsy and looked up at Isobel with a beatific smile.

"My name is Linnet. I know you are Lady Hume because Sir Stephen told me Lady Hume is as kind as she is beautiful."

Isobel gave a musical laugh that made Stephen's heart do an odd leap in his chest. Though he doubted the girl— *Linnet*—could keep up this pretense of good behavior, he winked at her to show he appreciated the effort.

It seemed unkind to mention the children's circumstances in front of them. Without thinking, he leaned close to Isobel to whisper in her ear. The smell of her skin sent him reeling.

When he remembered to speak, he said, "They are orphans in need of protection. I will take the boy as my page, but the girl..." He lost track of what he was saying. It was so very tempting to run his tongue along that delicate earlobe, to place a kiss in the hollow just below it.

Isobel jerked her head away before he could say—or do—more.

"Of course I will take her," she said, looking at him with wide, serious eyes.

She turned to the girl and took her hand. "This is fortunate, indeed! My maid asked leave to marry one of the king's archers. I would be so grateful if you would agree to take her place."

As Linnet looked over Isobel's fine clothes, her smile brightened. "I would fix your hair and help you dress in pretty gowns?"

Isobel nodded.

"And I could read you all the love poems men send you," Linnet said, her eyes glowing. "I am sure you have many!"

Many love poems? Or many men sending them? Either way, Stephen did not like it.

"You can read?" Isobel asked, surprise showing in her voice.

"Of course." Linnet gestured toward her brother. "As does François."

Stephen watched with sympathy as the boy melted under the warmth of Isobel's smile. He felt his own insides go soft when she said, "You are fortunate to serve a knight as skilled as Sir Stephen. Pay attention and you will learn much from him."

François gave her a solemn nod.

How had Isobel done it? Already she had these two little hellions in the palm of her hand.

Stephen heard a man clear his throat beside him and turned to find cold gray eyes upon him. The dark-haired man they belonged to inserted himself between Stephen and Isobel and tucked Isobel's hand into the crook of his arm.

So, this must be Isobel's delinquent Frenchman.

Stephen let his eyes drift slowly over the man. He knew just how he would take him. Years of practice taught him that. William had decided that a boy with a sharp wit and a big mouth had better learn how to handle himself in a brawl as well as on a battlefield. Each day, his brother assigned a different man to fight him. The lessons did not stop until Stephen learned to assess a man's strengths and weaknesses at a glance.

The man before him now was cocky, overconfident. He had a powerful build—the kind that would turn to fat as he grew older, Stephen thought cheerfully. Strong, but not too quick. Stephen would first grab him by the—

These happy contemplations were interrupted by Isobel. "Sir Stephen Carleton, may I present Lord Philippe de Roche."

Stephen waited, deliberately letting the silence fall between them. If he'd been a cat, his tail would have twitched.

"He is from Rouen," Isobel added, her voice tense.

Stephen knew damn well where the man was from. Since Isobel had not called him her betrothed, perhaps she was not yet irrevocably tied to this man with ice in his eyes. The man's too-perfect features made him look soulless.

Aye, a broken nose would add character to his face.

"You take advantage of my intended's soft heart," de Roche said to Stephen, then turned to Isobel. "You need not take some unknown girl this man has picked up off the streets."

Isobel put her arm about the girl's shoulders. "But

where shall I find another maid who can read poetry to me?"

Stephen wanted to kiss her.

The muscles of de Roche's jaw tightened, but he patted Isobel's hand. "Keep her if it pleases you, my dear."

The endearment reminded Stephen what this man would be to her. Her husband. Her bedmate. His chest began to ache.

"Come, I will show you my chamber," Isobel said to Linnet.

Isobel nodded her good-bye to François, but the smile left her face when she turned to take her leave of Stephen. As she looked at him with those wide, serious eyes, the ache inside him grew until he thought his chest might burst with it.

She seemed to startle when de Roche tugged at her arm. With a quick curtsy, she turned away.

He and François were still watching when Linnet turned to give them a sly wink over her shoulder. Linnet was an ally now, thanks to de Roche. As twelve-year-old girls went, she was not a bad ally to have.

Ally in what? Stephen took a deep breath and shook his head. What would he do if he won the prize? He wanted to take Isobel from de Roche, have her leave on his arm instead. And he most definitely wanted her in his bed. Badly. But since he did not want a wife, this was a battle he had no business trying to win.

He felt a light touch on his arm and turned to find Claudette at his side.

"What a foolish man you are!" she said in a low voice. "Stop staring after her. Do you want everyone to know?" She took his arm and firmly turned him toward François.

"Since it is better to have them think you lose your head over every pretty woman, try to look at me as this boy does."

When he looked down and saw the slack-jawed expression on the boy's face, he laughed and tousled François's hair. The poor boy was having quite the day.

"Do you want the king to banish you to the wilds of Ireland?" Claudette said between her teeth. She smiled and batted her eyes at him. "You do Lady Hume no favors by drawing attention to her."

Realizing, belatedly, that Claudette was right, he picked up her hand and kissed it. He let his gaze linger on her.

"Thank you," he whispered. "You are a wise woman."

"Of course you missed me," she said in a voice just loud enough to be overheard, "but you will make me vain with such compliments!"

"I do not deserve you, Claudette."

"You do not," she agreed and began walking him out of the hall. Dropping her voice again, she said, "There is that dreadful Marie de Lisieux, lying in wait for you near the door."

"I suppose I should cast lustful glances her way," he whispered back to tease her.

"I know how difficult that is for you, Stephen."

He gave Marie a broad wink and swiveled his head as they passed.

Claudette gave him a hard pinch for his efforts. "I did not say you must stare at her bosom."

He laughed with genuine amusement this time. "Marie would think something was amiss if I did not."

"Just looking at her makes my back ache," Claudette said, lifting one delicate eyebrow in disdain. "No matter what the fashion, men will always like big breasts."

"Not every woman can have your perfect proportions," he told her, as he knew she expected him to. "But, in sooth, I do not think I have ever seen a pair I did not like."

"Men are so simple." She heaved a sigh of feigned weariness that made him laugh again.

When they were safely out the door, she turned and wagged a finger in his face. "Now let us be serious. You must promise me you will use that clever head of yours and not get into a cockfight over Lady Hume."

He opened his mouth to object, but she held her hand up.

"You best remember," she warned, "the king has bet upon the other cock."

Chapter Fourteen

Thank God for the girl. If Linnet were not annoying de Roche with ceaseless chatter, he might notice how Isobel's hands shook. Isobel tried to make herself listen to what Linnet was saying but could not.

How could Stephen return just when she had put all thought of him behind her? That was not quite true. Not nearly true. But having him in Caen where she would see him every day made it so much worse.

She heard Linnet mention Stephen's name and almost missed the step. "What was that you said?"

"That my brother and I were very wicked to Sir Stephen."

How easy it was to be wicked with Stephen!

When she saw him coming through the crowd toward her, his smile like a swath of sunlight, her heart leapt in her chest. He looked so pleased to see her, too. For a moment, she thought he would sweep her into his arms.

She half hoped he would.

Perhaps more than half.

But then, Stephen could play her for a fool without even knowing it. As she left the hall, she turned to see whom Marie de Lisieux was watching so intently. It was Stephen, of course. He was already laughing and whispering with that breathtaking courtesan. While Isobel was shaken to her soul at seeing him again, he forgot her the moment she was out of sight.

He would be making his way around the room now, adoring woman to adoring woman. Making each and every one of them believe she was special.

Not that Isobel cared what he did.

She would think of her future. De Roche was a handsome man, every bit as attractive as Stephen Carleton. Surely she would find his kisses just as exciting. She would. Her mind was set on it. And for once, Robert was not here to interfere.

They were at her chamber door before she realized she had not spoken a word to de Roche since they left the hall.

"Wait inside," she whispered to the girl, giving her a gentle push inside.

She lifted de Roche's hand to cup her cheek and looked steadily into his eyes. Seeing how quickly the irritation in his eyes shifted to lust, she smiled, pleased with herself. It had been easy, after all. She would get her kiss now.

When he kissed her cheek, she was disappointed. Nay, annoyed. But then he began to work his way down her neck. She closed her eyes and tried to concentrate on the soft lips and warm breath against her skin. Instead, she found herself thinking of his heavy-handedness in trying to get her to change her mind about taking Linnet. And his utter lack of feeling for the poor girl's circumstances.

That Stephen had taken responsibility for the two

orphans surprised her. And yet... it did not. Wastrel, womanizer, drunkard that he was, Stephen did have a kind heart.

She'd forgotten de Roche when, suddenly, she was slammed against the door, the latch poking painfully into her back. De Roche's mouth was on hers, bruising her. With his tongue down her throat, choking her, she could not breathe. Panic surged through her as she tried in vain to push him away.

She fell backward with a shriek as the door opened behind her. De Roche caught her and leveled furious gray eyes at the cause of the interruption.

"M'lady, do you want these cleaned?" Linnet stood implacably in the doorway, holding a pair of boots in one hand. Not at all the humble maidservant.

"Thank you for escorting me," Isobel said before de Roche could shout at the girl. She straightened and held her hand out.

"Until tonight then," he said in a tight voice.

The gaze he fixed on her as he brought her hand to his lips held both anger and desire. She fought the urge to jerk her hand away when she felt his tongue on her skin.

As she watched him go, she wiped her hand against her skirts.

———

Claudette's serene expression gave nothing away, but Robert saw the glint of annoyance in her crystal blue eyes as she crossed the room toward him.

"Thank you," he said into her ear as he helped her into the seat beside him. "A woman's touch was needed."

"Stephen does need a woman's touch," she hissed. "That is precisely the problem."

She smiled and waved delicate fingers at an acquaintance passing by. "I tried to reason with him, but reason does not work on a man who is thinking with his—"

"With his heart?"

Instead of laughing, she gave a faint sigh. "Let us hope not."

Robert handed her the bowl of sugared fruit he'd taken from the table. "I must see what is taking de Roche so long to escort Isobel to her chamber."

"No need," Claudette said, glancing toward the entrance. "The snake has returned." Claudette had disliked de Roche from the moment she laid eyes on him.

From the way de Roche stormed across the room, Isobel had fended for herself well enough. De Roche went at once to join a small group in the corner, which included Marie de Lisieux.

"You know they are lovers?" Claudette said.

"'Tis a shame," he said, popping a sugared fruit into his mouth, "that murdering him would cause political complications."

She laughed this time—a lovely tinkling sound that always drew men's attention.

How he would love to catch de Roche in some treachery against the king. He drummed his fingers on his knee. "Tell me, do you think de Roche both clever and brave enough to play two sides at once?"

She turned to him and raised one perfectly shaped eyebrow. "Surely vanity and overconfidence would serve, as well?"

Claudette was right, of course. She always was about men.

"Tonight, however," she said, "he is too absorbed with looking down the front of Marie's gown to be conspiring about aught else."

Robert took a long swallow of his wine. Damn, it was too much to hope he could catch de Roche in some treachery in time.

How else could he save Isobel from this marriage? He narrowed his eyes, considering. All he had to do was stir the pot a bit. But the risks were high. High for all of them.

He chuckled to himself. What was life without a little danger?

Chapter Fifteen

You are a handsome devil," Stephen murmured, "the fastest of them all, a matchless wonder."

Lightning nickered his agreement.

"I think he likes me now," François said, brushing the horse with long, firm strokes, just as Stephen had taught him. "He only tried to kick me twice today."

Stephen rubbed Lightning's nose and fed him another carrot.

Sighing, he rested his head against the horse's. "I know she is to be wed. And truly, I have tried to stay away. But she will think me rude if I do not see her."

Lightning munched the carrot, unpersuaded.

It was not just good intentions that kept Stephen away. He hated to see her with de Roche. He did not want Isobel to suffer with a second husband who disgusted her, but did this Frenchman have to be so handsome?

Stephen thought of how Isobel's breath caught when he touched her. How her head fell back as he kissed her throat. Oh, God, how she pulled him down on top of her.

Would she do the same with de Roche?

Lightning jerked his head up as quick, light steps approached.

"Linnet, do not run or make sudden moves around a horse like Lightning," Stephen said as he patted the horse's neck to reassure him.

As soon as Stephen stepped around the horse, Linnet jumped into his arms and kissed him on both cheeks. "Thank you, thank you!" she squealed. "I love Lady Hume. She is as kind and beautiful as you said."

Her brother emerged from the horse's other side, and she ran to embrace and kiss him, too.

Stephen stepped between her and the horse and hauled her back to a safe distance. "Does Lady Hume know where you are?"

"She'll not mind that I come to visit my brother."

So, she had not told Isobel. "If I catch you going about alone again, I shall whip you until you beg for mercy."

Linnet rolled her eyes. "How silly you are! Maids do not require escorts."

All the same, he would speak to Isobel about it.

"I brought you a treat from the kitchen," Linnet said, reaching into the cloth bag slung over her shoulder. "Sir Robert told me these are your favorites."

The smell of the warm apple tarts diverted him from his lecture, just as she intended.

He grabbed François by the shoulder and pointed to the bucket of clean water. "The tarts will taste better after you wash the smell of horse from your hands."

The three of them sat on a pile of clean straw in the corner to eat their tarts.

"I like Sir Robert," Linnet said between bites and

licking her fingers, "but who is this...this de Roche?" She wrinkled her nose as though smelling dung.

Stephen liked the girl better all the time. "De Roche is the man your mistress is going to marry. He is from Rouen."

Through a mouth stuffed full of tart, François mumbled his own speculation that de Roche came from hell. These children were wise beyond their years.

Linnet furrowed her brows in a pretty frown. "I cannot go to Rouen and leave François. When is this marriage to take place?"

"I do not know." Stephen suppressed a sigh. "Let us not worry about that yet."

"We cannot wait until it is too late," Linnet objected.

"Perhaps you could marry her instead?" François said.

Stephen laughed and shook his head. "You want me to marry to please the two of you?"

"She is very pretty," François said, "and I know how much you like her." The boy leaned forward, mouth hanging open like a half-wit, in what Stephen took as an imitation of himself.

Linnet threw her head back and hooted with laughter.

Stephen rubbed his temples. What had he done to deserve these two demons? "I do wish Lady Hume a better husband, but de Roche is the man King Henry has chosen for her."

Linnet dismissed the king's wishes with a very French lift of her narrow shoulder.

"Come," Stephen said to her. "I shall take you back now."

He expected an argument, but Linnet jumped to her feet. After bidding adieu to François and Lightning—who

withstood her exuberance with uncharacteristic calm—
she was ready to go.

When they reached Isobel's chamber in the keep, Linnet pushed the door open and ran inside. Stephen followed, intent on speaking to Isobel about Linnet.

As he closed the door, he saw Isobel. She was standing
before the basin on the table against the wall, as if about
to wash her face. Her long, dark hair was in tangles, and
she wore just her shift.

The sight left Stephen dry-mouthed. When she turned
and met his eyes, heat scorched between them like a fire.

He'd seen countless women rise from bed wearing less,
but none stirred him as she did, covered neck to ankle in a
plain white shift. The thought came to him, unbidden and
unwelcome: He could see her like this every morning and
never tire of it.

He remembered the silky feel of her hair in his hands.
His fingers itched to touch it, but his feet were fixed like
stone weights to the floor.

His eyes traveled down the lovely curve of her neck. He
longed to run his tongue along the delicate collarbone just
above the edge of her shift. Then, shameless man that he
was, he let his gaze drop precipitously to her breasts. They
were round and full, the tips pressed against the cloth.

He could not get enough air.

Still, he followed the folds of the white cloth down,
pondering the sweet mysteries underneath. He was a
drowning man. Down, down, down he went, until he
reached slim ankles and bare feet. He wanted to hold her
delicate foot in his hand and kiss each toe. And then move
up her leg.

He dragged his gaze back up, savoring every inch in

reverse. When he reached her face again, he thought his heart would stop. Her eyes held that same look of longing he remembered from the first time they met.

Blood pounded in his ears. He wanted her so badly he could taste the salt of her skin. With this fire sparking between them, the first time would be hot and fast. But then he would take her behind those bed curtains and spend the rest of the day making slow love to her. He would run his tongue over every—

"Lady Hume, you must put this on!"

The voice penetrated his reverie. Vaguely, he realized he'd been hearing Linnet's voice for some time. Whatever was the child doing here?

"Lady Hume!" The girl was tugging on Isobel's arm. "Isobel!"

This time, Isobel heard her. Before Stephen could cry out in protest, Isobel snatched the robe from Linnet's hand and whipped it around her shoulders. She looked so beautiful with her cheeks flushed and her hair swept over one shoulder, Stephen could almost forgive Linnet the robe. Almost.

But the girl had to go. Now.

Linnet had to leave so Stephen could gather Isobel in his arms and take her behind those bed curtains—

Just what had Isobel been doing behind those bed curtains? Tousled and in her night shift in the middle of the afternoon?

Was there a man behind those curtains? De Roche? Nay, she would not. She could not. Jealousy settled in his belly like a corrosive poison.

"Are you ill?" he asked, keeping his voice calm with considerable effort. "Is that why you are abed at this hour?"

"I haven't slept well lately. After Linnet left, I decided to rest awhile," she said, pushing her hair back from her face. "But why are you here, Stephen?"

"I was returning Linnet."

"From where?" she asked. "She only went to the kitchen."

"You were here alone, asleep, with your door unbarred?" Stephen could not control his temper with so much emotion roiling inside him. "And you should not let the girl wander all over the castle on her own. For God's sake, Isobel, the place is filled with soldiers."

Isobel took Linnet's hand and spoke to her in a soft voice. "Sir Stephen is right; you must be careful where you go alone. Most of the castle is safe, but avoid the places where soldiers congregate and other women are unlikely to be about."

He was relieved Isobel was giving the girl sensible direction, though it was not as restrictive as he would like.

"An isolated area," Isobel continued, "is even more dangerous."

"Such as the storerooms along the outer wall," he could not help putting in.

With her practice partners gone to Falaise, had Isobel taken to going alone to the storeroom? He took her arm to pull her aside and ask. As soon as he felt the heat of her skin through the thin fabric, lust blazed through him again.

Whatever he meant to tell her was gone from his head. All he could think to say was that he wanted to see her naked.

Isobel jerked her arm away as if his touch burned her,

too. "Of course, the most dangerous place to be caught with a man is a bedchamber," she said between clenched teeth. "Stephen, you must leave."

Ludicrous as it was, he felt pleased that she was calling him just "Stephen" again. He loved to hear her say his name.

He bowed and left, baffled by his loss of control. If Linnet had not been there, he would have had Isobel on the bed before a word passed between them. Nay, they never would have made it to the bed. It would be on the floor, or against the wall—

The saints preserve him, he was light-headed from breathing so hard. He'd be better off lost to drink than lost in lust to a woman he could not have.

That was not quite the truth of it. Isobel was a woman he *should* not have. She may not know it, but he *could* have her. He did not mistake the look in her eyes. That made her all the more dangerous.

He truly must stay away from her now. God help them both if he could not.

Chapter Sixteen

March 1418

Stephen managed to avoid Isobel for a full week, though sometimes it seemed as if all the world conspired against him. How Robert found him here in the armory he could not guess.

"You must ask someone else," Stephen said without looking up from the blade he was sharpening. "I am busy."

"There is no time," Robert said. "All I ask is that you go tell Isobel I've been called away so she does not sit waiting for me all afternoon."

"She can wait."

Robert glanced at the men hammering metal at the far end of the armory and lowered his voice. "The king needs me to come at once, and I cannot just leave her there."

"I see I shall have to tell you the truth," Stephen said and slammed the blade down on the bench beside him. "'Tis for her own protection I cannot go. The lady is not safe with me."

Robert's mouth twitched with amusement, which annoyed Stephen more than he thought possible.

"Surely I can trust you not to attack Isobel in broad daylight in a common area of the castle?" Robert said, widening his eyes in mock horror. He leaned down and whispered, "The king wishes me to listen behind the secret door *while he meets with de Roche*."

That did it. Stephen wiped his blade and returned it to his belt. When he looked up, Robert was halfway out the door.

"You will find her," Robert called over his shoulder, "in the small garden behind the Old Palace."

The small garden! With tall hedges on three sides and a wall on the fourth, that garden was made for liaisons. Stephen should know. He opened his mouth to call Robert back, but his friend was long gone.

Damn, damn, damn. So much for good intentions.

A smile tugged at the corners of his mouth. Stephen fought it, but he could not prevent it from spreading into a grin.

A man could fight fate only so long.

Isobel. He could hardly wait to see her.

———

A rat scrabbled along the secret passageway behind Robert. God's beard, it was filthy back here! Three hundred and fifty years of royal spies and lovers traipsing through it, and he doubted it had ever seen a broom.

Robert pressed his ear to the hole again.

"I have persuaded my cousin Georges de la Trémoille to do all he can to keep Burgundy on your side."

Robert remembered the beady-eyed Georges from boyhood—a pompous ass if there ever was one, but a wily one. If Georges was taking the English side, it was for his own reasons.

De Roche droned on about various members of the Burgundy faction, all of whom he claimed he could influence. Not a word passed de Roche's lips that Robert could use against him. Damn the man.

At long last, the king dismissed de Roche and his guards.

"You were right to suggest I use common soldiers as guards today," the king said as Robert stepped through the hidden panel. "De Roche assumed they could not understand French and spoke freely."

The soldiers could not, in fact, follow the conversation. That was Robert's job.

"He told you nothing we did not know," Robert pointed out as he brushed a cobweb from his tunic. "He is a slippery one. We cannot know on which side he will land."

The king slapped his fist against his palm. "Then it is time to force his hand with the betrothal."

Robert did not believe it would be so easy to flush de Roche out. He would wait to share this insight, however, until the king was ready to hear it.

"At the pace you and de Roche are negotiating this marriage contract," the king fumed, "I may as well have asked the lawyers to do it."

Robert was rather proud of how long he'd managed to drag it out. He had to stifle a smile—until he caught the steely glint in the king's eye.

"I will have this betrothal settled," the king said, pointing his finger at Robert, "within a sennight."

Seven days. That did not give him much time to thwart

the king's plans. Rather, it did not give Stephen much time.

He hoped matters were progressing in the garden.

———

Isobel let her head rest against the wall behind her. It felt heavenly to be alone in this peaceful garden, knowing de Roche would not come looking for her. God bless King Henry for giving him a private audience today! It took constant vigilance to avoid being caught alone with de Roche again.

Stephen, on the other hand, she'd barely glimpsed since she sent him from her chamber. How close she had been to succumbing to temptation that day! She should have been insulted by the way Stephen's gaze moved so blatantly over her body. Instead, his hunger seduced her, made her insides go hot and liquid. Without a single touch, she was his.

Or would have been, but for Linnet. God would punish her for being such a sinful woman.

Stephen had avoided her ever since. When she did chance to see him, he was always occupied. Talking with merchants from the town. Drinking with local noblemen. And there was always a woman nearby—touching his arm, laughing at his jokes, following him with her eyes. It was as if Stephen wanted to show her she did not matter.

Sometimes, though, she felt his eyes upon her. But when she turned to look, his gaze was elsewhere.

"Isobel."

She looked up, and there he was, so handsome he took her breath away.

"Robert could not come, so he sent me to fetch you."

"Will you not sit for a while?" she asked, patting the bench beside her. "With the sun out, it almost feels like summer in this sheltered garden."

He pressed his lips together and shook his head.

"Are you angry with me?" She was embarrassed by the quaver in her voice, but she pressed ahead. "You almost run when you see me, as if you cannot bear the sight of me."

To her astonishment, Stephen threw his head back and laughed. He had a wonderful, infectious laugh. It filled the small garden and lightened her heart.

He dropped down beside her. Smiling his most wicked smile, he leaned too close and asked, "You will pretend you do not know why I keep my distance?"

She swallowed and shook her head. "I do not know."

"You lie, Isobel, but I will tell you all the same."

She could not breathe with him this near.

"I stay away because whenever I see you"—he kept his eyes fixed on hers as he ran his finger slowly up her forearm—"all I want to do is drag you off to bed, and keep you there for a week."

A week. Oh, my. Her mouth went dry, and she wet her lips with her tongue. Her stomach tightened at the desire she saw burning in his eyes.

"I cannot be in a room with you," he said, his voice thick and husky, "without imagining what it would be like to take your clothes off. To feel your bare skin, warm and soft beneath my hands, against my chest. To smell your hair, to taste—"

He stopped abruptly and closed his eyes.

Isobel tried to slow her breathing, but there was nothing she could do about her racing pulse.

He rested his forehead against hers and whispered, "Tell me, what is this between us?"

She had no answer, at least none that she would give him.

She felt weak and liquid as he took her face in his hands. *Kiss me. Please. Just once more.*

When he pulled away, she felt bereft, wanting.

Stephen fell back against the wall and rocked his head from side to side. "This is more dangerous for you than for me. 'Tis why I tried to stay away." He rubbed his hands over his face and muttered into them, "What am I to do with her?"

Kiss me, kiss me, kiss me. She clenched her fists to keep from saying it aloud.

He dropped his hands and asked, "Do you want to marry him?"

She blinked at him, startled by the question.

"Now that you've spent time with de Roche," he persisted, "are you content to be his wife?"

"It does not matter what I wish," she said, though he should not need to be told. She straightened her spine. "I must do my best to be content with the fate God gives me."

"That is no answer," Stephen said.

And not fair to her future husband, either. She felt a wave of guilt for her disloyalty.

"Truly, the king has chosen well for me," she said. "Philippe de Roche is far above me in both wealth and position. The match exceeds every reasonable hope I could have."

For a certainty, de Roche would make a better husband than her last. She shuddered to think what sort of man her father would have given her to this time. God forgive her for not being as grateful as she ought. For wanting more.

Stephen took her hand and squeezed it. "You deserve to be happy this time."

She did not bother telling him that what a woman deserved had very little to do with what she got, at least in this life.

Chapter Seventeen

The noisy clatter and conversation in the Exchequer hall came to an abrupt halt. Isobel barely had time to scramble to her feet before the king and his commanders left their places at the high table and filed out of the hall.

As she sat back down, Isobel risked a sideways glance down the length of the table. No woman sat next to Stephen tonight.

And it could snow in July, too.

What did Stephen mean, asking her those questions this afternoon? One moment he was teasing her, the next acting tormented.

"Isobel?"

She started at the sound of de Roche's voice beside her.

"I had to say your name three times," de Roche said. "Who were you looking at?"

"My brother," she said, relieved to have an excuse ready. "I worry he spends so much time at L'Abbaye-aux-Hommes."

That much was true. What was troubling Geoffrey that caused him to keep vigil with the monks so often?

And now he was desperate to tell her about a holy relic at some other abbey. What did he say the relic was? A saint's finger joint? She had promised to meet him later. Heaven help her, he'd probably written a poem about the shriveled finger.

"You can have no objection to your brother's devotion," de Roche said, interrupting her thoughts again.

Isobel did not mistake his pronouncement for an invitation to explain her concern. De Roche never asked her questions of a personal nature about her family. She was relieved, and yet... How different he was from Stephen. Stephen would not be content until he wheedled every dark family secret from her.

This time she was jarred from her thoughts by something warm and heavy on her leg.

"For once, your vigilant guardian has left us." De Roche was looking straight ahead, but his lips were curved up at the corners.

She glanced up and down the table. Both Robert and Stephen had disappeared. Off in search of amusement in the town, no doubt.

She grasped de Roche's hand to halt its progress up her thigh.

"You are tired, my dear," de Roche said. "Shall I see you to your chamber?" Without waiting for her answer, he gripped her elbow and hoisted her to her feet.

"I began to wonder if Sir Robert would ever leave your side," de Roche said in her ear as he whisked her out of the hall. "The man protects you as if you were an innocent virgin."

She felt uneasy and a little breathless as he marched her purposefully down the steps of the Exchequer and along the path to the keep. The night air was cold. Through the thickness of her cloak, she could feel de Roche's heat.

Could he not say something to soothe her?

He maintained both his silence and his brisk pace all the way to the keep. By the time they reached the corridor outside her chamber, her heart was slamming in her chest. His teeth gleamed in the rushlight as he spun her toward him. She tensed as de Roche ran his fingers down her throat.

When he reached the sensitive skin along the top of her bodice, she grabbed his wrist. "Someone will see us!"

"No one is here." He dipped a finger into the valley between her breasts. "Besides, we are nearly betrothed."

This man would be her husband. Soon she would share his bed as often as he wished her to. It seemed silly to protest this small familiarity.

The old hope returned. The hope that her new husband could make her feel the way Stephen did when he kissed her. That he could give her that feeling of being swept away, as if nothing else mattered so long as he touched her.

Was it possible? She needed to know.

"Kiss me," she said, lifting her face to him. This time, it would be different.

This kiss was different. Softer. Not frightening, like the first time. And not disgusting, like Hume's. Her mind was cold and clear as she waited for the thrill to seize her. And waited. The kiss felt...pleasant. But no more than that.

She could come up with no explanation. De Roche was handsome, young, healthy. True, the heavy scent he wore gave her a bit of a headache. But his lips were soft and warm. The tickle of his mustache did not bother her.

De Roche ran his hands up and down her sides. Her body began to respond to his caresses. But where was the mindless passion? What she felt was a dim candle to the roaring fire that burned through her when Stephen touched her.

She would try harder. Determined, she moved her hands to the nape of his neck and kissed him back. She opened her mouth to him and slid her tongue over his the way she remembered had brought moans from Stephen.

Before she knew it, she was crushed against him. She felt trapped, unable to move. She was so startled by the suddenness of the assault that it took her a moment to realize de Roche's hand was like an iron band around her wrist.

She made frantic little cries against his mouth as he forced her hand downward. He was so strong! She felt the hardness of his cock against her palm. Up and down, up and down, he rubbed her hand against it.

She bit his lip and tasted blood. Though he tore his mouth away, he did not release her hand. His breath was coming in horrid gasps against her ear. She was flooded with the memory of Hume's putrid smell gagging her in the darkness.

With a surge of strength, she wrenched her other arm free and swung at him. He caught her hand midair. They stood inches apart, staring at each other. Both were breathing hard, but she was choking back tears.

"Stop, please." Her voice was small, barely a whisper.

His eyes were black with rage. "After the way you kissed me, you will pretend you do not want me in your bed tonight?"

"I meant only a kiss," she stammered, feeling confused and ashamed.

"Ah, you mean to tease me." His voice was all the more menacing for its softness. "That is not a nice game to play."

Looking straight into her eyes, he cupped her breasts with his hands. She was too shocked and too frightened to move.

"Once I take you to bed," he said as he rubbed his thumbs in slow circles over her nipples through the cloth, "you will want to learn the kind of games that will keep me there."

———

There was a time when Stephen would have been pleased to be included in the king's meeting with his commanders. But not tonight. Although King Henry placed considerable importance on the just administration of his new territories, the other men looked bored as Stephen gave his report. And why not? Stephen was bored himself.

In sooth, he was not so much bored as anxious to leave. The moment the king released him, he made his escape. He pretended not to see William's signal to wait for him. As he ran along the dark path to the keep, he asked himself why he was going to find Isobel.

What would he say when he found her? He had no idea.

This was lunacy, even for him. If he wanted to forget all honor and seduce her, he could have done that already. He recalled the moment when he knew she was his for the asking—and almost forgot to breathe.

What she did to him! He felt better about himself when he was around her. More interesting. More clever. Certainly more virtuous! He wanted to protect her, to drive the sadness from her eyes.

He would not let himself think what that meant now.

He entered the keep and raced up the back stairs, two at a time. As he climbed, he thought of the last time he came here. When she leapt from the bed in her shift. His heart beat so hard now he thought it might burst from his chest.

He ran down the corridor and made the last turn.

And stopped dead in his tracks.

Despite the dim light, he could not fool himself into believing the woman was anyone other than Isobel. He'd spent too many hours studying that profile. And that foolish goatee could belong to none other than de Roche.

When Isobel slid her hands behind de Roche's neck and pulled him into a deep kiss, she may as well have reached into Stephen's chest and ripped his heart out. How could she? How could she do this?

Then he saw her hand, covered by de Roche's, reaching down. Sweet Jesus, he did not want to see this. Not this. When she began stroking de Roche's crotch, Stephen leaned against the wall and squeezed his eyes shut. And still he could hear the little sounds she was making. He had to get out of here. Now.

And yet he looked again. He could not help himself.

The lovers stood apart now, eyes locked. Stephen watched, transfixed, as de Roche covered her breasts with his hands and rubbed his thumbs over the tips. It was such a blatant show of sexual ownership that Stephen could stand no more.

He turned and fled without a sound.

————

Stephen drank with a purpose. Though his lips and even his fingertips felt numb, sweet oblivion escaped him. The drink had yet to loosen the knot of jealousy in his stomach. Nor had it dulled the loss that weighed down every muscle.

The woman was heavy on his lap—he had no idea who she was and how she got there. He wanted her gone, but it would take too much effort to make her move. The overpowering smell of cloying perfume, sweat, and sex turned his stomach. Even with his eyes closed, he could not pretend she was Isobel.

Quite suddenly, the weight was off his lap. He heard a sharp exchange of female voices, but he did not feel curious enough to open his eyes.

"You must be far gone to let that one near you! She'd give you the pox for sure, you fool."

"Claudette?" He opened his eyes to find her looking down at him, her hands on her hips. "It is you."

He was so glad to see her he leaned against her and put his arms around her waist. Though he was vaguely aware he should not have his face buried between her breasts, it felt comforting to be surrounded by all that softness.

Someone was pulling on his shoulders, and he heard a familiar voice behind him. Reluctantly, he released Claudette and fell back. All this movement was making his head spin.

"Jamie? What are you doing in this den of sin?" he asked. "William will have a fit."

"He is the one who sent me."

"William sent a fifteen-year-old to play nursemaid to me?" Stephen's voice sounded distant to his own ears.

"Aye, that is just what he did," Jamie said with a grin, "except that I am almost sixteen."

William sent Jamie with Claudette? More proof the world made no sense. No sense at all.

"How could she prefer de Roche?" he asked.

Jamie gave him a puzzled look, but Claudette—dear, dear Claudette—understood.

"She would be a fool to prefer him," she said and touched his cheek.

"But I saw her." The words came out of his mouth of their own accord; he could not stop them. "She was kissing him. And touching him, for God's sake. And—"

"Of course she was. She has to marry the man," Claudette interrupted. "Women must be practical."

Practical? Did women truly think that way?

"Kissing me was not practical."

"It certainly was not," Claudette agreed. "Not for either of you."

The next thing he knew he was in a carriage, bouncing over cobblestones, his head banging against the side.

Cold air woke him, and he got his feet under him. Snatches of conversation came to him, as if from a long way away: Jamie saying he could manage alone; the guards' loud jibes; his own voice suggesting they find Isobel.

When next he opened his eyes, he saw his feet dragging along the floor. Then some kind soul hoisted him onto the bed. He was sinking, sinking, sinking.

Jamie's voice brought him back from the land of the dead. "What did Claudette mean about women being 'practical'?"

"She means...a woman will bed a man"—he sighed because of the effort it took to respond, but Jamie shook his shoulder again—"because it makes sense to her . . . though she has no true feeling for him. They are all heartless, heartless."

"A virtuous woman would not do that."

"Virtuous ones are the worst!" God in heaven, even Catherine took a stranger to her bed.

Had he said that last part aloud? Nay, he'd never tell.

"You are drunk. She would never do that. No one could be a more devoted wife."

"Shhhe would neber do that to William. Nebber, nebber, nebber." But even Catherine . . . even she was practical once. Took a stranger to bed. A stranger.

"What did you say?" The voice seemed to be coming from inside his head. But it was damned persistent.

"Who was it? What happened?"

Stephen wanted the questions to stop so he could sleep.

"He could not get her with child. Her other husband. That cursed first one. So shhhe let someone else do the job. Thasss how she got ssweet little Jamie. Big sssecret. Shhh."

Chapter Eighteen

Stephen awoke with a bad feeling that had nothing to do with his hangover. A very bad feeling. Beneath the pounding headache, lurching stomach, and dry mouth, something more sinister lurked. He had the uneasy feeling he'd crossed a line. Committed some grave, unpardonable wrong.

Had he gone to bed with someone he shouldn't have? He turned his head, careful not to move too quickly, and let his breath out. If that was what he'd done, at least she was gone.

But he did not think that was it.

He crawled out of bed, poured cold water from the pitcher into the basin, and splashed his face.

What was it? He tried to piece together what happened after...The image of de Roche with his hands on Isobel was all too clear. His rising pulse caused his head to throb violently. He leaned over the basin and poured the rest of the pitcher over his head.

First he went to the public house nearest the castle gate. Then to the one near the old church. Sometime later, he ended up in the seamiest part of town. He remembered the smell of cloying perfume. Then Claudette appearing like an angel of mercy. And Jamie.

A carriage ride. Jamie dragging him to bed. Someone asking endless questions. About women being practical...

He squeezed his eyes shut. God help him, had he said those things about Catherine aloud? And to Jamie? He could not have. He had wheedled the secret out of an old servant years ago and never told a living soul. Never would.

He turned and looked about the empty bedchamber. Where was Jamie now? Trying not to panic, he threw on his clothes, grabbed his cloak and sword, and tore out of the room.

He had to find Jamie. God help him if he'd told Catherine's secret to her son last night. If he had, he would have to explain it to Jamie, try to make him understand.

And then he would have to tell William what he'd done.

———

Isobel looked everywhere for her brother. When she could not find him, she began to worry. Last night he said he had something important to tell her. Why did she not make him tell her at once? Of course, she did not expect de Roche to take her off so suddenly. And then, after what happened—she would not think of that now—she forgot completely about her brother.

Linnet's fair hair whipped about her face as they raced across the bailey yard. "We have not tried the stables yet," she shouted against the wind. "If his horse is there, you will know he has not gone far."

"You are a bright one," Isobel said, forcing a smile. She could not say why she was so worried.

Halfway to the stables, they saw François running toward them.

"Lady Hume, I've been looking for you," he called out as he drew near. He was as breathless as she. "Your brother asked me to give you a message."

"A message? What is it?"

François screwed his face up as if he were concentrating to be sure he got it right. "He and Jamie Rayburn have gone to an abbey two hours' ride from here to see a holy relic."

"You saw Geoffrey leave?" she said, fighting to sound calm. "With Jamie?"

"At first he was going to go alone," François said. "I told him it was too dangerous with all the brigands and renegades roaming the countryside. But he said, 'God will protect me.' I swear, that is just what he said."

Good Lord, she would kill him for taking such a risk! Even this child knew it was foolish to travel alone here.

"Then Jamie came tearing into the stable in such a state," the boy said, his eyes wide. "Your brother pulled him into a corner where I could not hear. Next thing I know, your brother gives me this message—and they ride off!"

"How long ago was this?"

François shrugged. "An hour? I looked a long time for you."

She must find someone quickly to ride after them and bring them back. By now, people would be gathered in the hall for breakfast. She ran headlong for the keep, the twins dogging her steps.

"Jamie is a good fighter," François called out in a valiant attempt to reassure her.

She would find de Roche. He came to Caen with a large contingent of armed men. Surely he could gather enough of them quickly to go after Geoffrey and Jamie.

She barely slowed to a walk as she entered the keep. "Wait here," she told the twins as she went through the great arched doorway to the keep's hall. She spotted de Roche at once and made straight for him.

"Philippe, help me!" she called out when she was close enough to be heard. She ignored the disapproval on his face; he would understand as soon as he heard what happened.

He held up his hand. With a laugh, he said to the man next to him, "My bride is anxious to see me."

"Geoffrey has gone off!" she cried. "You must go after him and bring him back."

"Calm yourself, my dear. Tell me you have not been running. You are quite out of breath."

"My brother is gone," she said between gasps. "You must go at once, or he'll come to harm, I know it."

"If you will excuse us," he said to the man. He took her arm in a bruising grip and led her to a corner.

"You should have asked to speak to me in private," he said, his eyes flaring with anger. "How dare you approach me in public making demands, telling me I must do this, I must do that!"

"I am sorry, but my brother—"

"Your brother is a grown man. He can make his own decisions and live with the consequences."

"But can you not go after him? He does not understand—"

"Good God, Isobel, do you think I have nothing better to do than chase after your foolish brother?"

"Do you?" As far as she could tell, he had nothing to do in Caen but negotiate the marriage contract with Robert—and that was going so slowly he could not be giving much time to it.

"I do not need to explain myself to you," he said. "Your brother is bound to think better of his actions and return. I suggest you go to your chamber and wait for him."

What sort of man was he? How could he refuse to help her? She had no time to argue. He would not be moved, in any case.

She rose up on her tiptoes to look over his shoulder for someone else she could ask. When she saw Lord Fitz-Alan, she shouted his name and waved her arms.

"Stop that at once," de Roche said. "You are making a spectacle of yourself."

FitzAlan was already striding toward her. Praise God! And that was Stephen, right behind him.

"Lord FitzAlan, Sir Stephen," de Roche greeted them as they approached.

FitzAlan ignored him. "What is it, Lady Hume? You seem distressed."

"François says my brother and Jamie have ridden out of the city alone," she said, trying to keep her voice under control.

Stephen gripped her arm. "Does François know their destination, or in what direction they rode?"

"To an abbey, two hours east." A fragment from one of Geoffrey's poems came to her. Something about a finger of a martyred saint and..."L'Abbaye de Saint Michele, could that be it?"

"I'll meet you at the stables," FitzAlan said to Stephen. "I must leave word for the king that I've gone."

"We shall find them," Stephen said and gave her arm a quick squeeze as they turned to go.

"Wait," she called after them. "I will come with you."

"Don't be foolish—" de Roche began, but FitzAlan cut him off.

"Keep her here," FitzAlan commanded, pointing his outstretched arm at de Roche.

Then they were gone.

Dropping her eyes on the floor, Isobel said, "I will wait in my chamber, as you suggested." She dipped a quick curtsy and left before he could say a word.

Linnet caught up with her on the stairs. As soon as they reached her chamber, Isobel opened her trunk and took out the clothes she had been mending for Geoffrey.

"Cut six inches from the sleeves and leggings, and help me change," she ordered Linnet. "Quickly now."

She brushed aside Linnet's objections. The voice in the back of her head told her what she was doing was foolish; she ignored that, as well.

Geoffrey was all she had in the world.

She could not sit here and wait. From the time Geoffrey was little, she was the one who protected him—from their father's criticisms, their mother's indifference, his own blindness to the world around him.

"If someone comes for me, tell them I am asleep," she said as she strapped on her sword. "Say I am unwell, a headache."

Thank goodness her cloak was a plain one. She told Linnet to fetch it as she pushed her hair under a cap. After giving Linnet a hurried kiss on the cheek, she pulled the hood over her head and ran out the door.

She got to the stables just as Stephen and FitzAlan were riding out. She ducked her head as they galloped past, then turned to see that they were headed toward the eastern gate, Porte des Champs.

When she found François inside, he was no more keen on her plan than his sister. Still, she made him help saddle her horse and swore him to secrecy. He looked so uneasy that she forgot her disguise and touched his cheek.

"I shall catch up to them in no time," she assured him. "They will keep me safe."

"Take good care, m'lady," François said. "They are going to be very angry."

She almost laughed—François was far more concerned about what Stephen and FitzAlan would do to her than the brigands and renegades.

Porte des Champs took her directly into the fields east of the castle. Far ahead, she could see two riders. She held her horse back, not wanting to close the distance too soon. Her plan was to wait to reveal herself until they were midway to the abbey, when they would find it easier to take her to the abbey than bring her all the way back to Caen.

Before long, she dismissed her fear of being discovered too soon. She was a good rider, but at each rise, the two men seemed farther and farther ahead. She lost sight of them altogether in the dips between.

When she crested the next hill, she could not see them at all. A surge of fear went through her as she realized how alone and vulnerable she was. She darted looks side to side and behind her. Should she go back? Heart pounding, she craned her neck and searched the empty horizon.

Suddenly, two riders burst out of the trees on either side of her. Her shrieks filled the air as they charged toward her. At the last moment, the two riders pulled their horses up. Their horses reared, hooves high in the air. Her horse shied away from them, nearly unseating her in its fright.

When Isobel saw who the riders were, she thought she might faint with relief. She pressed her hand to her thundering heart. "Praise God it is you! I thought you were brigands!"

"Isobel?" Stephen said, his eyes wide. "Isobel!"

She wanted to throw her arms around them both. The men were not nearly as glad to see her. In sooth, they looked as if they'd like to murder her.

"Are you possessed?" Stephen shouted at her. "Did you think we would not notice someone following us? If your screams were not so ... so ... so *female,* we might have run you through!"

He sounded as though he wished they had.

"You were a fool to come," FitzAlan said. "And that de Roche is a bigger fool for not making certain you did not."

"But I am here," she said quickly. "Geoffrey and Jamie cannot be far ahead now. We must keep going."

When she saw the look that passed between them, she knew she would get her way. But they were not happy about it.

"We shall take you to the abbey, and leave you there," FitzAlan said. "In chains, if need be."

With that, he turned his horse and galloped off.

"Stay close to me," Stephen ordered. "We'll ride behind until his temper cools."

They spurred their horses forward and rode side by side.

Stephen could not let it go just yet. "Truly, Isobel, that was foolish in more ways than I can name."

"Anyone seeing me will think I am a man," she said, though she was feeling worse and worse by the moment. "Surely 'tis safer to travel as three armed men than two."

"Safer, with you?" he said, turning and raising an eyebrow. "Your being dressed like that serves only to distract me. Why, I can see the shape of your leg all the way up to—"

"Be serious, Stephen."

She looked ahead, embarrassed. At least the anger was gone from Stephen's voice. Judging from the stiffness of FitzAlan's back, he would not forgive her so easily.

Stephen seemed to read her thoughts. "I've not seen a woman other than his wife provoke William this much before."

"He gets angry with her often? The poor woman."

"Poor Catherine?" Stephen laughed. "Believe me, she has the great commander wrapped around her little finger."

He was quiet a moment. "There is nothing he would not do for her," he said, his voice wistful. "Or she for him."

Who would have guessed the stern commander harbored a great love? Inexplicably, the thought made Isobel's eyes sting.

"Do not fret over William's displeasure," Stephen said. "He is so angry with me, he can have little left for you."

"What happened?"

"It is because of me," he said, staring straight ahead, "that Jamie ran off."

She averted her gaze from the naked pain on Stephen's face and tried to think of something she could say to comfort him.

"William!" Stephen roared.

She jerked her head up. Time stopped as she tried to make sense of the scene before her: FitzAlan slumped over his horse, a rain of arrows falling all about him. Was FitzAlan injured? How was it possible?

Stephen's shouts brought her to her senses.

"To the wood, Isobel! Now!" He pointed in the direction he wanted her to go and then shot forward on his horse.

She turned her horse into the field and galloped across it toward the wood beyond. When she risked a glance over her shoulder, her heart went to her throat.

Stephen had put himself between his wounded brother and the stand of trees from which the arrows were coming. As she watched, he leaned over, caught the reins of FitzAlan's horse, and took off again. Praise God!

Before she entered the wood, she looked for him again. Stephen was galloping, with FitzAlan in tow, in a wide arc that would bring them into the same wood, but farther up. She entered the wood and rode, as fast as she dared, to meet them.

At last she saw movement ahead through the trees. When she came upon the two horses, panic surged through her. Their saddles were empty. Then she saw Stephen beside a fallen log, hunched over his brother.

She leapt down from her horse and knelt beside him.

"What can I do?" She gripped Stephen's arm and peered down at FitzAlan.

Oh, my God. FitzAlan was drenched in blood. An arrow stuck out of his neck above his chain mail shirt.

"We should have taken the time to don full armor," Stephen said as he worked the arrow out of FitzAlan's neck. "Find something to bind the wound. Quickly."

Isobel removed the food bundle she had stowed inside her shirt. She let the bread and cheese fall to the ground, shook out the cloth, and folded it tightly.

"I am ready."

Stephen pulled the arrow free, and she pressed the cloth against the spurting wound.

God help them, FitzAlan was insensible and pale as death.

Stephen kept pressure on the wound while she cut a long strip from the bottom of her cloak. Then, working together, they wound the strip over the cloth covering the wound, around his back, and under his arm. Stephen tied the binding tight across his brother's chest.

As soon as it was done, Stephen gripped Isobel's arms and looked into her face. "Those men are still out there. I must divert them before they come into the wood."

"You are going back?" *Sweet Jesus, no. Please no.*

"I will come back for you as soon as I can." He pulled the sword and short blade from FitzAlan's belt and handed them to her. "But you must be ready should one of them get by me."

Oh God oh God oh God.

"You can do this, Isobel," he said, his eyes fixed on hers. "If a man does come, he will believe he sees a helpless woman. That is your advantage."

She looked down and saw that her hair fell loose about her shoulders. Where was her cap? It must have fallen...

Stephen took hold of her chin and turned her back

to face him. "Use his ignorance against him. Use your sword. Kill him, Isobel. Kill him."

Could she do it? Could she? His eyes drilled into hers until she nodded.

He took her face in his hands and kissed her hard. "Give him no second chances."

As Stephen's horse crashed through the underbrush, she gazed down upon the man entrusted to her care. King Henry's famous commander. Beloved of Catherine. 'Twas her fault he lay here grievously injured. She had distracted them from the real danger.

She took a deep breath and went to retrieve a blanket and flask from the horses. After wrapping the blanket around FitzAlan, she shooed the horses away so they would not give away their hiding place. Then she gathered armfuls of leaves and piled them around FitzAlan.

When she was satisfied FitzAlan was well hidden, she settled down beside him behind the fallen log. The smell of decaying wood and leaves filled her nostrils as she dribbled ale from the flask into his mouth. He swallowed without waking.

She alternated between checking FitzAlan and peeking over the top of the log. Though Stephen could not have been gone long, each moment seemed a day. She would not let herself think of what she would do if he did not return.

God, please keep him safe. Keep him safe.

She heard a twig snap. Gripping the sword in one hand and the short blade in the other, she inched up until she could see over the top of the log. Nothing.

She held her breath and listened.

There it was again.

She turned toward the sound, searching.

And then she saw him. A man, twenty yards off and coming straight toward her. She set down the sword to wipe the sweat from her hand.

Mary, Mother of God. She prayed under her breath that the man's presence did not mean Stephen was dead.

The man was coming closer. She had to think, to make her plan. He wore no armor, so she had a chance. She heard Stephen's voice in her head, saying, *Isobel, you can do this.*

She waited until he was ten feet from her.

She stood abruptly, keeping her hands behind her. "Sir! Please help me!"

The man's eyes went wide. "Now, here's a bonus," he said, relaxing his sword arm and breaking into a wide grin. "I was not told there would be a woman."

From his accent and his rough clothing, she could tell he was a French commoner. "English soldiers took me from my home," she called out, pretending to cry. "You must help me, please!"

The man came toward her slowly, as if she were a horse easily spooked. What if he was not one of the attackers? What if he was just some peasant who meant to help her? He had a sword, but—

The man raked his eyes over her, and she knew with utter certainty he meant her harm. And when he was finished with her, he would murder FitzAlan.

She stood very still and waited. One more step. One more step. When he was just on the other side of the log, not four feet from her, he lunged for her.

The shock of resistance as the point of her sword

entered his body made her arm shake. She clenched her teeth and pressed forward with all her weight. For a long, dreadful moment, he swayed on his feet, staring at her with eyes wide with surprise. Then he fell backward, ripping her sword from her hands.

She jumped over the log and stood over him, her heart thundering in her chest. The sword. She had to have it back.

Fighting back nausea, she took hold of the hilt with both hands and tugged. It would not give! Her hands felt cold and clammy. Sweat trickled down her back. She had to have it back.

She put her foot on the man's chest and pulled with her weight behind it. At last the sword gave way with a wet sucking sound. She fell back a step but kept her hold on it.

The blade was dripping with the man's blood. She could not take her eyes from it.

At the sound of a loud grunt behind her, she whipped around and saw FitzAlan. He had one arm over the log, trying to support himself. A chill ran through her as she realized his eyes were not on her. They were fixed on something behind her.

FitzAlan's free arm moved in a blur and something whizzed past her ear. When she turned back to look the other way, she saw a second man not five feet from her. FitzAlan's knife was in his chest.

She was behind the log before she knew she'd moved.

"My vision is not good," FitzAlan said in a rasping voice. The poor man's face was wet with sweat, and the bandage on his neck was soaked in blood. "But I think there are one or two more of them in the wood."

One or two more?

She swallowed hard. "I shall be ready this time."

"Good girl."

Isobel grabbed FitzAlan's sleeve to break his fall as he slid to the ground.

Chapter Nineteen

𝓘sobel kept watch as before. FitzAlan's color was not good. Not good at all. She leaned down and put her ear to his chest again. *Thump thump, thump thump.* The strength of his heartbeat reassured her. *Thump thump, thump thump.*

She heard a rustle and opened her eyes to see a man leading a horse through the trees. There was no use hiding. The log did not block them from this side, and the man had already seen them. She got to her feet and stood in front of FitzAlan.

The man halted several feet away, giving her time to notice the glint of silver on his horse's saddle and his fine clothing. This one was a nobleman. A French nobleman.

"Lord FitzAlan, the English king's great commander, reduced to having a woman champion." He shook his head and gave her a bemused smile. "It is quite splendid of you, dear lady. But hopeless, nonetheless."

So this was no random attack! These men knew their quarry. Somehow they must have learned FitzAlan rode out without his men today. But how was that possible?

Who could have told them? And gotten the word to them so quickly?

The man took a step forward, and she shouted, "Halt!"

"I will not hurt you," the man said, his voice calm. "'Tis FitzAlan I've come for."

"What will you do with him?"

"Take him for ransom." He took another step forward. "FitzAlan is quite a prize, you know."

Isobel did not believe him for a moment. These men had sought to kill FitzAlan from the start.

"Halt," she cried again as the man took yet another step forward. She kept her sword pointed at him.

"I may have to take you with me; otherwise, no one will believe me," he said, sounding amused. "I'll wager your husband will pay a hefty sum to have you back."

A cold calm settled over her as she accepted she would have to fight him. She felt a wave of gratitude toward Stephen. Every day he practiced with her had made her better. But would she be good enough? She looked the man over, to judge him as Stephen had taught her.

Nothing about him reassured her. He was taller and stronger than she was. What worried her more was that he walked with an easy grace that suggested he would be quick and light on his feet. Damn, damn, damn.

What did Stephen tell her? Find her advantage and use it. Too bad she had no skirt to lift to show her ankles.

She remembered Stephen's reaction to her leggings and unfastened her cloak with one hand. When she shrugged it off, the man dropped the point of his sword and gaped open-mouthed at her legs. Before she could overcome her surprise at how well it worked, he brought his gaze back up to meet her eyes.

"I'd wager your husband finds you a handful." His tone was still amused, but the glint in his eyes had her backing up. "I would love to be there when you explain to him how you happen to be traveling alone with FitzAlan and his brother . . . dressed as a man."

Her heel hit FitzAlan's prone form. She could step back no farther. With the man just two or three feet beyond the reach of her sword, she could wait no longer to begin her farce. She made a clumsy swing at him with her sword.

This time, she did not miss her moment.

When the man threw his head back, roaring with laughter, she lunged forward with her sword aimed straight at his heart. At the last instant, he jumped back and saved himself.

"You are full of surprises!" He was smiling, but he had his sword at the ready now.

She had no more tricks. There was nothing for it but to fight as best she could. He came at her hard and fast. The first attack she fended off. Then the second, and the third. But he was quick and strong, and more skilled than she.

"I see 'tis true that chivalry is dead among the French nobility," she jeered. "You are the worst kind of coward, to attack a man so gravely injured and a defenseless woman."

"You are hardly defenseless, my dear." He was circling, waiting for her to give him an opening. "I must ask, who was your teacher?"

She did have one advantage left, after all. From the way he was fighting, he was trying only to disarm her.

She fought with no such constraint; she would kill him if he gave her half a chance.

As they moved forward and back, swords clanging, he showed no concern he might lose. In sooth, the man appeared to be enjoying himself. He spun in a circle, returning in time to block her thrust. Good heavens, the fool was showing off!

The next time he spun about, she was ready. She lunged at once, putting all her weight behind it. Somehow he managed to duck below her sword, and she fell crashing forward. The air went out of her as he caught her around the waist.

"You tried to kill me!" the man said.

He hit her wrist with the side of his hand. The sharp pain made her hand go numb, and she dropped her sword.

"For that, I shall make you watch FitzAlan die," he said. "He must mean a good deal to you, for you to risk your life for him."

She kicked and screamed and bit as he dragged her with one arm back to where FitzAlan lay unmoving beside the log. Holding her against his side with one arm, he raised his sword arm over FitzAlan. The bandage around Fitz-Alan's neck looked like a bloody target.

"No, no!" she screamed.

He raised his sword higher. Desperate to stop him, she wrenched sideways, caught his raised arm, and clung to it.

The man threw her to the ground. Her head hit something hard, stunning her. When her vision cleared, she saw him raising his sword again. She scrambled across the rough ground on hands and knees and flung herself on top of FitzAlan.

The man above her was shouting a string of curses at her, but Isobel was screaming back. Suddenly, he jerked her to her knees by her hair. She looked up at the man's face, mottled with rage, and braced herself to be backhanded across the face.

As he swung his arm back to strike her, she heard a roar. The man turned, his arm frozen in midair. From the corner of her eye, she saw a blur of movement through the trees.

Thunk!

She stared at the hilt of a blade protruding from the man's left eye socket. Blood gushed from it, splattering on her. Even when his grip on her hair loosened and he fell to the ground, her mind could not yet grasp what had happened. She felt herself sway just before strong arms caught her.

Then Stephen was holding her against him. He was squeezing the breath out of her, but she did not care. As he covered her face with kisses, she sucked in gasps of air that came out as choked sobs. He murmured into her hair words she did not try to understand. But his voice comforted her.

She could not say how long he held her. It might have been an eternity, but it would never be enough.

Once her heart stopped pounding so violently in her chest and her sobbing subsided, a dense wave of exhaustion rolled over her. The leaf-strewn floor of the forest swirled beneath her.

"Thank you," she whispered and closed her eyes.

Stephen entered the wood riding at a pace that risked his horse, cursing himself for taking so long. Damn, there had been just too many of them. He charged into them, slashing his sword from side to side. He killed two in the first foray, but the next two took more time. While he fought them, the others scattered.

A few rode off across the fields, but he thought he saw at least two go into the wood. That was why he was riding like a madman through the trees.

He rode straight for the log where he'd left Isobel and William. When he saw them, his heart stopped in his chest. Isobel's body lay over William's. A man stood over them, holding a sword. God, no! They were dead! He was too late!

Over the sound of his horse crashing through the trees, he heard Isobel's screams as the son of Satan lifted her up by the hair.

Stephen was very good with a knife—he'd learned from William, after all—but could he risk throwing it with Isobel so close? When the man drew his arm back to strike her, a yell of rage and madness ripped from Stephen's throat. As he thundered down on them, he threw the blade through the trees.

Then, in one motion, he leapt off his horse and pulled Isobel into his arms. Nothing in his life would ever feel as good as holding her against him at this moment.

He wanted to weep with relief. God in heaven, what a woman! Fighting liké a she-wolf, screaming curses at the man. Jesus help him, she used her body to shield William!

When her knees gave way, he carried her to the log and held her while he scanned the woods. There could be one or two more in the wood. When he spotted two bodies lying on the ground, he blew his breath out with a whoosh. Thank God.

He turned to check on William. *Oh, God,* but William was pale. Moving quickly, he pulled the flask from inside his shirt and held it to Isobel's mouth until she drank. As soon as she was able to sit on her own, he dropped to his knees beside his brother.

William's pulse was strong, but he'd lost a lot of blood. If they got him somewhere safe—and soon—he could be saved. As he replaced the bloodied bandage with a strip of cloth from his shirt, he looked up at Isobel. She was almost as pale as William.

"We must go quickly," he said. "Where are the horses?"

His question seemed to startle her out of her daze. She got up at once, saying, "I shall get them."

As he cradled William's head to pour ale down his throat, William opened his eyes.

"Bit slow, weren't you?" William said in a weak whisper.

Good God, William was teasing him.

"I shall have to tie you to your horse," he said.

William attempted to nod and winced with pain.

Stephen looked up to see Isobel coming through the trees, leading the horses.

"Ready?" he said to William. "One, two, three."

William gasped as Stephen lifted him onto the log.

At Stephen's nod, Isobel brought William's horse around and held him steady.

"One, two, three," he said again to warn William and then hoisted him up onto the horse.

William got his feet in the stirrups before slumping forward over his horse's neck.

Just as well he is not awake for this.

As he tied his brother to the saddle, he looked over his shoulder at Isobel. She was mounted and awaiting his signal, her face serious and intent.

"The abbey is not far," he said, keeping his voice calm. "I don't want to frighten you, but we must get there with all possible haste. The monks will know what to do for William."

He did not tell her his other reason for haste. If this was not a random attack—and he suspected it was not—those men would not give up easily and move on to other prey. They could be part of a larger force, as well.

Stephen rode in front, leading William's horse. Twice Isobel called out that William was sliding off, and he had to stop. He told Isobel to stay mounted and kept his eyes on the horizon as he retied the ropes.

When the abbey finally came into view, he gave a silent prayer of thanks. Surely God was with them this day.

As they approached, the gates opened and Jamie and Geoffrey came running out. Jamie went at once to William.

"How badly is he injured?" Jamie had his knife out, ready to cut the ropes.

"Best to keep him on the horse until we are inside," Stephen said as he tossed the reins to Jamie.

Jamie swung up behind his father. Leaning protectively over William, he spurred the horse through the gates, across a narrow bridge, and up the short slope of the outer courtyard to the church. With monks trailing him now, he turned his horse and rode along the side of the church and through an arched doorway.

Stephen ducked his head as he followed Jamie through the arch. With a twinge of uneasiness, he realized they were in the monks' cloister. God might forgive them for bringing horses into this quiet place, but the monks would not.

"The infirmary is there," Jamie said, pointing to a doorway off the opposite side of the small courtyard.

Together they cut the ropes and lifted William down. Jamie blanched when William's head lolled back, revealing the bloody bandage around his neck.

Stephen met his nephew's frightened eyes. "There is no one stronger. He will make it." Stephen needed to believe it, too.

"With God's help."

Stephen turned to see who had spoken. It was an ancient monk with a bent back and pure white tonsured hair. The monk waved them through the low doorway Jamie had pointed to and followed them inside. As they laid William down on a cot in the corner, he moaned. He did not waken, but he was alive.

"Bring me the lamp," the monk said as he lowered himself onto a stool beside the cot.

While Jamie fetched a lamp from across the room, the old monk pressed his ear against William's chest.

"The heart is strong, and he is able to draw air," the monk said as he straightened. "Remove the bandage."

Stephen knelt beside the cot. As soon as he cut off the blood-soaked bandage, the old monk cleaned the wound from a basin of water he seemed to pull from the air. The monk snapped his fingers at Jamie and pointed to several pots on a shelf. Faster than seemed possible, he mixed a smelly paste.

"Does he have other injuries?" the monk asked as he spread the paste with flat, bent-back thumbs over the oozing wound.

"Just this one," Stephen said, "where he took an arrow."

"Has he wakened since?"

"Once, briefly, more than an hour ago."

"He awoke a second time," Isobel said behind him.

Until he heard her voice, Stephen did not realize she had followed them inside. He was grateful for her presence. It comforted him to have her near.

"There was a man I did not see," she said, a quaver in her voice. "Lord FitzAlan threw a dagger into his heart."

Stephen reached for her hand and squeezed it, then kissed her icy fingers. "'Tis so like William, to wake just when needed to save the day. He is the best man I know."

Stephen heard a choking sound behind him and got to his feet to put an arm around Jamie.

"'Tis my fault he is hurt," Jamie said in a cracked voice.

"Nay, the blame is mine, not yours," Stephen said, feeling the full weight of his misdeeds. "I am so sorry."

The old monk's ears were still sharp. "'Tis God's will this man was struck," he said without turning. "And with God's help, he will survive."

He turned on his stool and craned his neck to look up at them. "You are all big fellows, are you not? It will take time for this one to get his strength back, but he will heal."

"He will recover?" Jamie asked.

"He is not out of danger. But aye, I believe he will." The

monk made a shooing motion toward Stephen and Isobel. "Take the woman and leave the lad with me. I need only one pair of helping hands."

Stephen nodded but said, "I need a word with my nephew first." Best to get this over with.

"I know what I told you upset you," he said when he had Jamie in the far corner of the room. "It all happened a long time ago, when your mother was not much older than you are now. 'Tis not my place to tell you the whole of it, but neither is it yours to judge her. She did what she had to do to survive."

Jamie kept his gaze on the floor and his lips pressed tight together, but he was listening.

"William has been father to you since you were a child of three," he said. "You've always known you do not share his blood, but you are the son of his heart."

Jamie nodded and wiped his nose on his sleeve. "He is the best of fathers."

"And your mother?"

"I wish she were here," Jamie whispered. "The rest doesn't seem important anymore."

Stephen gave Jamie's shoulder a squeeze and led him back to the cot where William lay. Under the old monk's ministrations, William's color was already much improved. He appeared to be resting comfortably.

"Your father is in good hands," Stephen said. "He will be fine, I am sure of it."

This time when the old monk shooed them, Stephen thanked him for his care and left with Isobel. Outside in the cloister, they found Geoffrey waiting. The tall, distinguished-looking man with him could only be the abbot.

"We are grateful for your hospitality," Stephen said after Geoffrey introduced them.

The abbot took Stephen's arm and led him a few steps down the walkway. "We welcome travelers, of course, but these are troubled times," he said in a low voice and shook his head. "And we are a small abbey. It is...difficult...for us to accommodate...female guests...comfortably."

Stephen suspected the abbot was concerned not so much with Isobel's comfort as with the brethren's peace. Having a beautiful woman—dressed in leggings, no less—within the confines of the small abbey was a disruption the abbot did not want.

"We shan't stay long," Stephen assured him. "I intend to ride back to Caen under cover of darkness tonight and return on the morrow with a large contingent of soldiers."

The abbot's eyes widened in alarm. "We have but two small guest rooms—" he began in a querulous voice.

"If it is safe to move my brother," Stephen interrupted, "we shall all depart by midday tomorrow."

The abbot heaved a sigh of relief. "One of our brothers grew up in the next village. He can lead you the first part of the way in the dark."

The abbot wanted them gone.

"I will have food brought to you in the guest quarters," the abbot said.

"You are too kind," Stephen said. "Perhaps after we eat I could take Lady Hume outside for a walk?"

"A walk would be just the thing to soothe her," the abbot said, brightening at the prospect of having Isobel removed for the afternoon. "There is a lovely path that goes along the river and up to our orchard. The land is within the precinct walls, so it is quite safe."

Stephen ate with Geoffrey and Isobel at the small table in the woman's tiny guest room. As they ate, he questioned Isobel about what happened after he left her and William in the wood.

His stomach tightened as she told him. How close he'd come to losing them both! It took his breath away to think about it. He hoped Isobel did not realize the men would have raped her first; he wished he did not know it himself.

The image of her sprawled over William's body, when he thought them both dead, was burned into his memory forever. He took her hand, not caring what her brother might think.

"A walk would help take our minds off all that has happened," he said. "The abbot told me there is a path we can follow along the river."

"If we are to leave tomorrow," Geoffrey said, getting to his feet, "I would like to spend the remaining hours praying before the abbey's holy relic."

Isobel gave him a faint smile. "'Tis why you came."

"But please take Isobel," Geoffrey urged him. "It will do her good."

Isobel's brother was naive to the point of foolishness. Stephen knew damn well what would happen if they went out alone this afternoon. After their brush with death, neither of them was likely to exercise caution this time.

Stephen got to his feet as Geoffrey went to the door.

"I shall pray for Lord FitzAlan's recovery," Geoffrey said.

"Thank you," Stephen said. Looking down at Isobel, he added, "We are all in need of your prayers today."

As Geoffrey's footsteps echoed on the stone floor outside the room, Stephen held his hands out to Isobel. He knew what he wanted now. If she was willing, he would have her.

Isobel met his eyes, making no pretense she did not understand. She took his hands.

Chapter Twenty

Isobel saw the naked hunger in Stephen's eyes. If she were going to refuse him, she must do it now. She took his hands. Today she did not care what was right or wrong, wise or foolhardy. This one time, she would take the man she wanted, not the man she must. She would allow herself this gift and not think about what came after.

There was no falseness between them. No pretense as to what they intended to do. Without a word passing between them, Stephen took the woolen blankets from the cot and folded them beneath his cloak.

They followed the stone walkway past the kitchen. Beyond the kitchen garden, they found the gate that led to the river path. Thankfully, it was neither the season for harvesting apples from the orchard nor the time of day for hauling in the fish lines for the monks' dinner. There was no sign of another living soul on the river path.

Once they were hidden from view by the trees, Stephen put his arm about her shoulders. She sighed and leaned into him. It felt right, walking with him like this.

After the harrowing events of the morning, the chirping birds and gurgle of the river soothed her. The sun was out, and the air had none of the blister of March she was used to in Northumberland. Spring came early here. The trees were budding, and crocuses poked their bright heads out of the ground. An unexpected peace settled over her.

Neither spoke until they came to a fork in the path.

"Do we continue along the river, or go to the orchard?" Stephen asked, waving his arm first in one direction, then the other.

Stephen's lopsided smile made him look so handsome that, on impulse, she reached up to touch his face. As soon as her fingers grazed his stubbled cheek, his smile left him. His eyes darkened, sending a rush of desire through her that almost curled her toes.

"Come," he said and pulled her by the hand up the orchard path.

They moved with a sense of urgency now. As the trail went uphill, they left the scrub trees that grew near the river. They entered a field that would soon be planted with wheat or rye. Beyond the field was the apple orchard. An old croft stood between the two, its wooden door hanging at an angle.

"This is such a pretty spot," she said, looking around her. "What would make a tenant abandon this croft?"

"Likely he had to," Stephen said as he heaved the door open, "when his lord gave the land to the abbey."

As Isobel stepped over the threshold, she saw that the croft had not been abandoned so very long ago. The sun poured in through gaping holes in the thatched roof, but the walls had not yet begun to crumble. There were piles of leaves in the corners where the wind had blown them.

Her heart rose to her throat as she watched Stephen clear debris from the earthen floor with his boot and spread one of the blankets. Knowing it would happen now, she was suddenly gripped by nerves.

Stephen turned and took her hands. "Are you sure you want this?" he asked in a quiet voice. "We can still go back."

"I want to stay." How like him to make her say it. With Stephen, she could never pretend to herself she was seduced against her will.

She saw his Adam's apple rise and fall as he swallowed. He pushed a stray strand of hair from her face, following it with his eyes. "I do not want you to have regrets."

"I shall have none."

When this did not seem sufficient to reassure him, she said, "If I died today..." She ran her tongue over her dry lips and tried again. "What I would regret is never knowing how it feels to bed a man I want to touch me."

She could never have been so bold to say this to another man. Somehow, she knew Stephen would neither judge her nor make her feel bad for it.

When he still made no move toward her, she rose on her tiptoes and touched her lips to his. His lips felt so soft and warm, the kiss unbearably sweet. She had expected lust, not this tenderness that welled up in her chest until she felt she might burst with it.

When she dropped back onto her heels, he held her face in his hands and ran a thumb along her cheek. "You need only tell me if you change your mind."

Did he not want this as much as she did?

"But I hope to God you won't," he said before the

uneasy feeling could take hold. Then he scooped her up in his arms and held her across his chest.

Their eyes were locked as he dropped to his knees and lay her down on the makeshift pallet. As his mouth met hers, she felt as though she were still sinking back. The kiss was warm and deep, their tongues moving against each other.

When he broke away, she would have complained—except that the kisses he ran along the side of her face felt so good. A deep sigh escaped her, and she gave herself over to following the course of his lips. He pressed kisses along her jaw and behind her ear. As he moved down her neck, he unfastened her cloak and pushed it off her shoulders.

"I love this spot, right here," he said and ran his tongue along the hollow above her collarbone.

She forgot she wore her brother's clothes until she felt the warmth of Stephen's breath through the cloth at her throat. Wanting to feel his mouth against her skin, she began tugging at the tunic and shirt that were in the way.

"Let me," he said, taking hold of her hands. "Please."

Grinning, he rose to his knees, unfastened his cloak, and tossed it in the corner. He lifted her tunic and began to pull her shirt out of her leggings ever so slowly. The smooth linen fabric moved against her skin, followed by a rush of cool air.

She would never have guessed that his lips, his tongue, his loose hair, would feel so good against the bare skin of her belly. As he inched his way slowly upward, exposing more skin as he went, she felt a tightening in her womb.

Oh, my. She shivered with the sensations racing through

her body. When he abruptly stopped and pulled her shirt back over her stomach, she opened her eyes wide.

Stephen was on his hands and knees above her, a frown of concern on his face. "You are cold."

"Nay, I am not," she said.

The brocade of his tunic felt rough under her fingers as she took hold of it and pulled him down. Despite the deep, lingering kiss she gave him, he held his body away from hers.

"I want to feel you against me," she whispered.

"Oh, Isobel," he said, sliding down beside her and burying his face in her neck, "you will undo me."

He held her tight against him so that she could feel his warmth from her head to her toes. She pressed her face against him, blocking out the faint smell of rotting apples from the orchard and the heavier smell of mildewed thatch. She wanted to breathe in only his scent. Horse and healthy sweat and wool and leather. And just Stephen.

When he kissed her this time, he did not hold back. The passion exploded between them. She wrapped her arms around him and pressed against him until a blade of grass could not have fit between them. And still, she was not close enough.

When he rolled on top of her, he felt so good that she tore her mouth away to tell him. Before she could form the words, he slid down her body, kissing her through the cloth until, again, he found bare skin. His mouth felt as good on her belly as the first time.

As he moved upward, she breathed, "Don't stop this time."

He moved so slowly that her breasts were aching for

his touch long before he got to them. Hardly aware of what she was doing, she ran her own hands over them. She heard Stephen groan and felt his large, warm hands cover hers.

"Jesus, Isobel," he whispered, "you cannot expect me to go slowly when you do that."

"Must you go slowly?"

He gave a half-strangled sound and lifted one of her hands to press his mouth against her palm. When he ran his tongue in a circle over it, she felt her nipple harden through the fabric beneath her other hand. She drew in a sharp breath as he ran his thumb along the underside of her breast.

"Mmmmm," came from her throat as he dragged his tongue along the line his thumb had just traveled. She arched her back, lifting her breasts to him.

"Aye," she breathed as his other hand slid under her shirt, and "aye," again, when it finally covered her breast.

The rough skin of his thumb over her nipple sent ripples of sensation down to the depths of her belly.

She meant to offer another word of encouragement. But then he rolled her nipple between his finger and thumb, and the sounds that came from her lips would not shape themselves into words. She felt the warm wetness of his mouth on her other nipple and was lost in a swirl of sensation.

How did he know how she wanted to be touched before she knew it herself? The more he touched her, the greater was her need. Never, never did she imagine it would be like this.

He pulled her up to a sitting position, and they leaned against each other, both breathing hard.

"Stephen, that felt..." She tried, but she could not find words to describe it.

"Can we take this off?" he asked, fingering the bottom edge of her tunic.

"You first," she surprised herself by saying.

He rewarded her with a wide grin that lit up his eyes. Before she knew it, he whipped off his tunic and shirt together in one quick movement and sat before her bare-chested.

She drew in a long breath as she ran her eyes over the hard muscles of his chest. How many other women had looked at him like this and found him so beautiful it made them ache? She would not let herself think of those other women now. Today he was hers and no other's.

She reached out and ran possessive hands over his chest, feeling the roughness of hair over the sinewy muscle and warm skin. This close, she could see that black hairs were interspersed with the curly auburn hair on his chest. She followed the hair down to his flat belly.

Would it feel as good to him as it had to her to kiss him there? When she dropped her head to try, he gripped her shoulders and pulled her up onto his chest. She feared she'd done something wrong—until he smashed his mouth against hers.

"Your clothes now. All of them, off," he gasped against her ear. "I need to feel you naked against me."

She lifted her arms without a word and let him pull shirt and tunic over her head.

"My God, you are beautiful."

A small voice in the back of her head asked how a man who'd seen so many women's breasts could manage to sound awed. When he lifted his gaze to her face, though, he looked as though he meant it. Whatever he might think later, right now he wanted no one but her. It was enough.

When Stephen gathered her into his arms again, she understood. Skin to skin, it had to be. His chest felt so good against her bare breasts she had to close her eyes to bear it. The kiss he gave her was at once so gentle and so full of longing she felt as if he were squeezing her heart in his hands.

Stephen, Stephen, Stephen. No other man could kiss like this, she was sure.

A surge of lust ran through her that had her rubbing herself against him like a cat. Without lifting his mouth from hers, he rolled her until she felt the scratch of the wool blanket beneath her back. She ran her hands over him, reveling in the feel of skin and tight muscle beneath her fingers.

He kissed her throat, then moved down to suckle first one breast and then the other. Sensations tore through her until she was arching against him and begging for she knew not what.

When he began to ease down the top of her leggings, she felt a moment of panic. 'Twas a serious sin she was about to commit. At least she broke no vow, in this brief respite between marriages.

It was *possible* Stephen could get her with child. But how likely from just one time? Not once did she conceive in all her years of marriage. Surely the risk was small. In any case, she would be married soon enough.

Stephen ran his tongue along her abdomen, wiping all such thoughts and fears from her mind. If she never felt this reckless joy and passion again, she would have it now.

She lifted her hips to help him slide the leggings down. As he pulled off first one leg, then the other, he paused to kiss her thigh, her knee, her calf. He sucked her toe into his mouth as he ran his hand slowly up the inside of her leg. A shiver ran through her.

He had her completely naked now. She watched his chest rise and fall as he raked his eyes over her. His slow perusal sent her pulse beating so hard she thought he must hear it.

When she shivered again, he lay down beside her and spread the other blanket over them.

"Are you warm enough, sweetheart?" he asked and kissed her shoulder.

She nodded and tried to concentrate on the feel of his callused hand running up and down her side. And not on how easily "sweetheart" and "love" rolled off his tongue.

"What is it, Isobel?"

So much was right, she did not want to ruin it. She rested her hand on his shoulder and met his troubled brown eyes.

"I did not know it would feel as good as this," she said and felt the taut muscles relax beneath her fingers.

He nuzzled her neck and playfully bit her earlobe. But that was not what she wanted now. She moved his hand from her side to her breast and turned in to him to give him an open-mouthed kiss. His playfulness vanished.

With a fierceness that matched her own, he kissed her back. He gripped her hip, and she liked the strong, possessive feel of his hand there. When he slid his other hand up the inside of her thigh, her whole body tensed with anticipation. Surely it would not be long before they committed the final act of sin.

The thought of having him inside her sent a spasm through her even before his fingers reached her center. Once he touched her, his fingers moved in ways that did magical things to her.

"What are you doing?" she asked, a little breathless.

"If you do not know, then your husband truly was a swine," he murmured. "Do you wish me to stop?" From the humor in his tone, she could tell he was confident of her answer.

"But... but ...," she tried to speak but could not hold her thought long enough. "I never... this feels so ... so ... so very..."

She rubbed the back of her hand against his hard stomach. When she brushed against the rough cloth of his leggings, she grabbed his forearm to stop his hand. "Will you not take your leggings off, as well?"

"What is it you want, Isobel?" His voice was soft, but she heard the tension in it.

"I—I—" She fell silent, embarrassed by what she'd been about to say.

"You must feel free to tell me anything, love," he said, touching her cheek. "Especially when we are in bed."

If she were going to have only this one time with him, she wanted it just right. She could not have explained why, but she could not bear the thought of him just pulling it out of his leggings to take her.

Though it made her cheeks flush hot, she told him. "I want you as naked as I when we are joined."

"I can bring you pleasure, sweetheart, without putting my cock inside you."

The crude directness of his words startled her. 'Twas

hard to think past "bring you pleasure" and "cock inside you."

"If we are to avoid the risk of getting you with child, 'tis best I leave my leggings on." He ran a finger along the side of her face and said, "Believe me, it will be harder for us to stop in time if they are off."

She looked into those melting brown eyes and heard herself ask, "Must we stop?"

He coughed, then said in a choked whisper, "I want you to be sure. This is a serious choice we make here."

From what she heard about him, it was a choice he made all the time. She felt her heart constrict. "Do you not want to?"

His eyes flashed, and he broke into a wolfish grin. "Oh, aye, without a doubt I do," he said. "In sooth, I can think of nothing but being inside you."

His words sent a jolt of desire through her.

"'Tis all I can do," he said, tracing her bottom lip with his finger, "to keep myself from employing every argument I have to convince you."

In a voice just above a whisper, she asked, "What arguments would you make?"

"Not the kind you hear with your ears." He gave her another of those devilish grins that nearly stopped her heart.

He kissed her senseless then. When he guided her hand to the fastening of his leggings, she felt a lurch of awareness as her fingers touched the hardness of his shaft through the cloth. She rubbed her palm down its length, reveling in the moan he made. She sucked on his tongue as she rubbed up and down, pulling new sounds from deep in his throat.

"You will have me spilling my seed like a youth," he said, grabbing her wrist.

She smiled, pleased at the desperation in his voice. "You said you would take your leggings off."

He sat bolt upright. After a couple of quick movements under the blanket, he raised his arm aloft with the leggings and threw them across the room. This time when he took her into his arms and kissed her, he was fully naked against her.

And heaven above, he felt good!

The feel of his shaft pushing against her belly sent a thrill through her, right to her core. She bit his shoulder as she ran her hands down the small of his back and over the firm, rounded muscles of his buttocks. He slipped his hand between her legs. As his fingers went round and round, he swallowed her moans in deep liquid kisses.

His breath was hot in her ear. "How does this feel?"

"I—I . . ." *What did he ask?* She could concentrate on nothing but what he was doing to her with his hand. "Don't stop. Please."

"I won't," he said in a husky voice, "not until you cry my name in your pleasure."

She did not understand what this feeling was welling up inside her.

"Trust me."

She did trust him. She did.

He lowered himself to pull the tip of her breast into his mouth, his hand never stopping. Tension grew and grew in her. She could feel it in him, too. In the tautness of his muscles, the pulsing shaft against her thigh, the heat vibrating off his skin. As he sucked her breast harder, she pressed herself against his hand, her body wanting still more from him.

When she thought she could bear no more, her body spasmed in wave after wave of pleasure that shook her to her very soul.

Oh God oh God oh God.

After, her limbs felt weak and limp. Stephen's head rested against her chest; his heart beat wildly against her stomach. With an effort, she lifted one hand and ran her fingers through his hair. She felt a small squeeze inside her when she felt his hard shaft against her leg.

Just when his head began to feel heavy on her chest, he turned with her so that they were on their sides, face to face.

"I never felt that before," she told him.

He took her face in his hands and gave her a kiss that was slow and deep. When he hooked his leg around her, she ran her hand over the taut muscle of thigh and buttock. All the while, they kissed, tongues sliding against each other.

She wanted to touch him. When she reached down and ran her finger along the length of his shaft, he drew in a sharp breath.

"Could you?" he asked in a tight voice. He wrapped her hand around it and moved their hands together to show her what he wanted.

Even she realized where this was going. She stopped her hand. "You said you wanted to be inside me."

He drew back to peer into her face. "You have given yourself to no man but your husband." He paused, then asked, "Why choose me, Isobel? Why me?"

Why did the reason matter to him?

"I've come this far in my sin. I want to know all of it," she said. That was part of it, but far from all.

Was that disappointment in his eyes? Hurt? What did he want her to say? That she knew no other man could make her feel this way?

"You are the only one I would have." Her pride would let her confess only this much. "The only one I want."

Feeling uncertain, she kissed his cheek and guided his hand to where he had touched her before. She wondered uneasily if he would jerk his hand away when he felt how wet she was. Instead, he groaned with what sounded like almost painful pleasure.

Soon she was lost in his kisses, his touches, the burning heat between them. She hardly noticed when he rolled her onto her back. When she felt the tip of his shaft against her opening, all she could think was *at last, at last, at last.* She may have whimpered the words aloud.

They both gasped when he pushed into her. She wrapped her arms and legs tight around him. She clung to him as he moved against her, slowly at first and then faster.

"Sorry. I cannot . . . last too long . . . this time," he gasped, "I . . . can . . . not."

He was ramming into her, harder and faster with each thrust. *Harder, harder, harder,* she egged him on. A burst of pleasure hit her, even stronger than the one before, and she cried out.

He was trying to pull away from her, but she held on to him with all her strength, refusing to let him go. And then he was moving inside her again and she was weeping and calling his name, over and over. He cried out with her, and she felt his seed empty inside her.

When he finally lay still in her arms, she held him to her, saying his name again and again and kissing his face and hair.

"Jesus," he said without lifting his head. He rolled to the side, pulling her with him, and tucked her head under his chin. In a fading voice, he said, "Isobel, my love, my..."

She heard his breathing grow steady. Could he possibly have fallen asleep? Nothing short of a wild boar could have gotten her to move, but she was too awash in emotions to sleep. A hundred questions spun through her head as she tried to fathom what had happened between them, and to her.

She leaned back, taking advantage of his dozing to study him in repose. In the shaft of sunlight that fell upon his hair, she saw that what looked auburn from afar was in fact a hundred shades of red and gold.

His face was near perfect, to her mind. She liked his straight dark brows, his strong jaw and cheekbones, the blade nose, the glint of bristles from a day's growth of beard. His generous mouth. Even at rest, the corners seemed to tip up.

She felt an overwhelming tenderness toward him. Was it merely gratitude for the unexpected pleasures he gave her? Was it something else? Something more?

She brushed a lock of hair away from his face and sighed. What did it matter? She recalled her mother's last words to her: *We women are born to suffer.*

Aye, she would suffer for this.

But she would not regret it.

———

Stephen kept his eyes closed, not wanting to waken and find it was all a dream. A smile spread across his face. Nay, that could not have been a dream. He'd always known Isobel had a passionate nature beneath that sober exterior, but God in heaven, he was a lucky man.

Aye, he must admit to one disappointment. He was not so foolish as to expect her to profess abounding love. But she did not even admit to a particular fondness for him. Did she simply desire him? Surely that alone would not be enough for a woman like Isobel to cross the line and commit herself.

Even at the end, he tried to pull out to preserve at least some possibility she could change her mind and avoid the marriage. God knew how hard that was! Surely she understood why he did it. Her answer was unmistakable: she wrapped her legs around him like a vise.

It had been heaven.

Other men could give her pleasure, so that could not be the only reason she chose him. Since the only other man she'd been with was that ancient husband of hers, it was possible she did not know that. Well, she would never know it now. No man but he would touch her again. He'd cut de Roche's hands off if he tried.

Strong mutual desire was not a bad start to marriage; it was more than many had. She enjoyed his company. Still, he hoped she saw more in him than a charming jester who could please her in bed. He wanted her to think better of him than that. Nay, he wanted to *be* a better man than that for her.

He opened his eyes. The sight of her was like a sharp stab

to his heart. She looked unspeakably lovely, with her tousled dark hair, smooth pale skin, and serious green eyes.

"Did I sleep long?" he asked.

A softness came into her eyes, and a hint of a smile lifted the corners of her mouth. She shook her head a fraction.

"I am a lout to let you get chilled," he said, gathering her into his arms. "Good Lord, you are covered in gooseflesh!"

He rubbed her back and arms until she laughed and begged him to stop. As he held her to him, he glanced up through the holes in the roof to judge the light.

She must have heard his sigh, for she asked, "What is it?"

"We must return to the abbey in another hour," he said. "The monks have their supper early. If we are not back before then, someone is bound to notice we are still gone."

She shrugged one fine-boned shoulder.

"Surely you do not want to be the cause of even more sinful thoughts among these poor monks?" he chided her with a smile. "You'll have them doing penance for months."

When she laughed at his joke, he had to kiss her. And just like that, he was hard again. From the way her eyes widened when he leaned back to look at her, she'd noticed. Her lips curved upward. A very good sign.

"You need do no more than look at me, and I want you." He breathed in the summery smell of wildflowers in her hair and felt her nipples harden against his chest.

This time, he intended to take her slowly. He did not know when they might have opportunity to sneak away again, so he wanted to be sure she would not soon forget.

As he kissed her, he wondered vaguely if the king would truly banish him to Ireland for this. If so, their next time together might be on a boat.

"Do you get seasick?" he asked between nips at her earlobe.

"Mmmm?" she asked, but when he stuck his tongue in her ear and pressed his shaft against her thigh, he knew she forgot his question.

When she reached down and took him in her hand, he forgot it, too.

He was a man who knew how to please a woman; usually he went about it with deliberation. This was different. With her, he went on instinct and emotion. From touch to touch to touch, he followed her sighs. He sought to make every inch of her his own.

There was no need for caution this time. When he finally entered her, he thrust all the way into her. She welcomed him, moved with him. This time, he made it last.

"You are mine," he told her as he moved inside her. "Only mine."

She was his. Now and forever.

After, he was flooded with such tenderness toward her that he could find no words to tell her. He could not speak at all, except to whisper into her hair, "Isobel, my love, my love."

As they walked hand in hand back to the abbey, he felt relaxed, happy. Surprising, how content he felt at the prospect of being bound for life. "Forsaking all others" gave him no twinges of regret. Truth be told, he was relieved to have done with that part of his life. Isobel was all he wanted.

Stephen began to make his plan. To win the king's

blessing, he must have all his ducks in a row. It would be wise to have William with him when he approached the king. A shame Catherine was not here to play on her childhood friendship with King Henry. But Robert would speak for him, too.

The king would insist on questioning Isobel. That could not be helped, but he would prepare her.

All would be well. He would see to it.

Chapter Twenty-one

*I*sobel lay on the hard cot in the small, windowless guest room. The long night stretched out before her. At midnight, Stephen left for Caen, promising to return with twenty armed men two hours after first light.

She did not see him alone after they returned from the orchard. When they went to check on FitzAlan, they could hear him arguing with the old monk from outside the infirmary door. Reassured, Isabel left Stephen to spend the remaining hours at his brother's bedside.

She was so exhausted she felt light-headed. But how could she sleep when the rough blanket still smelled of him? She held it to her nose and drew in a deep breath. She wanted to remember every moment of their afternoon together.

Every touch, every look, every word. The way her stomach fluttered as she watched him spread the blanket. The solicitude and longing warring in his eyes when he asked if she was certain. From that first soft kiss, there was no chance of her changing her mind. She brushed her fingers over her lips now, remembering it.

Though vivid, her memory after that was a jumble

of sensations and emotion. She'd had no notion being with a man could be like that. It was a wonder couples who had that kind of passion between them ever left their beds.

Perhaps it was rare for it to be so perfect.

Regardless of what others might have, all she had was one afternoon. One afternoon of her life! She balled her hands into fists and pounded the thin mat beneath her.

After her burst of frustration, the bleakness of her future settled over her like a heavy weight. Tears trickled down the sides of her face and into her hair. Perhaps tomorrow she could be hopeful about her life with de Roche, but not tonight. Not when the smell of Stephen was on her blanket and her skin still burned with the memory of his touch.

Would it have been better not to have gone with him? Better not to know what it was like? He could not have been kinder or more passionate. He gave her such pleasure she thought she might die from it. And happily so.

Nay, she could not wish she had not done it. She was a sinful woman. And an unrepentant one.

Stephen made her feel as if she were special to him. Perhaps that was his secret, the reason women were so drawn to him. He made each one believe it. For once, she felt sympathy for Marie de Lisieux. She understood why Marie could not let him go, even when it was plain to all he was done with her.

Isobel had too much pride for that. And she had her duty. Even if she had a choice—which she did not—she was bound by her promise to the king. She was not like her father. She would not abandon loyalty and honor with every change in the wind.

Soon she would make her pledge to de Roche. A sacred pledge.

Just for a moment, she let herself imagine joining hands with Stephen instead.

Unbidden, a childhood memory came to her. A memory of her father gazing at her mother, his expression one of pain and unbearable longing. Her mother never cared for him. Isobel had always known it, as a child knows without understanding. Her father loved his wife with a hopeless, helpless passion. She met it with cordial indifference. After their lands were lost, that indifference shifted to complete unawareness.

It must have killed him.

For the first time, Isobel saw her father with an adult's insight. The great wrongs he committed were desperate acts. He sacrificed both his honor and his daughter in the vain hope that wealth and position might finally gain him his wife's love.

How much more unhappy she would be, wed to Stephen! Unlike her mother, who devoted herself to God, Stephen would share his affections with woman after woman after woman. Surely that would be worse.

Stephen was a man who gave in to temptation readily. And temptation fell into Stephen's lap at every turn. If he were her husband, how would she bear sharing him with other women? She could not. She could not do it.

How ridiculous she was! Lying here on this cot, furious with Stephen over imagined slights in an imagined future. He was not her husband; he made no pledge to her. Though he showed her warm affection, he spoke only of the moment.

He never even said he loved her. Not once.

In any case, her future was set. Locked in place and bolted shut. In the morning, Stephen would take her back to Caen. To de Roche.

She rolled onto her side and held herself in a tight ball. And wept for all that she wanted and could not have.

Isobel awoke to the sounds of voices and hurried footsteps outside her door. A moment later, her brother knocked and stepped in, fully dressed and sword in hand.

"A dozen armed men are riding hard this way," Geoffrey said in a rush. "They are not English soldiers."

She bolted upright, heart racing, and saw Jamie in the doorway behind her brother. She was on her feet and strapping on her sword by the time Jamie was in the room.

"I fear it could be the men who attacked you yesterday," Jamie said, "and that they've come to take my father."

Geoffrey got her cloak for her from the peg behind the door, and they raced out behind Jamie.

As they ran across the cloister, Isobel grabbed Geoffrey's arm. "Surely they would not take FitzAlan by force from a holy place?"

The grim set of Geoffrey's jaw told her that was just what he thought they would do. And worse.

"You cannot believe the abbot would give him up?"

Geoffrey nodded and charged ahead of her through the archway and along the path. When she reached the front of the church, she saw the abbot and several monks gathered below by the open canal that ran inside the perimeter wall. On the other side of a narrow bridge that crossed the canal, two lay brothers were lifting the heavy bar that held the gate.

"Do not open the gate to them!" Geoffrey shouted.

The abbot glared over his shoulder at them as he signaled for the men to continue.

"Get FitzAlan into the church," Geoffrey called back to her as he raced down the hill after Jamie.

Isobel saw the sense in it at once. Even godless men would hesitate to take a man from the sanctuary. She hurried back toward the infirmary, wondering how she would get FitzAlan into the church. As she rounded the corner, she nearly collided with two monks carrying FitzAlan on a litter.

The old monk hobbled beside the litter, admonishing the two men to make haste. Praise God the old monk saw the danger! She took his arm and helped him the last few steps.

He shook her off the moment they were inside the church. "Cover your hair, woman!"

Though it seemed unlikely God would care at such a moment, she swallowed back her panic and yanked her hood over her head.

"How does your patient fare?" she asked.

"He would not stay abed," the monk complained, shaking his head. "So I gave him a sleeping draught."

Hearing a burst of shouting, she turned to see monks were pouring into the church. Holding her hood in place, she pushed past them to the front steps of the church. What she saw below sent her heart to her mouth.

On the other side of the bridge, crowded between the canal and the front gate, were at least a dozen armed men. Geoffrey and Jamie stood on this side, swords drawn, looking like the men of ancient Thermopylae holding off the Persian hordes. Behind them lay the abbot. A four-foot shaft stuck up from the center of his chest.

Fearing she would see her brother and Jamie meet the same fate, she clasped her hands together and began praying aloud. "Mary, Mother of God—"

A voice rolled out like thunder across the grounds: "You violate this holy ground at your peril!"

At first Isobel did not recognize the voice as her brother's. But it was.

"God has put his strength into our swords," Geoffrey shouted. "We are the instruments of His wrath!"

Isobel could swear she felt the ground shake. The men on the other side of the bridge must have felt it, too, for they stopped dead in their tracks. At the back of the group, the only man in full armor jerked his helmet off and shouted at them. The men still hesitated, exchanging nervous glances. Only when their leader called them by name did the first two men start across the bridge.

To Isobel's amazement, Geoffrey and Jamie cut the two down so quickly her eyes could not follow their swords. She flicked her eyes back to the leader. His black hair whipped about his face as he hurled curses at his men.

This time, three men came across the bridge.

Geoffrey's sword flew as if the wrath of God truly did move his arm. Never had Isobel seen her brother fight like this—nor had she suspected he could. He dispatched two more rapidly than she thought possible. While Jamie fought the third, Geoffrey came behind the man, lifted him by the collar, and threw him into the canal. Splashing and crying out in terror, the man scrambled up the other side to safety.

"God has seen into your hearts!" her brother shouted. "He knows you intend to murder these holy men. Turn and go, or he will strike you down where you stand!"

Her brother was acting like God's own raging angel. Despite their leader's angry shouts, the men turned as one and fled past him out the gates.

The black-haired man held his horse in place. Without hurry, he swept his eyes over the abbey grounds and up the rise to where Isobel stood alone before the church. A chill of fear went up her spine as their eyes met and held across the distance. He could not harm her now. And yet she could not breathe until he turned his horse and rode out the gate.

Isobel ran down the hill so fast she nearly fell head over heels. When her brother saw her coming, he opened his arms and caught her in midair.

"You were magnificent!" she said, burying her face into his neck. When he set her down she asked, "How did you ever think to say those things to them?"

"I spoke the truth," her brother said. "God's truth."

She was taken aback. Everyone spoke to God in prayer. Few, however, claimed God spoke to them—at least not with such clarity. She did not quite know what to make of it.

Geoffrey smiled, showing he both understood and forgave her doubting nature. With all the righteous fire gone from him, he was her sweet brother once again. They walked arm in arm up the hill to the church.

Jamie caught up to them, his eyes shining. "We did well, did we not?"

"Aye," Isobel said. "Your father will be proud of you."

"Those men may get their courage back." Jamie squinted at the early morning sun, still low on the horizon. "'Tis less than an hour since daybreak. I hope to God Stephen returns before they do."

"I shall pray he does," Geoffrey said.

"You do that," Jamie said, slapping Geoffrey on the back. "He seems to hear your prayers."

The three of them went into the church and huddled around FitzAlan. He was awake, his color much improved. When he looked at Jamie, the fierceness of the love in his eyes caused Isobel to suck in her breath. Isobel looked away; it felt intrusive to observe that moment between them.

The sanctuary felt crowded with all the monks gathered inside. With Jamie hovering over FitzAlan and the old monk close at hand, there was no need for her ministrations. Geoffrey was on his knees in one of the alcoves. Having no occupation herself, she told Jamie she would act as lookout.

She climbed the narrow stairs that led to the small gallery overlooking the nave. From there, she had to duck her head to go up the even narrower set of stairs above. She pushed a wooden door and found it opened onto a perch at the peak of the church roof. When she stepped out onto it, her stomach filled with butterflies and her palms grew sweaty. She looked at the slats for climbing the spire above her and nearly swooned.

The perch was high enough.

From here, she had a bird's-eye view of the fields and woods on all sides of the abbey. Her eyes followed the winding river and the path that led up to the orchard. She sighed, remembering the sound of birds and Stephen's arm about her. Squinting, she picked out the abandoned croft. If only she could go back with Stephen one more time. Just once more.

That was pure foolishness! No matter how many times, she would always want more.

A fine lookout she was. Annoyed with herself, she turned her back on the croft and scanned the horizon to the west.

What was that? In a copse of wood she thought she saw the gleam of metal. She watched until she made out the shapes of horses and men, tiny as ants, through the trees.

Their attackers had not fled far. Would they go on their way, or return for a second attack? It was impossible to tell. She decided not to panic the others until she knew.

She grew cold and stiff as she watched and waited. Surely it was a good sign they took so long. She imagined the black-haired leader ranting at his men down there under the trees. *Please, God, let the men resist him until Stephen returns.*

She risked taking her eyes off the wood to glance to the northwest, in the direction of Caen. Two hours after dawn he would come. How long had she been watching? An hour? Surely Stephen would come soon.

She saw first one rider, then another leave the cover of the wood. "God, no, please, no."

They rode straight toward the abbey. She waited, muscles taut, to count them. Four, five, six. Their line strung out, the space between increasing with each horse that left the wood. She read reluctance in their slow trot. Still, they came. Ten, eleven, twelve.

She must warn the men below.

She cast one last look in the direction from which Stephen would come, willing him to be there.

God be praised! Stephen was coming!

The riders cresting the faraway hill were no more than dots on the horizon. They were twice the distance from the abbey as the others, but they swept down the hill, moving fast.

Isobel flew down the narrow stairs.

"He comes! He comes!" she shouted as she ran across the sanctuary to Jamie and FitzAlan.

"The men who attacked us are returning," she said when she reached them. "But Stephen rides hard behind them."

FitzAlan pulled himself up on one elbow with a grimace, then commenced to fire questions at her. "What is the distance between them? How many men in each?"

Feeling like one of his soldiers, she gave him her report. She was rewarded with a nod of approval.

"Stephen will chase them off," FitzAlan said, "but we'd better get to the gate on the chance he needs help."

Despite Jamie's efforts to hold him down, the fool man tried to heave himself up.

"Lord FitzAlan, lie down at once!" she said, standing over him, hands on her hips. "I shall not forgive you if you reopen that wound and bleed to death after all we've been through."

"Geoffrey and I can hold the gate until Stephen comes," Jamie said, his voice quiet and sure.

FitzAlan and Jamie locked eyes. Then FitzAlan gave his son a tight nod.

As Jamie ran past her, he squeezed her arm in thanks.

"Take me outside where I can see," FitzAlan shouted at some monks hovering nearby.

Four of them rushed to do his bidding. At his insistence, they carried his pallet out the door and propped him up against the wall. The monks almost knocked Isobel over in their haste to get back inside the church.

She sat down beside FitzAlan. From their high spot, she could see over the abbey's wall to the first rise beyond.

Looking out, she said, "There is fresh blood on your bandage."

"I've fought in worse shape."

FitzAlan's sword lay beside him on the pallet; his hand was on the hilt. If the need arose, FitzAlan would find the strength to charge down the hill, sword swinging. She had no doubt of it.

If it came to that, she would go with him.

Over the chanting of the monks' prayers inside the church, she heard the faint sounds of shouts and galloping horses. She jumped to her feet. As the sounds grew louder, she rose on her tiptoes, straining to see. A group of riders broke over the hill. A moment later they streaked past, riding along the wall of the abbey and into the woods on the other side.

Then a second, larger group came thundering over the hill. As they rode in front of the abbey, the lead rider broke away and waved the others on. It was Stephen; she knew it before he rode through the gate. He pulled off his helmet and looked up the hill, his eyes searching, until he found her.

Now that the danger was past, she felt tears welling up. She remembered how Stephen comforted her after the killing in the wood. How she longed for that now! To feel his arms so tight around her she could not breathe. To hear him mutter soothing, senseless words into her hair. She clenched her fists until the nails dug into her palms, to keep from running to him.

Stephen tossed his reins to Jamie. With a lightness that belied his long journey and heavy armor, he trotted up the hill. Afore God, he was a beautiful man, with the sun glinting off his armor and shining on his hair.

But he was coming straight for her. Panic seized her as she saw the intention in his eyes. Surely he knew better than to embrace her here, in front of everyone? Did he not care if they all knew?

As he came near, she took a quick step back and said in a voice much too loud, "Your brother is able to sit up, as you can see, Sir Stephen!"

Had she truly said that? After he rode through the night and back again to save them?

"Thank you. Thank you so very much." Her words fell awkwardly from her lips, showing her for the idiot that she was.

Stephen raised an eyebrow, but he came no closer.

Now that she knew he was not going to do anything foolish, she wanted to say something more to acknowledge his feat. "I—I saw you coming from the church roof."

He leaned his head back and squinted up at the church, a smile playing at the corners of his mouth. "Watching for me, were you, now?"

Isobel glanced down at FitzAlan. Could the man not save her from further embarrassment and offer some word of greeting?

When she noticed the sheen of sweat on FitzAlan's brow, she dropped to her knees beside him. *Where is the old monk?* She looked about but did not see him.

"How are you, William?" Stephen's voice above her was soft, worried.

FitzAlan was saved from answering by the arrival of Jamie and Geoffrey.

"Better late than never," Jamie said, slapping Stephen on the back.

Stephen gave Jamie a puzzled look. "Late?"

"These same men attacked us at dawn," Jamie said. "Geoffrey and I sent them running like scared rabbits."

"This was God's doing, not ours," Geoffrey said.

Stephen looked from one to the other. The light left his eyes as he realized they were not having a joke on him.

"Forgive me, I came as fast as I could."

"You came when you were needed," Jamie said. "We could not have held them a second time."

Stephen did not look any happier.

"One of the men lived long enough to confess," Jamie said. "They meant to sack the abbey, murder all the monks, and blame the English army."

FitzAlan dozed off before Jamie was done giving Stephen a full account.

"He is bleeding through the bandage again," Isobel said, looking up at Stephen.

Stephen sent Jamie and Geoffrey to fetch the old monk and knelt beside her. "How bad is he?"

"He has lost too much blood," she said. "He is weaker than he would have us know."

Chapter Twenty-two

Stephen's men gave up the pursuit and returned shortly. Their mission was to return FitzAlan to Caen as quickly as possible. Within an hour, the horses were watered and fed, the men had eaten, and FitzAlan's wound was freshly bound.

Isobel found Stephen supervising four men loading FitzAlan's litter onto a cart. To her relief, FitzAlan was awake and complaining loudly that he could "damn well ride." Still, the pallor of his skin made her anxious.

When she touched Stephen's arm, he turned and fixed worried eyes on her. He looked tired. She wondered if he'd had time to sleep at all.

"Thank you for the gown," she said. "'Twas very kind of you to bring it."

With all he had to do in his short time in Caen in the night, how had he thought to retrieve a gown for her? He saved her a good deal of embarrassment. Monks might try to avert their eyes, but soldiers were another matter. It would have been a long ride back with all the men staring at her legs.

Stephen acknowledged her thanks with a nod. "I want

you to ride in the cart with William," he said in a low voice. "He will not fight you as he would Jamie or me."

"Of course."

Her breath caught as Stephen placed his hands on her waist. When he hesitated, she sensed he wanted to pull her against him as much as she wanted him to do it. Then her feet left the ground, and she was beside FitzAlan in the cart.

The journey back to Caen took forever. Though Fitz-Alan did not complain of the pain, he flinched each time a bump in the road jarred his wound. She tried to get him to rest.

The usually taciturn man, however, was set on passing the time talking with her. Since it seemed to distract him, she gave in. He plied her with questions until she told him every detail of what happened the day before, after he was hit with the arrow.

FitzAlan closed his eyes, a smile on his face. "There is no man I'd rather have at my back in a fight than Stephen."

"Aye," she said, "he was a wonder to see."

FitzAlan opened his eyes a slit. "My brother has the heart of a hero, always has," he rasped. "He only wants for opportunity to show it."

She wondered why it was so important to FitzAlan she understand this. Speaking cost him considerable effort.

"A man could not do better for a brother or a friend," he said, ignoring her attempts to shush him.

Despite the pain he was in, she did not think these were the ramblings of an addled mind. FitzAlan's speech seemed to be directed to some purpose, but what?

She thought he was finally drifting off to sleep, when

he spoke again. "He will make some woman a fine husband one day."

As she wiped his brow, she muttered under her breath, "If a woman does not mind sharing."

His ears were sharper than she credited. When his bark of laughter turned into a groan of pain, she regretted her remark.

As she leaned over him to check his bandage, he opened his eyes again. They were honest eyes, the color of golden amber.

"'Tis only the follies of a young man," he said between harsh breaths. "Stephen needs—"

"Lord FitzAlan, please, you must lie still." His wound was bleeding again, and she was truly worried. "We shall speak no more now. You must be quiet and rest."

He closed his eyes, a faint smile on his lips. "Catherine...she would like you. I promised...Catherine...I would come home..."

'Twas true, then. The great commander did love his wife. Isobel could hear it in his voice. This was not the offhand affection most men felt for their wives. This Catherine was the joy of his life. The reason he wanted to go home again.

Tears stung at the back of Isobel's eyes. Perhaps it was all the emotions of the last two days hitting her now. It seemed a lifetime since she left Caen, so much had happened. She was so tired! And worried half to death about FitzAlan.

"Isobel." It was Stephen's voice.

She wiped her eyes and turned around to where he'd drawn his horse next to the cart.

"Are we near Caen yet?" she asked, her voice breaking. "I fear he grows worse, and there is little I can do for him here."

Stephen's face was grave as he looked at his brother. "Another hour, perhaps. We cannot go faster with the cart."

Isobel sensed the tension beneath the calm of his voice.

"Take Jamie and a few others ahead," Stephen called out to the nearest man. "Get a physician and have a room prepared at the castle for Lord FitzAlan."

She understood Stephen's purpose. He did not want Jamie to see how grave FitzAlan's condition was before they had him safely inside the city walls.

Stephen rode beside the cart for the remainder of the journey, but they spoke little. When at last they reached the city, the king's own physician was waiting at the gate. The elegantly dressed man waved at the driver not to stop and leapt into the moving cart.

"To the keep!" the physician called out as he began to examine his patient.

Jamie was waiting at the steps to the keep. Before she knew it, he and Stephen lifted FitzAlan's litter and carried him inside the keep. The physician trotted behind in their wake.

Quite suddenly, Isobel found herself alone, relieved of responsibility. She leaned back and let out a long breath. Now that the ordeal was over, she felt so weary! She could not convince herself to rise and get out of the cart.

"Lady Hume."

She opened her eyes to see King Henry and Robert standing beside the cart. It was the king who had spoken.

"Thank you for caring for my good friend," King Henry said, holding his hand out to her.

She glanced at her blood-encrusted nails. When she hesitated, the king flustered her completely by lifting her bodily from the cart. It was easy to forget the king was a strong and athletic young man.

"Thank God you are safe," Robert said, greeting her with a kiss on each cheek. The lines on his handsome face had deepened since she saw him last. "Until Stephen returned last night, I could only guess what happened to you."

Her heart constricted as she realized she was the reason he looked so haggard. "I am sorry I worried you."

"That little Linnet, I wanted to strangle her," Robert said. "I could not squeeze a word out of her."

Despite his words, Robert sounded impressed.

"I can see you are weary from your ordeal," the king said and held his arm out for her to walk with him. "But as soon as you are rested, you must tell us everything that happened."

"As you wish, sire." What would the king want to know from her that Jamie or Stephen could not tell him?

"Women often notice things that men do not," the king said.

"Try to recall every detail you can about the men who attacked you—horses, clothes, weapons. An unusual piece of jewelry. Anything that might reveal who these fiends are."

"I shall do my best, Your Highness."

"We must learn who these men are," he said, biting off each word. "These cowards who would lie in wait to murder my commander and commit sacrilege *in my name*."

She could feel his rage vibrating through her fingers resting on his arm.

"I shall have their heads on pikes." More calmly, he said, "You shall tell Robert everything you can remember. Later, I may wish to question you again myself."

Exhausted as she was, she could not help noticing the king and Robert were on friendlier terms than she thought. 'Twas odd, too, that the king relied upon Robert to help discover the identity of the attackers.

Just what role did Robert play for the king?

Perhaps she underestimated Robert, just as she had Stephen. There was more to both men than met the eye.

Chapter Twenty-three

*I*sobel awoke weighed down by guilt. There seemed no end to the consequences of her rash decision. FitzAlan was injured, Robert's feelings were hurt, Linnet was barely speaking to her. She hardly knew where to start making amends.

Since Linnet was close at hand, she would begin with her.

Just as Isobel opened the bed curtain, Linnet came through the door with a rush of cold air and a tray laden with food. The smell of warm bread made Isobel's stomach growl. She'd slept through supper last night.

"Thank you, Linnet, that was thoughtful of you."

Linnet kept her eyes on the tray and did not speak. Isobel sighed and wrapped her robe around herself. Motioning Linnet to join her, she sat down at the small table.

"You must have been frightened when I did not return by nightfall," she began. "I am sorry for that."

Linnet lifted eyes swimming with unshed tears. "You did not need to go," she said, accusation sharp in her voice. "Sir Stephen and Lord FitzAlan would have brought them back."

"I was too afraid for my brother to think clearly."

Linnet pressed her lips together. After a long moment, she nodded. "For François, I would do the same."

Linnet forgot her annoyance as Isobel related the story of the first attack.

Eyes wide, Linnet said, "'Tis something to see Sir Stephen and Lord FitzAlan fight, is it not?"

"I forgot you saw them fight in Falaise—"

Someone pounded on the door so hard it shook, startling them both to their feet.

The door swung open and de Roche stood in the doorway, his eyes black with fury. "What kind of fool woman has this English king saddled me with?"

Linnet flew to Isobel's side and clutched her hand.

De Roche slammed the door, causing them both to jump again.

"Foolish *and* disobedient," he said. "Did I not tell you to wait in your chamber for your brother's return?"

He strode across the room. When he stood not a foot from her, he asked again. "Did I not tell you?"

As a girl, Isobel had played with the boys. She knew about bullies. Cowering emboldened them.

"Aye, you did," she said in a clear, unapologetic voice. Anger welled up in her, fast and hard. She opened her mouth to call him a coward for not going after her brother himself.

Just in time, she remembered de Roche would be her husband and bit her tongue. No man could forgive being called a coward, especially if the words were just. If she were to have any hope of a cordial relationship with her husband, she must not say it.

De Roche stared at her tight-lipped. Then, quite

suddenly, the anger left his face. She let her shoulders relax. The awful moment was past, thank heaven.

"I begin to see the appeal of a spirited woman," de Roche said, letting his gaze slide over her.

He pushed Linnet away and slammed Isobel against him. His mouth was hungry on hers, his hips ground against her, his erect shaft pressed against her belly. Beside them, Linnet was shouting and pulling on Isobel's arm.

De Roche released her just as suddenly.

"Perhaps you are worth the trouble, after all," he said, smiling. He gave her cheek a hard pinch, then turned and left.

As soon as the door closed behind him, Linnet drew her to the bench under the arrow-slit window. Linnet sat close beside her and held her hand. Isobel could not stop shaking.

"Must you marry him?" Linnet asked in a small voice.

"Aye, 'tis the king's command," Isobel said as calmly as she could. "You mustn't judge him by one angry moment. He had cause to be displeased with me, and he was over it quick enough."

Isobel cursed her dead husband under her breath. Must she suffer for the rest of her life for Hume's foolishness? She should be mistress of her own home, living in peace in Northumberland.

"Help me dress," she said, patting Linnet's hand. "I must see how Lord FitzAlan fares."

A short time later, she stood outside the door to Fitz-Alan's sickroom. She lifted her hand to knock, hoping and dreading she would find Stephen within. The door was ajar. She could hear voices.

One of them was Stephen's.

After a deep breath, she rapped lightly. The people inside were talking so loudly, no one seemed to hear her. When they broke into laughter, a flood of relief ran through her. FitzAlan must be out of danger. Smiling, she poked her head through the door to ask permission to enter.

She froze as she took in the scene before her. On a stool beside FitzAlan's bed sat a breathtakingly beautiful woman. The woman leaned over the injured man, holding his hand in both of hers. Lady Catherine FitzAlan. The woman was fair, where Jamie was dark, and she looked far too young to be his mother. Still, Isobel had no doubt that was who the lady was.

The three men in the room leaned toward her like sunflowers toward the sun. The usually stern FitzAlan was beaming up at her like a boy in his first puppy love. Jamie stood behind, a hand resting on her shoulder. Completing the circle, Stephen sat beside her, a hand on her other shoulder.

It was not Stephen's hand on the woman's shoulder that made it impossible for Isobel to breathe—though that did not help. It was what she saw in his face as he gazed at the woman.

Bits of what she had overheard Stephen say about his brother's wife spun through her head. *But I adore Catherine. There is no woman like her.* Worse still, she remembered the wistful tone of his voice when he spoke of her.

Suddenly, it all made sense. Why Stephen avoided a betrothal. Why he wasted time with worthless women like Marie de Lisieux. She swallowed against the pain rising in her chest.

Stephen was in love with his brother's wife.

Though Lady Catherine had to be several years older than Stephen, she was yet a great beauty. Isobel's heart might hurt less if she could believe physical beauty was all that drew him. But when Stephen spoke of her, it was not of her beauty.

Nay, he loved this woman for herself.

Lady FitzAlan must have felt Isobel's stare, for she turned and looked at Isobel with eyes as blue as Jamie's.

"Come in," she called out. She rose to her feet and held her hands out to Isobel, saying, "You must be Lady Hume."

Caught like a rat in a trap. Isobel stepped into the room and took the woman's hands, for she could do naught else.

"I am Catherine," the woman said, kissing Isobel's cheeks. "Forgive my familiarity, but I've just heard how you saved my husband's life. God bless you!"

She startled Isobel further by pulling her into a full embrace. Isobel could not recall the last time she was embraced by another woman. She had no sisters, no close aunts or female cousins. It must have been when she was a small child, before her mother lost her warmth and laughter.

Isobel let herself be enveloped in the softness and breathed in Lady FitzAlan's light, feminine scent. Much as she might want to, she could not hate this woman now.

Lady FitzAlan pulled her into the room and made her sit on the stool Stephen gave up for her. Though Isobel felt Stephen's eyes on her, she could not look at him.

She sat mute, stunned by her discovery. *He loves her.*

He has always loved her. The words went round and round in her head. She struggled to follow the lively talk in the room but could not.

She tried again to listen, determined to leave at the first break in the conversation. Lady FitzAlan was speaking of a premonition so strong that she sent her children to her mother-in-law. Then she paid the owner of a fishing vessel an exorbitant amount of gold to carry her across the channel between winter storms.

"'Twas foolish to risk yourself," FitzAlan said. He had not once taken his eyes from his wife since Isobel sat down.

"'Tis good she came," Stephen said behind her. "Catherine is the best medicine."

Isobel could not bear to hear his voice.

When Stephen started to say something about the Fitz-Alans moving into a house in the town, she got to her feet. She had to get out. This very moment.

Murmuring a feeble excuse—she hardly knew what she said—she went out the door before anyone could stop her.

Clamping a hand over her mouth to keep from sobbing aloud, she hiked up her skirts and ran down the corridor. She did not get far before Stephen caught her arm.

"Isobel, we must talk," he said, spinning her around. "I am sorry you are upset with me for not speaking to the king yet. I could not leave my brother, and then Catherine came. But I will do it today, now, if the king will see me."

"The king?" What was he saying?

"If the king insists on questioning you separately," he said, "I shall ask Catherine to go with you."

"Why must you speak to the king?" She had to hear him say it to be sure.

"Because of de Ro—" A look of distaste passed over his face, and he began again. "Because the king made other plans for you, 'tis best to obtain his permission before we marry."

"I know you feel honor-bound to do this," she said, "but I will not let you."

He was chivalrous enough not to show relief. But perhaps he did not yet believe she meant it.

"Do not fret," he said, giving her arm a squeeze. "The king will blame me, not you. I'll not lie to you, he will be angry. Quite angry, for a time. But all will be well in the end, I promise."

"You shall not speak to the king about me."

Stephen drew his brows together. "Isobel, surely you know we *must* marry."

He did not call her "love" now.

"I know no such thing," she answered, her voice tight. "If bedding a woman meant you must wed her, then you would have a great many wives by now."

As soon as the words were out of her mouth, the easy, familiar Stephen was gone. The man glaring at her was the other Stephen—the dangerous one who would ride into shooting arrows or throw a blade into a man's eye.

"We shall marry as soon as—"

Stephen stopped at the sound of someone calling his name. Isobel turned to see François running toward them down the corridor.

"Stephen," François said between gasps of breath, "Madame de Champdivers says you must come at once. She has something you want."

Isobel's blood turned to ice. She would be a fool to risk all and marry this man. Between his hopeless love for his brother's wife and his constant affairs, there would be no end to her suffering. He would crush her heart worse than her father had.

"I shall find you when I return, and we shall talk," Stephen said, his tone as hard as granite. "And then I shall go to the king."

She jerked her arm away and glared at him.

"We shall do what is right here, Isobel."

Chapter Twenty-four

I thought you would never come," Linnet scolded Stephen as she let him and François into Isobel's chamber. "You must save her from that horrid man."

Stephen sighed. At least the twins were on his side. Isobel had been so angry when he tried to apologize for not yet speaking to the king. Damn, he should have stayed and talked with her instead of going on that wild-goose chase.

Claudette had sent François to fetch him after overhearing de Roche and Marie de Lisieux having a furious argument. As Claudette passed by a window in the Old Palace—Stephen did not ask Claudette what she was doing there—she noticed de Roche and Marie in the garden below. Claudette caught only a few words of the argument, but she heard Marie say both Stephen's name and "abbey."

Stephen tried telling Claudette that, by now, everyone in the castle knew of the attack. But Claudette was certain Marie knew something. And she was equally certain that Stephen was the only one who could worm it out of her.

When he finally tracked Marie down, she was pleased

to see him. Too pleased. He did not believe Marie was involved in planning the attack, but she did know something. He was not willing, however, to go to bed with her to find out what. After all, he was almost a married man.

Whether his wife-to-be knew it or not.

Where in the hell was Isobel? It was late; they had no more time to waste. His head was throbbing long before he heard voices outside the door.

The twins ran to meet Isobel at the door.

"François, 'tis nice to see you," Isobel said as she came in. She sounded tired.

"I must go with François," Linnet said as she and her brother scurried past Isobel.

"Linnet!" Isobel called as the door closed behind them. Isobel collapsed onto a stool and buried her face in her hands.

Stephen felt himself softening toward her, but he fought it. He must be firm with her.

When he stepped into the circle of light from the lamp on the table next to her, she looked up, startled. She looked so lovely he could not speak.

"Did you get what you wanted from Madame de Champdivers?" Isobel snapped her mouth closed, as if the words had slipped out before she could stop them.

Was it possible she was jealous? Of Claudette?

Ridiculous as it was, could that be the reason for her reluctance? The thought cheered him. Much better she be jealous than indifferent.

"Claudette is a friend, nothing more."

Isobel made a dismissive snort and looked away.

"We must go talk with William and Catherine about how best to approach the king. 'Tis late, and my brother needs his rest, so we mustn't tarry." He held out his hand to her.

She rose without taking it and stood toe to toe with him. "I will not," she said flatly.

He sucked in a breath to calm himself before speaking. "We must accept the consequences of our actions. I'd prefer you entered into this marriage gladly. Regardless, I will try to be a good husband to you. I hope, in time, I can make you happy."

"I will deny anything happened between us."

He was stunned. "But why?"

She clamped her lips together and refused to answer.

"You cannot wish to have de Roche as your husband."

It was bad enough that she was less than enthusiastic about marrying him. But surely she could not prefer that smarmy Frenchman over him?

"I made a promise to the king," she said, crossing her arms, "and I will make good on it."

"And what of our promise to each other?" he asked. "We made a promise by what we did in the old croft at the abbey."

"From what I hear, Stephen Carleton, you give such 'promises' to women all the time."

"Those women were different."

"How?" she demanded, giving him a hard look.

Why did he need to explain this to her? "Those women took me to their beds for pleasure only. It was understood between us. I misled none of them. Most were not even free to marry."

"Then I am no different," she said. "I took you for pleasure, and I am not free to marry."

Her words were like a knife to his heart. Had she really

used him like that? Had he been so mistaken in believing what happened between them meant as much to her as it did to him?

At least he knew how to play it now. This was a game he was good at. He would take his own advice. In a fight for your life, you must use the advantage you have, not the one you wished you had.

He pulled her roughly against him and slowly, deliberately, ran his thumb over her full bottom lip.

"De Roche would disappoint you."

She looked up at him with wide green eyes and blinked once, twice. Already, her breathing changed.

"I want you naked." He held her gaze and let her see how much he meant it. He did want her that way, he just wanted her heart more.

Her lips parted, and her gaze dropped to his mouth. "I...I..." She tried to speak, but her words drifted off as he ran his finger along the side of her neck and down her throat.

When he reached the top of her gown, her breath hitched. He could almost hear her thoughts, they were so plain on her face. She was telling herself she should back away, but she wanted his touch too much to listen.

He would make sure of it.

He brushed his finger ever so slowly along the delicate skin at the edge of her bodice, across the rise and fall of her breasts. Like warm beeswax, she melted against him.

"You want to be kissed?" He tried to hang on to his cool calculation, but it was hard with her looking at him like that.

When she rose onto her tiptoes to meet him, his heart leapt in his chest. What kind of fool was he? Who was seducing whom? Who would be vanquished? He feared it would be him again.

Stephen never suffered from a lack of courage. Truth be told, he threw himself into danger with nary a thought. But his knees trembled as he leaned down to take this gamble.

As soon as his lips touched hers, there was fire. As there was every time they kissed. He let it envelop him, lap all around him, as he sank into her. He wanted to touch all the places he loved: her face, the enticing curve of her back, the long line of her thigh. Her hair, he had to have his hands in it. Without lifting his mouth from hers, he began pulling the pins that held her headdress.

"Let me," she gasped, breaking the kiss.

While her hands were busy with pins and coils, he moved down her body. He pressed his lips to the soft skin above her bodice, then dropped to his knees to kiss her breasts through the cloth of her gown. When her hair fell over his hands, he sighed with pleasure and rested his head against her.

But he could not afford to let her catch her breath and reconsider. He rose to his feet and spun her around to unfasten her gown.

"We should not...," she began, but her voice trailed off as he reached around and cupped her breasts. Soft and full, they fit perfectly in his hands. She leaned her head back against his shoulder, making little sighs and moans.

He kissed her neck, then whispered into her ear, "I want to feel your skin against mine again."

This time, she made no pretense of objecting. As soon as he unfastened her gown, she pushed it off her shoulders and let it fall in a pool at her feet. As she turned around to face him, he pulled his tunic and shirt over his head. He drew in a sharp breath when she put her arms around his waist and he felt her breasts against his chest.

She looked up at him, eyes dark and serious. "I know it is wrong, but I cannot help myself."

"There is no wrong in it, if we are to marry."

"I would rather sin than suffer every day—" Her voice broke in a sob.

He could not begin to understand her. What could she mean? "We would have joy between us, can you not see that?"

She shook her head violently from side to side. With the passion broken, he could feel her slipping away from him. Before she could change her mind, he lifted her in his arms and carried her to the bed.

This was no time for fighting fair.

He began by kissing her senseless.

When she slipped a hand under the top of his leggings, he grabbed her wrist. Holding both her hands over her head, he nipped at her ear and ran his tongue along her collarbone. By the time he reached her breasts, she was squirming and arching her back.

Slowly, he circled her nipples with his tongue. Round and round, then flicking with his tongue until she slammed her fist against the bed.

Good. He ran his fingers up the inside of her thigh, inch by inch, as he continued teasing her nipple with his tongue. When he reached her center, she was hot and wet and he wanted her so badly he nearly forgot his purpose.

With renewed determination to control himself, he drew her breast into his mouth and pleasured her with his hand. Every sigh and moan made him want her more.

When he stopped to run his hand along the inside of her thigh again, she opened her eyes.

"Good things come to her who waits," he said, grinning down at her. He set to teasing her, moving his fingers in circles ever closer to her center until he brushed it with each turn with a feather touch.

The saints preserve him, she had beautiful breasts! He kissed the one closest to him. She made a little high-pitched sound when he took the nipple between his teeth. As he increased the pressure between her legs, her breathing grew ragged.

"Stephen, don't stop," she said, her voice urgent as she tried to pull him down to her.

When she cried out, he wrapped his arms around her and buried his head in her neck. He felt overpowered by emotions so strong he did not know what to do with them.

He squeezed his eyes shut as she ran her fingers along the side of his face. He was tight as a bowstring. When she turned in to him to kiss him, the tips of her breasts touched his chest. This was the way to ruin. He let himself enjoy a painfully languid kiss before he broke away.

"On your stomach," he told her and sat up.

Giving him an uncertain look, she turned. He gathered her mass of dark hair and swept it to the side. As he kissed her neck, her lips curved up. He leaned back and let his eyes travel down the graceful line of her spine. To let her know how much he wanted her, he rubbed his cock against her buttocks.

In truth, that was just for him.

It did get her attention. She looked at him over her shoulder, eyes wide and lips parted. She looked so beautiful he had to fight the urge to part her legs and enter her right then.

Whoa! He shook his head.

He gave her buttocks little bites that made her laugh, even while they aroused her. Then he turned her over to kiss her breasts again. How did she smell so good?

He played with her nipples as he worked his way down. He paused to stick his tongue in her belly button. As he moved lower, he felt her tense. He rose up to kiss her for a long while, his hand between her legs.

"You will like this, I promise," he said next to her ear before he moved back down to show her.

She did. Her release was so exciting he thought he would have his own against the bedclothes. Sweet Jesus, she was going to kill him.

Sometime later, he once again had her on the edge, just where he wanted her. She was clinging to him like warm honey. He hovered over her, teasing her—and torturing himself. It took all his strength of mind not to plunge into her.

"Now." She wrapped her legs more tightly around him, her voice was urgent. "I want you inside me. Now."

"Say you will marry me first."

She made an indecipherable sound.

"You must say it, Isobel," he insisted. "I will not again risk giving you a child unless I have your word."

"I cannot!" she half moaned, half cried. "Do not make me, Stephen. Please. Please. Do not make me."

Even in the midst of passion, she would not give in to him.

A man can take only so much. When she lifted her hips to him, he let his shaft slide over her. He closed his eyes and moved against her, again and again, until he spurted his seed over her belly.

He rolled off her and lay on his back, arms crossed over his face. He'd never felt worse in his life. The humiliation alone might kill him. But it was nothing to this aching hole in his chest where his heart had been. He wanted to crawl off into a corner like a wounded animal. But he could not move with this heavy sadness lying over him like a great weight.

Though they did not touch, he felt the heat of her body next to him and heard each shallow breath she took. There was one demand he had to make. Though she won all else, he was determined to have his way in this one thing. He gathered his strength and what little pride he had left, and said it.

"I will not allow another man to raise my child."

He let the silence linger to give her time to absorb this before he told her how it would be.

"'Tis unlikely," she said in a bare whisper. "I have never conceived. I—I may not be able to."

He was resolved in this, and he would have her know it. Fixing his eyes on the ceiling, he let the coldness he felt show in his voice.

"You will find a way to delay your marriage to de Roche until you know for certain," he said. "If you are with child, I will give you two choices. You can marry me, or you can have the child in secret and give it to me to raise."

He got up from the bed. As he pulled on his clothes, his hurt and disappointment turned into something cold and hard within his chest. The silence was thick between them as he sat and methodically put on one boot and then the other.

He was not going to slink out of Isobel's bedchamber half dressed. He was not that kind of man anymore. He had tried to do the right thing. He still wanted to.

Gritting his teeth, he strapped on his belt and sword. Only then did he look at her. She was sitting with the bedclothes clutched to her chest, her hollow eyes fixed on him.

"Understand me. I will not allow you to pass my child off as de Roche's," he told her. "I would kill him with my bare hands before I let that unworthy piece of shit have a child of mine."

She nodded.

It was enough. He turned and left her.

Chapter Twenty-five

Stephen waved aside the guards' cautions and rode out the gate. Brigands and renegades be damned.

Lightning liked galloping in the dark. Stephen gave the horse his head, though it risked both their necks. The cold helped clear Stephen's mind. When Lightning slowed to a walk, he looked up at the star-filled sky and tried to draw hope from it.

After he left Isobel, he was in such a tangle he awakened Catherine for advice. She showed no surprise at his intention to marry Isobel. Good God, was he so obvious?

Catherine demanded he tell her all. He was not about to confess he'd just tried to seduce Isobel into agreeing to the marriage. Tried *and failed.* As it turned out, all Catherine wished to know was what he *said* to Isobel.

"You told her you 'must' marry?" Catherine said in her most exasperated tone. "Not that you *wanted* to marry her? That you love her? That you cannot live without her? For God's sake, Stephen, what were you thinking!"

Obviously, he had not broached the subject in the best possible way. He should have mentioned how much he cared for her. But how could Isobel not know it?

Those ugly remarks she made about other women were insulting. He'd not gone to bed with another woman since he met her, for God's sake. And it was not as if he had no offers.

The simple truth was he did not want any woman but Isobel. He'd told her he was done with other women... or had he? Surely his determination to marry her said as much?

Stephen and Lightning rode through most of the night. He did not turn around until he was sure he could speak with Isobel without getting angry again—no matter what foolishness she might say. A storm rolled in with the dawn, soaking him to the skin before he reached the castle gate.

He rode straight for the keep, hoping to find the king at breakfast in the hall. This time, he meant to talk with the king first. Then, when he spoke with Isobel, he could assure her the king was willing to release her from her promise.

The king would not like it, but he would approve the marriage. Being a pious man, what else could he do when Stephen told him what they'd done?

———

Last night, Linnet had found Isobel naked and weeping on the floor. The girl wrapped her in blankets and frantically pressed her with questions. Distraught as she was, Isobel made the mistake of telling her Stephen wanted to marry her.

Linnet was still furious with her this morning for her "utter, utter foolishness" in refusing him.

Was she being foolish?

What should she have said to Stephen? That she loved him so much her heart ached every moment of every day? That this, more than anything, frightened her? That she wished with all her heart he loved her back?

Yet even that would not be enough. She wanted the impossible. Unless he loved her *always,* being his wife would cause her too much pain.

Isobel felt ill from so much weeping. If she could, she would remain in bed for days with the curtains closed. The king, however, sent a message summoning her to join him for breakfast. Vaguely, she recalled he wished to know about the attackers. She tried to turn her mind to it. But misery engulfed her, leaving her thoughts disjointed and scattered.

Linnet maintained her stony silence while helping Isobel dress. For spite, the girl chose the green velvet gown Isobel wore on the day of Stephen's return from Falaise. Blinking back tears, she ran her fingers over the soft fabric.

When Robert came to escort her, she forced a smile. Taking his arm, she said, "You look well today."

"I should. Somehow I managed to sleep all of yesterday." He frowned at her. "But I can see you have not recovered from your ordeal. You look pale, my dear."

"I am sorry I caused you such worry," she said. "It was thoughtless of me not to leave you a message."

Robert laughed. "A message would not have helped, unless you had the good sense to lie to me."

"Has the king summoned me to ask about the attackers?"

"I can think of no other reason," Robert said with a

shrug. "I was supposed to question you yesterday, so he must have grown impatient."

When they entered the hall, Isobel took a quick look up and down the tables. Stephen was not here, praise God. She needed time to think. Now, that was odd—de Roche was in the honored place next to the king. Her brother was seated at the far end of the high table, looking anxious.

After the king acknowledged her and Robert, he gestured for them to sit beside de Roche. Isobel sat without meeting de Roche's eyes. After his volatile and offensive behavior of late, the prospect of sharing a trencher with him made her queasy.

Isobel could not think of a single word to say to him. She was relieved when the king rose to speak.

"This is a happy occasion," the king said, holding his arms out. "Today we celebrate the symbolic joining of England and Normandy . . ."

Isobel barely heard a word the king said. She was startled to attention, though, when Robert leapt to his feet beside her.

"But, my good sire, I must beg you to put off this betrothal a little longer," Robert said, his voice tense. "We have not yet completed negotiation of the terms of the marriage contract."

"Since you proved unable to accomplish this simple task, I took it upon myself to assist her brother," the king said. "The three of us met an hour ago. Agreement was easily reached."

"With your good guidance, I'm sure it was readily done," Robert said in a clipped voice.

"Lord de Roche has been exceedingly generous," the

king answered in an even tone. "I assure you, Lady Hume can have nothing to complain of."

Isobel felt as if she were watching events unfold from a great distance. Surely this was not happening. Not now.

She was vaguely aware of Robert cursing under his breath as he sat down. With his hand on her arm he whispered, "I had no notion the king meant to do this today."

"Lord de Roche wishes to have the marriage ceremony take place in his home city of Rouen," the king announced. "The banns will be posted there."

"Merde!" Robert hissed beside her.

Isobel kept her eyes fixed on the untouched food in front of her while the king talked on and on. She flinched each time she heard the word "betrothal" but took in nothing else.

God help her. It was too late.

When the king finished speaking, de Roche stood and took his turn. His words flowed like thick honey of the bonding of two great kingdoms, God's will, the king's destiny.

Isobel started at the sudden weight of a hand on her shoulder and looked up into hard gray eyes.

"'Tis time to sign the marriage contract and pledge our troth," de Roche said.

To the sound of halfhearted clapping, he pulled her to her feet. Geoffrey walked to her from the far end of the table.

"I am sorry to surprise you," he whispered as he laid the marriage contract before her. "The king would brook no delay."

She took the quill and signed without reading it.

De Roche signed with a flourish, then took her hand.

His deep voice filled the room as he made his formal promise to her.

All eyes in the hall turned to her. Panic seized her. She could not do this. Not now. Not yet. Not ever. She took a step back, her eyes on the door.

King Henry stood before her, blocking her way. She opened her mouth to tell him—

Tell him what? That she could not do this now? Surely the king would demand a reason.

I must wait until I know if I am with child. I have committed the sin of fornication, with a man other than the one I agreed to wed.

She could not tell him that. Not before all these witnesses.

The king cleared his throat. When she looked into his magnetic hazel eyes, Isobel felt the full force of his will for the first time. Before her was the king who united England, the commander men followed gladly into war. His every aspect exuded utter certainty that he knew what was right.

King Henry was relentless in pursuing the destiny God set out for him. Every day, he did his duty with all of his being. With his steady gaze, he was telling her that today he expected her to do hers.

The king prompted her, telling her what she should say. She did as he bade her. She repeated back the simple words of the promise to marry.

It was done.

A gush of wind went through the hall, causing the lamps and candles to flicker. Isobel turned and saw a dark figure at the entrance, rain dripping from his cloak. Her heart caught in her throat. Even before he threw his hood back and pushed the wet hair from his face, she knew it was him.

"Sir Stephen," the king called out, a smile lighting his face. "Come, we will make room for you here."

Stephen strode up to the high table and made his bow to the king. But when he lifted his head, his dark eyes were fixed on Isobel.

"You are just in time to hear the good news," the king said, gesturing toward Isobel and de Roche. "Lord de Roche and Lady Isobel Hume are betrothed. They leave today for Rouen."

Isobel felt faint under Stephen's gaze. Though his face was expressionless, she saw the muscles in his jaw working. How angry he must be with her! Only hours since he demanded she delay this marriage, and already she had bound herself. Only hours since she lay naked with him, and she stood beside the man who would be her husband. She wanted to cry out that it was not her fault—the king gave her no choice.

But none of it mattered. What was done was done.

"I wish you every happiness," Stephen said between his teeth. Without another word, he turned on his heel.

Isobel watched the dark drops of rainwater fall from his cape and hit the gray stone floor as he walked across it. Long after he was gone, she heard the echo of his boots in the silent hall.

Isobel sat on the bench in her bedchamber, staring blindly out the window slit as Linnet packed her chest. Glancing down, she saw she was dressed in her traveling clothes. She had no memory of changing.

Now and then, Linnet asked a question about the packing. Isobel could not muster the strength to answer. When she saw Linnet carry her sword to the chest, though, she forced herself to speak.

"I shall have to give that up." Her voice came out as a croak. "My new husband will not approve."

Linnet glared at her over the top of the chest as she laid the sword inside it. Then she stalked over to Isobel.

"We shall wear our daggers." Linnet flipped up the skirt of Isobel's gown and strapped a dagger to her calf.

"But we'll be traveling with twenty of de Roche's men—"

"I stole an extra for each of us." Linnet slapped a second dagger into Isobel's hand. "Find a place to hide it on you."

It was easier to slip the dagger through the fichu of her gown and fasten it to the belt underneath than to argue.

"You need not come with me," Isobel said, though the thought of losing the girl, too, brought her to the brink of tears again. "You will want to stay with François."

"We are both coming," Linnet said. "Sir Robert said you will have need of us."

Isobel took Linnet's hand and squeezed it, unable to find words to tell her how grateful she was.

Linnet jerked her hand away, still furious with her for letting this happen. Isobel leaned her head back against the stone wall and let the tears slide down the sides of her face. She could not seem to stop weeping. Perhaps if she were not so very, very tired.

Linnet brought a cold, wet cloth for her face. As Isobel took slow, deep breaths through the cloth, she told herself that if she could survive eight years married to Hume, she could survive anything. Even this. She drew in one last deep breath and set the cloth aside.

"Thank you, Linnet." She rose to her feet, dry-eyed at last. "I am ready."

It was still raining, so they made their good-byes inside the keep. Somehow, she managed to make the expected nods and murmurs as she moved from group to group with de Roche.

She faltered only twice.

The first was when she saw Lady Catherine Fitz-Alan. Isobel could not help thinking Stephen would not be happy, either, in love with his brother's wife. Though Lady Catherine had been kindness itself when they met, she offered no good wishes now. The blue eyes fixed on her, as if asking a burning question.

Isobel faltered again when she bade farewell to her brother and Robert. How she would miss them! All that kept her from breaking down was Robert's promise to visit her soon.

"Do not tell de Roche, but I go in secret to Paris now," Robert said in a low voice when de Roche turned to speak to someone else. "I shall come see you upon my return."

She felt certain Robert knew what was between her and Stephen, though they never spoke of it. When he embraced her for the last time, she could not help whispering in his ear, "He did not come. He did not come."

"You will be happy yet, Isobel, I know it."

Despite Robert's effort to hide his worry behind a smile, she saw it in his eyes as he waved good-bye to her.

They had two days' ride before them, and de Roche was anxious to be gone. With a twin on either side of her, Isobel urged her horse forward with the rest of their party.

As they crossed the bailey yard, she turned for a last look at the storeroom along the wall where she spent so many happy hours practicing. Where she and Stephen first kissed.

A movement on top of the wall drew her eye upward. A dark, hooded figure stood against the gray sky, black cape flapping in the wind.

Stephen had come to see her off, after all.

Though she could not make out his face, she felt his eyes burning into her long after she rode out the gate.

God help her, she loved him. Her life was in ruins.

Chapter Twenty-six

Even with an escort of twenty men, the road to Rouen was dangerous. They rode hard, rarely stopping, except to camp a few hours overnight on the bank of the Seine. Isobel was past exhaustion by the time she saw the towers and church spires of Rouen on the horizon at dusk on the second day.

A formidable city. The city walls went on forever and had more towers than she could count. Weary as she was, she could not help wondering how King Henry hoped to take it.

The others must be tired, as well. The entire party slowed to a sluggish pace now that Rouen was within sight. By the time they passed through the city's massive gates, it was full dark.

De Roche dropped back to ride beside her. "Follow close behind me," he told her. "The house is not far now."

Isobel fought to stay awake as she followed de Roche's horse through the narrow, winding streets. Every few yards, she turned to check on the twins, who rode, heads bobbing, just behind her.

At last they came to a halt before the gate of a massive,

walled house. De Roche helped her down. Her legs, stiff from riding all day, gave way as he set her to the ground.

Strong arms lifted her. The man's smell was wrong, but she could not summon the strength to open her eyes. She heard hushed voices around her. Then there was nothing but the lulling, rocking motion of being carried upstairs.

Isobel sat straight up, heart racing, not knowing where she was. When she saw Linnet amid the tangle of bedclothes beside her, she put her hand to her chest. Thank God. She took a deep breath to calm herself. But then the events of the last days came back to her.

Slowly, she lay back down on the bed.

Memories of Stephen ran through her head. Stephen, speaking in a cold voice of what she must and must not do. Strapping on his belt and sword, too angry to look at her. His face when he understood what she had done. The echo of his boots as he left the hall.

And the last time she would ever see him: A dark figure on the wall, cape flapping in the wind.

God give her strength.

She wept silently, trying not to waken Linnet, but her sobs shook the bed. She forced herself to take slow, deep breaths. Nothing was to be gained by more weeping. Blinking back her tears, she sat up and pushed the heavy bed curtain aside.

It was late, judging by the light. Though she was grateful de Roche had saved her from meeting his mother last night, she must not delay making the acquaintance of her mother-in-law any longer. The woman would think badly of her.

Isobel stood on the cold floor, hugging herself, and looked about the bedchamber. It was a dark and austere room, the only furniture the bed, a bench, and a table with pitcher and basin. What light there was came from the adjoining room.

Isobel stepped through the doorway into a cozy solar. It had a coal brazier for warmth and was comfortably furnished with a small table, a chair, and two stools. The best feature was the large double window that bathed the room in late morning light. Beneath it was a window seat with colorful cushions.

Isobel stepped up onto the window seat to look out. Her rooms, she saw, were on the third floor overlooking an interior courtyard. A single tree filled the courtyard, its branches rising higher than her window. A row of small brown birds perched on the slender branch closest to her, heads twitching back and forth as they chattered.

At the sound of a light knock, Isobel hopped down just as a pretty maid opened the door.

"The lord awaits you in the hall, m'lady," the maid said, bobbing a curtsy. "I am to help you dress."

Isobel decided to let Linnet sleep. A short time later, she followed the young woman down two sets of stairs and through several rooms to the hall. There, she found de Roche sitting alone at a long table set before the hall's huge hearth.

He rose and greeted her with a kiss on each cheek. "Your rooms are satisfactory?" he asked as he helped her sit.

"They are lovely, thank you, especially the solar."

Several trays were on the table, piled high with food. De Roche pushed his trencher toward her and nodded for her to help herself. All this food for just the two of them? The rest of the household must have long since broken their fast.

She nibbled at a piece of bread. "I am sorry I missed your mother. When shall I meet her?"

"My mother is not here just now." De Roche stabbed a slab of ham with the point of his knife and stuffed it into his mouth.

Not here? His mother must already be out visiting friends in the town.

"I'm afraid you shall not see much of me for the next week or two," de Roche said, chewing.

He surveyed the tray of steaming bread, picked a thick slice, and dipped it in the bowl of honey. Dribbles of sticky honey ran down his chin and fingers, reminding her disturbingly of Hume.

Between bites of the bread and licks at the honey running down his hand he said, "I will be busy persuading the men of the town to take King Henry's side in this fight."

This, at least, was good news.

"I'm glad you will speak for our king," she said. "You can assure them he is a just ruler who cares for all his people."

De Roche snorted. "That is hardly an argument that will persuade the men who matter."

"I do not understand the resistance to King Henry," she said. "There can be no sincere dispute as to his right to rule Normandy." His right to rule all of France was not so clear, so she did not mention it.

De Roche patted her hand. "Do not trouble yourself with such matters."

"But I want to be your helpmate in all things," she protested.

"Leave the politics to me," he said. "Your other duties will more than fill your time."

At his signal, one of the servants brought a small bowl of water for him to rinse his fingers. De Roche kept his eyes on her as he wiped his wet fingers on the cloth the servant held out to him. Uncomfortable at the intensity of his gaze, Isobel set down the slice of bread.

"Come," de Roche said, rising from the table. "I shall show you the house. I have an hour to spare before I must leave."

The smell of ham and warm bread wafted up her nose. Stomach rumbling, she stood and took his arm. He was an important man with duties to attend to; she would not keep him waiting.

De Roche walked her past several rooms without giving her a chance to look in. There must be some part of the house that he was particularly proud of, a set of rooms he wished to show her first.

"Shall I meet your mother at supper, then?" she asked as he hurried her past yet another room.

"Hardly. She is in Paris."

"Paris? Your mother is in Paris?"

"'Tis safer for her there, while Normandy is unsettled."

Surely de Roche would not bring her to stay in his house without a female family member present.

"If your mother is not in the house, who is?" When he made no immediate response, she said, "You know I cannot stay here with no one to serve as chaperone."

"It is a huge house," he said, putting his arm around

her waist and guiding her forward. "And with all the servants, you cannot say we are alone."

How could he put her in this position? It was all she could do not to shout at him. Not that it would do any good now. After one night under his roof, the damage was done. People would think what they would.

"Come, I want to show you the new wing of the house, where I have my rooms." He opened a heavy wood door and motioned for her to precede him.

She folded her arms and turned to face him. "You should have told me your mother would not be here."

"We are betrothed," he said, leaning down until his breath was hot against her ear. "As good as wed."

Before she could get the words out to object, he hoisted her up and carried her through the timber-framed doorway.

"Put me down! Please!"

De Roche carried her through a large, richly furnished solar and into an adjoining room. Centered against the wall of this second room was an oversized bed with a dark wood frame and heavy burgundy curtains tied back with gold cords.

This was quite obviously de Roche's bedchamber. And his bed.

He set her on her feet and walked her backward until she felt the high bed behind her. She arched back against it to keep from touching him; his sickly sweet scent filled her nose.

Reaching past her, he patted the bed behind her. "Your most important duty is here."

Her heart thundered in her chest. She did not want this. When she turned her head away from his kiss, he ran his mouth down her throat. Then suddenly, he was all over her—hands squeezing her breasts, knee pushing between her legs, mouth sucking on her neck.

"Stop, you are hurting me!" she cried as she tried in vain to push him away.

He was pulling at her gown, yanking it up.

"You must let me speak!" she shouted at him.

He leaned back, breathing hard. "I beg you, be brief."

"I am not well."

He smiled. "Oddly enough, I feel feverish, myself."

"I'm having my courses." The lie tumbled out of her mouth before she thought it. Blushing, she added, "They began this morning."

"I see." De Roche stepped back and straightened his tunic. "Well, then, we can wait a few days."

"Aye," she said in a voice just above a whisper, "we should wait."

Hume had followed the church's admonition to abstain from relations during her monthly bleeding. She'd used the excuse as often as she dared. From the expression of distaste on de Roche's face, she suspected this reprieve was due to a perverse squeamishness rather than a desire to avoid sin.

De Roche marched her back to her rooms, not bothering to hide his displeasure. As if she could help having her courses! She lied, but he did not know that.

Well, she was angry with him, too. And she had good cause! Displeasing him, however, would not serve her well in the long run. The man could make her life a misery in a thousand ways, if he chose.

So why did she lie to put him off? If she carried a child, then bedding de Roche now was the safest and wisest course. The only sensible course. If her husband suspected the child was not his...She closed her eyes. Nothing could be worse.

Still, she could not make herself do it. She could not yet take that final step. A betrothal plus consummation made a marriage, regardless of the formalities.

She would honor Stephen's demand, as best she could. Though she was not able to delay the betrothal, she would forestall completion of the marriage until she knew if there was a child. Stephen's child.

'Twas foolish, for Stephen could not save her now. Even if he wanted to, he could not.

Chapter Twenty-seven

$\mathcal{A}$s if being punished for her lie, Isobel awoke the next morning with a damp stickiness between her legs.

Nay, it could not be! She closed her eyes and tried to pretend she did not know. But it could mean nothing else. She rolled to her side and hugged her knees to her chest.

There was no baby.

Only now could she admit to herself how much she had wanted it. If she were with child, there would be no way for Stephen to know of it, no way for her to get word to him. Still, she harbored the hope that somehow he would know. And come for her.

It made no difference that he would have married her for the child's sake. Nor that she would make a pathetic wife, always hoping to make him love her. In her secret heart of hearts, she wanted to be forced to take her chances with him.

Regardless of all else, she wanted this baby. Stephen's child. A part of him she could love and keep.

Linnet stirred on the bed beside her, bringing her sharply back to the present. There could be no escape from her betrothal now. Her life was here in Normandy. With de Roche.

Isobel was lost in such despair that days and nights blurred together. She did not stir from her rooms, refused to dress, and ate only what Linnet forced down her.

Although she told herself she must gather herself and face her future, she simply could not do it. It took all her strength to drag herself from her bed to sit in her solar. She spent most of her time there, gazing out the window at the tree in the courtyard. It was in blossom now.

She ignored the tug on her arm. When it persisted, she turned her gaze from the tree to find Linnet at her side.

"I've been trying to tell you!" Linnet's voice was urgent, upset.

Isobel tried to make an effort, for the girl's sake. "What is it?"

"I told them all you have a raging fever, but it has been a week and de Roche is asking for you."

How could Linnet believe she cared about this?

"Listen to me!" Linnet put her hands on her hips and stamped her foot. "I swear, I shall slap you if you do not quit looking at that damnable tree. François and I need your help."

Before Isobel could drift off again, Linnet lifted a cup of wine to her mouth and held it there until she drank. She felt the wine hit her stomach and travel down her limbs. With so little in her stomach, she felt light-headed when Linnet hauled her up from her chair.

Could the girl not leave her in peace? She looked longingly over her shoulder at her tree. The sharp slap on her cheek startled her.

"Linnet!"

"I warned you," Linnet said without the slightest show of remorse. "Now you shall eat the food I brought you, and then you shall wash and dress. Did you not promise the king you would keep watch on de Roche? I tell you, he is up to something. We must find out what it is before it is too late."

Too late? It was already too late, for her. But Linnet was right. She was neglecting her duty. If de Roche was changing loyalties, she must try to turn him back. She was so bone weary, though, she did not know how she would do it.

"I will get dressed and do my duty," she told Linnet. Bleak as her future looked, she did not want to add traitor's wife to her list of burdens.

As if by some signal, there was a knock on her door the moment she was dressed. She heard whispers, and then François appeared before her. He must have grown half a foot since Stephen first brought him from Falaise. Overnight, he'd gone from boy to youth on the brink of manhood.

"'Tis good to see you up and about, Lady Hume," he said in a new, deep voice. "Are you feeling better?"

"I am, thank you." She did feel a bit better for having eaten. "Linnet tells me you have some news I should hear?"

"'Tis about Lord de Roche," François said. "Linnet and I believe he is plotting against King Henry. Late at night, he meets with men in the small parlor, where none of the servants can overhear them."

"This means nothing," Isobel protested.

"But we heard them from the bushes outside the window," Linnet said.

Good heavens, what had the two of them been up to? Isobel felt a surge of guilt for her neglect.

"We did not hear much," François admitted, "but they kept mentioning King Henry and—"

"—Burgundy and the Dauphin," Linnet finished for him.

"So they speak of politics? In these times, men talk of little else. I am sure de Roche is only doing what he pledged to do. He is persuading these men to support King Henry."

The twins shook their heads in unison.

"De Roche sounded as if he wanted to spit each time he said the king's name," François said, as if that settled the matter.

Though there was no reason for the late night meetings to make Isobel suspicious, the twins' certainty made her uneasy. Had de Roche changed loyalties? To find out, she would have to join him in the hall and learn whom he entertained as guests.

The thought of seeing him caused her palms to sweat and her throat to go dry. There was no point, however, in delaying the inevitable.

She stood. "I shall go speak with him now."

"There is something else you must know," François said.

Was there no end to this? Isobel nearly snapped at him before she noticed his gaze was on the floor and he was shuffling his feet.

"What is it?" she asked, touching his arm.

François's voice was so low she had to lean forward to hear him. "No one in the city knows of your betrothal."

"That cannot be," she said. "By now, the banns must have been read in church at least once."

François shook his head, then looked sideways toward the door, as if longing to escape.

To what end did de Roche delay? News traveled slowly between the English- and French-held parts of Normandy, but it did travel. He could not hide her forever.

Isobel found de Roche sitting behind a table scattered with parchments in his private parlor. When he saw her in the doorway, he leapt to his feet and crossed the room.

"I'm glad to see you are well!" he said, taking her hand and kissing her cheek. He seemed genuinely pleased to see her. "You look lovely, if a little thin. Come, you must sit."

He put his arm around her and guided her to the chair closest to the brazier. His solicitude made her feel guilty for letting the twins' wild speculations run away with her.

"I am sorry to interrupt you," she said.

"I am glad to see you before I leave. 'Tis a shame I must go just as you are better, but I cannot delay visiting my mother any longer." Roche shifted his gaze and pulled on his ear. "I cannot have her hearing of our betrothal secondhand. You see, she rather dotes on me."

So this was the reason for his delay in having the banns read! No excuse was adequate, to be sure. Still, she was relieved his motive was no more sinister than consideration for his mother.

"You are a good son," Isobel said, pleased to learn it was true. "But should I not go with you?"

"Don't be foolish! You've just risen from your sick-bed," he said. "I would not have you risk the roads again, in any case."

They were interrupted then by one of his men-at-arms. "Lord de Roche," the man said from the doorway, "the men are ready and await you outside."

"I shall join you shortly," de Roche said, dismissing the man with a nod.

Isobel sighed with relief; she could delay the unpleasant task of questioning him about politics a little longer.

"I can escort you to your chamber before I leave," de Roche said, rising to his feet.

At the door he stopped abruptly, as if he had forgotten something, and went back into the room. His back was to her, but Isobel saw him take one of the parchments from the table and lock it in the drawer.

He took her straight to her rooms, his brisk steps conveying he was in a hurry now. Outside the open door of her solar, he kissed her hand and bade her an abrupt adieu.

When he turned to leave, something inside the room caught his attention. A wave of unease passed through Isobel as she followed the direction of his gaze. What caught de Roche's attention—and held it still—was Linnet.

The girl sat on the window seat, head bowed over her needlework, sunlight shining on her fair hair. How had Isobel failed to notice? Linnet, like her brother, was growing up. Her emerging shape was a trifle too apparent in the too-small gown.

Isobel drew in a sharp breath when Linnet looked up and fixed her deep blue eyes on them. Heaven help the child. A girl so alone in the world should not be this lovely.

As Linnet's mistress and lady of the house, Isobel could

protect her from most men. But not from de Roche. If he was dishonorable enough to take advantage of a dependent, Isobel was powerless to stop him.

Well, perhaps not completely powerless.

"Philippe," she said, pointedly using his Christian name.

He dragged his gaze away from Linnet to look at her. Forcing a smile to her lips, she took a half step closer and rested her palm against his chest.

She had his attention now.

Coy did not come easily to her. She tilted her head and looked up at him from under her lashes. "Must you go?"

De Roche wrapped his hand around hers and brought it slowly to his lips. "I fear I must," he said, regret tugging at his voice. "I can delay no longer."

Isobel took a deep breath and let it out on the single word "Alas."

Roche ran his tongue over his lips as his gaze dropped to her breasts. For a long moment, she feared her act had worked too well. When he gave his head a shake and stepped back from her, she sent a silent prayer of thanks to every saint she could think of.

"I shall return in a week," he said, raking his eyes over her one last time.

As Isobel watched him disappear down the stairs, she thought about what was in his eyes when he looked at Linnet. Not just lust, but possession. De Roche felt he had a right to take her. Isobel was not naive; she knew how it happened. The lord might give the serving girl a few trinkets or coins, but he would not allow her to refuse him.

Isobel would delay the inevitable no more. She would not protest that the banns must be read thrice.

When de Roche returned, she would go to his bed.

She was not vain enough to believe she could divert de Roche forever. Eventually, she had to get the girl out of his house. But she could buy time. When Robert came to visit, he could take Linnet away with him. How long before Robert's promised visit? A few weeks? She could distract de Roche that long, if she tried.

Isobel could not save herself. But by the saints, she would save Linnet.

Chapter Twenty-eight

April 1418

Rouen was a prize second only to Paris. From La Chartreuse de Notre Dame de la Rose, the Carthusian monastery set on a hill to the east of the city, Stephen could see over Rouen's walls and watch the bustle of this prosperous city of 70,000 souls.

The city's defenses had been strengthened since English forces last tried to take it, some thirty years ago. Stephen scanned the long line of the wall, with its sixty towers. To lay siege here, King Henry would have to bring an army large enough to encircle the city and guard all six gates. He would also have to block supplies from reaching the city from both the south and the north via the Seine, which flowed beside the city.

Besieging Rouen would be an arduous task. All the same, the city would fall. Stephen did not hold out much hope he could convince the men of Rouen of that truth, though.

As the king's envoy, he was tasked with putting a single question to them: Would Rouen submit willingly, or would its people be starved into submission?

Stephen wondered again why the king chose him for this mission. He sensed his brother's hand in it. Perhaps it was Robert's. Stephen had plenty of time to contemplate that puzzle on the two-day ride to Rouen. Instead, all he thought of was Isobel—and what he was going to do about her when he got here.

It had been two weeks. Two weeks since she lay naked beneath him. Two weeks since she refused him.

Two weeks since she made her pledge to another.

For the thousandth time, he asked himself why she did it. How could she? How could she do it right after she agreed not to? She did it so soon after he left her bed, his smell must have been on her skin as she made her pledge to de Roche.

Somehow the king had suspected Stephen's intentions toward Isobel, or so Robert believed. The king was not the only one to guess. Apparently, Robert, William, and Catherine had planned to speak to the king on Stephen's behalf that very day. King Henry acted swiftly, before his friends could approach him.

Robert insisted the king surprised Isobel, as well. But still, it was she who spoke the promise of marriage. Stephen's only comfort was that Isobel did not look the happy bride that morning, with her eyes swollen and her skin as pale as death.

A betrothal between a man and woman of consenting age was very nearly irreversible. But surely pregnancy by another man was a valid ground for breaking it. Time was short. Her marriage to de Roche could be completed in a week or so.

If Isobel was with child, it would be a simple matter. Stephen would carry her off and deal with the consequences later. If she did not agree to marry him at once, he would wear her down by the time the child was born.

What would he do if she did not yet know if she carried his child? Or worse, if she were certain she did not? He would not let himself think of that.

"Stephen!"

He turned to see Jamie and Geoffrey hurrying toward him.

"The city has replied to the message you sent today," Jamie said, holding out the rolled parchment.

Stephen scanned the long and flowery missive.

"The city will graciously welcome King Henry's envoy on the morrow," he summarized for Jamie and Geoffrey. "But they 'invite' my escort of English knights to remain here at the monastery while I conduct my business in the city."

"You cannot agree to go alone," Jamie protested. "At least take Geoffrey and me with you."

"They will not permit it," he told them. "And there is no need, since they have guaranteed my safety."

"Their guarantee!" Jamie scoffed. "These Frenchmen murder even sworn allies and close relations."

"If they mean to violate their guarantee," Stephen said, "one or two men could not save me."

He would ride into Rouen alone on the morrow. Within a day or two, he would know the city's fate. And his own.

———

Linnet rushed into the solar and slammed the door behind her. "De Roche has returned!"

Isobel's stomach clutched; her reprieve was over.

"The servants are all abuzz, because no sooner was he in the house than he left again," Linnet said, her cheeks pink with excitement. "You'll not believe it! 'Tis even worse than we thought!"

"Slow down, Linnet. What will I not believe?"

"François overheard the men talking while he helped with the horses," Linnet said. "De Roche was in Troyes, not Paris!"

Isobel tried to make sense of this news. "Troyes? Is that not where the Duke of Burgundy and the French queen are?"

Linnet nodded her head vigorously up and down. "Proof that de Roche betrays the king!"

Word had reached the city that Burgundy had captured the queen and set up a sham government in Troyes. Everyone expected Burgundy to break his alliance with King Henry any day now.

"François heard the men say Burgundy parlays with the Armagnacs, proposing terms to join forces against King Henry."

"What was François doing—hiding in the straw? I wish he would not take such risks! Where is he now?"

"He followed de Roche, of course," Linnet said. "I told him to."

"Do you wish to get your brother killed?"

For the hundredth time, she wondered about the twins' background. They refused to tell her anything except that they were orphaned. One thing was certain. Linnet was not raised to be anyone's servant. She was every bit as willful as Isobel was at that age.

They sat up past midnight sewing—or pretending to sew—while they waited for François. Just before Isobel heard a light tap on the door, Linnet tossed her sewing aside and ran to open it.

"Where did de Roche go?" Linnet asked François as soon as she closed the door. "Did you see whom he met?"

"I followed him to a house where Armagnac supporters were meeting."

"You should not do everything your sister tells you," Isobel scolded. "These are powerful men with much at stake. That makes them dangerous."

"De Roche never saw me," François said with a cocky grin.

Why was de Roche meeting with Armagnacs? Was he in league with both factions against the king? Aloud she said, "'Tis possible de Roche attempts to persuade them of the rightness of King Henry's cause."

Linnet gave an unbecoming snort.

"He was never loyal to the king," François said.

King Henry was not beloved here as he was in England, so she sometimes wondered at the reason for the twins' fervent loyalty. But this, like their parentage, was not something they shared with her.

"The king must be warned," Linnet insisted.

"Of what would we warn the king?" Isobel asked, trying to reason with them. "Even if we knew something worth the telling, how would I get a message to the king?"

"There is a way," François said, beaming at her. "King Henry has sent an envoy to Rouen."

"The king's envoy is in the city?"

François shook his head. "He is outside the city, awaiting permission to enter. The garrison commander and the city leaders spent the whole day arguing over what to do with him."

"How do you learn these things?" Isobel asked. "You mustn't go everywhere about the city as you do."

"Someone must bring us news, and you will not let me go," Linnet said. "Now, how shall we get a message to the envoy?"

"But we have no proof de Roche acts against the king," Isobel argued. "You expect me to betray him on so little?"

Linnet lifted her chin. "If we find the proof, will you do it?"

Isobel looked from one pair of bright blue eyes to another.

Would she betray her king, or de Roche? Before she could answer that, she must learn the truth. But how?

In bed. Aye, that would be the best time to ask him. Tonight, after their first time together.

Chapter Twenty-nine

In the morning, Stephen dressed in the clothes he brought to play the part of king's envoy. Elaborate liripipe hat, knee-length velvet tunic, jeweled rings and brooch. Even particolored hose, God help him. As he fastened a heavy gold belt around his hips, he heard a low whistle. He looked up to see Jamie grinning at him from the doorway.

"'Tis certain they'll notice you, Uncle."

"Only doing my duty," Stephen said with a wink. "Now, you be sure to get out of here fast if there's trouble."

"Trouble?" Jamie asked. "You mean when the ladies start to fight over you?"

Stephen laughed and put his hand on Jamie's shoulder.

"The worst they will do is hold me for ransom," he said in a hushed voice as they walked outside together. "If I do not return or send word before nightfall tomorrow, ride hard for Caen. Wait no longer, or they may come to the monastery and take you, as well."

"I shall do what needs be done," Jamie said.

"I know it. You always make me proud."

Stephen did not think the good citizens of Rouen would

throw him over the wall and set him afire. But they might. So he embraced his nephew, not caring if he embarrassed him before the other men. Ready now, he mounted Lightning and rode down to the city's main gate.

He arrived just as the bells of the city churches rang for Sext, the agreed-upon hour. An escort of two dozen knights met him at the gate and accompanied him the short distance to the Palais de Justice. At the Palais, he was received with all the tedious protocol due the English king's representative.

It was better than throwing his lifeless body over the wall. But they could always do that later.

After the welcome, he was taken to a room in the Palais and left there "to rest from his journey." Since the ride from the monastery was no more than half a mile, this meant the important men of the city were not yet agreed on what to do with him.

News of the arrival of King Henry's envoy would have spread to every corner of the city by now. If de Roche was still the king's man, he should find a way to have a private word with Stephen. Stephen did not expect him.

Since de Roche was a man of influence here, Stephen needed to settle the king's business before his own. De Roche must not suspect Isobel was leaving with Stephen before the city gave its formal reply. Better still if de Roche did not learn of her departure until they were a good half day's ride away.

There was little Stephen could do now but pace. After an hour or two, a servant appeared at his door to advise him there would be a reception in his honor that evening.

De Roche was bound to attend with the other local

notables. Which meant Isobel would be there, too. Stephen had to find a way to speak to her alone so they could make their plan.

————

Isobel stood at the top of the stairs, dressed in her green silk gown with silver trim and matching slippers and headdress. She smoothed the skirt one last time. Then, with trepidation in her heart, she went down the stairs.

Last night she'd been so sure de Roche would come to her that she sent Linnet to sleep with the kitchen maids. She lay awake for hours listening for the scrape of the door. Near dawn, she heard voices below. When the house grew silent again, she finally drifted off to sleep.

This morning, Linnet woke her with the news that de Roche had already left the house "to commit more treachery." François came later to tell them the city was rife with rumor that the envoy was locked up or murdered in the Palais.

All day she was tense, waiting for de Roche's return. Finally, an hour ago, de Roche sent a servant to tell her to dress for a grand reception at the Palais. That must mean the envoy was at the Palais—but alive and well.

The reception would be her best—perhaps her only—opportunity to give a message to the king's envoy. If de Roche was involved in some treachery against King Henry, she must try to learn what it was before they arrived at the Palais.

De Roche was waiting for her in the front entry. His eyes widened when he saw her.

"I would much rather stay home with you this evening,"

he said as he took her arm. "But the reception is for King Henry's envoy, and he will expect to see you."

"Who is the envoy?" she asked. "Do I know him?"

He shrugged. "I did not hear the name. Come, the carriage is waiting. We are late."

She had so little time! What would be the best approach? Flattery? Pouting? She was off playing with swords when the other girls learned these useful skills.

"'Tis a shame," she said once they were settled in the carriage, "you could not even come to greet me after being gone a week."

De Roche's teeth flashed in the dim light. "You missed me."

She looked up at him through her lashes and nodded. In sooth, his almost constant absence was all that gave her hope of surviving this marriage.

She turned her head away and gave a sniff. "I hope you had good reason to neglect me."

He put his hand on her thigh. "I told you the men here are hardheaded," he said, leaning closer. "It takes much effort to persuade them to the right course."

He began kissing her neck. When his hand went to her breast, she panicked and blurted out, "Are you with the Armagnacs now?"

De Roche sat back abruptly. In a voice so cold it sent a shiver through her, he said, "What is it that you think you know, Isobel?"

"Nothing, I know nothing," she said in a rush. "'Tis only that I worry about you. These are such dangerous times."

He remained silent, examining her with narrowed eyes.

"You cannot think the Dauphin would ever make a

proper king!" Though a part of her knew she should be quiet, the arguments spewed out of her mouth of their own accord. "By all accounts, the Dauphin is a weak and unworthy youth. And after all the queen's affairs, many doubt he is the mad king's true heir."

God help her, what made her say it! 'Twas too late now for pretense.

"If you are planning to break with King Henry, I beg you not to do it," she pleaded, "for your sake, as well as mine and our future children."

"Which one of the servants is telling you these lies?" he demanded. "I promise you, he will regret his loose tongue."

"Please, Philippe, you must tell me if you have changed loyalties."

"I must tell you nothing." His voice was tight with barely controlled rage. "There is but one thing a man must do with his wife. In that you have thwarted me, but not for long."

"I fear for your safety if you cross King Henry," she tried again. "He will prevail in the end."

"Do you intend to tell tales on your husband tonight?" Bits of his spittle hit her face as he spoke. "Do I have a spy in my own home?"

"Nay!" Her voice was high-pitched, panicked. "I would never be disloyal. I want to make a good wife."

"Then you are unwise to displease me." He grabbed her wrist. "I warn you, Isobel, do not leave my side tonight."

Chapter Thirty

Stephen stood before the crowd of well-dressed merchants and nobles in the great hall of the Palais. The reception was to begin with his formal speech pleading King Henry's case. The king had drafted it himself, taking only a few of Stephen's suggestions.

As Stephen unrolled the parchment, he scanned the room again. De Roche and Isobel were late.

"King Henry comes not as your conqueror, to take plunder and lay waste to the land, but as your rightful sovereign lord," he read in a loud voice. "To all who pledge loyalty to him, he will welcome you to his bosom with great joy and generosity.

"But be warned! If you defy him, he will crush you without mercy. He shall claim what is rightfully his. The victor of Agincourt is rolling across Normandy, and none can stop him. God is with him. He will prevail."

Stephen took a deep breath, glad to have the formal speech over. From Henry's mouth to their ears: "Crush without mercy." He hoped the people listening in the hall tonight knew King Henry meant every word.

For the next two hours, Stephen stood at one end of the

hall as the city notables took turns coming to pay their respects.

Where is Isobel?

He made himself pay attention to the useless platitudes of each person, listening for hints of what lay beneath. So far, they seemed an overconfident lot. It mystified him how they could believe their city walls could withstand English cannon when the famed "impregnable" walls of Falaise could not.

He heard them boasting to each other. "Burgundy will come to our defense." "The Armagnacs will never let the great city of Rouen fall." What made these men think either faction would bring their armies to save Rouen? For months, both stood by as city after city in Normandy fell.

Stephen saw the uneasy expressions on the faces of their wives. If only the decision were in the pragmatic hands of the women, instead of these strutting cocks.

Where was Isobel? The crowd was thinning out, and she and de Roche still had not arrived.

And then he saw her. Politics, war, his official duties—all flew out of his head as Isobel and de Roche came into the hall through a side entrance. Stephen forced his gaze to drift past them. Eventually, de Roche would have to come to him.

De Roche did not delay but came straight to him. And then Isobel stood before him—so close he could have touched her if he reached out his arm. After so long away from her, it took all his will not to sweep her into his arms. He could almost taste her.

How was it possible she was so beautiful? Her skin was pale, though, and she looked thin.

"Have you been ill?" he asked her.

"I am well now, thank you. And you, Sir Stephen?"

Her voice. He wanted to listen to it and nothing else. But de Roche was blathering something to him, like a gnat buzzing about his head.

"What?" he snapped. He let his eyes burn over de Roche, letting the man see that Stephen thought he was a worthless sack of horseshit. "The king will be displeased to hear you've made little progress with the city leaders. Your failure will bring the people of Rouen to grief."

De Roche's face flushed a deep red. When he opened his mouth to speak, Stephen cut him off.

"Lady Hume, you are much missed in Caen," he said as he took her hand and lifted it to his lips. Her fingers were trembling and icy cold. "The king sends his warmest greetings."

Keeping his eyes on hers, he said, "I hope Lord de Roche will permit me to speak with you in private before I leave the city, for I have news of your brother." Switching to English, he added, "And a question to ask."

She sent a furtive glance at de Roche, who was staring fixedly at the wall above Stephen's head. Then she gave her head an almost imperceptible shake. That tiny movement hit Stephen like a heavy blow, knocking the wind out of him and sending him back a step.

"Of course you may speak with her, if time allows," de Roche said, unaware that Isobel had already given Stephen the only answer that mattered.

There was no child. Stephen watched in a daze as de Roche took Isobel's arm and led her away.

No child, no child. He'd been so certain.

Somehow he managed to gather himself and pretend the world was not crashing around his ears. He did his duty by his king. But it was the longest evening of his life.

When the reception finally ended, he retired to his room and collapsed upon the bed. He stared at the ceiling. To see her and not touch her. To talk with her and not be able to say the things he needed to say to her. It had nearly killed him.

He was so sure she was with child. Because he needed her to be. It shamed him that he wanted to use the child to force her hand, to make her wed him instead of de Roche. In time, she would have seen it was for the best...

He heaved a sigh. What would he do now?

He could not leave without telling her what was in his heart. If she wanted him, he would find a way. How, he did not know. But he would.

There was a rap on his door. Please, God, make them go away! When the knocking persisted, he rolled off the bed. He opened the door and found himself looking into a pair of blue eyes beneath a head of shaggy blond hair.

"François!" He pulled the boy into the room and closed the door behind him. "'Tis good to see you! I swear you've grown still more since you left Caen. How is your sister?"

"Truth be told, she is a constant worry to me."

"Nothing new in that," Stephen said, slapping the lad on the back. "You are just the man I need. Where is Isobel staying? I need to speak with her."

François flushed and dropped his gaze to the floor. Unease rolled through Stephen.

In a low voice the boy said, "She stays in de Roche's house."

Blindly, Stephen found his way to the nearest chair and

fell into it. Isobel was living in the man's house? He had not expected this. How could she agree to it? A betrothal was difficult enough to break, but a betrothal plus consummation made a marriage.

"'Tis a very large house," François said, stretching his arms wide and speaking in a quick, nervous voice. "Her rooms are in a separate wing, and Linnet stays with her."

"But he must have family there, some married woman responsible for guarding Isobel's virtue."

When the boy dropped his eyes again, Stephen was suddenly so angry he wanted to punch his fist into the stone wall. Good God, it could not be worse.

"What was she thinking, agreeing to this...this... arrangement?" he said, throwing his hands up. Was she *trying* to torture him?

Had she done it? Had Isobel slept with the man? This time he did slam his fist against the wall. God's beard, that hurt!

François's eyes went wide as Stephen shook his hand out and muttered curses.

"I need to speak to Isobel alone. When is the best time to find de Roche gone?"

"He is often out late," Francois said with a shrug. "He rarely shows himself in the hall before the midday meal."

"And Isobel," Stephen asked between clenched teeth, "does she rise late, as well?"

"Nay, the lady is always up early."

He was a lost man, that he would take heart from so little. Though it seemed a lost cause now, he would go see her. He had to.

"Tell me what you know of de Roche's activities," he said to change the subject.

"He's always meeting in secret," François said. "Sometimes with Armagnac sympathizers, other times with the Burgundy men."

"What is he up to?" Stephen asked.

François shrugged again. "Lady Hume says we have no proof, but Linnet and I believe he is involved in some treachery against King Henry."

Isobel, married to a man like her father, whose oath of loyalty meant nothing. A man of no honor.

———

Isobel squeezed her eyes shut, grateful for the darkness of the carriage. Her hands would not stop shaking. Stephen. How it tore her heart to see him! She was grateful de Roche dragged her from the Palais without introducing her to anyone.

"There was a rumor in Caen about you and this Carleton." De Roche's voice was low, menacing. "I did not believe it at the time, but now I wonder."

De Roche grabbed her chin and jerked her face toward him.

"Were you bedding him, while you played the virtuous lady with me? Were you, Isobel?"

"You insult me grievously and with no cause," she said, forcing herself to speak in a steady voice. "I have gone to bed with no man, save for Hume."

He released her chin and sat back. "In sooth, I could not imagine you risking marriage to me for a dalliance with that wastrel. I vow I do not know what women see in him."

That he is ten times the man you are.

At least her anger kept her from weeping now.

De Roche did not speak again until the carriage came to a halt before the front gate of his house. "I must return to the Palais for more discussions," he said, sounding distracted.

Discussions over the city's response to King Henry. Which side would de Roche argue? She hardly cared anymore, so long as he was away from her. Her foot was on the carriage step when de Roche's voice stopped her.

"Leave your door unbarred tonight."

She took a candle from the sleepy-eyed servant who opened the front door and assured him she could find her way to her rooms alone. As she walked past de Roche's private parlor, she recalled talking with him there. She stopped in place. In her mind's eye, she saw the scattered papers on the table...de Roche returning to lock something in the drawer...

The locked drawer. If he had something to hide, it would be there. Perhaps she could find a clue as to his true allegiance. She had a right to know something that affected her future so significantly.

Should she look now? De Roche was gone, the servants abed. Heart pounding, she stood still and listened. No sound of anyone moving about. She eased the parlor door open and slipped inside.

She felt her way through the dark room to the window on the courtyard. Looking out, she saw no light in any of the rooms save for her solar, where Linnet waited up for her.

It was safe, then, to light the lamp.

She lit the lamp on the table with her candle, then tried the drawer. Locked. As she looked about for something to use to pry it open, a small vase on the corner of the table caught her eye. Would de Roche be so obvious? She turned the vase over onto her hand. She smiled as the key fell onto her palm. The man was wholly lacking in subtlety.

The key made a satisfying click as she turned it in the lock. Aha! A single sheet of parchment lay in the drawer. When she began to read it, her sense of satisfaction drained from her.

She sat down on the chair and smoothed the parchment with shaking hands to read it again.

> *Cousin,*
> *All is arranged. We are assured the pious H will insist on hearing Mass on such an occasion. Thus the great H will die on his knees. I shall be there to see it.*
> *The complicity of others comes at a high cost. Have your share of the gold ready when I arrive.*
> *T*

Murder. That was what de Roche's cousin intended for "H." Who was this "H"? She sucked in her breath. King Henry, of course! He was both "great" and "pious," to be sure. And it was well known he had Masses said on every possible occasion.

And the cousin "T"? That could only be de Roche's wily and powerful cousin Georges de la Trémoille.

But what was the "occasion" at which they intended to murder the king? She had a vague recollection of Robert complaining of how dull Caen would be with the king spending all of Lent in fasting and prayer. But at Easter, there was to be a grand event at which scores of men would be knighted.

Mass was a central part of the knighting ceremony.

A number of nobles who followed Burgundy—Henry's supposed ally—would be invited to this important event. Trémoille could easily attend.

A shudder ran through Isobel at the thought of King Henry murdered on his knees in church. The greatest king England had seen in generations, struck down by a coward's blade. If it was his fate to die young, such a king should fall in glory on the battlefield.

She had to get word of this conspiracy to Stephen so he could warn the king. But how? Carefully, she put the letter back as she found it, locked the drawer, and returned the key to the vase. She blew out the lamp and sat in the dark, trying to think how she would do it.

Stephen had asked de Roche's permission to visit her. If he did come, she could tell him then. She bit her lip in frustration—de Roche would never allow her to meet with Stephen alone. If she could find François, she could send a message with him...

But François was already in danger. De Roche raged about finding the servant who told her of his secret meetings. She must get both the twins to safety. But how?

She could think of no way to accomplish all that she must. A feeling of hopelessness took hold of her. She buried her head in her arms on the table and let herself weep. For her king. For the twins. For the misery of her life. For Stephen. How she longed to see him, to hear his laugh, to have his arms around her one more time.

How long had she been weeping when she heard voices?

She wiped her face on her sleeves and got to her feet. What had she been thinking, remaining in Roche's parlor? As she started toward the door, she heard the voices again. She went to the window and listened.

A scream reverberated through the courtyard. Isobel's blood froze in her veins. Linnet.

Isobel was out the door and running for the stairs. *Please, God, let me not be too late.* De Roche was the only one who would enter Isobel's rooms at night without permission.

The memory of Hume taking her the first time came to her sharp and clear as she raced up the stairs. There was nothing Isobel would not do to save Linnet from that. Nothing she would not do to save the girl from being forced to lose her innocence to a man she loathed.

Her heart was beating wildly in her chest as she reached the top of the stairs and flung open the solar door.

De Roche had Linnet pinned against the wall, holding her wrists over her head with one hand.

"Stop it, stop it!" Isobel screamed.

Linnet looked at Isobel with wide, terrified eyes. There was a studied casualness to de Roche's expression as he turned to her.

"A man must make do when he cannot find his bride." He spoke with a cold calm that was more frightening than if he had raised his voice. "Where were you, Isobel?"

"I...I was just in the courtyard," Isobel stammered. "Let her go, Philippe. Please, I beg you, let her go."

"Waiting for the banns, the formalities...it all seems... so...unnecessary to me," de Roche said. "Does it not to you, my sweet?"

"Let Linnet go, and I will do whatever you want."

"Whatever I want." His white teeth gleamed in the candlelight. "That is just what I hoped you would say."

The moment he released Linnet, the girl ran to Isobel and threw her arms around her waist.

De Roche took out a handkerchief and wiped the blood from the scratches on his cheek. "I should have the girl whipped."

"No, Philippe."

"You will find," he said, wiping his hands on the handkerchief, "I can be as agreeable as you are."

Isobel pushed Linnet's hair back and kissed the girl's forehead. "Go now."

"I'll not leave you," Linnet whimpered against her.

"I shall be fine," Isobel said in a firm voice. She led Linnet to the door and removed the girl's arms from around her waist. As she pushed Linnet out the door, she whispered, "Go to your brother and do not return until morning."

The bar made a *thunk* as Isobel slammed it into place. She closed her eyes and rested her forehead against the door. Nothing could save her now. She would be the wife of this dark and treacherous man until the day she died.

She would, however, get Linnet out of Rouen. She gathered herself and turned around to face her husband.

De Roche was already unfastening his belt.

Chapter Thirty-one

When the knocking continued, Isobel spun around.

"Linnet, stop this!" she called out loudly enough to be heard through the door. "You must go away now."

A male voice answered, "Is Lord de Roche with you, m'lady?"

De Roche fastened his belt as he stomped to the door. After pushing Isobel aside, he slid the bar and jerked the door open. An elderly servant stood on the other side, rubbing his bony hands together and blinking nervously.

"What is it?" de Roche demanded.

In a high, quavering voice, the servant said, "The visitor you were expecting on the morrow, m'lord...he...he has just arrived and...and he is asking for you."

Isobel was startled by the sudden change in de Roche. The angry impatience was gone, replaced by a palpable fear.

De Roche turned hard gray eyes on her. "Do not leave your rooms tonight."

Without another word, he followed the servant out.

Isobel lay awake most the night, dreading the moment of de Roche's return. She must have eventually drifted off, for she was in a deep sleep when Linnet returned in the morning.

Linnet looked sharply about the rooms with narrowed eyes. "Where is he?"

"De Roche had a visitor shortly after you left," Isobel said. "He did not return."

The tightness in Linnet's face eased. "François did not come back, either."

"Come, I do not know how long we have," Isobel said as she led Linnet to the window bench. "I must tell you my plan."

As Isobel expected, Linnet objected to the plan at first.

"We must save the king," Isobel told her. "I shall have your promise that you will play your part, for there is no other way."

They spent the rest of the morning holding hands and talking quietly of small, unimportant things. Nothing could be gained by talking more about the difficulties ahead.

Isobel prayed de Roche would not come to her bed-chamber before Stephen's visit. She did not want to have the memory of de Roche touching her when she saw Stephen for the last time. But what if Stephen did not come today? What if he did not come at all?

It was midafternoon when a servant came to tell Isobel that Sir Stephen Carleton was waiting in the hall to see her. De Roche, too, would be told of Stephen's arrival. If she could get to the parlor first, she might have a moment alone with Stephen.

"Hurry, please," she urged Linnet. Isobel tried to help with the headdress, but her hands were shaking so violently that Linnet slapped them away.

Isobel stared, unseeing, into the polished brass mirror as Linnet worked. She was so caught up in planning how to get the news of the murder plot to Stephen that she'd given no thought as to why Stephen wanted to see her. What reason could he have? Any news of Geoffrey he could have told her at the reception.

Could he be here to ask if she carried his child? She closed her eyes and swallowed. She'd been so sure Stephen understood her silent message.

"If I do not get to speak with Stephen alone, Linnet, tell him"—she said it with her eyes still closed—"tell him...there is no child."

It hit her again. There was no child.

Isobel opened her eyes. In the mirror's reflection, she saw her fist clutched against her chest and slowly lowered it to her lap. Did she hope Stephen cared? That he would suffer as she was suffering? Nay, she would not wish this pain on him.

Linnet touched her shoulder. "I've finished."

Isobel met Linnet's eyes in the mirror. "Wait outside the door until I call you."

Linnet nodded.

"Trust me." Isobel stood and took the shawl Linnet held for her. Taking a deep breath, she hurried out the door.

She was within a few steps of the entrance to the hall when a voice behind her stopped her.

"I was just looking for you, my dear," de Roche said, taking her arm in a firm grip. "We should welcome our guest together."

She would not have even a moment alone with Stephen. Before she could prepare herself, de Roche led her in.

Her heart stopped at the sight of Stephen. Last night, he

looked like an impossibly handsome prince, bedecked in jewels and gold trim. Today he was in the sort of clothes he regularly wore. Their very familiarity made her ache to run her fingers along his collar, down his sleeve.

The usual humor and mischief were missing from his expression, however. His face was drawn, the laughter gone from his deep brown eyes. How could she have found fault with the easy, lighthearted Stephen of before? The man who made her laugh. She missed him now more than she could say.

It was evident Stephen's purpose in coming was to speak to her alone. It was equally clear de Roche would not permit it. After straining to make small talk for a few minutes, Stephen rose to his feet.

"I leave the city today," Stephen said, "so I must bid you adieu now, Lady Hume."

"Wait!"

She said it more loudly than she intended. Both men looked at her expectantly. De Roche's eyes were narrow, suspicious; Stephen's hand was on the hilt of his sword.

"Sir Stephen, I must ask you to take back the two servants you loaned to me," she said in as cool a voice as she could manage. She lifted her chin. "My new husband has more than enough servants to meet my needs."

Stephen furrowed his brow. "You are welcome to keep Linnet and François all the same. I am sure they are a comfort to you in your new surroundings."

"My husband provides for my comfort," she said. "I do not wish to have the girl here. She is headstrong and difficult. Her behavior is an embarrassment to me."

Stephen visibly stiffened. The shocked disapproval on his face almost made her falter.

She kept her expression hard and called out, "Linnet!"

On cue, Linnet came quietly into the room. The girl played her part to perfection. She stood, eyes cast down, tears rolling down her cheeks.

"You and your brother are leaving with me," Stephen said. Lips pressed together, he grabbed Linnet by the wrist and charged out. At the door, he turned to cast a scorching look at Isobel that nearly knocked her from her feet.

The hall was silent, save for the muffled sound of retreating footsteps. De Roche stood, mouth agape, staring after them. It happened so quickly he had no time to object—or to speak at all.

She had done it.

She had saved Linnet and François. They were in Stephen's hands now, and he would protect them. And she had uncovered the plot to murder King Henry. The twins would tell Stephen, and he would warn the king. It was enough.

———

After collecting François, Stephen strode ahead, barely aware of the twins trailing at his heels. Every now and then, Linnet's sobs penetrated his stormy thoughts, and he was angry all over again.

How could she dismiss Linnet so coldly? Little Linnet, who was wholly devoted to her. What she said about Linnet was surely true, but Isobel was always patient and tolerant with the girl before. What happened to her? Was it possible for a woman to change so much in so short a time?

Her new husband provides all the "comfort" she needs!

Comfort, indeed. That remark was meant to cut him to the quick. It had.

He did not notice until he reached the Palais that François and Linnet had fallen behind.

"Sorry, we could not keep up," François said as they caught up to him on the steps. It was not François, whose legs were nearly as long as Stephen's, who could not keep up.

Stephen's blood was still pounding in his ears. He took a deep breath in an attempt to calm himself. "I apologize, Linnet. Come, we shall go to my room now."

Linnet blew her nose loudly and half coughed, half sobbed. Stephen narrowed his eyes at her—something was not quite right here. Deciding not to press her at the entrance, where anyone could be watching, he led the way to his room.

The servant assigned to watch him was frantic. "Where did you go, sir? You should have told me—"

"Be gone until morning," Stephen said as he shoved the man out of the room, "or I shall tell them how easy it was to slip by you."

As soon as he slammed the door, Linnet threw her arms up and danced around the room. "Was I not wonderful? You did not guess! François, you should have seen his face! And de Roche's!"

He clenched his fists to keep from strangling the girl.

"How could you believe Isobel would throw me out?" Linnet asked, rolling her eyes at him.

"Tell me the reason for this farce," he demanded.

In the blink of an eye, Linnet's face changed from delighted self-congratulation to anguish. "Isobel sent me away so I could tell you that de Roche and his cousin are plotting to kill King Henry."

What? His head was spinning. "How does she know this?"

"By spying on de Roche, of course," Linnet said.

Stephen sat down and closed his eyes. Alone, without a friend in this city, Isobel was spying on de Roche while living in his house? He shook his head. "What can she be thinking?"

"She is only doing her duty," Linnet said.

"Is Isobel quite certain of this plot?"

Linnet nodded. "Aye, she found a letter from his cousin in a locked drawer."

God help her, she was taking chances!

"The cousin writes that all is set to murder the king in church upon some grand occasion."

Murder the king! He stopped to think. "I wonder if they mean to do it at the knighting at Easter..."

"That is what Isobel believes," Linnet said. "And she says the cousin is Georges de la Trémoille, because the letter is signed 'T.'"

Stephen nodded, his thoughts on Isobel. "But why did Isobel devise that ruse to send you away? Surely she could have found another way to get a message to me."

Linnet's fair skin went red, and she would not meet his eyes. Stephen turned and raised an eyebrow at François.

Blushing as fiercely as his sister, François stepped next to him and whispered, "As we were walking here, Linnet told me de Roche was...that he was...after her. She thinks Lady Hume used the message as an excuse to get her away from him."

God's blood. Stephen wanted to kill the man with his bare hands.

François straightened and said, "She is right to trust you to protect my sister."

But who would protect Isobel when de Roche discovered the games she was playing? What could Stephen do now that she was living with the man? Nothing! Nothing at all. She was de Roche's wife now, beyond his reach.

He must go quickly to warn the king. Easter was still two weeks away, but men would begin arriving sooner. The conspirators could be in Caen any day, ready to act. He swallowed hard at the thought of leaving Isobel, of perhaps never seeing her again. Still, he had to go. He could not let his king be murdered.

But how could he leave her?

His thoughts were interrupted by a knock at the door.

It was one of the Palais guards. "This young woman says you arranged a...meeting...with her." The man waggled his eyebrows and jerked his thumb behind him.

Before Stephen could protest, a stunning woman with smoky dark eyes emerged from behind the guard. In a voice rich with unspoken promises, she said, "Claudette sent me."

Stephen winked at the guard. "Claudette knows the best."

He put his arm around the woman and let his hand slip down to squeeze her nicely rounded bottom as he pulled her inside. With another wink and a grin, he tossed a gold coin to the guard and kicked the door closed.

He moved his hand to the woman's arm and guided her to a seat. With languid ease, the woman sank into the chair.

Linnet was scowling at him furiously.

"My name is Sybille," the woman said in her sultry voice.

"You are a friend of Claudette's?"

The woman nodded. "I've just come from Paris, where I saw her. She asked me to carry some news to you. Something she thought you should know."

An hour later, Stephen walked her to the door.

"Thank you, Sybille," he said. "I hope coming here has not put you at risk."

The woman shrugged her shoulders and gave him an unconcerned smile. "The guards know me. I have visited important guests at the Palais before."

Stephen reached into the pouch at his belt, wondering how much a woman like this cost.

Sybille put her hand over his and shook her head. "I owe Claudette a favor."

She ran her tongue over her top lip and leaned forward until her breasts were a hair's breadth from his chest. She smelled divine.

"Since it is a very big favor I owe her, I could..."

"I appreciate the offer, and you are breathtaking," he said, putting his hand to his heart, "but I cannot."

She gave a soft laugh. "You made me lose my wager with Claudette."

With a saucy wink at François that made the boy blush crimson to his ears, Sybille went out the door, hips swaying.

Stephen sat down to think. What the courtesan told him changed everything.

Chapter Thirty-two

Stephen donned his showy clothes—the heavy gold belt, particolored hose, and all the rest—for his grand departure. He had no choice but to leave the city. A dozen heavily armed men waited outside to make sure he did.

Guy le Bouteiller, the garrison commander, rode beside Stephen to the gate. Stephen liked le Bouteiller and was glad for the opportunity to have a few words with him.

"I am flattered," Stephen said, glancing at the column of men armed to the teeth, "but how much trouble do you think these two children and I could cause on our way to the gate?"

"'Tis not what you would do that concerns me," le Bouteiller said, returning the smile. "Let's just say there are men in Rouen who might wish to answer the king of England by returning his envoy without his head."

"I tell you," Stephen said, "an honorable man like you would be happier serving King Henry."

Le Bouteiller did not dispute the point.

Before they parted at the gate Stephen said, "The men of this city make a grave mistake by spurning his peaceful offer."

"Return in a few months," le Bouteiller said in a low voice. "Much could change by then."

"The city should take the generous terms he offers now," Stephen said, not bothering to keep his own voice down. "Next time, King Henry will come himself, and he will bring his army."

With that last warning, Stephen turned his horse. He signaled to the twins to follow and galloped out the city gates.

———

Isobel felt Linnet's absence so keenly in her rooms that she simply had to get out for a little while. She slipped down the stairs, intent on reaching the courtyard unseen. Perhaps everything would not seem so very hopeless in the sunshine.

Seeing Stephen again—and then having him leave her in anger—left her ragged and shaken. Losing the twins at the same time was more than God should ask of her. The gaping hole in her heart would never heal.

After Stephen and Linnet left, de Roche had taken her hand and told her all was settled. As if it still mattered to her. It gave her no comfort to know de Roche was prepared to go through the formalities to finalize their marriage now.

She stepped lightly as she passed the door to de Roche's private parlor. Just when she thought she was safe, the parlor door creaked open behind her.

She closed her eyes and stood perfectly still, wishing him away. Did God hate her so much that he would even deny her an hour of solace in the courtyard? Now she would have to listen to de Roche lecture her about not following his command to wait in her rooms for him.

She had a vision of her life constantly alternating between terror and tedium. Pride had led her to this. She would have been better off in her father's care than under the thumb of this tyrant.

He cleared his throat behind her. Slowly, she turned to face him. If she could have drawn breath, she would have screamed. It could not be! The man standing before her was not de Roche, but the black-haired man who had led the attack on the abbey.

She knew she was not mistaken. The distance from gate to church had not been far in the small abbey; the piercing eyes and hawkish face were chiseled in her memory.

With the slightest inclination of his head he said, "I seemed to have startled you, madam."

He did not know her.

"I—I expected Lord de Roche," she said.

His black eyes seemed to go through her. Panic closed her throat as she waited for him to recognize her. Then she remembered: She wore her brother's clothes that day at the abbey. He had no cause to guess the finely dressed lady before him was the same person.

"My name is LeFevre," he said.

She forced herself to offer her hand to the monk killer. When he touched his lips to it, she swallowed the bile that rose in the back of her throat.

"And you, madam, are . . . ?"

"Lady Hume," she said. "Lord de Roche's betrothed."

His eyes widened. "Philippe's betrothed?" He paused, as if expecting her to contradict him, then said, "I shall chastise Philippe for not sharing his good news with me."

She could not remain in his presence a moment longer.

Aware she was making an awkward departure, she gave him a stiff nod and turned back the way she had come. The courtyard would not do now. She wanted a barred door between her and the black-haired man. With his eyes burning into her back, she fought not to break into a run before she turned the corner.

She sat on her window seat, shaking and holding her arms across her belly until she was calm enough to think. LeFevre. LeFevre. Where had she heard the name before?

Then it came to her. One day she overheard Robert and Stephen speaking in low voices about men associated with the Dauphin and the Armagnacs. They mentioned several names before they noticed her and abruptly changed topics.

LeFevre had been one of the names.

So it was the Armagnacs who were behind the attack on FitzAlan and the abbey. What was she doing, sitting here? King Henry was adamant about how important it was for him to have this information. Somehow she had to get to the Palais and tell Stephen before he left the city.

She was reaching for her cloak when she heard angry voices echoing through the courtyard. One of the voices was de Roche's. Whoever was arguing with him could not be a servant, because both of them were shouting.

Damn him! She could not risk attempting to leave the house with de Roche just below. When the shouting faded, she stood on her window seat and leaned out the window. Had they moved into another part of the house? Or were they simply speaking too quietly for her to hear? She would have to take her chances.

No sooner did her feet hit the floor than the solar door banged open with a crash. De Roche filled her doorway.

"My Lord," Isobel said, dipping her head. How would she get to the Palais with him barring her way?

De Roche stood glaring at her with hard, angry eyes. "I thought you would wish to know," he said, his voice slow, taunting, "Carleton has left the city."

Though she tried to cover her reaction, she felt herself pale. *He has left me, he has left me, he has left me,* ran through her head like a chant. She wanted to sink to her knees and cover her face in her hands.

"I must say, Carleton looked rather grim during his visit to our fair city." De Roche walked around the solar, picking up things and setting them down again, as though what he said held little interest to him. "Still, I don't believe it will take him long to forget you."

He made a tutting sound with his tongue. "No time at all. In fact, I'm told he looked considerably more cheerful when he rode out the gates this afternoon. But then, he'd just spent an hour with the highest-priced courtesan in the city." He gave a loud sigh. "Sybille would cheer any man."

A courtesan? Without thinking, she parroted the words Robert once told her: "A man may enjoy a courtesan's company in public without employing her services in private."

Roche laughed aloud, appearing to be genuinely amused. "But he did 'enjoy her company' in private. The hour they spent together was in his bedchamber at the Palais."

"Since Sir Stephen is neither married nor betrothed," she said through her teeth, "he is free to do as he pleases."

De Roche laughed again. "You are mistaken if you think betrothal or marriage will cause a man to forgo other pleasures."

A courtesan. Stephen went to a courtesan right after leaving her.

De Roche cupped her cheek, forcing her attention back to him. "My betrothal will not stop me from taking you."

His words made no sense.

He ran his hands down her arms and encircled her wrists. "You look puzzled, Isobel."

The heat in his eyes told her what he wanted from her. With Linnet safely away, she could try to put him off.

"The banns have not yet been read thrice," she said.

He forced her back until her heels struck the wall. Holding her wrists against the wall on either side of her head, he leaned down until his nose nearly touched hers.

"The banns? The banns?" She felt the moisture of his breath on her face as he spat the words out. "Did you believe I would marry a woman so beneath me?"

He released her and spun away. "Me, a de Roche! I am blood relation to the greatest families of France! My wealth is ten times that of your father's."

Isobel rubbed her wrists as he stormed up and down the room, ranting. She was good and truly frightened now.

"Marriage to you would bring me no titles, no land. A pittance of a dowry. And yet your king thought I should be grateful—" He was so angry he choked on the word. "Grateful, because you are an *English* noblewoman."

He stopped his pacing. A cold stillness settled over him that frightened her more than his ranting. As he started toward her, a shiver ran up her spine.

"I shall make your father pay a ransom three times

the paltry sum he offered as dowry," he said, jabbing the point of his forefinger against her chest. "And while I wait for him to pay it, I shall make you my whore."

"But we are betrothed!" Her voice shook, despite her effort to keep it steady. "I cannot be your...your..."

"My English whore."

Why was he talking ransom and saying such horrid things to her? "You know very well that if you take me to bed, I will be your wife in the eyes of both the church and the law."

"That would be true," he said, speaking slowly, "if I did not already have a wife."

"A wife? You have a wife?" She shook her head from side to side, unable to take it in. "You cannot. It is not possible."

"I assure you, it is. I made a very advantageous match with a young lady whose family is close to the Dauphin. Since her father was not entirely...supportive...of the marriage, we wed in secret shortly before I came to Caen."

"Then why did you come to Caen?"

"What better way to persuade King Henry of my loyalty than to agree to a marriage alliance?" de Roche said with a shrug. "I never intended to go through with it."

She was too shocked to speak.

"Your friend Robert was no more anxious to settle the marriage contract than I, so it was easy to put Henry off." He took a deep breath and shook his head. "I needed but a few weeks more."

"But you made a formal pledge to me," she said. "Before witnesses. Before the king."

"I admit Henry surprised me," he said. "He cornered

me before I had a chance to slip out of Caen. I had no choice but to go through the sham betrothal."

How could any man be so wholly lacking in honor? And she, what had she done?

"Is that not bigamy?" Was it? Was she guilty of the sin, as well? "And what of the other lady? I cannot think she or her family will be pleased with the news of a second betrothal."

"I went to a good deal of trouble to ensure they would not learn of it," he said. "'Tis a shame you told my cousin."

"Your cousin?"

"Aye, you met Thomás today, downstairs." He shook his finger at her. "My cousin is a dangerous man. You should have stayed in your rooms as I told you."

"Thomás? You mean LeFevre? LeFevre is your cousin?" She sucked in her breath. Was Thomás the "T" in the letter? Had she warned the king of the wrong man?

"So many questions, Isobel. Fortunately, it is as much in Thomás's interest as mine to keep the secret." He tilted his head and said, "Still, he is quite angry with me. You see, it is his young half sister who is my wife."

She was reeling from all the revelations. One thought rose above all the others clamoring in her head. If de Roche was married and her betrothal false, *she was not bound to him*.

Roche lifted her chin with his forefinger. "No matter what Thomás says, I shan't give you up soon."

She slapped his face, hard.

He regarded her with icy gray eyes as he touched the red mark she left on his cheek. "Your king has quaint notions of chivalry. Since he told me he would send an envoy—and I could not yet risk offending him—I had to take care with you before."

He took her wrists and held them in an iron grasp in one hand. Then, his expression cool, he swung his other arm and backhanded her so violently that her ears rang.

"But now?" he said. "Now there is nothing to keep me from doing whatever I want with you."

He kissed her hard, bruising her lips and grinding his hips against her. Still stunned from the slap, she did not fight him. When he released her, she fell back against the wall. She focused on the hair's breadth between them and pressed herself against the wall.

"I shall not be able to return to you until late." He rubbed the back of his fingers against her stinging cheek. "I suggest you spend the time thinking of ways to please me."

He gave her cheek a pinch that made her eyes sting before finally turning to go out the door. She heard the key scrape in the lock as she sank to the floor.

How long did she lie there, clutching her knees and shaking so hard her teeth chattered? The room grew pitch-black, and still she could not make herself get up.

How would she bear it? How could she live until her father sent the ransom? Would her father pay it? Or would he leave her here forever? If she went home, it would be in shame—perhaps with de Roche's child in her belly. The blemish on her virtue would be no less for not being her fault.

She pounded her fists on the floor. How could she have mistaken de Roche's stern nature for honorable character? His arrogance for seriousness of purpose? The man was an oath breaker of the worst kind. And he was related by blood—and by marriage—to that monk killer. She could hardly breathe thinking of LeFevre being under the same roof.

As she lay on the floor in the darkness, bits of what de Roche told her floated through her head. Then the bits began to fit together.

Did de Roche know of his cousin's attack on the abbey? God preserve her! Was de Roche the traitor who sent men to ambush FitzAlan that day? Isobel covered her face and rocked her head back and forth against the floor. If he did it, then de Roche was the vilest of men. As vile as his cousin.

A memory came to her of Linnet, eyes bright with anger, slapping a dagger in her hand. Isobel sat up. She would have de Roche's blood before she let him touch her again!

Her thoughts returned to LeFevre as she hurried to light the lamps. If Thomás LeFevre was the "T" who signed the letter, then he was the cousin involved in the plot to murder the king, not Trémoille. Would Trémoille's head be on a pike because of her false accusation?

She stood stock still. If she had the wrong man, she could have everything else wrong, as well. She thought the murder was planned for the knighting ceremony only because of Trémoille. Armagnacs, however, would choose some other occasion—and the king would have no warning.

To have any hope of saving the king, she must first save herself. Somehow she had to escape from the house and steal a horse. Once she got out of the house, she would figure out how to get to Caen.

After trying the locked door, she jumped onto the

window seat and leaned out the window. She might just be able to reach the top branches of the tree and climb down. If she did not break her neck, she could escape through the house from the courtyard.

She needed her weapons. She ran to her chest and tossed gowns and slippers to the floor until she found her daggers. Then, through the layers at the very bottom, her fingers touched the scabbard of her sword.

When she leaned down to strap a dagger to her calf, she caught sight of dull brown in the midst of the colorful silks and velvets heaped on the floor. Her brother's tunic! She would be far less conspicuous traveling as a man than as a silk-clad noblewoman.

She slid her sword into the narrow space between the mattress and the frame of her bed for safekeeping while she changed. It was out of sight but within easy reach, should de Roche return before she was ready.

The blade of her dagger served as lady's maid. One long stroke and she stood naked, the cold sweat of fear on her skin. Moving swiftly, she donned her brother's shirt, hose, tunic. Then she rammed her feet into her boots and hooked one dagger into her belt. As she slid the other dagger into her boot, she heard voices outside the door.

There was no time! Heart in her throat, she dashed into the solar and leapt onto the window seat. She heard the muffled rattle of keys as she heaved herself up onto the window ledge. She had one leg dangling outside before she realized she'd left her sword behind. Damn, damn, damn!

She heard the soft *click, click* of the key turning the lock. Heart thundering, she swung her other leg over the ledge. She peered through the darkness, trying desperately to judge the distance to the nearest branch. It looked much farther than before.

The door scraped against the floor.

"God's blood!"

De Roche's voice rang out behind her as she pushed off, flinging her arms out. She grasped at leaves and branches as she fell crashing through the tree. For a moment she hung, suspended in the air, clinging by the fingers of one hand to a spindly branch. It snapped, and she fell again.

"Ooof!" The breath was knocked out of her as she landed on her stomach on a thick lower branch.

De Roche was shouting above her for help. Since most the servants were abed, she still might have time to escape. Circling her arms around the branch, she slid over the side, hoping to hang down and drop safely. Her palms stung from being scraped. Before she was ready, her hands let go.

Arms and legs flailing, she fell the last few feet to the ground. She tasted blood and dirt. Squeezing her eyes shut against the throbbing pain in her ribs, she dragged herself up to her hands and knees. The next thing she knew, her feet were dangling in the air.

"I cannot breathe," she squeaked to the man holding her up by the collar.

"Lady Hume?" the man said, surprise in his voice. "I thought you were an intruder."

A cold chill of fear swept through her. The man holding her was Thomás LeFevre.

He set her down so that her feet rested on the ground, but he did not release his hold.

"Send the servants back to bed and wait there," he

called up to de Roche. "I shall bring you what fell out of the window."

Turning back to her, he said, "I take it you were as displeased as I to learn of my cousin's duplicity."

He must think she jumped because she learned of de Roche's prior marriage. Thank God, neither man had reason to suspect she knew about the murder plot!

Isobel tried to clear her head. Though shaken and bruised, she was not seriously injured. She must try to get away before LeFevre took her upstairs. However poor her chances, they were better with one man than two. She must choose her moment carefully.

LeFevre stood behind her, calm but alert, his hands resting on her shoulders as if he were a friend or lover. It was odd, both of them waiting and listening. The sounds of voices and people moving about the house gradually subsided. One by one, the rooms on the courtyard went dark, save for her solar.

LeFevre clamped a hand over her mouth and pulled her roughly to the doorway. Isobel grabbed the doorframe with both hands and tried to scream. Barely breaking his stride, he jerked her hands free. She struggled against him, kicking and biting as he dragged her relentlessly up the stairs.

When they reached her solar, LeFevre kicked the door open. He hauled her across the room and shoved her into the bedchamber. She fell sprawling across the floor. When she looked behind her, alarm pulsed through her. Both LeFevre and de Roche were staring at her.

"I've never seen a woman clad in men's leggings before," de Roche said, examining her from head to toe. "I shall have to ask you to wear them for me again."

She could not defend herself against both of them. But if she waited until the last minute to pull her knife, she might succeed in killing the first who tried to touch her.

De Roche took a step toward her. Fine. It would be he who felt her blade. He deserved to die at her hand.

"Wait!" LeFevre put his arm out to stop de Roche.

That was not lust in LeFevre's eyes. Still, his penetrating gaze frightened her even more than de Roche's.

"Pull your hood up and push your hair into it," LeFevre ordered her. "Do it now, or I shall do it for you."

If he took hold of her, she could lose her chance to pull her knife. She did as she was told.

LeFevre narrowed his eyes. Then his expression cleared, as if he found the answer to a question that had been puzzling him.

"She was with FitzAlan at the abbey," LeFevre said.

"What?" de Roche said. "How could she?"

"She was there, dressed as she is now," LeFevre said in a flat tone. "And she saw me."

De Roche started to speak again, but LeFevre cut him off. "You recognized me from the first, when we met outside the parlor," LeFevre said to Isobel. "It was a mistake for me to dismiss the fear I saw in your eyes."

"What shall we do?" de Roche asked, the edge of panic in his voice. "We cannot have our involvement in the abbey attack known. The Dauphin would distance himself from us without a second thought."

LeFevre's black eyes never left Isobel's face.

"We shall have to kill her, of course."

Chapter Thirty-three

When do we sneak back to get Isobel?" Linnet asked.

Stephen sat with the twins and Jamie at a simple wooden table in the abbey guesthouse. While the other men were preparing to ride, he was giving Jamie a brief recounting of events and advising him of his plan.

"*You* are not going, Linnet." He wished he did not have to take François, either, but he needed the boy's help to get into de Roche's house. Damn, damn, damn.

Ignoring Linnet's glower, he told Jamie, "I shall go back into the city after dark."

"How many of us do you want to go with you?" Jamie asked.

"François and I will go alone. I need you to lead the men back to Caen."

When Jamie started to object, Stephen held up his hand. "This is a command, Jamie. The king must be warned of the murder plot without delay. He needs to know of the Burgundians' treachery. I shall follow as soon as I am able."

How he would manage to get to Caen with Isobel and François he did not know. He would worry about that after he got Isobel out of de Roche's house.

Jamie seemed resigned. Within a quarter hour, he had the men mounted and ready. Linnet was another story. Lips pressed tightly together, she refused even to bid Stephen and François good-bye before riding off with the men.

Stephen changed into his regular clothes and wiped mud onto his and François's boots to give the illusion of long travel. At dark, they mounted and headed toward the city. A cold wind picked up with nightfall, giving them excuse to draw their hoods low and wrap their capes close about them as they approached the gates.

If the men at the gate thought the merchant on the fine horse unwise to travel outside of the city accompanied by a single servant, they did not bother telling him.

"Once you get me inside the house, come back and wait for me near the gate," Stephen told François. "We need to make a plan for you in case I do not return."

Stephen ran a hand over his face and tried to think. Damn, damn, damn. "I wish I knew one soul in this wretched city I could trust," he muttered half aloud.

"What about Madame...er, Sybille?"

Stephen rolled his eyes heavenward. Lord above, was this wise? The courtesan had something else in mind when she whispered her address in Stephen's ear. Nonetheless, he had it.

"If I do not return by dawn, her house is on Rue St. Romain next to the small church," he said. "Sybille can get a message to Robert, and he will figure out how to get you back to Caen."

They took a circuitous route to the narrow lane that abutted the back of de Roche's house and stables. Then Stephen hid in the shadows with the horses while François called out at the gate.

"'Bout time you showed your face, boy."

The gruff greeting was followed by the creak of the gate. Luck was with them—the man had not been informed François was no longer in de Roche's service. Stephen eased his grip on his sword.

"You been gadding about the town again when you're s'posed to be working?" the gruff voice continued.

"Of course!" François said. "How else would I have stories to tell you? I've brought you a flask of wine, as well."

The man's laugh rang out in the darkness. "Come in, then, you rascal." Their voices faded as the gate clanked closed.

François was in.

Stephen paced up and down the dark lane, wondering how long he would have to wait. François said the man would be well into his cups by this hour. The waiting seemed endless.

Would he find Isobel alone? God, please, he did not want to find her in bed with de Roche.

Killing de Roche would be satisfying, to be sure. But not in front of Isobel. She would suffer shock enough when he told her the news Sybille brought. After hearing whispers in Paris of de Roche's secret marriage, Claudette confirmed it with de Roche's mother, of all people. Stephen knew he would have to tell Isobel to convince her to leave with him.

When the gate creaked again, every muscle of Stephen's body tensed. The outline of a figure appeared, leaning out the gate.

"Stephen," François called out softly into the darkness. When Stephen joined him at the gate, François said,

" 'Tis safe. He's drunk as a bishop. He'll not wake 'til morning."

"Good work." Stephen squeezed François's shoulder as he slipped through the gate. "Let us hurry."

"The door into the house from the stable yard is not locked," François said in a hushed voice as they trotted across the yard. "But Isobel's rooms are at the top of the house. I can show you from the courtyard."

Stephen touched the rope wound around his waist. It would be safest to bring her down from the window; the less time the two of them spent walking through the house, the better.

"No talking inside," Stephen warned when they reached the door. "As soon as you show me which window is hers, leave for the city gate."

Stephen barely heard the soft click and swish of the door. François had a talent for this. Once inside, François led Stephen down a short corridor and around a corner. He stopped in front of a large window and eased a shutter open to reveal a square courtyard of perhaps fifteen feet across. An overgrown tree filled the small space.

He heard a shout from the lit window above as something fell crashing through the tree.

"Get out, now!" he said to François. When the boy did not move, Stephen took hold of the back of his cloak and turned him around. "Go!" he said, giving François a shove in his back.

Dear God, those were Isobel's screams echoing off the walls of the courtyard!

Stephen spun around. He was halfway out the window before he saw the man standing in the shadows. Another man was leaning out of the window above, bellowing his head off. It was all Stephen could do to make himself wait.

When the man in the courtyard pulled Isobel roughly to her feet, Stephen clenched his jaw so hard his teeth ached. He decided he would kill this man before he left the house tonight.

"Send the servants back to bed and wait there," the man called up. "I shall bring you what fell out of the window."

Good. Better to have the servants abed when he and Isobel made their escape.

When the man in the window turned his head to bark orders at someone behind him, Stephen recognized de Roche's ridiculous pointed goatee. But who was the man in the courtyard? Not a servant. The voice was cultured, used to command. He thought he'd heard it before, but where?

The man was experienced; he did not lose patience and move too soon. Instead, the devil's spawn waited until the rooms went dark and the voices stilled before dragging Isobel into the house. At least Isobel was not badly injured from the fall. She was scratching and kicking like a madwoman.

What a woman! Jumping out the window!

She must have learned about de Roche's wife.

Stephen followed them up two sets of stairs. With Isobel struggling at every step, the man did not once look behind him. At the top, the man kicked a door open and carried Isobel inside.

The door closed behind them. Damn.

Stephen padded up the last steps and pressed his ear to the door. The two men were talking. He could not make out the words, but something in their tone had the hair on the back of his neck standing up.

Stephen drew his sword from its scabbard. Though de Roche was a skilled swordsman, he was not as good as he thought he was. His arrogance would lead him to make a mistake.

The other man worried Stephen more. If he had a choice, Stephen would take him first. Having made his plan, such as it was, Stephen eased the door open with his boot.

Nothing happened. He nudged it a few inches wider. Now he could see the room—a small solar—was empty. The voices were coming from the adjoining room.

Stephen stepped lightly across the room and pressed himself against the wall next to the open door. He could hear more clearly now. De Roche was saying something about an attack on an abbey. An abbey? Could de Roche—

As the other man spoke, Stephen's speculations came to a jarring halt. His words turned Stephen's blood to ice.

"We shall have to kill her, of course."

Stephen stormed through the door.

In that first instant, he saw where each person in the room stood in relation to him and to each other. Isobel was farthest away, her back to the bed. Though her face was scratched, the fire in her eyes told him she had her wits about her. Thank God. De Roche was two steps from Isobel.

Fortune placed the other man closest to Stephen. A black-haired man.

"Stephen," Isobel called out, "he is the one who attacked the abbey."

"You blasphemous pig, murdering unarmed holy men,"

Stephen spat out as their swords clanked together. "I shall send you to the devil!"

Stephen thrust his sword toward the man's heart. At the last instant, the man leapt to the side. He was right to worry more about this one than de Roche. Still, he would take the man.

From the corner of his eye, he saw de Roche take a step forward to join the fight. The fool had his back to Isobel. She was already reaching for her dagger. Stephen wanted to shout at her not to take the risk, but his warning would draw de Roche's attention to her.

Stephen whirled around to parry behind his back. While the wild stunt did keep both men's eyes on him, the black-haired man's sword nearly caught him. Stephen felt the blade slash the back of his tunic as he spun out of the way.

De Roche screamed and threw his arms up, arching his back. Eyes bulging and mouth agape, he looked caught between shock, outrage, and agony. God's blood, Stephen hoped it was a death blow. If not, the man would turn on Isobel with a vengeance.

Damn, he needed to finish this monk killer and help her. But the man was good. Too good. De Roche's scream reverberating in the small room did not distract him.

The man did not even flinch.

Their swords flew in a blur of movement as they parried and thrust back and forth. Stephen worked his way closer to Isobel. When de Roche turned and staggered toward Isobel, Stephen gave de Roche a kick that sent him sprawling at her feet.

"Isobel, here!" He tossed his short blade onto the bed and shouted at her, "Kill him now! While he is down!"

Stephen dropped to the floor. As he rolled, he felt the wind from the blade passing over his head. It would do Isobel no good to kill de Roche if he let this son of Satan get the better of him. She stood no chance against a man as skilled as this.

With Stephen on the floor, his opponent committed fully to his thrust, believing it to be the final one. Stephen sprang to his feet, sword forward. Before his opponent could recover and withdraw, Stephen slashed the man's sword arm.

The man did not spare a glance at the blood soaking his sleeve. The wound was not fatal, but his eyes held a fury that might serve, as well. Rage could cloud a man's judgment and make him rash.

Not so with Stephen. His anger was hard and cold. It sharpened his senses and focused his mind.

He pressed the worthless scum, attacking again and again and again, until he pushed him into a corner. His opponent had no room to maneuver, no means to escape Stephen's sword. Stephen saw his opening. Right through to the heart, in one swift thrust. Just as he was poised to deliver the piercing blow, Isobel cried out behind him.

Stephen fell a half step back and took a quick look over his shoulder. Sweet Lamb of God! Isobel's chest was covered in blood! The breath went out of him.

De Roche was sliding down her body to the floor, leaving a swath of blood. Isobel stood, a bloodied knife raised in her hand. The blood was de Roche's. Not hers, praise God! The realization took no more than an instant.

But it was time enough for his opponent to knock the sword from his hand.

Stephen backed up slowly, one step at a time. For a certainty, he could not save himself. What he must do is live long enough after the first blow to take the man with him.

"You cannot save her," the man said with a thin smile, guessing Stephen's intent. "No man is that good."

The man inched forward, backing Stephen closer to the bed and Isobel.

"'Tis a pity I cannot spare her, since she saved me the trouble of killing de Roche," the man said. "I came to regret helping him wed my half sister."

"Odd that bigamy should offend you when murder does not."

"What are a few monks more or less?" the man said, lifting an eyebrow. "I have but one sister, and I would not have her shamed."

Stephen decided how he would do it. He would deflect the sword from his heart with his left arm and grab the dagger from the man's belt with his right. By the time the man brought his sword back, Stephen would be plunging the dagger up under the man's breastbone.

Neither would live, but Isobel would get away.

Stephen took another step back from the point of the man's sword. He felt Isobel just behind him. It was time.

"Your hand," she whispered.

Cautiously, he brought one arm to his side. When her hand brushed his, he felt a rush of gratitude. One last touch before he died. He sucked in his breath and prepared to make his move.

Chapter Thirty-four

With LeFevre's attention riveted on Stephen, Isobel side-stepped to the foot of the bed as quickly as she dared. One half step. Then another. And another.

LeFevre closed in slowly, as if approaching a cornered animal that might prove dangerous and unpredictable. The end of the deadly dance was near, and both men knew it.

Isobel slipped her arm under the folds of the half-fallen bed curtain. She reached back between the mattress and the bed frame until she felt it. Cold steel, welcome and familiar.

The mattress held the scabbard in place as she slid the blade free. Under cover of the fallen curtain, she brought the sword to her side. Stephen was so close now she could feel his heat, feel the tension running through him.

And then she knew, as clearly as if he said it aloud. Stephen was about to sacrifice himself to save her.

"Your hand," she whispered.

When the side of his hand brushed hers, she pressed the hilt of the sword against it.

Stephen moved so fast then, she did not even see him strike. But LeFevre was falling, mouth open in surprise, the telltale spot of blood over his heart. His head made a dull thud as it hit the floor.

Stephen whirled around and crushed her against him.

Like a rushing river, the terror she had held at bay flooded through her. She buried her face in his shoulder.

"I thought you were gone," she whispered.

His arms tightened around her. "I could not leave you."

She drew in a deep breath. His familiar smell comforted her. Wrapped in the strength of his arms, she felt safe for the first time since leaving Caen. Safe. She was safe at last.

Much too soon, he pulled away.

Stephen's face was strained, but he gave her a small smile. "You must be brave a little longer. Someone may have heard us. We must be gone."

She straightened and nodded. This was no time for weakness. When she felt the chill of wetness and looked down, she faltered. Her shirtfront was soaked with de Roche's blood.

"I will give you a clean shirt when we are out." Using the torn curtain, Stephen wiped the blood from her face and neck. Then he kissed her forehead and squeezed her hand.

"I have horses waiting outside," Stephen said and handed her sword to her.

"That is—was—de Roche's cousin, Thomás LeFevre," she said, pointing to the other body on the floor. "The letter was from him, not Trémoille."

Stephen wiped his dagger clean of de Roche's blood and stuck it in his belt.

"We must warn the king," she said as he led her into

the solar. "Others may go forward with the plot. They are Armagnacs, so it will not happen at the Easter knighting, as I believed."

By this time, Stephen had unwound a rope from his waist and fastened one end of it to the bench under the window. He handed her the other dagger, cleaned of blood.

"We'll talk later," he said and lifted her onto the bench.

Isobel held on to Stephen as he instructed. Hand over hand, he took her down the rope. As soon as her feet touched the ground, he took her hand and led her from the courtyard into the house. It was pitch-black inside.

Relief flooded through her as she stepped out the door to the stable yard. They made it! She saw the outline of horses in the shadows by the gate.

Wait, was there a rider on one of the horses? She tightened her grip on Stephen's hand. He cursed under his breath but did not slow his pace.

When they reached the horses, he said in a harsh whisper, "I told you to wait at the city gates!"

"I heard the shouts and thought you would need me."

François! She wanted to weep for joy at hearing the boy's voice. Before she could run to him, Stephen lifted her onto a horse. In another moment, the three of them were out the gate and trotting down a narrow lane away from the house.

"We must stop at the house on Rue St. Romain," Stephen said to François. "'Tis on the way."

She saw the gleam of François's teeth in the dark and wondered what on earth could make him smile tonight. And why Stephen would take the risk of stopping somewhere.

They rode down back streets, with François leading and Stephen at the rear keeping watch to see that no one followed.

When they drew their horses up before the door of an elegant house, François piped up, "Let me get her for you."

Stephen said, "Stay here and keep quiet."

Stephen spoke in undertones to the servant who answered the door. A short time later, a woman appeared. Her long, fair hair fell loose over a red silk robe. As she drew Stephen inside, her husky laugh drifted through the night air.

"Who is that?" Isobel whispered to François.

"A friend of Madame Champdivers."

A "friend" of Marie's! Despite all his other lies, had de Roche spoken the truth about Stephen and the beautiful courtesan? What hold did the woman have on Stephen that he would come here now, in the midst of their escape?

"She is very, very beautiful," François said with a sigh.

The door opened again, casting a wedge of light on the narrow street. As Stephen kissed the woman's cheek, Isobel saw her press a pouch into his hand. Without a word of explanation, he mounted his horse and signaled for François to lead.

Isobel should have expected the city gates to be barred at this late hour. Still, her bowels turned liquid when the guards came out of the gatehouse, weapons drawn.

"My good fellows!" Stephen called out. He held a hand up in a calming gesture as he dismounted.

After a brief exchange, Stephen held up the pouch the

woman had given him and swept his arm toward the other men circled about them. Then he shook the pouch into the outstretched hand of one of the guards. Glittering coins overflowed the man's palm and spilled onto the ground.

When the guard grabbed Stephen's shoulder, Isobel broke out in a cold sweat.

What? Were they laughing? The guard pounded Stephen on the back as if they were old friends sharing a merry joke. Soon the other guards were snickering and snorting, as well.

Stephen's voice grew louder and she caught a few words. "...then the Englishman said, 'Why do you think we raise so many sheep? For wool?' "

Good heavens, Stephen was telling them jokes! Obscene jokes, from the sound of it. After another round of laughter, Stephen remounted his horse, and the men opened the gate just wide enough for them to ride through single file. They departed the city amid calls of "baa baa" and a spate of good-natured obscenities.

Stephen turned and waved as they headed down the dark road.

"How did you do that?" Isobel asked.

"Night-guard duty is dull work, and the men are always grateful for a few jokes," Stephen said. "But it was the coins that opened the gate. The guards' job is to keep attackers out of the city; they can see no harm in taking a little silver to let someone out."

Isobel suspected Stephen had not been nearly as confident the guards would let them pass as he pretended.

"They will be repeating those awful jokes for hours," he said. "With luck, that will divert them until we are well away."

"When those guards came out, I imagined your head on a pike," she said. "And I would wager you did, as well."

"Aye," he said. "And you imprisoned, guarded by an ugly hunchback who gives you lewd looks."

François burst into laughter, but Isobel was thoughtful.

"We will camp in those woods for the rest of the night," Stephen said, pointing into the darkness ahead.

"Where is Linnet?" Isobel asked, guilt-stricken that she did not think of the girl sooner.

"I sent her back to Caen with the men who came with me."

Until this moment, she'd given no thought to the journey back to Caen. They had a long and dangerous road to travel.

But Stephen was here. He would keep them safe.

Chapter Thirty-five

*S*t. Winifred's beard, that was close at the gate! Isobel thought he was joking when he said he imagined her held captive by a hunchback. The image was so real he'd almost forgotten the end of that absurd sheep joke.

Because their lives depended upon it, he carried off the facade of easy bonhomie. But the sweat ran down his back.

And now? He rubbed his hand over his face and cursed himself. Riding through the countryside with no other men-at-arms was an open invitation to the worst kind of trouble.

He felt better as they neared the wood. At least they would be safe here for the night. In the morning, he would watch the road for a large party they might join. It would be a long night for him, keeping watch alone. He might have to tell himself stupid sheep jokes to stay awake.

What was that? It sounded like the snort of a horse coming from the wood. He put out his arm, signaling for the other two to stop. Praise God, they had the sense not to speak.

His head hurt from the strain of listening so hard.

What was that? A rustle of leaves? A footfall? He drew his sword soundlessly and urged his horse forward.

"Stephen? Is that you?" came out of the darkness.

His nephew should be halfway to Caen by now. And yet it was his voice coming from the high grass just off the road.

"Jamie?"

Jamie rose up from the grass, as beautiful to Stephen as Venus rising from the water.

Jamie shouted over his shoulder, "'Tis my uncle!"

Several shadowy figures came out of the trees, calling greetings. The tightness around Stephen's heart eased, and he laughed.

"I see you ignored my orders," he said as he dismounted. He put his arm around his nephew's shoulders. "Thank God you did!"

"In sooth, I never intended to follow them," Jamie said. "If you did not come by morning, I was going to ride into Rouen and get you."

"François! Isobel! Stephen!"

Stephen heard Linnet's shouts as she ran toward them, her fair hair shining in the darkness.

The ride back to Caen was a nightmare. Every hour, Stephen had to weigh the exhaustion of his charges and horses against the need to reach Caen before the king departed for Chartres.

The Armagnac men who controlled the often-mad French king had proposed a secret meeting between the two monarchs at Chartres in just a few days' time. King Henry agreed, since such a meeting could lead to a negotiated end to the conflict. To keep the meeting secret, King Henry would leave his army behind and travel to Chartres with only a small escort.

If the Armagnacs intended to murder King Henry, the rendezvous in Chartres provided them with the perfect opportunity.

Stephen had allowed his group only two or three hours' rest in the wood outside Rouen. This morning, they rose early and rode hard all day. He called a halt tonight only when darkness made riding too dangerous for the horses.

He found Isobel sitting before the crackling fire with Linnet's head in her lap. She looked up as he approached and gave him a weary smile.

"I hate to wake her to finish her supper," she said.

"I'll see she gets an extra portion in the morning." He knelt to lift the girl. "You should sleep, as well. We'll break camp at first light."

It hurt him to see how drawn Isobel's face was.

"I have never been so tired," she said, pushing her hair from her face. "Still, I cannot sleep just yet."

Linnet's arms and legs hung limp against him as he carried her to the blanket she would share with Isobel. When he returned, Isobel was gone. He looked across the fire to where Geoffrey, Jamie, and François were rolling out their blankets.

"She went to the stream to wash," Geoffrey said.

"Watch over Linnet," Stephen ordered, irritated that they let Isobel go alone.

By moonlight, he followed the bank of the stream away from the camp. All day he had wanted to speak with her. But the ride was too strenuous for serious talk, and he had to keep constant watch. Now that he finally had his chance, he was uncertain how to broach the subject with her.

He heard a splash of water and spotted a dark shape squatting at the edge of the stream. He hurried to her and helped her to her feet.

"Isobel, you will freeze to death!" He wrapped his cloak about her and held her until she stopped shivering.

He leaned back to look at her face, but the moonlight was not bright enough to read her expression. Surely she knew what he wanted to say? He took her hands and waited, hoping she might say something to encourage him.

Finally, he simply told her what he wanted: "As soon as we arrive, I want to ask the king's permission for us to marry."

He heard her sharp intake of breath.

"We must act quickly, before the king decides upon another husband for you." He was determined not to let the king outflank him again.

"I thought you understood," she said in a halting voice. "I do not carry your child."

Her words were like a knife to his heart. "You see that as the only reason for us to marry?" Hurt rang in his voice, but he could not help it.

When she did not deny it, he swallowed his pride. "But you still need a husband; de Roche may have given you a child." He kept his voice soft, though the thought of the villain's hands on her wrenched his guts.

"You need not rescue me from that, as well." Her voice was high, tense. "I am in no danger of having his child."

Stephen sagged with relief. God be praised, the vile bastard had not taken her.

Still, the conversation was not going as he had hoped.

"I wish to have you as my wife," he said, belatedly recalling Catherine's advice, "because I love you."

"If that be true," she snapped, "I am sorry for it."

His hopes were like dust in his mouth. Fighting to keep calm, he asked, "Do you not care for me at all?"

"Not care?" Isobel raked her hands through her tangled hair. "If only I did not care! If only I did not love you!"

All the tension and tiredness fell from him. He felt light, happy. All would be well. Isobel loved him!

But when he tried to pull her into his arms, she threw her hands up.

"'Tis because I love you I could not bear the betrayals," she said, backing away.

"How can you think I will betray you?" he said, reaching out to her. "I love you."

"Do you think I do not know about all your women?" she said, her voice rising. "I was there. I saw you every day in Caen."

"I will honor my marriage vows," he said, an edge to his voice. Did she not see how she insulted him?

"One day in Rouen, and you have courtesans giving you money, doing you favors!"

"I can explain about the women—"

"If it is not women, it will be something else." When he tried to speak again, she covered her ears and shouted, "Have I not suffered enough?"

He grabbed one of her hands and pressed it to his heart. "For you, I will be the best man I can be. I want to make you proud of me, to be proud of myself. I will be a good husband, a good father. Isobel, please. Trust me."

"I cannot, I cannot!" She jerked her hand away and ran from him into the darkness.

When he started after her, Geoffrey stepped out of nowhere to block his way.

"Let her go," Geoffrey said with his hand pressed against Stephen's chest.

"But I must tell her—"

"Not now," Geoffrey said, holding his ground. "Not tonight. Can you not see how weary she is?"

But he needed to tell her about the spying so she would understand about the women. "She is upset, I—"

"For heaven's sake, Stephen, she still has the last man's blood on her!"

Stephen shuddered as he recalled the moment he turned and saw her chest drenched in blood.

"She was trying to wash it off," Geoffrey said.

Stephen knew what it was like to be covered in that much blood. Though he gave her a clean shirt and a bucket of water last night, nothing short of a full scrubbing in a steaming hot bath could get the blood out of all the cracks and crevices.

Geoffrey took Stephen's arm and turned him around. "You must give her time to recover."

"You are right, of course," Stephen said, feeling wretched. Less than a day after she escaped rape and murder by her last betrothed, he was pressing her to marry.

"I see more than my sister gives me credit for," Geoffrey said. "Sit down and I will try to help you."

Stephen slumped down beside Geoffrey in the tall, wet grass by the stream. "Does she not believe I love her?" he asked, desperation rising in his throat.

"You concern yourself with the wrong question."

Geoffrey picked up a stone and tossed it into the water. "What Isobel wants to know is, can she trust you? Will you be there when she needs you? Or will you sacrifice her for something you want more?"

Stephen stared at the dark, moving water. He heard the splash of another stone and watched the ripples in the reflected moonlight.

"I was too young to remember our mother before our family's fall from grace," Geoffrey said. "But it was different for Isobel. Both she and our father felt abandoned."

"Isobel told me something of it."

"That loss made their bond closer still," Geoffrey said. "They enjoyed each other's company and liked to do the same things—sword fight, ride fast. She became both companion and the kind of son he wished he had. 'Tis lucky Isobel has a good heart, for our father could not tell her 'nay.' He adored her."

"And still," Stephen said, "he traded her happiness for a chance to have his lands back."

"It devastated her," Geoffrey said, shaking his head. "I worry for her soul, for she has yet to forgive him."

"So, no matter that I love her, she believes I will betray her, too?"

"'Tis worse than that," Geoffrey said.

"Worse?"

"Aye. She loves you."

"How can that be worse?" It was the one thing that gave Stephen hope.

"That is why she is so determined not to marry you," Geoffrey said, patting Stephen's shoulder. "She knows the more she cares, the more you can hurt her."

"Isobel would not throw happiness away for lack of courage," Stephen argued. "Would she?"

"She has courage to spare," Geoffrey said, getting to his feet. "The problem is, she has an equal measure of stubbornness."

Damn! Stephen leaned back on his hands and gazed up at the moon. Somehow he must find a way to convince her she could trust him. But how?

"I suggest you pray," Geoffrey said, above him.

He heard Geoffrey walking through the brush in the direction of their camp.

"Pray without ceasing," Geoffrey called out from the darkness. "That is your best course."

Chapter Thirty-six

Caen Castle was a glorious sight, the distinctive stone of its high walls pink in the light of sunset. At long last! When Stephen finally led his bedraggled group through the gates, one of the king's guards was there waiting for him.

"The king had us watching for you from the towers," the man told him. "You must come at once."

When they reached the Exchequer, Stephen helped Isobel dismount. She was so exhausted, she fell into his arms.

"I cannot see the king like this," Isobel pleaded.

Poor Isobel, she still wore men's clothes. Despite her attempts at washing, she was as filthy as the rest of them.

"I'm sorry, but the king will want to hear of the plot from your own mouth," Stephen told her. "He'll tolerate no delay."

She had dark circles under her eyes and looked so weary he was tempted to carry her. Instead, he fastened her cloak for her and pulled her hood low over her face.

"Now no one will see what you wear," he said, "except the king, and he will not notice."

They were ushered into the king's private parlor behind the great hall. To Stephen's relief, the king was unattended save for Robert, William, and Catherine.

"God be praised you are safe," the king said before Stephen could exchange greetings with the others. "Once we learned de Roche was involved in the attack on the abbey, we feared for you both."

"How did you learn of de Roche's role?" Stephen asked.

The king smiled at Catherine. "Your sister-in-law got it out of Marie de Lisieux."

Catherine smiled back. "I could not let the men risk their virtue by questioning her, could I?"

Stephen gave them a brief recounting of the events in Rouen. The king seemed more intrigued than disturbed by the news of the murder plot. After peppering Stephen with questions, he turned to Isobel.

Stephen was worried. She was swaying on her feet, and the king had to ask her repeatedly to speak up. After she recited the critical letter from "T," the king narrowed his eyes and stared off into the distance.

"The Dauphin is behind it," the king said, rubbing his chin. "He has the most to lose, and this is just the sort of cowardly act he would favor."

"He would not act without key Armagnacs behind him," William said.

"Perhaps not," the king said. "But I doubt King Charles—or that depraved queen of his—had any part in this scheme."

"That would make for awkward relations when you wed their daughter," Robert put in.

The king broke into laughter. "Too true!"

The king's expression grew serious as he turned his attention back to Stephen and Isobel. "I am most grateful for this service and wish to reward you."

Stephen bowed. "'Tis an honor to serve you."

"Lady Hume," the king said, "I owe you a husband."

Damn! Could Henry not give him even a day to get matters settled with Isobel?

Stephen caught Robert's wink and looked to his brother. William's nod confirmed it. They had already spoken to the king on his behalf. Isobel was his.

"I apologize for my first choice of husband," the king said, "but I believe you will be happy with my next."

The king's eyebrows shot up as Isobel fell to the floor at his feet.

"Please, I beg you, sire," Isobel said. "Do not make me do it. If you are grateful for my service, release me from my promise."

The king glared at William and Robert. "You told me she would be pleased."

Robert motioned to the king, urging him to continue.

"Please, do not make me," Isobel wailed and pounded her fist on the floor. "Can I not be left alone!"

"Lady Hume is past exhaustion," Stephen said, ignoring William's signal to be quiet. "Please, sire, can this wait until tomorrow, when she is rested?"

The king gave Stephen a curt nod.

"Thank you, sire," Stephen said.

He made a quick bow and helped Isobel to her feet. As he half carried her out of the hall, he tried to speak to her. She made no response to his entreaties.

William caught up with them at the bottom of the steps. "Lady Hume," he said in a gentle voice as he took her arm. "My wife and I want you to stay with us at our house in the town."

Catherine appeared behind them and pushed Stephen aside to take Isobel's other arm. Without a word to him, husband and wife walked away with the now-placid Isobel between them.

William turned to give Stephen an exasperated look over his shoulder. As if the scene inside had been his fault! Stephen clenched his fists in frustration.

He felt a hard thump on his back and turned to find Robert standing beside him on the steps.

"That did not go as well as we had hoped," Robert said. "Did you not realize the king has chosen you to be her husband?"

"I guessed as much." Stephen sank to the bottom step and rested his head on his arms. It was all too much. He was bone weary. "But I could not take her like that."

"Come, come," Robert said, settling down next to him. "Isobel thought the king was marrying her off to another scum like Hume or de Roche. Who could blame her for objecting?"

"She does not want to marry me."

"Isobel will come around, once she realizes how much she cares for you."

"She says she loves me," Stephen said without lifting his head from his arms. "It does not help my cause."

Chapter Thirty-seven

*I*sobel could not breathe! De Roche's hands were around her throat, squeezing with a ferocious strength as he leaned her backward over the bed.

"You! You!" he croaked, his eyes bulging.

Panic surged through her, giving her the strength to do what she should have done before. With one sweep of her arm, she brought the double-edged blade across his throat.

For one horrifying moment, de Roche hovered above her, gushing blood like a fountain. Blood splattered her face, soaked her shirt, and ran in rivulets down the sides of her neck. Then de Roche collapsed against her, trapping her against the bed. He was so heavy! Gagging convulsively, she fought to push him off.

Isobel sat up in bed, her heart racing.

A dream. This time, it was a dream.

Gingerly, she touched her fingertips to her chest to be sure. The cloth was dry. She looked down and let her breath out when she saw the clean white shift.

De Roche and LeFevre were dead. She was safe.

She heard a door scrape, and her hand flew to her throat.

"Lady Hume?" a cheerful voice called out. "Are you awake?"

Isobel pulled the bed curtain back as a plump older woman entered the room carrying a steaming tray.

"Feeling better today?" the maid asked over her shoulder as she set the tray on a table near the door.

"I am, thank you," Isobel answered. "Did I sleep long?"

"A full night and day, m'lady," the maid said with a laugh. As she came toward the bed, she pinched her brows together. "Tsk, tsk, those are nasty bruises."

Isobel dropped her hand from her throat.

"Such a tired lamb! You gave me quite a turn, you did, falling fast asleep in the tub."

"You scrubbed the blood from my fingers," Isobel said, remembering.

She was so grateful she could have kissed the woman. For two days, every time she looked down at her hands on the reins, she saw de Roche's blood crusted under her nails. She couldn't get it off, washing in the dark with no soap.

How could Stephen and the king speak to her of marriage when she still had de Roche's blood on her boots and leggings and matted in her hair?

"I would have let you rest longer," the maid said, "but your brother has come to take you to the king."

"To the king?" It felt as if she had just left him.

She closed her eyes. Damn that old fool Hume! If he'd not been taken in by Bartholomew Graham's lies, none of this would have happened. She would never have met de Roche, she would not have had to kill anyone, and she would not have bruises on her throat. She would be living peacefully in Northumberland, running her household.

What would be her fate now? That a marriage alliance had failed to ensure de Roche's loyalty would not deter the king from trying again. Which French nobleman did King Henry wish to bind to him now?

Or would it be Stephen? Could he convince the king? If he did, what would she do?

She would agree. Of course, she would.

How long would it be before he broke her heart? A few weeks? Six months? A year? Regardless, she would rather be unhappy with him than be with another man. If God were kind, she would have children to comfort her.

An hour later, she entered the Exchequer hall. Her heart dropped to her feet when she saw that Stephen was not there.

She stood before the king, once again waiting to hear her fate. Geoffrey and Robert stood on either side of her.

Where was Stephen? If he wished to claim her, surely he would be here. Perhaps he had already spoken to the king, and it was all settled.

"I hope you have recovered sufficiently to discuss your future," the king said, kindly enough.

Isobel flushed, recalling how she had flung herself at his feet, begging. She as much as told the king he owed her a debt of service—and how he should repay it. She never would have done it if she had not been utterly exhausted.

"I leave Caen at dawn and want to settle this matter before I leave," the king said, unrolling a parchment in his hands.

She turned her head to see if Stephen had come in.

"I have a letter from my uncle, Bishop Beaufort."

Bishop Beaufort! Had he not caused her enough grief?

"He spoke to your father about increasing your dowry."

Why? What were they planning now? How many times must she suffer the choices of men who held power over her? She was sick to death of the decisions they made on her behalf.

"The bishop prevailed upon your father to increase your dowry to a handsome sum."

She could imagine Bishop Beaufort "prevailing upon" her recalcitrant father. If she were not so tense, she might be amused.

"Your Highness, if I may?" her brother said. When the king nodded, Geoffrey said, "Our father will increase her dowry further when he learns I am joining the Cistercian order."

Isobel tried to smile at her brother. Though it was an unlikely choice for an only son, she was happy for him.

"I admire the Cistercians' devotion to poverty, prayer, and arduous labor," the king said. "Your father should be proud."

Ha! The king might hear their father's shouts all the way from Northumberland when he heard the news.

"'Tis a shame the dowry won't be needed now," the king said, shaking his head. "I am releasing you from your promise to marry a man of my choosing."

"Your Highness?" Isobel was too stunned to be sure she heard him correctly.

"If you will not take a husband, you must have an income," the king said. "So I'm granting you the Hume property, as well."

She blinked at him. "But the Hume lands belong to Bartholomew Graham now."

"Graham was caught consorting with Scottish rebels," the king said. "So the bishop confiscated the lands for the crown."

She stared at him. Was it possible?

"I intended to give the property to your new husband as a wedding gift," the king said, frowning.

Isobel felt dizzy. The Hume lands were hers, at long last. It was what she'd waited for all these years. Never again would she suffer the humiliation of being sold like cattle for land or political need. She could run her own household, dependent on no man.

Quite suddenly, she was struck by the loneliness of the life before her. The life she had prayed for since she was a girl of thirteen.

"Surely this is the best of news," Geoffrey said as he led her out of the hall.

"Aye, the best," she murmured.

She could not remember if she thanked the king. Or made the proper curtsy before leaving his presence.

"You look pale," Robert said on her other side. "Are you unwell?"

She turned to look at him. "Do you think the twins would go to England with me?"

Robert made a face and shook his head. "'Tis best they stay here. Sooner or later, a relative is bound to turn up and claim them. Until then, I'll look after them."

She was unaware they had left the castle grounds until they stood before the door to FitzAlan's house.

"I would like to be alone now," she said.

"But the FitzAlans are waiting to hear your news," Robert said.

"They have been so kind," Geoffrey added, "surely you can visit with them for a little while?"

She nodded, knowing her brother was right.

"The family is expecting you," the servant at the door told them. "They are in the solar."

"Thank you," Robert said. "We can find our own way."

"The king has released me to escort you home to Northumberland," Geoffrey said as they went up the stairs. "You will need to say your good-byes to the Fitz-Alans soon."

Isobel felt the prick of tears at the back of her eyes. She'd become fond of the FitzAlans, especially Jamie.

"You've visitors!" Robert called out as they reached the top of the stairs. He stepped aside to let Isobel enter the solar first.

She stopped dead at the threshold. Leaning against the wall opposite, arms folded across his chest, was Stephen Carleton. Long and lean and perfect. When he turned and met her eyes, the breath went out of her.

The sad, sweet smile he gave her as he came to greet her made her insides go soft. When he touched his lips to the back of her hand, she had to close her eyes against the wave of emotion that washed through her.

"We must let Robert and Geoffrey come in," he said in a soft voice.

She moved on stiff legs as he drew her away from the doorway. The warmth of his hand on her arm was so comforting, she longed to rest her head against his shoulder.

She stood mute as Robert and Geoffrey told the others of her good fortune. No one showed surprise at the news.

"So, you shall be a wealthy landowner in your own

right," Lord FitzAlan said with false heartiness. Despite his words of congratulation, the look he gave her was full of sympathy.

"You will return to England soon?" Lady Catherine's voice, unlike her husband's, was cold, and her eyes were angry.

"Aye, we will," Geoffrey answered for her.

"We go home ourselves," FitzAlan said. "Perhaps we can travel together as far as London."

"I am leaving, as well," Stephen said beside her.

The tightness that had been around Isobel's heart like a vise eased a bit. She would not have to say good-bye to Stephen until they reached London, and that would take at least a week.

"You travel to England?" Robert's tone was casual, as if this were a matter of little concern. "To Northumberland to claim the Carleton lands?"

Northumberland! Why, they would journey together for two or three weeks. If Stephen remained in Northumberland, she might even see him at gatherings from time to time.

"I stay to fight with the king," Stephen said. "I am taking command of William's men."

Isobel's stomach gave a lurch.

"I must bid you all adieu now," Stephen said. "We march at dawn."

March? At dawn? Isobel felt herself sway on her feet.

As Stephen left her side, she felt a rush of cold where his hand had rested on her arm.

Stephen and FitzAlan slapped each other's backs.

"I know you will watch over Jamie for us," FitzAlan said and pulled Stephen into a fierce bear hug.

Jamie was leaving, as well? Would she have no chance to bid him good-bye?

Lady Catherine fell into Stephen's arms, weeping openly. "Promise me you will come back. Promise."

"Give my love to the children," Stephen said and kissed her cheek.

After saying his farewells to Robert and Geoffrey, Stephen returned to stand in front of Isobel. His eyes were soft as he took her hands.

"Isobel, I wish you every happiness."

"You have a command, as you wanted," she said, her voice cracking.

"I told you what I want." He attempted a smile, but his heart was not in it.

He gave her hands a final squeeze and was gone.

Isobel flung the water jug against the wall. It bounced instead of smashing to bits, giving her no satisfaction at all.

Now that she finally had what she wanted, why was she not happy?

She paced the small bedchamber until her legs ached. Finally, she crawled onto the bed and lay on her back. The bed curtains encased her like a tomb. Tears of frustration slid down the sides of her face and into her hair, making her head itch.

If not for Stephen, she would be content. Nay, she would be overjoyed! He had taken that away from her.

What did he mean, telling her he wanted her and then leaving? She pounded her fists against the bed. And then she cried in earnest until her head ached and her throat was parched.

The door opened with no warning knock. A moment later, someone jerked the bed curtain back with a snap and thrust a candle in her face.

"How can you be so foolish!"

Lady Catherine. Could the woman not leave her to her misery? Isobel locked her arms over her eyes.

The mattress sank as Lady Catherine sat on the bed.

"Please go," Isobel groaned.

"If it were only you who suffered, I might." Catherine's voice was sharp. "Have you no sense of what you are doing to Stephen? I fear he will not survive the first battle."

Isobel sat up. "But he is a skilled fighter."

Ridiculous as it was, her confidence in Stephen's abilities was such it did not occur to her until now he might be killed.

"'Tis a dangerous thing," Catherine said, "to send a man off to war when he does not care if he lives or dies."

Isobel felt as though a fist squeezed her heart. "You do not truly think—"

"I do," Catherine said.

"Then he must not go," Isobel said, wriggling out from under the bedclothes.

When she tried to squeeze past, Catherine caught her arm and held it. "Stephen will not take you if you only wish to save him. He told me he tried to force your hand before, and he will not do it again."

"Then you know he only wanted to wed me because he thought I might carry his child."

Catherine blew out a long breath. "Of course, Stephen

would do the honorable thing. But are you such an idiot you cannot see he loves you?"

Isobel shook her head violently from side to side, though she did believe Stephen loved her now.

"Stephen is such a good man, kindhearted and thoughtful," Catherine said, her voice growing softer. "You could not ask for a better father for your children. 'Tis a rare man who is so good with little ones."

Isobel's heart ached, because all that Catherine said was true.

"I can see you love him, too," Catherine said.

"Of course I love him! He could not make me so very wretched if I did not." Isobel looked hard at Catherine, willing her to understand. "I promised myself I would never let another man have the power to hurt me as much as my father did."

"It is too late for that." Catherine brushed the hair back from Isobel's face. "Come, tell me what it is you fear."

"That he will fail me when I need him most," Isobel blurted out. She drew in a shaky breath and then added in a whisper, "That he will abandon me, as both my parents did."

"I see I shall have to tell you," Catherine said, shaking her head, "though Stephen made me swear not to."

Isobel leaned forward. "Tell me what?"

"You know Stephen has been spying for the king?"

Spying? Stephen spied for the king?

"The king is exceedingly grateful for the service," Catherine said. "He offered the Hume lands to Stephen— and he wanted Stephen to take them."

How naive she was! Hume Castle was a border castle; of course, the king would want a strong man to hold it.

"The king decided to throw you into the bargain, as men will do, when we told him Stephen wished to wed you."

"The king chose Stephen for my husband?"

Catherine nodded. "But Stephen asked the king to free you from your promise and to give the Hume lands to you."

"Why? Why would Stephen do this? He said he wants to marry me."

"Because he wants your happiness more," Catherine said, gripping Isobel's arms. "Stephen wants you to choose him freely—or not at all."

Stephen sacrificed his own gain, his own happiness, so that she might have hers.

He had the heart of Galahad, strong and true. Time and again, he proved it. In his devotion to his family, his kindness toward the twin orphans, his willingness to risk his life for those he loved...including her.

Honor would always mean more to him than position or power. His loyalty ran deep. It did not waver.

He would not fail her.

"How near dawn is it?" Alarm had Isobel leaping from the bed. With impatient hands, she jerked at her gown. Thank heaven she had not bothered to take it off!

"I waited as long as I dared," Catherine said as she knelt to help Isobel into her slippers. "'Tis yet an hour before dawn. Robert is waiting downstairs to take you to the castle."

"Robert is waiting?"

"Robert always had faith in you," Catherine said. "Now give me your other foot so we can get you on your way."

As Isobel raced down the stairs, she called back, "The angels should sing your praises, Lady Catherine!"

Robert caught her in his arms. "I knew you would choose happiness in the end, but did you have to take so long?"

Horses were saddled and ready outside the door. Robert flung her on one, and they rode hard through the empty streets. When they reached the castle gates, the guards waved them through.

Isobel slid off her horse at the steps of the Old Palace.

"Stephen is in his old chamber," Robert said, taking her hand as they ran down the corridor.

They skidded to a stop before Stephen's door.

"Tell Stephen not to worry about the men," Robert said, gasping for breath. "William is sending orders to put someone else in command."

After the headlong rush to get here, Isobel stood staring at the closed door. What would she say to Stephen? Would he still want her after what she put him through? Could he forgive her?

"Don't make the poor man wait any longer!" Robert opened the door and pushed her inside.

The door closed behind her with a loud thump.

Stephen sat at the small table beneath the arrow-slit window. From the state of his clothes, he had not been to bed. A single candle glowed on the table, its holder resting in a pool of melted wax.

With a rush of regret, she realized it was an hours candle. Stephen must have used it to count the hours until his departure—and the hours remaining for her to come to him. Only a stub remained.

He rose to his feet and put his hand on the back of the chair, as if to steady himself. Though he did not take his eyes from her, neither did he come to her. His handsome face was etched with lines of tension and fatigue.

"Why are you here, Isobel?"

To think she might never have heard this voice she loved so well again. A sob caught in her throat when she attempted to speak. Still, he waited.

She swallowed and tried again. "I've loved you for a long time, but I was afraid to trust your love for me. I feared you would betray and abandon me."

"I would never do that," Stephen said. Still, he made no move toward her.

"I understand that now."

"Isobel, tell me why you are here."

She took a single step forward. "I come because I choose you, Stephen Carleton, to be my husband." She took another step. "I choose you because you brought joy and love back into my life, and I do not want to lose them again."

With each step she took, her voice grew stronger.

"I want to sleep beside you each night and wake to see your face each morning. I want to meet your mother."

His eyes crinkled at the corners.

"I want to know the nieces and nephews you speak of with such fondness. I want to go home with you to Northumberland. I want us to raise our children there."

She took the last step and stood before him. "I do not want to waste more time or spend another day apart."

"I love my mother, but I think we should wed before you meet her," Stephen said, his face lit by the smile she loved so well. "I can't risk having her scare you off."

In the next instant, she was in his arms.

"I tried to keep my hope," he said into her hair, holding her tightly. "But it was hard."

He lifted her off her feet and twirled her in his arms.

With his eyes warm on hers he said, "Every day of my life, I will thank God you chose me."

He kissed her then. A soft, warm kiss that made the world swirl around her. She pressed against him, glorying in the joy and comfort of having his arms around her again.

Stephen was hers. Always and forever.

She leaned back and fiddled with the collar of his tunic. "'Tis hard to see why we should wait for the ceremony, since we've already..." She let her voice trail off, having no doubt he understood what she was proposing.

"I'll take no chances with you," Stephen said, laughing. "We shall make our pledges before witnesses tomorrow, but I shall hear your pledge to me now—*before* we do aught else."

———

Stephen had attended numerous betrothals over the years, but he'd never paid the slightest attention. Still, he was fairly certain all he had to get right was the essential promise to make it binding.

"Lady Isobel Hume, I pledge you my troth and take you as my wife."

Isobel raised an eyebrow—in appreciation, he believed, of his admirable simplicity.

"Sir Stephen Carleton," she said in turn, "I pledge you my troth and take you as my husband."

"Now I have you!" With immense satisfaction, he pulled her into his arms.

He felt awash in his love for her. He smiled, thinking of hardheaded little girls with bouncy dark curls and serious green eyes. And, God forbid, wooden swords in their pudgy little hands. Girls like that would need brothers to keep them out of trouble.

Isobel pursed her lips and tapped her finger against her cheek. "Is there not something more we must do to make the promise binding? Something that makes it...irrevocable?"

Irrevocable.

"I believe," he said, his voice turning husky as he leaned down to touch his lips to hers, "'tis consummation after the promise that does it."

They kissed for a long, tender moment. When she opened her mouth to him and pressed against him, his desire grew into an urgent, pulsing need. He lifted her in his arms to carry her to the bed.

"Come, wife, we are to bed." He smiled—he'd waited a long time to say that.

He awoke hours later, suffused with contentment. Nothing and no one would ever take Isobel from him now. With her at his side, he was ready to take his place in the world. He would claim his lands, serve his king, be a husband and father.

His life was full of golden promise.

Epilogue

Ouch!" Isobel sucked on her finger and set her needle-work aside.

He should be here by now, should he not? She paced up and down the empty hall, glancing toward the entrance at each turn.

Where was he?

Sunlight fell across her face as she passed one of the long windows, reminding her how much she loved this house. She and Stephen built it on the Carleton lands. It held only good memories for her.

Only this last remnant of discontent from her old life remained. Both Stephen and Robert urged her to put it to rest.

When she turned again, he was standing at the entrance.

"Father!" Her heart constricted. When had he become an old man? She gestured toward the table set up near the hearth. "I have sweet wine and cakes for you."

"You remember my sweet tooth." He pulled a handkerchief from inside his tunic and blew his nose.

After pouring him a cup of wine, she took a cake for herself from the platter between them. There were so many unspoken words between them, she did not know where to start.

"I am grateful to your husband," he said, "for bringing the children to visit me from time to time."

Isobel's cake caught in her throat.

"Sir Stephen is well respected on both sides of the border," he said. "He seems an honorable man."

The word "honorable" hung between them like an accusation.

"His eyes shine when he speaks of you," her father said, his voice cracking. "I need to know you are happy, Issie. Tell me you are."

Her happiness mattered to him. She nodded. When she could speak, she asked, "Why did you do it?"

Even after all this time, she wanted to know.

He ran his hands through his white hair. "We lost everything. Everything. I was responsible for the three of you. Geoffrey was so young, and your mother...she was never strong like you. You were the only one who could restore the family. I could think of no other way."

He took a deep breath and shook his head. "I did not believe Hume would live through the winter."

Isobel folded her hands on the table and fixed her gaze on them. "I know men marry off their daughters for such reasons all the time," she said, keeping her voice steady. "But you did not raise me like other girls. You made me believe I was special."

"You were special from the day you were born," he

said, wrapping his big, warm hands over hers. "God knows I've made more than my share of mistakes, but the one thing I did right was to claim you as my own."

Isobel's eyes flew to his face. Could he know the truth?

"Your mother gave birth six months after we were wed." He gave Isobel a bittersweet smile and shrugged. "I can count as well as the next man, but what was I to do? Send her away?"

He never considered it, Isobel was certain.

"She seemed happy enough in those first years," he said. "But when our lands were taken, she saw it as God's punishment for her sins. I thought if I could get them back, she . . ." He sighed and shook his head over long-ago regrets.

"His name is Robert," Isobel said in a quiet voice. "I met him in Normandy."

His eyebrows shot up, but he knew whom she meant.

"He would not have made her happy, either," she said.

After a quarter century of traveling and philandering, Robert finally settled down. Thank God he found Claudette.

"He is a good friend now. But when I was a child, he would not have been as good a father to me as you were."

As soon as she said the words, she knew them to be true. For the first thirteen years of her life, he was the best possible father she could have had.

He was looking at her with such hope, such love, she felt the bands of anger around her heart give way. She leaned down and pressed a kiss against his rough knuckles. When she looked up, tears were running down the crevices of his weathered cheeks.

A squeal of laughter tore her attention from her father to the arched entrance of the hall.

"They escaped their nursemaid again," Stephen called out as he came through the doorway carrying one child under his arm and holding the other by the hand.

"I found the little one outside eating dirt," he said, tilting his head toward the giggling boy under his arm. "His big sister told him to do it."

Their daughter, Kate, gave Stephen a mischievous grin so like Stephen's that Isobel felt her heart swell. Lord help her, that child was a trial to raise.

Stephen gave his father-in-law a cautious greeting. Kate, however, ran to her grandfather, blazing red hair flying out behind her. In another moment, she was dragging him across the room, pointing at something out the window.

"You are back early, love," Isobel said as Stephen settled down on the bench beside her.

"I was worried," he said and kissed her cheek. "But I assume all went well, since I did not find your father with your blade in his heart."

She smiled at him. "Tell me about your day."

Stephen rubbed his hand over his son's head as he gave his report. "We've lost no more cattle to raiding, and the fields look good after yesterday's rain."

"Who would have thought my wild young man would make a contented farmer?" She pinched the hard muscle at his side. "I expect you'll go to fat soon."

He leaned close until she felt his warm breath in her ear. "We shall both be contented, once I have you alone."

Isobel turned at the sound of Kate's happy shrieks ringing through the hall. As she watched her father toss the giggling girl into the air, the last of the resentment she held in her heart cracked and melted away.

Forgiveness made her feel light, happy. She turned, smiling, to Stephen.

He gave her one of his slow winks, full of the devil. "As soon as your father leaves, we'll lock the wild heathens in with their poor nursemaid, and..."

Isobel threw her head back and laughed for the sheer joy of it.

Historical Note

The map of Europe might be different today if Henry V had not died in the prime of his life at the age of thirty-five. At the time of his death in 1422, he controlled all of Normandy and was well on his way to becoming the ruler of France. To make peace with Henry, the French king agreed to marry his daughter to Henry, disinherit his son the Dauphin, and name Henry as his heir.

Under this arrangement, Henry permitted the ailing King Charles to remain the nominal king during his lifetime. This would have been a politically astute move had Henry outlived his father-in-law and been crowned king of France. The long years of fighting, however, took a heavy toll on Henry's health. During the lengthy winter siege of Meaux in 1421–1422, he fell ill, probably with dysentery. By July, he was so ill he had to be carried on the campaign in a litter. He was dying when he was brought to the castle at Vincennes, outside Paris, where his French princess waited. He died August 31, 1422, predeceasing his father-in-law by two months.

Henry left a nine-month-old babe as heir to two kingdoms. The men who ruled on his son's behalf were for the most part good men who did their best to carry out Henry's vision. However, none was Henry's equal.

If Henry had lived, he might have succeeded in securing all of France. He might, on the other hand, have cut his losses and settled for Normandy when Joan of Arc came along. It seems extremely unlikely he would have lost it all, as his son eventually did.

I should mention that there is some dispute among historians as to whether there was a massacre when the English took Caen. I assumed there was one because it served my story. If a massacre did occur, it would have been contrary to the king's orders. Henry V prohibited his soldiers from committing the rape and mayhem that was common for victorious armies at the time.

Henry V was held up as the ideal to which later kings should aspire. For many years after his death, men sought to preserve his legacy and carry out his will. They continued to be The King's Men.

Margaret Mallory's
All the King's Men series
continues in her next passionate
medieval romance!

❦

Please turn this page
for a preview of

Knight of Passion

Available in June 2010

Chapter One

The stench of the Thames made Sir James Rayburn's eyes water as he rode through the angry crowd. The "Winchester geese," the prostitutes who worked this side of the river under the bishop's regulation, would not do much business today. The men filling the street were not here to seek pleasures banned inside the city; they were spoiling for a fight.

Earlier, Jamie had crossed the river to gauge the mood within the city of London—and found it on the verge of riot.

The crowd grew thicker as he neared London Bridge. Men glared at him but moved out of the way of his warhorse. As he pushed through them, his thoughts returned to the evening before. There had been far too many men-at-arms at the bishop's palace.

Over supper last night, Jamie had tried to discern the bishop's intent in bringing so many armed men to Winchester Palace. Under the bishop's watchful eye, however, no one dared speak of it. Instead, they pressed Jamie for news of the fighting in France.

He obliged them, telling them of the recent battle against the Dauphin's forces at Verneuil. As he warmed to his tale, the ladies leaned forward, hands pressed to their creamy bosoms. He liked to tell stories. Just when he had begun to enjoy himself, Linnet's words came back to him.

What you need, Jamie Rayburn, is a dull English wife who will be content to spend her evenings listening to you recite tiresome tales of your victories.

After all these years, Linnet's ridicule still rankled. He had brought his story to an abrupt end last night and left the bishop's hall for bed. Damn the woman. Five years since he'd seen her, and she could still ruin his evening.

Calling him boring was the least of Linnet's crimes against him. No matter that she was not even sixteen at the time. Next to her, he'd been a babe in the woods. It embarrassed him to recall how he had worn his heart on his sleeve back then. While he professed eternal love and adoration, Linnet used him without a shred of guilt or regret.

After the debacle, he left Paris at once in the hope of reaching England before his letter. But nay. He had to suffer the additional mortification of telling his family he and Linnet were not betrothed, after all. Someone should have told him that men value a woman's virginity far more than women do themselves. He had mistaken the gift of hers as a gift of her heart—and a pledge of marriage.

Never again would he let a woman humiliate him like that.

That did not mean he'd sworn off women. In sooth, he

had bedded any number of them in his determination to wipe Linnet's memory from his mind. Most of the time he succeeded.

Thinking of her now put him in a foul mood. Suddenly, he could not breathe with all these people around him. He had seen enough. The message he must send back to France was clear: the situation at home in England was far worse than they had feared.

The conflict between Gloucester and his uncle, the Bishop of Winchester, had been simmering for months. This dispute between two members of the royal family was far more dangerous now that it had spilled over into the streets.

As Jamie turned his horse to head back toward the bishop's palace, someone grabbed hold of his boot. He lifted his whip but checked his arm when he saw it was an old man.

"Please, sir, help me!"

The old fellow's eye was purple with a fresh bruise. From the livery he wore, he was not a part of the rabble, but a servant of a nobleman.

Jamie leaned down. "What can I do for you?"

"The crowd separated me from my mistress," the man said, his voice high and frantic. "Now they've taken my horse, and I cannot reach her."

Sweet Lamb of God, a lady was alone in this mob? "Where? Where is she?"

The old man pointed toward the bridge. When Jamie turned to look, he wondered how he had missed her before. London Bridge was three hundred yards long, with shops and houses projecting off both sides. But in the gap where the drawbridge was, Jamie had a clear view of a lady in a bright blue and yellow gown. She sat astride a white palfrey, sticking out from the horde around her like a peacock atop a dunghill.

"Out of my way! Out of my way!" Jamie shouted, waving his whip from side to side above the heads of the crowd. Men flung themselves aside to avoid the hooves of his horse as he forced his way forward through the throng.

As he rode up onto the bridge, he heard the familiar sound of an army on the move. He turned and saw men-at-arms marching up the river from the bishop's palace. God's blood, the bishop had even sent archers.

Jamie had heard a rumor that Gloucester intended to ride to Eltham Castle to take custody of the three-year-old king. Such a move might well cause the bishop to fear Gloucester meant to usurp the throne. Apparently, the bishop had decided to stop his nephew at the bridge by force of arms.

God help them all.

But in the meantime, Jamie needed to rescue the fool woman caught between the forces of the two feuding royals in the goddamned middle of London Bridge.

The mass of people caught on the bridge began to panic as word spread of the men-at-arms marching toward them. As Jamie pushed his way over the first part of the bridge, their shouts echoed off the buildings that connected overhead.

He was still twenty yards from the lady when he heard her scream. Sweet Jesus, hands were grabbing at her, attempting to pull her off the horse. She fought back like a savage, striking at them with her whip.

Someone caught hold of her headdress. Despite the

noise on the bridge, Jamie heard the gasps of the men around her as a cascade of white-gold hair fell over her shoulders to her hips.

The air went out of him. There was only one woman in Christendom with hair like that. Linnet.

And she was in grave danger.

"Do not touch her!" he roared. He raised his sword and pulled the reins, making his horse rear to clear his way. He pushed forward with vicious resolve.

As he fought his way the last few yards through the seething mass, he heard Linnet's voice over the clamor, cursing the men in both French and English.

A burly man gripped her thigh with a filthy hand, and murder roiled through Jamie. Linnet looked up then and saw him. Her eyes went wide and her lips parted, and all the sounds around him faded away.

In that moment when she was diverted, the burly man caught her arm that held the whip. Another man yanked at her belt. Through the blood pounding in his ears, Jamie heard her bloodcurdling scream as they pulled her off her horse.

"Hold on, Linnet!" he shouted.

She was hanging off the side, clutching at her saddle with both hands. God help him, she would be trampled to death in another moment. Her horse had remained remarkably steady until now. With its rider unsaddled, however, it was wild-eyed, tossing its head and sidestepping into the crowd. Jamie's heart went to his throat as Linnet swung sideways and slammed against her horse's side.

The men, whose hold was snapped by the horse's movement, were grasping at her skirts as the horse flung her from side to side. She was hanging on by one hand when Jamie finally broke through. With one sweep of his sword, he slashed the two men as he leaned down, caught Linnet around the waist with his other arm, and lifted her up onto his horse.

Praise God, he had her! Now he just had to get her off this damned bridge before arrows started flying.

"My horse!" she said, twisting to look over his shoulder.

Without warning, she leaned over the side of his horse with both arms outstretched. Was the woman mad? He gripped her tighter as she reached out to catch hold of her horse's loose rein with her fingertips.

She sat up and gave him a triumphant grin as she held it up in her hand. Good God, she hadn't changed a bit. She was happiest in the midst of tumult and trouble. He wouldn't be half surprised to discover it was she, and not Gloucester, who caused the riot.

"Don't gloat," he said in a harsh voice. "We could be killed yet."

Her eyes flicked to the side, and she brought her whip down on an arm reaching for her horse's bridle. She was as fearless and bold as when she was a girl. He resented that he still admired her for it.

He turned his horse and shouted at the crowd, "Get off the bridge! Get off the bridge!"

The panicked mass of people surged against them like rolling swells against a ship at sea. Linnet ignored his repeated command to "Let go of the damned horse and hold on." Instead, she held tight to her horse's reins, slashing at anyone who tried to grab them.

Since she was doing nothing to hold herself on to his

horse, he held her tight—so tight his fingers would probably leave bruises on her ribs. She felt so slight against
him. It seemed a miracle she had been able to fight off
those men and stay on her horse for so long. Anyone who
touched her now would be a dead man. He was a battle-
hardened knight. Now that he had her, he had no doubt he
could protect her from the rabble.

Flying arrows, however, were another matter.

Somehow, he managed to reach the end of the bridge
a hair's breadth before the bishop's men-at-arms got
there and blocked the way. He rode east along the river,
away from the bridge and the crowd, until his heartbeat
returned to normal.

They were a quarter mile down the river before he said,
"What in God's name were you doing on the bridge? An
idiot could see that was no place to be today."

Linnet turned around to look at him. This time, with
the danger past, his heart did a flip-flop in his chest. In
addition to everything else she was, did she have to be so
beautiful? It was the curse of his life.

"'Tis nice to see you, too, Jamie Rayburn." She cocked
her head and raised an eyebrow. "After all this time, I
expected a better greeting."

He fixed his gaze dead ahead and grunted. God in
heaven, how could she be so cool after what happened on
the bridge?

When she leaned lightly against him, his chest prickled
with sensation. Lust and longing took him like a fever. He
should put her on her own horse now. He wanted to pretend she was too distressed to ride alone, but the thought
was ridiculous. This one small weakness he would allow
himself. It meant nothing.

"I heard you were with Bedford in France," she said.

"Mmmph."

"When did you arrive in London?"

"Yesterday."

After a long pause she said, "Are you going to tell me what you are doing in England?"

"Nay."

"Or ask why I am here?"

"Nay."

He felt her sigh against his chest. Against his will, he remembered other sighs, other times...

He had to get rid of her. "I trust your man will make his own way back. Where shall I deliver you?"

"The bishop's palace," she said. "I can find someone there to escort me back to my lodgings."

Good. 'Twas best he not know where she was staying. Not that he would seek her out, but a wise man avoided temptation where Linnet was concerned.

Taking a different route to avoid the mob, he worked his way back to the bishop's palace. Even over the stink of the city and the river, he could smell the lavender in her hair.

He saw Linnet safely inside the palace and left her.

After that, he was far too busy to dwell on seeing her again. He went to the bishop at once to offer his services to help mediate the dispute with Gloucester. He and the other emissaries traveled back and forth across the river eight times, trying to forge a compromise. It was late in the night before Gloucester and the bishop finally agreed to terms.

Jamie fell into bed exhausted. With the country on the brink of civil war, he had managed to push all thought of

Linnet aside while he was awake. But near dawn, he was tormented by a dream of her. Not the annoying, sentimental sort of dream he often had in the early days after he left Paris. Nay, this was a raw, sensual dream of her writhing above him, crying out his name. He awoke gasping for air.

He needed a woman, that much was clear.

But first, duty called. The Duke of Bedford, the eldest surviving brother of their dead and glorious King Henry, had sent him home from France with two tasks. His first assignment was to report on the conflict between Bedford's brother, Gloucester, and their uncle. Late last night, he had sent his first message to Bedford.

This morning, he must attend to the second task: keeping the young, widowed queen safe in the crisis. This was a duty he owed not just to Bedford, but to his dear dead king. Perhaps he would be able to combine duty with pleasure. If past experience was any judge, one of the ladies at court would be pleased to keep him company.

He started the short six-mile ride to Eltham Palace as soon as he broke his fast. Shortly after he arrived, he was taken to the queen's private parlor. As he entered, Queen Katherine, a fragile-looking woman of twenty-four, rose to greet him.

"Your Highness," he said, dropping to one knee.

When he looked up, he caught the flicker of sadness in her eyes and knew she was remembering that awful day at Vincennes, outside Paris. He was one of the knights who had carried the dying king into the castle, where the queen waited for him.

"I am so very pleased you have come, Sir James," she said, holding her hand out for his kiss. She looked past him and smiled. "As I believe my friend is also, no?"

He turned to follow the queen's gaze.

Linnet swept past him to stand beside Queen Katherine. With her stubborn jaw and her chin tilted up, she looked more regal than the queen. And here he was on his knees, groveling at her feet once more.

At the queen's nod, he got up.

"My friend says you would not tell her what brings you back to England," the queen said with a coquettish smile. "But you dare not refuse me."

"I have come at the behest of the Duke of Bedford, who is concerned for your comfort and well-being." He could not tell her of Bedford's other charge to him.

"He has always been kind to me," the queen said in a soft voice. She did not need to add, *unlike Gloucester.*

"I have an errand of my own, as well," Jamie added, surprising himself. "I have come home to marry."

Linnet's quick intake of breath was quite satisfying.

The queen clapped her hands. "How delightful!"

"I have so many tiresome tales of my victories to tell," he said, "that I really must take a wife."

The queen laughed, though she could not have understood the jest. Turning to Linnet, she asked, "What sort of lady should we find for our handsome James?"

Linnet looked at him with her direct, ice-blue eyes and said, "I think he should please himself."

Oblivious to the edge in Linnet's voice, the queen clasped her hands together and beamed at him. "Tell us, Sir James, what lady would please you?"

"A dull English lady," Jamie said, turning to meet Linnet's steady gaze. "The kind who makes a virtuous wife."

THE DISH

Where authors give you the inside scoop!

♥ ♥ ♥ ♥ ♥ ♥ ♥ ♥ ♥ ♥ ♥ ♥ ♥ ♥ ♥

From the desk of Susan Kearney

Dear Readers,

I came up with my idea for RION, the second book in the Pendragon Legacy Trilogy, in the usual way. As the sun dipped below the horizon, a time machine landed on the aft deck of my yacht. And another hunky alien, muscles rippling, climbed up the ladder and joined me on the third deck.

Rion.

Damn. How lucky could a girl get? After LUCAN's story, I was filled with excitement at the prospect of hearing about the next installment in the Pendragon Legacy series.

Rion had even arrived at my favorite time of day. As the sun cast slashes of red and streaks of pink across the Gulf of Mexico, the sunlight kissed Rion's skin, accenting his sharp cheekbones. And shadowing his eyes—eyes that really got to me. Eyes that were both kind and hard. Eyes that revealed past heartaches and perhaps a newfound sense of peace.

Did I mention the guy was also hot? From his casual jeans to his open shirt that revealed a ripped chest, he looked more like a treasure hunter than a king from the planet Honor. Between his five o'clock shadow, the dark gleam in his eyes, and the bruise at his temple, he could have just stepped off a battlefield.

And as twilight deepened into darkness, as the waves lapped gently against the hull, Rion told me his story.

He spoke in a sexy rumble. "Lucan said that you're interested in love stories about the future."

"I am." Pulse escalating with excitement, I sipped my wine.

"In the future, my planet will be attacked, my people will be enslaved."

Uh-oh. "But you saved them?" I asked.

"I couldn't do it alone."

"You needed the help of a woman?" I guessed, always a romantic at heart.

"A special woman from planet Earth. In fact, she's Lucan's twin sister."

"Marisa?" Oh, this story sounded exciting. Lucan had told me how his sister had given up a job as a reporter to train dragonshapers. How she'd longed for children of her own. And I could envision the feisty woman with this man. They'd have cute babies . . . "Marisa agreed to help save your world?"

"Not at first." A smile played over Rion's lips. "I had to kidnap her."

Wow. "I'd imagine it took her a while to get over that." While Rion was quite the catch, still . . . he'd kidnapped her. I swallowed hard. Maybe it wasn't so bad. The woman in me told me he'd more than made it up to Marisa. "You mentioned a love story? So she forgave you, right?"

Lucan's face softened. "Marisa, she didn't just help me. She helped my people, too."

"And you made her your queen?"

His eyes sparkled. "First she ran away and almost got herself killed."

"But you saved her?"

He grinned. "We saved each other."

If you'd like to read the story Rion told me, the book is in stores now.

You can reach me at www.susankearney.com.

Enjoy!

Susan Kearney

♥ ♥ ♥ ♥ ♥ ♥ ♥ ♥ ♥ ♥ ♥ ♥ ♥ ♥ ♥ ♥

From the desk of Margaret Mallory

Dear Readers,

I love to catch characters on the cusp of change—on the verge of disaster, falling in love, or just growing up.

At the start of my current release, KNIGHT OF PLEASURE, Sir Stephen Carleton is disillusioned, drinking too much, and going to bed with all the wrong women. I think we have all known someone like that—a bright young man with so much potential that you want to scream or cry when you see him slipping into a downward spiral and wasting all that talent. What Stephen needs, of course, is the right woman. He is at a crossroads—with one foot on the wrong path—when he meets the no-nonsense, strong-minded Isobel. She is just the inspiration Stephen needs to step up and become the man he was meant to be.

If you read my first book, KNIGHT OF DESIRE, you already know Stephen has a hero's heart beneath all that charm. In that book, he is the hero's younger brother, an endearing youth of thirteen, full of gallantry and prone to trouble. By the time I finished writing KNIGHT OF DESIRE, I was so attached to Stephen that I simply had to give him his own story.

While I was writing Stephen's story, KNIGHT OF PLEASURE, the same thing happened with Jamie, Stephen's fifteen-year-old nephew: Jamie had to have a book. But Linnet, a young French girl, is such a strong character that she fairly jumped off the page, begging for a leading role. It was not until I tried outlining a book for each of them that I realized these two characters were meant to be together. And so they will be, in KNIGHT OF PASSION. Look out, Jamie, because the fiery Linnet has revenge—not marriage—on her mind.

Now, as I write KNIGHT OF PASSION, I am keeping a close watch on the teenagers who seem to pop up of their own accord in my books. I wonder which one will demand a love story of his own . . . Whoever my next hero and heroine turn out to be, I'm bound to put them on the verge of disaster before I reward them with their happy ending.

I hope you enjoy all three books (so far) in my medieval series, All the King's Men: KNIGHT OF DESIRE, KNIGHT OF PLEASURE, and KNIGHT OF PASSION.

Margaret Mallory

www.margaretmallory.com

Want to know more about romances at Grand Central Publishing and Forever? Get the scoop online!

GRAND CENTRAL PUBLISHING'S ROMANCE HOMEPAGE

Visit us at www.hachettebookgroup.com/romance for all the latest news, reviews, and chapter excerpts!

NEW AND UPCOMING TITLES

Each month we feature our new titles and reader favorites.

CONTESTS AND GIVEAWAYS

We give away galleys, autographed copies, and all kinds of fun stuff.

AUTHOR INFO

You'll find bios, articles, and links to personal websites for all your favorite authors—and so much more!

THE BUZZ

Sign up for our monthly romance newsletter, and be the first to read all about it!

VISIT US ONLINE

@ WWW.HACHETTEBOOKGROUP.COM.

AT THE HACHETTE BOOK GROUP WEB SITE YOU'LL FIND: